ABOUT RAGE

by

Erin Ban

Disclaimer

Any opinions, statements of fact or fiction, descriptions, dialogue, and citations found in this book were provided by the author, and are solely those of the author.
This is a work of fiction entirely which contains graphic descriptions of violence and is not meant for the eyes of persons under the age of 18.

Copyright 2022 by Erin Banks
2nd edition April 19, 2024

All rights reserved. No part of this book may be reproduced in any form or by any means without the prior written consent of the author, excepting brief quotes used in reviews.

Cover design 2024 by Erin Banks
Interior Formatting by Erin Banks

Content Disclaimer

The fictional serial killer tale ABOUT RAGE entails depictions of violence, among them physical, verbal, emotional and mental abuse as well as mentions of sexual abuse, neither of which are intended for nor advisable to be read by persons under the age of 18. This is a work of fiction. With the exception of public figures, any resemblance to persons living or dead is coincidental. The opinions expressed herein are those of the characters alone and ought not to be confused with the author's.

Acknowledgements

I would like to thank my friends and beta readers for all their constructive criticism and encouragement.

Liesl, for these past ten years, you have been the best friend everyone needs but only I have, and I'll never stop marveling about the one reason that happened being…snow.

I owe eternal gratitude to Kevin M. Sullivan, and also thank the Fallen Angels crew: Linda Graham, Jana Haney, and Jori Daniels; my siblings in Kemper: Candace Caspers, Christina Murphy Pyman, Paul Hobson, and Elissa Kerrill; the Guilty girls: Ang D. Jones, Patty Sullivan and Gail Morrongiello; as well as Kathleen Littell, Aaron Pyman, Sondra Nowicki, Lorre Westhaver, Cheryl L. Bullock, Matt Martinek, Sam Hobson, Pilar Spechtold, Kelly "Cupcake" Madison, Annika Kaufert, Dr. Z, and the CrimePiper brigade: Tabitha Kent, Sabrina Holmes and C. Cortez.

Special thanks to the incredibly talented Peter Douglas, who offered to translate the poetry for this novel musically, in order to create a compelling soundtrack, and to Mirko Swo, Helena Roth, Anja Axelsson. In the same vein, I appreciate everyone who kept a straight face while reading back the quote to me for the song *"Hold Your Hooves & Horns"* on the soundtrack of this novel – Aaron Furlong, Robert Bryce, Kacy Williamson, Dwayne Letson, Markus Brooks, Jeff Ignatowski, Chris Morgan, Chris K., William Dathan Holbert, Mike Hines, Gryff Nowicki, Mikki Allen and Joe Kellerman, as well as to their respective spouses for being such good sports about it.

I am also thankful to psychologists Emma Louise Brooks and Caralyn Dreyer for their expertise, to Erma from Uncle Jim's Worm Farm, as well as Tina from the Church of Latter Day Saints. And always, always, my better half…

June 21, 2022

Dedication

"…Mystery Rider,
What's your name?
You're a killer,
A drifter gone insane.
Mystery Rider,
What's your game?
You're a rebel
No one else can tame…"

~Danny Rolling, "Mystery Rider"

Index

Content Disclaimer 4

Acknowledgements 5

Dedication 6

Index 7

Chapter 1 It's Not Easy To Explain, But It's Not Difficult
To Live With 9

Chapter 2 A Being Driven By Instinct Alone 15

Chapter 3 Let's Not Get Ahead Of Ourselves Here 20

Chapter 4 Purging Their Bodies Of Their Souls 29

Chapter 5 The Marriage Of Passion And Pain 35

Chapter 6 Humanity Weakening Me Like Poison 43

Chapter 7 Excitement Lighting Up His Eyes Like
Napalm 51

Chapter 8 I'm Coming For You, Michael 58

Chapter 9 Good Faith 70

Chapter 10 To That End, You May Do Whatever You
Please 80

Chapter 11 Violent Love, Pure Rage 91

Chapter 12 Run 102

Chapter 13 Always 109

Chapter 14 This Is Why, And This Is How 119

Chapter 15 A Fierce Cacophony Of Contrary Forces ... 130

Chapter 16 Kate 140

Chapter 17 A Welcomed Distraction 149

Chapter 18 Back Into The Rider's Den............................160

Chapter 19 Awake, Dreaming, Or Dead 171

Chapter 20 All Ducks In A Row, All Eggs In One Basket 180

Chapter 21 Anything You Can Do, I Can Do Better.....189

Chapter 22 Ocean Shores...203

Chapter 23 Georgia...213

Chapter 24 The Cavalry 225

Chapter 25 Rob..229

Chapter 26 We Owe Loyalty To No Man......................241

Chapter 27 Anything You Can Dig, I Can Dig Deeper 249

Chapter 28 Rage, Pristine & Simple, Healing & Merciful 258

Chapter 29 Razor Sharp Tongue 265

Chapter 30 The Heart Is Deceitful Above All Things ..278

Chapter 31 Decrescendo 290

ABOUT RAGE – The Soundtrack....................................303

Glossary..328

About Erin Banks...333

Chapter 1
It's Not Easy To Explain, But It's Not Difficult To Live With

As I awaken, I immediately experience *the discontent*. It is akin to sunburn, my skin leathery, too tight around my flesh, and my brain a few sizes too large for my skull, because the Rider is clawing his way out of the pit. I can feel he's hungry to merge. And all I know is…we must kill. Today.

It's not easy to explain, but it's not difficult to live with. At least not anymore. Despite the physical discomfort, a small smile bends the corners of my mouth. There is a faint bitterness on the back of my tongue. Adrenaline seeping through every fiber and pore inside out. Pushing, pushing forward in the form of anticipatory sweat, and manifesting itself in that strangely bitter, sour battery acid taste.

As much as I enjoy the kill, I enjoy the process of choosing a victim far more.

I am a hunter.

It's not grandiosity to state with certitude that I am among the best there is, as no prey has ever escaped me thus far, and I remain unsuspected of any crime.

I remember that when I began killing, many years ago, I believed the panic that overcame me afterwards to be remorse. It took a long time to understand that my early qualms were merely the fear of being caught and caged, never being able to do again what I had just begun to do.

I can mentally comprehend the components guilt consists of and what conventionally triggers it in others. And of course I can mimic it quite expertly by now. I can feign any human emotion, thanks to hours of practicing my mimic, gestures and posture in front of the mirror, and with the humans. And I suppose the theater and makeup classes I took in my early twenties have also aided me.

I still wonder though. Sometimes. On days like these when I feel the urge.

Because I believe I recall that I was once capable of feeling guilt and remorse as well as the full range of human emotions, and not only for myself either, but for others too. Empathy they call it.

But if I ever did, and wasn't just childishly deluding myself, I at least haven't felt any of it since I returned home from the hospital when I was nine years old. I remember looking into mother's deeply creased face on that day, her lopsided mouth conveying her contempt for me. From that day forth, she would look at me with this mask of regret and silent condemnation until the day she died. After the humanity had died inside me as though someone had simply switched it off, she became "the mother," rather than "my mother," in my mind.

We all have a shadow self, they say, though I wouldn't call him that. The Rider is my better half. People nod wisely, thinking of the time they told a white lie, or even a more profound lie, such as when they engaged in infidelity or gave false testimony, engaged in theft or bullied a co-worker threatening their status.

But they only scrape alongside the edges of what they call shadow and darkness. That which I call the wildness – true freedom from all constraints of this world.

I began understanding that when I read Hermann Hesse's Steppenwolf. People, the novel teaches, are both light and dark, yin and yang, and have a million facets in between. Most of them dance back and forth on paler shades of gray in their lifetimes.

I don't.

Not anymore.

I am neither man nor wolf. I am the freedom that lingers beyond the distinction of light and dark or the judgment of good and evil. What is evil, anyway? Being so radically good to yourself that the welfare of others is inconsequential.

The hospital happened twenty-eight years ago, to the day, I

realize, as I lazily stretch in bed. "Happy birthday," I whisper to the Rider, giggling inaudibly, a sound deep in my throat, like pebbles hitting water.
Whoever it will be today, or tonight, they will search my eyes for a hint of humanity but find none. They'll find that I am all about rage.

Once I have peeled myself out of my weighted blanket, I almost trip over my own feet, chuckling at myself. I'm not a klutz, in fact, I cannot afford to be. But if it serves me well, I may act clumsily. Ordinary folks who only know that shrinking violet facet of me consider me "adorable," which particularly counts for the males of their species. Truly, it is them who are "adorable" in their gullibility.
Eventually, I tiptoe over to my spacious wardrobe and upon opening it, let out a happy sigh. My kill closet consists of unassuming clothes. Cargo pants, sweat pants, an assortment of caps, wigs, plain shirts, fat suits, and shoes with different types of weights worked into the sole. Shoes which will make it appear as though my feet were larger or smaller than they are. I'm not particularly fond of the latter ones, as they're painful to wear and prohibit me from running, should the need for me to do so arise. They're mostly for clean-up and trolling jobs.
Across the room is another closet, my façade's clothes. Costumes, essentially. Frilly dresses in bright and happy colors are for church. I'd considered joining a different religion many decades ago, mainly because I found their self-adulation and near-professional self-victimization hilarious. Ultimately, there were too many rules and regulations, the communities they refer to as tightly knit gave me Big Brother vibes. Church is splendid entertainment, however, though I am careful that my attendance is unpredictable enough for no one to try and befriend me.
Should I, upon my own demise, find that there is a God, I would

follow Buddha's advice. I'd stab God through the jugular. After all, I'm not fond of competition.

Almost all members of the congregation are Sunday-Christians, too busy "sinning" to take any genuine interest in each other. I'm amused by their weekly professions to change, once the corpse upon the cross guilt-trips them into wanting to deny their primal urges. No thing on earth can change, least of all the humans. Merely, they become more secure in their insecurities; they cloak their negative traits with righteousness or victimhood. It is that which mimics change.

Slipping into the role of believer, modern hippie, the smart business woman with a heart of gold, the self-confident vixen, or really, much of anything in between, serves as another time-filler to hold myself over with during those agonizing weeks during which I cannot kill.

I enjoy the stares I'm being met with when playing the vixen, too. But before you entertain simple-minded musings, such as that I likely enjoy appreciative glances by males, and envious ones by females, let me stop you right there.

Certainly, I am a hunter, but most importantly, I'm a perverter and corruptor. Whenever the opportunity presents itself, I enjoy corrupting women into questioning their sexuality and leaving their partners – often those who'd given me lusty glances or outright relaying to me that their wife and them had "an understanding."

The destruction of "love" is a favorite of mine. Love is but a biochemical cocktail in the brain, raging hormones, a drug much like cocaine in effect. Yet people act as though it had sacred, yes, healing properties even. But I have witnessed how fickle and flimsy love truly is.

I've had crack heads offer me their newborn to rape and murder just so I would spare them. Which, for the record, I never did. I've

had a husband tell me he himself would kill his wife, if only I would spare him.
That is what love is. A drug to ascertain the continuance of the species, which is yet easily overridden by the instinct of individual self-preservation.

Today, I opt for gray cargo pants and an olive green T-shirt. The trick is to choose colors found in the natural world, and combine them in more unusual ways. Many people may even remember I wore cargo pants, but will automatically think "olive green," rather than gray, and likely confound the color of my pants with that of my shirt, inadvertently aiding me, and making it more difficult for law enforcement to find me.
The rule of thumb is no labels, no logos, no band shirts. Those are for amateurs who let their egos get the best of them.
It's mid-June, and I will prowl the mall today, I decide. I pull my caramel blonde hair up into a ponytail and pin each stray hair flat to my skull before carefully adjusting the chocolate brown bob cut wig. A baseball cap perfects the outfit.
I used to kill long before I ever even paid any attention to other serial killers. You are likely asking yourself why I kill. This question – to someone with my brain makeup – is as though I asked you why you breathe. You do not actively contemplate it; it is not constantly on your mind that you do so. You just do it. You only start thinking about it if you try not to breathe, or, alternatively, cannot breathe. You can hold your breath for a while, until you realize that it's not just a compulsion or an addiction like some self-appointed experts claim. And should anyone or anything prohibit you from breathing, you instinctively struggle, you convulse, you fight, for it is a necessity. It's survival.
Of course, living in Washington, my life had been sporadically peppered with mentions of Ted Bundy's name, but it wasn't until I had developed a habit as well as my own modus operandi, that I

developed an interest in him, too.

I hide in plain sight. It's a tad risky, managing a social media group dedicated to his case, perhaps, I realize that. But I am rather known for the austere, sterile and almost joyless manner in which I discuss the subject matter.

Sometimes it irks me that I am dependent on the group, as it is the only way for me to covertly share my true self and murder addiction with the world. Most often however, the duping delight reaches orgasmic proportions.

Chapter 2
A Being Driven By Instinct Alone

During the first few hours that I am perched on one of the plastic seats of the round commercial sofas at the mall, I pretend to read while scanning the crowd through my fake tinted reading glasses. My phone buzzes every three minutes, whenever it's time to turn the page, just in case anyone's watching, wondering why I've been staring at the same page for half an hour straight.

Today, the mall is my own personal á la carte menu to choose from.

I know I will need to take a girl today. There is something about their softness that is enticing. A softness that I don't have, no matter how hard I pretend.

Even a few of the "boyfriends" used to comment on it, that I seemed to be missing something. I could go through the motions, and in everyday life no one's ever suspected me of being able to hurt a fly, but the more personal it got with anyone, they at some point grew aware I wasn't quite right. Which is when I typically break it off. I don't keep boyfriends because I have an interest in them as people or in building a life together. The idea rather disgusts me, and, strangely enough, I always feel as if I were cheating on the Rider. I merely keep them to appear normal, to build a wall of human flesh and emotions around me so that no one would ever suspect what I actually am.

There were a few boyfriends that I would have loved to kill but I am loathe of the term "Black Widow." It was just my luck that one of the previous partners lived abroad and I got to give him the surprise of his life. The last surprise of his life, that is. He entirely deserved it by the way. His accent was abominable. Who pronounces "car" like "care?" The entire country is one filled with linguistic barbarianism I find myself unable to tolerate.

She almost walked past me without my really noticing her. It's her scent that prompted me to stare after her, watching her stubby legs break into a light jog, as she tries to catch up with her taller friend who is taking long, deliberate strides towards the exit.
I don't actually know how I choose my victims when I'm feeling spontaneous. When I see or sense them I just...know. It is as if someone shone a spotlight on them from high up above; they somehow appear brighter and more in focus than everyone else. They make my heart stop for just a second.

As a hunter, I specialize in the fine art of knowing which victim will react best to what particular ruse. I can tell who is a fighter and who a screamer.
She is. I only need to take one look at her, calloused feet in cheap cork wedge sandals, her faux leather purse, the large dangling hoop earrings, to know everything about her. The poor ones are quite often screamers. The rich snobs more often remain business-like and try to regain control.
The back of the jean cut-offs she is wearing are littered with cat hair. Oddly enough, I experience responsibility towards my victims' pets. I sometimes make an anonymous call and see to that they're being taken care of and won't starve to death after their owners' demises.
Some of my fellow population control specialists began their murderous journey by torturing and killing animals. I started with those I perceived to be a waste of space. A few of the boys always lurking at the bus stops or in alleyways, drinking and throwing their empty bottles at the neighborhood cats or waddling towards the crows and pigeons to clumsily kick at them in a pathetic show of pseudo-virility.
But that was when I was much younger, much shorter too. I have fond memories of that time because the surprise in their eyes was even more pronounced, the sense of betrayal they felt was often

verbalized in amusing ways, because they did not expect a minor to do this to them.

I discriminately murdered until I realized that everyone is a waste of space, which may just be the only pro-social and politically correct thing about me. Males, females, one of the newer gender identities, are all among them. Just no animals. It should also be noted that I consider children animals.

Perhaps my aversion to hurting animals is because I consider myself an animal. A predator of course, but nevertheless, a being driven by instinct alone, with no finer tuned or so-called higher emotions.

I'm reminded of the dangerously inaccurate statement that *all* serial killers used to torture animals, specifically cats, in their youth. Some do, some don't. Many of us owned pets, tending to them with great care. I merely lack the time for one, but I still donate large sums of money to different animal shelters each year. As a boy, Ian Brady was deeply perturbed when he witnessed a horse put down in the street while on his way home. When his pet spaniel died, he was inconsolable, and later while already tending to the wildness in him, he owned a dog with whom he is depicted on various images on the internet.

Ted Bundy's mother Louise reported how her son had brought home a myriad of small animals whom he had nursed back to health, and never harmed his pet dog, Lassie.

Even Carl Panzram admitted to only having one regret in life, that of having mistreated a few animals in his lifetime.

I could continue, but I believe I have adequately made my point.

I make sure to keep an even distance between us, staying some 26 feet behind *her* and her friend.

Although I know I must keep watching, must observe my surroundings for possible boyfriends joining them, possible witnesses, I'm suddenly mentally transported to the backyard of my childhood home.

I'm ten years old and hiding from her again. I can hear her yelling. "You better get over here now!" Her voice still causes a physical reaction in the form of goosebumps. I felt – and feel – no fear, make no mistake. My hiding was self-preservation, the goosebumps the early stirrings of the Rider who had saved me at the hospital.

Whenever I heard her voice as a child, anger enveloped me like a straightjacket. It was anger, and not rage, because then it was justified. And righteous anger is still such a docile human beast in comparison to rage.

"Good grief, you little swine!" she shouts in my memory, stomping her foot.

Her name was Grace. She'd been one of my nurses at the hospital but the mother never believed me that she'd had any involvement with what had occurred there. The mother felt she had to make up to Grace for my alleged lies, offering her, who only worked part-time, another part-time position to care for my daddy. She was supposed to aid the mother, who was overwhelmed with caring for him, after cancer had left the once dignified man a slobbering, incontinent mess.

I understood Grace and the mother were close, bonding over their shared tasks. It took me a little while longer to understand that Grace shouldn't have slept in bed with the mother.

My daddy died several months after I had learned to walk again. Mother died not even half a year later. The pathologist's report listed her death as a heart attack. Grace disappeared from my life days later.

The term people use for me is 'orphan,' which has such tragic connotations, but in truth I don't think I would have been able to thrive in a symbiotic system like a family. Symbiosis is subjugation. I am not orphaned, I was the strongest cell casting off

all the weaker and diseased cells of my family.
Every time I remembered the day of my daddy's funeral throughout the years, something was slightly changed, though I could often not even tell what it was.
Eventually, I couldn't even see his face in my mind anymore. Nowadays I don't even try.
I cannot even see Grace's face anymore. It was always a blur, even when I had known her. As soon as she turned around, I could not recall its features.
Yet Grace is everyone I ever killed, every female, and strangely enough, all the men as well.

I glance up again as my current prospect victim is trudging up to a dusty, wine red Ford. I only laid eyes on her in profile as she walked past me but her mere physique sends stabbing waves of rage through me, courtesy of the Rider. Her mild demeanor, the beauty of it, offends me.
The two women walk side by side now, her friend, the tramp as I call her in my mind, easily five or six inches taller.
In the distance I hear people laughing, someone kicking a beer can, children screaming in delight.
But those few people who went to the mall this morning, rather than going to sunbathe at a nearby lake, are too far away to see our faces and are not paying us any attention. And that tells me that it is time.

Chapter 3
Let's Not Get Ahead Of Ourselves Here

I have, on occasion, lured victims into my car, but today I have a different ruse in mind, which is why I took the bus to the mall. I know what you're thinking now. What about cell phone tower pings? Do you seriously believe someone like me wouldn't have cell phone jammers, stingrays, dirtboxes and a whole lot more at her disposal?
I fish for the broken smartphone prop in my oversized purse, and approach the women as both of them begin putting away their shopping bags in the trunk.
I neither wanted nor needed her friend but I know how to get rid of her, regardless.
"Excuse me," I whine, trusting that my face is a perfect mask of wide-eyed concern. "I don't mean to bother you but my boyfriend left to get something from his car, and it's been hours. He's not anywhere to be found, and neither is his car. Is there any way I could get a ride home? It's not far – by Idylwood Park."
"Oh wow. Well, we're driving past there. Huh. Have you tried calling him?" Grace asks.
"Dropped my phone earlier today, and it won't power up." I hold it up, presenting its cracked black screen to them. "I'm really sorry for asking but you're the first girls I see in the parking lot and…well, I didn't want to ask a guy, you know?"
With this, I will my lower lip to quiver just ever so slightly, then glance down at my feet as though ashamed of my having gotten overemotional. Out of the corner of my eye I see the two women looking at each other. The tramp is rolling her eyes, asking, "You can just take the bus, right?"
"I can't," I sigh. "The item my boyfriend was to retrieve from the car was my wallet. I took it out when digging for something in my purse." The tramp groans in reply. Grace gives her a slight frown

and shrugs apologetically. "We could drive you up to a police station? There's one about a mile from here."

I make a mental note to ask her how exactly she knows this, later in the car.

One of the dangers of taking someone spontaneously is that you never know whether they have any connections to law enforcement or similar agencies. This is a tremendously exciting yet perilous road to go down, obviously.

I pretend to deliberate for a bit, manage an embarrassed giggle. "Actually, I'd like to check home first? I don't want to call in the cavalry if it's not necessary."

Grace shoots me a sympathetic look and when our eyes meet we make *the connection*. It doesn't matter she is yet unaware that in this moment we are one, that I own her.

"Of course we'll take you." The warmth of her voice sends chills down my spine. It tickles something deep down in the bottomless pit.

And I know her last thoughts on this earth will be of this moment. It will not be the unspeakable physical pain, it will be the sense of betrayal. She will die feeling angry – outraged, in fact - with herself.

"Yeah? You'll take me?" I shyly ask. One gracious nod, one casual motion of her hand for me to enter her car, and she has decided her own fate.

The ugly one throws up her hands in the air, "As long as you drive me home first. Whatever."

"I'm really sorry for inconveniencing you," I say conciliatorily, inclining my head and glancing up at her submissively. "I know how odd this whole situation must be for you."

Playing on people's, especially women's, social obligations, and the guilty conscience that comes with not fulfilling them, usually does the trick. But she does not meeken. She simply looks back at me, empty-eyed, and I wonder if she might be similarly hollow.

I've never had an opportunity to take another killer like me, and had occasionally pondered whether it would be or make me feel any different. Would there even be any joy in this? If I didn't kill animals because they were kindred spirits, would I be able to kill another human animal like me?

I turn my attention back to Grace. "I'm Emily, by the way," I smile. She reaches for my outstretched hand. "Emma."

I close my eyes while repeating her name, "Emma." The name rolls off my tongue, another E, and so close to my own name. It was supposed to be her.

It was supposed to be her!

How I cherish these little intimate moments when I'm yet being reminded that the universe runs on synchronicity. She was always supposed to be mine. She was alive only so I could take her life and make it mine.

I have of course acquainted myself with the concept of magical thinking, Schizoaffective and Schizotypal Disorder, as well as all types of psychoses. But as knowledgeable as I am, as it pertains to human behavior and psychology, there are so incredibly many things science neglects to take into account that it leaves me baffled.

I see through it all, I see everything. I have hence forged my own marque of psychology. As it has never failed me, I see no reason to question it either.

"I'm not riding in the back," the tramp states, violently yanking open the car door to the passenger's seat. The car bobs up and down as her chunky body hits the seat.

"Gosh, I'm so sorry about Charity," Emma whispers to me conspiratorially as she opens the back door for me.

Charity. How ironic.

"Hey, I know you want to drop off your friend first," I call to the front of the car where Emma - really: Grace - is just putting her seat belt on. "So where do you live, Charity?"

Charity suspiciously glares at me in the front mirror as she learns that Grace must have just revealed her name to me without her realizing so.

"Um," she says aggressively, obviously not wanting to reveal it. Silly, really, since I would have known in a little while anyway. "A little past where you wanted to go, and you know, then southwest."

"Bellevue?" I inquire excitedly, pretending I don't notice her growing irritation.

"Mh."

I'll take that as a yes.

For the first few minutes, we ride in silence after I had provided Grace with the location of my alleged boyfriend's cabin. The girls will likely experience the silence as awkward but I welcome it, for it allows me to let my thoughts wander.

My daddy's motto had been to build early on, then delegate, and thanks to inheriting both his business as well as business smarts, I own little strategically placed hideout spots all over the Pacific North West.

I'm in no way rich by any stretch of the imagination, though I would be were I not a murderer. I mainly finance my costly recreational activities by renting out cabins, apartments and the occasional "business space." In case of the latter, these are in part associates or customers of my old acquaintance Robert Bryce.

I certainly enjoy the steady influx of cash, but a large part of why I play landlady is for kicks. It's a brain thrill, sexually gratifying, that I experience when thinking about the occupants setting up their lawn chairs above some of the graves. Obliviously tanning, drinking, eating. Fornicating in the master bed above the secret basements, further humiliating my spirit whores.

No intake of alcohol or drugs could ever match this slow burn of knowing that others unwittingly continue my abuse.

Initially, I viewed my landlady obligations as a distraction from the Rider and I tenderly growing the wildness. But although I mostly delegate by now, I have come to see its merit, as well as the fun of it all. My landlady persona is a superior character to play because at church everyone is on their best behavior, masking their darker human nature, their animal selves, similar to the way I have to in all of everyday life. Of course, they have less to conceal, less to lose. Just their faces, rather than their lives. There is seldom friction amongst the members of the congregation, giving me little to work with. But as a landlady, handling whiny housewives, entitled rich snobs and disgruntled elderly people on a bi-weekly basis schooled me in which voice to speak with, what face and clothes to wear and what dose of feigned empathy to apply to whom.

Eventually, the women had launched into a casual conversation, which I now interrupt.

"Oh, Emma, since this is me almost," I say in my best little girl voice as Grace turns a corner. I lean towards Charity's seat. "You think we could just take the next exit real quick, since my boyfriend's cabin is perhaps five minutes away?"

"I don't have time for this," Charity snaps.

"Of course. I understand," I offer with a smile. "It's just five minutes of your time, and I could imagine Emma would be grateful not to have to have to drive one and a half hours back and forth unnecessarily."

Charity aggressively sighs and shrugs in response.

I can't risk her being able to give police a description of me despite my costume, in case I can't hunt her down fast enough after I slaughtered her friend.

The moderately aggressive interaction prompts Grace to attempt more small talk to placate her friend, and Charity soon steers the conversation towards a wildly inappropriate story about their last community college party, and her exploits with two of the guys she had left with. And so I resort to listening, taking in every word, as it might aid me later on while torturing them to death. Any information is good information if only one knows how to apply it.

It's cute. They think sleeping around and dropping the f-bomb is edgy. I wonder what they would make of the tales I could tell about my own college experiences. Is stalking a renowned psychology professor, and raping him while forcing him to look at photos I'd secretly taken of him with his boyfriend during an intimate encounter, considered edgy? I merely found it necessary. That professor had the most offensive views about my kind. My actions didn't change that, but I'd known he would be less outspoken about it afterwards. In fact, he wasn't teaching anymore at all. I rarely release my prey, but if I do, naturally I see to it that my identity and face remain a mystery to them.

Once the cabin is in sight, Grace asks, "Is this it? That's -"
"Creepy." Charity mutters under her breath and Grace can't help a small chuckle. "Well, it's very rustic," the latter offers more politely.
Sure enough, my cabin doesn't compare to the other properties built around the wider lake area. It's tiny in comparison, at least not counting the extended basement. Its wood is dark and slightly mossy. It looks like a dump left over from the 70s and is conveniently surrounded by shrubbery and trees.
"My boyfriend is a very private person, one of these survivalist and prepper types, you know?" I sigh.
"Ah, okay," Grace replies absentmindedly while slowly rolling up to the front porch, her mouth twitching with ill-concealed amusement.
"Do you mind waiting a second? I'd like to check the house and our messages real quick. Well, and," my voice grows thick, "if he's not here, maybe you could give me a lift to the police station after

all? Oh, by the way, do you know anyone at the station? It's so rare to meet someone who knows exactly where the nearest one is located."

Charity gives me an icy look. "If his car's not here, he's not either, right? So what exactly do you want to check?"

Oh shut your whore mouth, Charity. I'm going to have a lot of fun with that mouth later on, I decide.

"I'd like to check our messages," I repeat calmly though the smile will not return to my face as a claw of Rider rage slices through my insides. He hates her, too.

My eyes shift to Grace. "He's been having trouble with his car, so he sometimes hitches a ride when he breaks down somewhere." The lie comes easily, thanks to years of practice.

Grace nods. "We'll wait. And no, I don't know any cops personally or anything. I just like to keep informed in case of emergency. Seems wise being, you know," she awkwardly points at herself, "a woman."

I slowly nod while watching Charity cross her arms in front of her bulbous chest, as though with that gesture she could contain her own inner rage.

I notice Charity hasn't answered if she knows someone on the force, but to press the issue now would come across as strange. Suddenly, I feel the combination of painkillers I took earlier today, the alcohol I consumed before going to the mall, as well as the anticipation, all rolled into one. I'm aware many serial killers similarly calm their nerves before going on the prowl. We've often discussed this in my group but ordinary people, it seems, cannot grasp the concept. They seem to believe calming our nerves means we are nervous, might even have second thoughts due to an onslaught of a guilty conscience. No, the nerves, that's an entirely different animal, it's all about the excruciating wait. The drugs just ensure that I won't attack my prey right on the spot. It's artificial patience. They don't dull my senses, they only curb the want which would otherwise make me see red and prevent me from being in full control.

As I reach for the doorknob, my eyes fall onto the house number. 74E.
E like Emma. E like Emily.
Are they watching me? I strain my ears. It sounds as if they are talking among themselves while listening to some eighties pop dreck on the radio. I swing the door open nevertheless.
"Hello?" I call out to my non-existent boyfriend. "Charles! Chuck, are you here?" Hopefully the frantic tone in my voice will get the girls' attention. I can't look back of course, so I repeat myself, only louder and even more frenzied this time around.
I hover in the doorway, shyly taking a step forward, then one back again, finally turning around and waving at Grace and her friend, both of whom are staring back at me through the windshield.
I have already taken them but it's the moments leading up to them learning that they were taken that are among the most arousing.
I jog down the porch steps towards the car. Grace is already half out when I whimper, "The door is open. I'm, I'm kind of afraid to go in alone?"
"Call the police," Charity's tone is authoritative when addressing Grace.
"No!" I plead, my voice breaking. "Please, not yet. I'm just really emotional right now, and..."I start sniffling again, trying to look as embarrassed as I can, and my agitation attempting to fight its way through the drugs actually aids me in this. "If I'm wrong, I'm going to feel so, so silly. I just...I just don't want to go in alone?"
Charity cusses, adding "This is all so pointless."
Well. Let's see if you'll still think so in half an hour, shall we? But let's not get ahead of ourselves here.
Grace rubs her nose, turns around to Charity. She still has one foot in the car – just one more step, just one choice. Shall she ignore her

better instincts or fulfill the social contract of always being helpful, patient and kind?

The tension is killing me, no pun intended. I know you want this, Grace... You deserve a spot amidst my spirit whores.

"Maybe we can just go in real quick, see if anything looks disturbed?" Grace suggests as Charity lets out a howl of frustration.

This imbues the Rider with yet more triumphant strength. Scratching at the fence I had built around his pit with intoxicants, he beats his tail so wildly I can see its smoky features waft upward behind him. Impatiently, he rattles at the pickets, ready to breech through the weak defense.

And then it is decided.

"Come on, Charity, don't be a jerk now," Grace nudges her friend, her voice gentle despite her words.

Chapter 4
Purging Their Bodies Of Their Souls

As we make our way up to the cabin together, Charity declares, "I'm going to wait out here."
This...is not going to work. I reach deep, deep down into a small pocket of myself that I keep stored for emergencies like this one. It has become part of my inner kill kit. Echoes of humanity.
Where are you... where are you...? I rummage around inside what I've mockingly dubbed "the rootkit," the chest in the darkest corner of the Rider's pit, until I find my most harrowing memory. The hospital.
The humiliation of still being helplessly, godforsakenly human.
I let the memory wash over me until it brims over inside me and emerges in the form of tears.
"Oh!" Grace exclaims. "Oh, no. Come here, you, it's all good?" She glares at her friend despite addressing me. "We got your back. It'll be okay, you'll see?" She pulls me into an awkward embrace and - of course - I let her.
I obsessed about this on the drive, about what she would feel like in my arms. Also wondering what sound the knife would make as I rammed it into her lower abdomen.
It sounds crazy but it's a different noise every time. Not physically, just mentally, and perhaps spiritually? With almost all of my murder spouses, it's like a bell in my mind, its purifying ring purging their bodies of their souls.
With others, it could be a metallic sound, as sterile and unpleasant as their personalities were, or a deep dark crackle like a large log in a fireplace.
It's a bit like cleaning crystals, I surmise. The mother used to be into all sorts of things esoteric, indulging in an extensive phase of exploring healing crystals after daddy had fallen ill. They were all over the house, and she cleansed most of them in the sink, letting

lukewarm water rinse over them, "feeling" their sounds and state of cleanliness.

Grace smells clean, of an indistinguishable flower maybe, and her hair is lush and soft against my cheek, as she carefully rocks me back and forth. I will rock her limp body back and forth like this once she's sacrificed unto the Rider.

"Charity, are you just going to come in now!" Grace adds an unpleasant expletive that makes me jump a little.

Reluctantly, Charity does as asked, resorting to leaning against the wall panel by the door, blocking the concealed switch that will have the metal shutters come down, once activated.

I could quickly step around her and activate them nevertheless, but I know with two women in my house, one of them with the stature and demeanor of a Valkyrie, I had better be sly, lest I be physically overpowered.

"I think I need a glass of water," I breathe, swaying back and forth a bit for emphasis. "Would you both come to the kitchen with me?"

As Grace guides me by the arm, Charity's loud, aggressive steps echo a few feet behind us. Why, I believe the only realistic chance I have got is to use this dead-eyed freak against Grace, not vice versa.

I slump down on a chair at the round kitchen table, palms pressed to my temples. I'm one deliciously apprehensive wreck inside, knowing how vulnerable I am in this present state, where absolutely nothing is determined yet, and anything and everything could happen.

"There are glasses in the upper kitchen cabinets," I murmur. "Could you...?"

"Charity, get her a glass of water," Grace commands, one hand on my shoulder. Suddenly, she blinks, realizing that there's cause for concern. "Should we check the house first? You know, since the door wasn't locked."

"Of course, you're absolutely right. Just one sip?" I plead with her, still red-faced and puffy-eyed.

"Oh, okay. Yeah," Grace replies uncertainly, fidgeting her hands and ultimately putting them in her pockets for comfort.

Now.

It's going to happen *now*.

Charity turns on the faucet but no water will come. Of course not, the water main is shut off. It always is because it's part of this type of spontaneous abduction ruse.

"What the -?" She asks irately, her fake pink plastic nails repeatedly flipping the faucet on and off.

I slowly stand up, directing an apologetic smile at an ever more weary growing Grace, and stroll over to the sink.

"Here, let me help you," I offer placidly as I reach over to activate the switch that will lock the cabin's door down from the kitchen. "Cabin kinks, you know, it's an old house."

Cabin kinks! How am I even staying upright, not rolling on the floor laughing?

"Yeah, let's all have a drink while there might be a serial killer in the house," Charity snarls just a second before the shutters come crashing down. I yank her back by the backcombed helmet of bleached blonde hair, while reaching for my favorite knife in the butcher's block, placing it against her fleshy neck.

"There actually *is* a serial killer in the house," I say quietly. All traces of girlish helplessness gone from my voice, it is but a low hum, beautifully accompanying the staccato of my beating heart. 'Our beating heart,' the Rider chides me, a hand on my shoulder. 'Let me ride you now.'

And when he enters me, my moan turns into a hysterically screamed laughter of delight, my unnerved victims screaming along with me in fright, until we bellow, "Silence! – Now. Grace?" we address the girl who used to be Emma. "We have one favor to ask of you."

"Wait, wait, what. Wait a minute!" Grace's breaths come quick and shallow. She's nearing a state of hyperventilation and we like what this is doing to us. Mentally. And sexually.

We picture their brains lighting up like a Christmas tree, even observable on fMRI brain scans. Prey animals' - such as ordinary humans' – brains show heavy activity in the limbic system, primarily the amygdala, empathy central, when presented with unpleasant imagery, descriptions or situations.

Grace's voice interrupts our musings. "Oh my God, what is this?! What are you doing!"

Watching the immediate tension in her body is delicious, and part of the foreplay. She's backing away, then turning right and left, not quite knowing where to turn or what to do.

"Grace," we say, willing our heart to beat more steadily again. "Focus."

Charity's body quivering against ours sends little ripples of pleasure through us.

"Who are you talking to?!" Grace whines. "I'm Emma!" Our lack of response emboldens her to continue. "Look. Nothing has happened yet. We can just leave. We're far too shaken up to recognize you again anyway, and even if we did? I promise you -"

We cut her off. "I promise you," we laugh insouciantly. "Oh, Grace, your promises are as vacant as your mind."

"I'm not Grace..." the confused girl starts again. It's time to put her in her place.

"Do you really think it wise to argue with us, all things considered?" Our voice is low. We admit we never bothered to research it, but our theory is that once we begin speaking in a low yet firm voice with prey animals, their brain recognizes what we are. Collective memory is in part stored in, and passed on, via DNA, after all.

"Tell me who you are," we demand.

Her admission, "I am Grace" is like heroin shot straight into our vein. Our lids are heavy, blinking slowly, we are so high. For some reason we are reminded of these boring social media memes about living in the moment. But at this present time there really is no future, no past, only now. It's an almost meditative state. Eventually, we address her again. "Grace. We won't lie to you. One of you can make it out of this alive."

Charity's body is immediately shaken with sobs and we instinctively pat her with the knife. We're not even sure whether it's to be consoling or to silence her. Regardless, the gesture must have startled her, for she first slumps forward into the knife – which breaks her skin – then pulls back with a shriek, echoed by Grace's own. We hope she won't leave anything but blood on it. It's not that we won't, but we are not particularly fond of killing overweight people. For one, their flesh is marbled with little islands of fat, which we find aesthetically unpleasant during the dismembering process. However, the key component is that it's incredibly strenuous to take apart, transport and bury the weightily challenged.

"Now," we breathe, licking our lips, "it boils down to you having two simple choices. Do you understand?"

"Yes," Grace exhales, a tear dancing on the rim of her lower lid.

"Choice number one, you kill Charity."

Charity erupts into Banshee-like wails. She better not get any snot on the blade, we swear to God, her nose will be the first thing to go if she does.

"Option two, Charity kills you," we conclude. Almost as an afterthought we add, "We can imagine what you are thinking right now. You wonder whether you can overpower us and get away. But let me tell you this, even if you killed us, there are multiple traps in place to ensure you will die here. You'll need a code to open any of the windows and doors. Any attempt to open them without entering the correct code in time will result in the house being filled with gas. Have you ever watched footage of concentration camps?"

In truth, there is no Zyklon B in this cabin, just a homemade concoction that would briefly render anyone unconscious. There are no further traps either, but after a few hiccups, we have come to find these types of threats rather effective.

"I can't!" Grace howls hysterically. "I can't kill my friend! Why would you even want this?"

Just before we can cut in, we hear Charity whisper a prayer under her breath. We bring our ear closer to her mouth and feign shock. "Well, your friend Charity just said she would have no problem killing you if it guaranteed her survival. Should we give her the knife? What do you think."

"I never said that!" Charity shrieks in response but we see the doubt on Grace's face. Planting the seed of distrust is on my top five list of brain thrills.

The next few steps are mere technicalities. We instruct Grace in how to unlock the downstairs entrance to the kill room off of the kitchen that we refer to as the "tunnel," due to its shape.

Once the two girls are in the tunnel, we toss the knife in after them, and activate another button. The wall comes down hard in front of us, locking them inside.

We take our usual seat in the control room on the Western wall of the tunnel, aching to witness their anguish without a two way mirror between us, but first things first.

For now, we wait.

Chapter 5
The Marriage Of Passion And Pain

We press our hand and cheek against the mirror, foggy traces of our breath waxing and waning on it. Watching the struggle, the friction inside their very souls reflected in their wide, teary eyes is, in its own way, an act of penetration. We always get deep inside, emotionally and physically, until we come out on the other side – sometimes literally. If they want to believe they can survive, they have to become us.

They say there's nothing more beautiful than a woman giving birth. But it is not the actual birth that is miraculous or beautiful, neither aesthetically nor biologically speaking. It's an organic process devoid of any meaning, other than what we assign to it. No. What makes the birthing woman beautiful is that in her most unspeakable anguish, she lets go. The restrictive mask sanctioned by society, only allowing for limited expression, is torn off, revealing the raw core of what humans are made of. Agony, the marriage of passion and pain.

Birth and death are siblings. And we are overcome with a certain degree of mental tenderness whenever we look at our victims just before the liberation, as they open up enough to share with us who they truly are.

Now you understand. We do not merely murder people, we murder pain embodied, and we believe that makes us a sort of humanitarian in our own way.

The girls are still sobbing hysterically, each of them comically holding on to their own torsos. They're a few feet apart, glancing back and forth between each other and the knife on the ground.
"I won't do it." Grace pants. "I can't kill my friend."

Charity's swollen eyes cannot hide the calculation flaring up in them, a split second before she scrambles to pick up the blade. Called it.

Our finger finds another button on the console in front of us, and a portion of the wide wooden cabinet slowly opens. As it reveals its contents to the corpse-brides-to-be, they gasp in unison. We take their reaction as a compliment. It really *is* an extraordinarily neatly arranged array of torture instruments.

Eyeing each other suspiciously, the girls' sobs come less frequently now. We planted the seed of distrust between them. They will water it themselves.

"C-can I just get a hug?" Grace hiccups eventually. Is that her ploy? – Should Charity agree, will Grace reach for the closest knife at hand from the kill cabinet behind her and literally stab her friend in the back? Charity looks as though she were pondering the same thing. Finally though, her shoulders slouch, the blade clutters to the ground. "I can't do it. I know I can be…but I'm just not…"

"Then…let's not do this," Grace concludes with relief. "Let's be in this together. As sisters. Chances are she's going to kill me or you anyway if one of us kills the other. We stand a better chance if we work together."

Ah. The bargaining stage.

Charity steps around her friend, closer to the two way mirror. "You hear that, you sick freak? We won't do it!" she shouts.

Well, this is regrettable. We watched someone starve to death in one of our other kill rooms before but it's a slow and mostly boring process, during which you have to supply the victim with water to make sure they'll wither over a few weeks, rather than days. And we're really just not feeling it right now with these two.

We sigh and heave ourself out of the chair, biting down on our lip as the pain shoots through our hip. Our narrow pelvis bone, once broken in two places, reminds us of how far we have come in life.

It's still tying Emily to her past, cautioning both of us to never forget where the Rider had come from, and that vulnerability is only ever a lack of preparation, the consequence of a lazily trustful mind.

We yank out a gun from underneath the console, quickly checking the safety, and enter the tunnel.

Their cries swell to a chorus as Charity is forced to strip for us, before being tied to the chair sitting atop the hole, the basement below the basement. In a flash of genius, we realized what to use her clothes for later on, and neatly fold them up, placing them in the far corner of the tunnel, lest they get sullied.

Our own heart, relentless and quick like a tribal drum, provides the beat to this exquisite soundtrack of terror. It is spiraling down, down, down between our legs, to a pit just as vicious and voracious as the Rider's.

The stainless steel knife handle is smooth and cool in our hand when we pick it up. It's an average WMF butcher knife that Emily once bought on the recommendation of a church friend. The Germans are experts at crafting long-lasting quality tools for cooking and killing, indeed.

We can't but close our eyes in reverence, because we remember so vividly the things this knife has done for us. Yes, this knife has sliced, cut and fucked large red holes into already bent and broken bodies. We've pleasured ourself with the bloody handle too. For the record, Emily is averse to swearing, but the Rider has his own will and life, and once we are one, there's no accounting for any bad language.

Quickly, we trace the knife across Charity's cheek. For a moment, there's nothing but an empty gash. Blood can be awfully shy. But once it starts pushing through the wound, Grace cries, "Oh!" before burying her face in her hands.

"Oh!" we imitate her hoarsely, adding, "Will you look at that!"

Charity seems yet too perplexed to dare utter a sound. Her eyes are turned inward, as if trying to determine how severe the wound is by focusing on the sensation of the steady flow of blood oozing from it.

"We want you to watch this, Grace."

"Who is she talking about?!" Charity gulps, her eyes darting back and forth between us and Grace.

"I-I don't know, maybe she's psychotic," Grace whimpers. Now, that's a big word for a community college mattress, kudos!

"Grace," we laugh softly. "If you keep looking away, you won't get the chance to save her anymore."

"What do you want me to do in order to save her?"

A sly smile lifts our cheeks. "But we already told you. The only way to save her is to kill her."

To emphasize the meaning of our words, we hook a finger into the side of Charity's mouth. One swift cut and her face is beautified by half a Glasgow smile. This time, with her senses heightened, body on high alert due to the earlier knife attack, Charity feels the pain at once. She's screaming at the top of her lungs, which gives us the opportunity to slash at the other corner of her mouth to complete the Glasgow smile. Her mouth is a gaping red hole. She looks like a creature from the Predator movies.

"What is wrong with you?! Why are you like this!" Grace howls while Charity's eyes are rolling back in her sockets, head bobbing back and forth in an attempt not to faint.

We grab her limp cheek flesh between two fingers, wiggling it back and forth a bit, eliciting more low pitched groans from Charity. "It's like she's a ventriloquist's dummy!" In a mock male voice we continue, "E.T. phone home," before bursting into a happy laughter.

"You're insane... you're insane..." Grace whispers to herself.

We understand. Humans do that. They call others names in order to elevate and separate themselves from them. She's trying to confirm that *she* is still sane after witnessing what she has.
"Come here." Just as we wonder whether it is fear or courage prompting her to take a few hesitant steps in our direction, we smell the urine before we see it. There's our answer. The bitterness of it mingles with the metallic stench of fresh blood.
We pull her into us by her belt, wrapping our arms around her midsection, one bloody finger pressed to her quivering lips.
"Lick it off," we whisper in her ear as our lips brush against her soft skin. We enjoy that it erupts in goosebumps too, little flesh bubbles of fear made corporeal.
"No," Grace bawls, her head almost violently falling onto our shoulder. An act of passive rebellion.
"She's counting on you to save her."
Her jaw unclenches, accepting our offering. "That's it, let us in," we whisper, resting our forehead against her cheek. Naturally, she gags once the blood hits her taste buds.
We pout at her. "It's an acquired taste. Do you know what that means?"
She's confused, shakes her head.
"It means you can acquire that taste if you try. Close your eyes." Upon her doing so, we kiss her. It takes a few whispered promises in between until we finally feel her respond to our kisses. Her eyes close, she relaxes, even if only slightly. She is in the moment. That is the vulnerability, the level of trust, we needed from her.
"We're going to rape you now," we smile tenderly, our face inches from hers. Let the words sink in. We can tell the message doesn't immediately compute in her brain, takes even longer to reach her heart.
"You're a woman, you can't rape me," she sputters. Her voice is just a tad more high-pitched on the last word, revealing her uncertainty as much as her words reveal her unoriginality.

We don't know how many hours we spend with Grace and her friend in the tunnel. At the end of it all, we lie in pools of coagulated blood on the floor, whose coldness we barely feel in our state of overheated exhaustion from pleasure.

We cannot form a coherent thought, struggle to remember the correct order of events that unfolded, and just let go, allowing individual, unfiltered images to wash over us.

Charity's breast leaking a gel-like substance after we'd retracted the knife. Silicone. A novum for us, and another memory to call upon whenever we'd need a good laugh.

Another flash of Grace's head between a dead Charity's legs, obeying our orders.

A corpse's fingers inside us, a flash of bright light before our eyes when the Rider climaxes.

And another. Grace screaming, "Why are you killing us?"

It was that particular wording that made us look up at her. Her having accepted her fate. We're not going to lie, we had hoped that she might have something poignant to offer when we asked her, "Why not?"

Expectations are fertile ground to disappointment, thus resentment. And so her frantic ramblings only served to enrage us further.

"You can't play God like this."

"Why not?"

"It's just wrong," Grace had whimpered.

"Why? Is a lion wrong for slaying a gazelle?"

"The lion doesn't enjoy this!"

We had chuckled then. "Yes, they do. Seals rape baby otters to death. Cats play mice to death and leave them to rot, undevoured."

"But," Grace had scrambled to argue, "but why do I have to be the gazelle?"

"Because you are not the one who lured us to your abode today with the intent of killing us. Because you did not even entertain the idea of throwing any of the knives or other weapons from the cabinet at us as soon as we stepped inside this room."

"Oh my God, oh my God, please save me," she had feebly cried.

"What God are you calling upon?" we'd asked. "Odin convinced one of his followers to tie his daughter, Rindr, to her bed so he could rape her. The Biblical god murdered the entire world with a flood. Gods have demanded blood sacrifices, abortion, stoning, hanging, incest. Have you not read the so-called holy books? Gods are monsters. I see none of them stepping down from their divine thrones to stop us. It would appear they are either not powerful enough to do so or applaud us. Were we not created in their image, after all?"

She'd started murmuring something to herself. A prayer? We'd approached her to spy on her most private conversation between her and her delusion of an invisible friend.

Only, she had murmured, "Mommy, mommy, I'm coming" over and over. We understood. Still asked. "Is your mother dead?"

"She's an angel," Grace had whispered, an otherworldly, far too peaceful smile on her face.

"What did your mommy die of?" We'd asked in mock concern.

"She died of cancer," she simply breathed, no tears following that statement. That had irked us even more, the audacity of depriving us of her passion in that way.

"So you watched her suffer. Possibly over multiple years. You're cruel, Grace."

Grace's objection came in a whisper. "No. No, I was never cruel. I never would have harmed my mother in any way. I wanted her suffering to end."

We had her.

"And if you look at your friend here now? Knowing that in just mere seconds we will ram this knife up her vaginal cavity, does that make you want to save her? Or will you let her die like you let your mother die?"

Her eyes went blank. She was ready.

The first stab had accidentally punctured Charity's lung, prompting her to spew up blood. She was drowning in her own human life juices, an irony we much appreciated. For we all do not live but die our lives.

But rather than shrink away, Grace had put her foot onto the seat of the chair between Charity's legs, pulling the blade out of her friend's breast plate with such vigor that it trembled like a leaf of grass in the wind. Stabbing, stabbing again, as Charity kept spitting blood. Despair had given way to rage when Grace roared, "Why won't you die already, die! Die!"

Now she was starting to understand…

After the Rider had untangled himself from me to haul himself down into his den to rest, I'd decided I considered Grace entertaining enough to keep her a tad longer.

After the hours-long cleanup, I'd left Grace in the hole below the tunnel with the promise to return on the next day. I'll have to dispose of the trash bags containing Charity's remains anyway. For now, they safely rest inside one of my freezers.

As I walk out the cabin door, I hum a tune. It's June 18th now, just after 7 A.M. Everything is light as a feather inside me, though my body is sore and I am ravenous. Time to hit the food court at a mall. There's this new boutique in Olympia I was alerted to, and from which I've just been dying to buy this pretty pastel lemon-colored sundress I saw the other day. It has butterflies on it too, which I just adore. I also adore the shop assistant that I spotted a few times while walking past the store.

She just doesn't know it yet.

But she will.

Chapter 6
Humanity Weakening Me Like Poison

She'll have to be between eighteen and twenty, I estimate. Her name, the tag on her chest informs me, is Elysia; likely related to the Elysian Fields of Greek mythology, and very ironically the final resting place of the virtuous. Though completely outside of her control, her ridiculously melodramatic name alone makes me want to choke the life from her.

The wig isn't precisely the same color as Charity's hair was, but pulled up and tucked into the baseball cap I found in Grace's bag, it should still be convincing enough. The attempt of cutting up a few of my fat suits and taping them to my body in such a way that they wouldn't be visible underneath Charity's skimpy outfit proved more time-consuming than first estimated. I had draped a shawl around me in an attempt to conceal my lack of arm-, shoulder- and chest fat. I'd also opted to wear leggings to hide the bottom fat suit. It wasn't perfect but neither are the grainy CCTV cameras at the mall. Another condemning piece of evidence would be the fact I had parked Grace's vehicle in the car park, wiping it down for fingerprints.

Once the girls' disappearance is being investigated, all of this ought to point to Charity as a person of interest. Particularly if Elysia goes missing shortly after an interaction with "Charity." Elysia keeps an eye on me at the store, approaching only to ask if I was "okay with sizes." I am fully aware the question implies I look too robust for the size clothes I am perusing, which is a delightful confirmation of my fat-suit craftsmanship. I resort to informing her that I am picking up a dress for my friend, and after a fake smile that doesn't quite reach her eyes, she leaves me to my own devices. At the cash register, I ask whether she's going to be in the next day, in case I needed to exchange the dress for a different size.

"Oh, I'm always here," she squeaks. "Yeah. It's only me for now, the owner is still looking for part-timers." I always marvel at the amount of information people unwittingly give up to complete strangers.
"Thank you, Miss –" I pretend to only just now notice her name tag. "Miss Elysia."
Her giggle is genuine. "Just Elysia, it's my first name. We're more of a modern store for modern people."
I accept the slight with a smile, and make eye contact for a few more seconds, in case she wanted to surrender her last name to me, alas, she does not. Either way, thanks to her atrocious name I shan't have much trouble finding her on social media to adequately stalk her a while.

One of the most tedious elements of serial homicide is the disposal of evidence. Bodies are dismembered effortlessly enough, their individual parts buried, burned and strewn all over the country, alas, cars are not. And with the increase of traffic cameras and humankind discovering even the most secluded areas in nature so as to escape city life, this task has on occasion made me want to shout at the heavens.
There's safety in solitude when one is a serial killer, and yet, regrettably no one required more assistance than someone engaging in such murderous tasks. And help is surprisingly easy to find if you know how to network, and amongst what groups of people to look.
On the bus back home, I send a quick confirmation text to Rob, head of the group of people who aid me on occasion and sit back in the uncomfortable plastic seat, resting assured that Grace's vehicle, freshly cleaned and re-painted with its plates missing, is being stripped for parts right now as we speak, and that I can catch up on some much deserved sleep. As so often though, I lie awake for hours, reveling in the previous night still fresh in my

mind, until I enter a strange state of unconscious unrest, waking disheveled and wondering how much of it all was memory as opposed to dreams, or whether I had slept at all.

It is just past 8.30 P.M. when I pull up to the cabin in one of my own vehicles, checking for tire tracks of Grace's battered old Ford that could be used against me. But no, I got them all earlier this morning during the clean-up.
The grocery bag casually dangling from my left wrist, I enter the tunnel.
Freeze.
There is a dead woman on the chair.
It isn't Grace.
The hatch on which the chair normally sits is wide open.
I still cannot move, am momentarily incapable of comprehending what happened, don't even reach for the gun in the back of my pants. I am all but unprepared for the first time in years, and my physiological response attests to it. Worse still, there's something happening inside me that I cannot quite make sense of.
Occasionally, I joke with friends about being an old soul, which is code for possessing but proto-emotions, courtesy of my reptilian brain. I don't experience fear. Perhaps a physical jolt, after which I quickly settle back into my logical routine, is a more adequate way to describe it. Right now, however, I *feel* fear, though I'm not even sure of what.
After what may very well have been a good five minutes, I move again, albeit only because the grocery bag has slid down onto the concrete floor with a loud thud, yanking me out of my state of paralysis.
I draw my gun, let down the wall behind me, creep along the Southern wall as silently as possible. The gaping hole in the floor worries me somewhat, as it provides excellent shelter to whoever might possibly be armed and ready to fire at me from down there,

but first I'll need to establish a) whether the woman is actually dead or if this is a ruse and b) who on earth she is.

Never in my life have I yearned for the Rider to merge with me as much as I do now. I listen inside, calling down into the pit. Silence. Fully satisfied with our earlier kill experience, he is fast asleep.

Her face is stained with crusted blood, a few gaping wounds on the top ride side of her head give the impression she was bludgeoned, though I can't say with what. Judging by the shape, it may have been the blunt side of a hammer. I'll have to wipe the blood off of her face in a bit in order to determine if I even know her.

While establishing that she has no pulse and the restraints aren't ruses either, I wonder if I may have had a psychotic break during which I did all this.

I recall reading about a case of a man who'd indeliberately murdered members of his family while sleepwalking. After all, I had suffered from severe bouts of insomnia lately, only to collapse after a few days of being awake, as I'm prone to do during the depression, murdering and totem phases - three of seven phases of serial killing. I have indeed sleepwalked a handful of times in my life in this uncontrollable state as a youth.

My palms are sweating profusely. The gun slippery in my fingers, I inch closer to the hole, embarrassingly aware of how hard I have to clench my butt cheeks in order not to sully myself.

Conventionally, there's neither any reason for me to avoid physical and armed confrontation, nor does the thought of death intimidate me, though I'd prefer for the process to be a swift and painless one. It's the bizarreness of this whole scenario that has the rootkit inside me spring open – its contents of humanity and uncontrollable human reactions spilling into me, weakening me like poison.

After determining that the hole is empty, which does nothing to alleviate my stress, I stare at her limp features, the complete lack of muscle tension making them appear somewhat bloated. I lift her chin with my finger, and this is when the wig slides off of her head.

As soon as I lay eyes on the short ruby red hair, I know. For confirmation, I check her nose, and there, underneath the blood pudding, it is – her septum piercing.

It's Elysia.

I don't understand. This had to be my doing, but if it was, then where is Grace?! Like an automaton, I stumble towards one of the two freezers, yank open the lid and discover that the trash bags containing pieces of Charity are also missing. Close to fainting, I tear at the lid of the second freezer. Wispy tendrils of frozen air rise up, teasing my cheeks and forehead, making my eyes water. Once they clear, I stare at the emptiness before me in disbelief.

My thoughts are racing. Did I, in my orgasmic delirium, reveal to Grace my next target? But I would never! In the right state of mind at least. Did Grace somehow free herself and take Elysia?

Why, why would she though? As a gift to me? As a threat? Did she start to enjoy killing but wanted me out of the picture? So she put a dead body in my basement and perhaps already informed law enforcement about this cabin and its contents?

None of my frantic musings are realistic though. I have no explanation and don't even know how to begin looking for one. I understand that time is of the essence and that I must get rid of the body as soon as possible.

Close to tears from equal parts fatigue and confusion, I open the wall cabinet, plug in the electric hacksaw and get to work, ultimately hosing down the tunnel top to bottom.

Mostly, I humorously refer to stuffing body parts in Glad trash bags as the "bag and tag" phase but tonight is no laughing matter. In fact, I am shaking, feeble, hungry. There are two very different types of primitive Steppenwolfesque beasts warring inside me.

One whose flight reflex is violently wrestling with the one that demands certainty. The latter one's name is Impulsivity.
Although I know I chose the safest option, I crawl down into the hole defeated and embarrassed, trembling from exhaustion. The Rider had thought of everything, though I had often thought him paranoid: I insert the key into the metal bars that would lock the hatch from the inside, ascertaining no one possibly lurking somewhere inside the house would be able to come down here to kill me. A prisoner in my own cell, I am left to shiver on the narrow cot, no blanket to warm me, frantically gulping down half a quart of water originally intended for Grace. I fall asleep quickly but wake often, jerking upright and reaching for my phone, which at some point only shows 3% left. I decide to turn it off. What would I do with it anyway, call the police to come to my rescue?

I'm nowhere near well-rested when I decide to rise from my cave to face whatever it is that may await me upstairs. I had briefly pondered using the exit tunnel to escape the cabin, but I know I would not have been able to stop obsessing unless I had searched it thoroughly to assess if anyone was still lurking inside, had removed or altered something, or had even left me more clues – or bodies – to tend to.
The food and water have at least supplied me with enough energy to ignore my sore neck and muscles, and I do a few stretches to get limber again.
I sigh with relief once the wall comes up, for I had had absurd nightmares about being locked in here and succumbing to thirst and hunger. I have an entire arsenal strapped to me and a strategy on how to effectively search the house. The one thing I have not is a bulletproof vest, and I make a mental note to add one to the kill cabinets of each of my homes.
The control room on the Western wall is empty. My steps are quiet but I can hear myself breathing. My clothes, rubbing up against

each other as I sneak up the stairs, thunder in my ears. I'm paranoid that whoever might hide in the cabin might hear them too. I make a right, into the kitchen, my back half turned to keep an eye on the living room. I open the first two bottom doors of the kitchen cabinet. But no one's hiding in any of them. They look undisturbed, as does the living room. No one's hiding underneath the bed or behind the shower curtain either.

One after the other, I grab the heavy duty trash bags, heaving them up the stairs and into the trunk of my car. As I switch on my phone, it is June 19th, 5.22 A.M. The battery is at 1% now but before it goes black, I detect no missed calls, urgent emails or notes written to myself in a psychotic state, which would help explain my current situation.

I bury the toothless head just outside of Issaquah, the extremities as well as each quarter of the torso are laid to unrest in different locations between Counties Snohomish, King, Pierce and Mason, and I change clothes and shoes that I keep in the trunk of each car each time I depart from a dump site.

The only reason I don't kill more often is that it's immensely time-consuming work, which, I think, ordinary people do not appreciate enough. In order to bury an entire body I would have to spend about six to seven hours, short breaks included. There are some obvious risks connected to that. To be frank, though I'm in excellent shape, I simply lack the stamina for this type of laborious effort.

Instead, I spend about an hour dismembering a body, three to clean up – "bag and tag" included. Driving back and forth between locations takes anywhere between three and five hours, and after each burial of a body part, I am grateful to be able to sit and rest, listening to music while on my way to the next burial site. I probably spend more time burying each limb individually, but it's overall a more convenient experience. Most pressingly, it may stall or entirely prohibit the body parts' as well as my own discovery.

I always hope that the lye will do its part in speeding along decomposition, though Washington soil West of the Cascades is already quite ideal in this regard. As plastic has a decomposition rate of ten to twenty years, I cut open the trash bags, placing the human waste directly into the soil, just lightly covering them with the plastic. The graves ought to be deep enough, but I hope the material will do its part in deterring animals to try and dig up any remains.

Surprisingly, webpages dedicated to forensics, such as the Forensic Anthropology Center, offer little to no insight on how to best dispose of a body, and so many of the post mortem rituals I dutifully carry out were – and partly still are – trial and error.

Back in my Seattle apartment, I do a quick sweep of each room, still suspicious I might find a corpse waiting for me there, too. When that is not the case, I take a hearty swig from the whiskey bottle in the kitchen and decide to take a hot shower to alleviate the pulsing discomfort in my hips.

As I shampoo my long locks, I ponder turning myself into a sleep clinic to check for abnormalities such as sleepwalking. The more I think about it, the more it makes sense that I am responsible for the oddity I'd encountered in the tunnel last night.

That is why it aggravates me to no end that when I walk back towards the bedroom, I find a strange man sitting on my living room couch, sucking on a vape pen.

Chapter 7
Excitement Lighting Up His Eyes Like Napalm

One look at his relaxed posture, legs crossed, his flat palm resting next to him on the green velvet Chippendale couch, tells me that he is in complete control of the situation.

The only control I have is not giving him what he'll likely expect. And so I resist the urge to fasten the towel around my torso, waiting for him to introduce himself as my hair keeps dripping shower water all over my dark hardwood floors.

"Miss Sand, I am Detective Michael Pennington." His eyes remain trained on mine, searching for any signs of human weakness, as law enforcement are wont to do. I give him nothing, my veneer remaining in place.

"It would appear that at the very least we share an appreciation for the darker side of human nature," he adds, uncrossing his legs to lean forward, resting his arms on his thighs. "Fascinating, no?"

"Do you have a card, Detective?" I ask back. "I'd like to inquire whether King County Police is now generally in the habit of breaking into law-abiding citizens' homes."

His mouth twitches with irony. "Did you like my gift, Emily?"

Son of a...

"What gift would that be, Sir?"

"Wow, you kinda rule. What a great response," he says so wholly without irony, his hoarse voice full of warmth, that I'm relieved my face was already flushed from the shower.

The choice of words and tone serve several functions. For one, it's supposed to make me question my reality because this isn't a sane response to the turn this conversation has taken. There's also a finality to his words that puts the ball in my court. It prompts a question, rather than a mere 'thank you.'

Lastly, it is a gross spin on the Reid method. Which is virtually a manual teaching law enforcement to employ isolated cluster B behaviorisms to break a suspect – love bomb, devalue, discard. Rinse and repeat.

"Elysia was my stepdaughter."

The words ring through the silence, stunning me. That's…not something I would have ever seen coming.

"It would be my pleasure if you called me Michael," he says. "And not to appear patronizing but I'll gladly wait for you to don some clothes, after which we can continue our conversation."

I had fully expected them to be gone, yet still investigate whether the Detective had removed my weapons, conveniently hidden all over the apartment. The fact that each and every one of them was in its designated place in the bedroom reinforce the message that he was "the man."

My brain is going haywire, trying to decipher the meaning of all this, yet I remain uncertain about how to tackle this situation. All I know is that I need more time to think, which means – and don't laugh – I will blow-dry my hair.

Ten minutes later, I'm dry but still none the wiser.

It doesn't appear that the Detective is out for a physical confrontation but just in case, I opt to wear clothes that cannot be used against me. Your opponent is on the ground and you're trying to get away? Tight clothes will make it more difficult for them to grab or yank you back by them. Long hair is another issue, but I'm too vain to shave mine off.

"Would it be alright if I poured myself a drink?" the Detective calls from the next room. I feel silly shouting back at him, and I'm afraid I can't stall any longer, so I return to face him.

"I'll pour us a drink each," I offer nonchalantly. "Whiskey?"

"You read my mind."

I wish…

I sit down in the King George armchair across from the sofa, placing the Detective's glass on the far other end of the table. As we quietly sip the amber-colored brew, I take him in – and he lets me.

He's not a handsome man by society's standards but he is compelling, so compelling I feel as though I already knew him, despite it being a ludicrous split second thought. The glabellar frown lines between his lively ocean blue eyes are the only wrinkles visible on his pale face. He'll probably be in his early forties. His posture is excellent, like that of many overweight people – a way to appear thinner than they are. His choice of clothes speaks to this as well. A silver gray suit - pants and a vest, no jacket – with a white dress shirt underneath. I estimate that he is one of the ones who'll give their height as six feet – the national average for white males – despite being just one or two inches short of it.

The hair remaining on either side of his head is cropped so short I cannot tell its natural color. It's darker than his eyebrows, so it probably used to be blond earlier in his life. I fish a cigarette out of the pack on the table and concentrate on lighting it.

"Did you like what you saw?" he calmly inquires. Is he talking about his 'gift' or his face?

"Yes." I say before even thinking, not quite sure what I'm responding to. Perhaps both.

He smiles, his cheeks parted by long narrow dimples that let him appear even younger - like a rowdy little rascal – excitement lighting up his eyes like napalm.

"I have to say," he resumes, "it's rare to make a connection of any sort with a female who is also into the twisted nature sometimes found in the mind."

Another mysterious statement. I'm increasingly tiring of whatever it is he's ultimately playing at.

"How may I be of service to you, Detective?"

"I don't intend to alarm you, but I've been watching you a while. You have left me profoundly impressed, not solely as it pertains to your own methodology of disposing of those you deemed worthy of briefly meeting your true self. I also noticed – perusing your bookshelves earlier - that you are well-read, which is rare these days. Moreover, you are so…uniquely in control of every action, every word, every emotion you pretend to feel – you continue to intrigue."

Flattery is one of the coarser attempts of human manipulation, which have no effect on me. To hear someone praise my modus operandi, alongside the carefully crafted façade I hide behind, is a novelty however. It unnerves and thrills me in equal measures, though I do my best not to show it.

"What was the purpose of your gift, Sir?"

"I understand that my proposal may cause initial hesitancy on your part, but ask only that you take ample time to think it over." Wow. The audacity of this man is matched only by his grandiloquence. He clears his throat. "I would like to get to know you. I intend to do it right, Emily. In brief, I just need to take you out."

"Take me out as in murder me?" I stupidly ask before I can stop myself.

He chuckles, sucks on the vape pen again. "I'd also like to show you who I am, does that put you at ease? I believe you may eventually have to concede that we are but mirror images of one another. Mayhap more."

I want to respond 'I doubt that,' but had I intended to make the acquaintance of someone like myself, I would likely have left a surprise token challenge in the form of a dead body in his basement as well.

I had taken into consideration that the Detective might try to blackmail me into killing someone for him. But his 'gift' indicates otherwise. Clearly, he isn't averse to doing his own dirty work. Had he intended to book me on charges of murder, he wouldn't have had to slaughter his own stepdaughter to frame me for it, and he wouldn't have come alone.

"Well," he says as he rises from the couch. "Notify me of your decision at your earliest convenience." He tucks his vape pen back inside the pocket of his vest. "To that end, I shall now let you rest. I know you've had an…adventurous night."

He doesn't leave a card, demonstrating that not only is he aware I can find him if I so desire, but also that he's not worried about me finding anything on him that I could use to my advantage.

I do not rise from the chair, do not even turn around to watch him leave. I'm so completely stumped, I'm barely aware the cigarette has burnt down to the filter, scorching my fingers.

As soon as I have somewhat recovered from this unforeseen revelation, I get to work on my laptop, opening tab after tab of databases, genealogy sites, social media, articles, image results. After an hour of perusing multiple pages, I believe I have most of the basic information on the correct Michael Pennington – no social media accounts – who is the adopted son of military veteran Jason Pennington and Dottie Farmer Pennington, no occupation listed. Based on her age, she may have been a homemaker. There's no information online about his family of origin, merely his place of birth. He's Southern-born but has no accent, meaning he will likely have been adopted very early in life.

I notice that the only PDF publication referencing his name is one from a small town Southwest of Seattle, on the Olympic peninsula. I cannot stress this enough, it always pays to have a Whitepages premium membership and become a member of genealogy, yearbook and similar sites when you are a serial killer.

Alas, there are no high school photos of Pennington online, merely his name – Mikey Pennington – appears in a long list of students in a Washingtonian high school yearbook from 1987. I cannot even imagine calling him Michael, let alone Mikey. The innocent playfulness of the nickname doesn't jibe with his posture, mimic and overall demeanor in the slightest.

It would appear he lives with one Isobel Cutter, which is an ironic name for a killer cop's girlfriend. Her daughter Elysia Reichert is listed as having lived at his address but now resides – resided – at an address in Olympia.

I don't like that the news of Pennington living with someone deflate me the way they do. On the other hand, I appreciate the level of his perversity, wondering if he is at home holding Miss Cutter's hand as she weeps over the disappearance of her only child – which he murdered.

I try to envision what a slow burn it would be to find myself in that very same situation, and cannot help feeling aroused. What would he be saying to her? Remembering his raucous voice, the words of comfort and reassurance I imagine him to utter, tighten my chest and quicken my breath. Did his intense blue eyes flare up with lust when he brought the tool down on Elysia's head? The way they'd done when looking at me?

The notion alone was so preposterous, that I'd never entertained the prospect of finding a serial killer companion. I couldn't say with any degree of certitude that this was even Pennington's intention. However, his actions weren't congruent with a frame job. And while I was devoid of just a shred of loyalty myself, I was dyspathetic to the idea of playing second fiddle alongside Miss Cutter, for reasons inexplicable to me at present time.

My mood sour, I erase my search history and retract to the bedroom. Indeed, I had more dire matters to tend to than mere mortal jealousy. The situation at hand called for a little reconnaissance of my own.

Just as I begin to form a plan of action for the next day, my phone buzzes. His first name appears above a number I distinctly remember not saving to my phone. He did while I was in the shower.

The message reads, "Good night, Emily Sand."

Chapter 8
I'm Coming For You, Michael

After I'd spent the morning on more research, as well as ordering the bullet proof vests for my various cabins, I listen to my kill playlist on the drive down towards the wider Olympic area. Not because I have any intention of taking anyone's life just yet, but to get amped up and ready for my stalking adventure.

I don't know much about the town Pennington lives in, other than it is referred to as crackhead central by Washingtonians, but I wonder if I should eventually employ my friend Kate Bauer to look into my new acquaintance. She is a class "A" stalker if ever there was one, having access to various databases and websites no one else has, thanks to her occupation as an archivist. I say this not only with the utmost respect but with gratitude, recalling all the times she's helped me out without asking any questions whatsoever. Kate has been helping to keep my destructive side somewhat satisfied during the weeks and months I have to abstain from my lonely debaucherous art, redirecting my sadism into something constructive and orderly, and giving me little tasks to do while we were targeting individuals we'd decided to deconstruct. Most True Crime consumers and self-appointed authorities were intellectually impaired to a point I wish it were fatal. I do not fancy myself a vigilante in the slightest, but I could also not claim that I did not believe Kate's choices weren't justified.

We target interior designers misrepresenting themselves as criminal profilers, a term and profession that doesn't actually exist the way it is portrayed on television, ghost hunters pretending to hold séances with Ted Bundy's deceased victims and making the True Crime community as a whole look like a den of lunacy, female misogynistic psychologists enviously discrediting aspiring writers with refreshing new takes on human behavior, anger excitation readers projecting their impulse control issues on the offenders in question.

None of it was personal, and we had conveniently framed another woman for our shenanigans, who had dared get on my bad side when she had extensively flirted with one of the boyfriends we kept as pets.

We worked on our projects for as long as we kept feeding each other's obsessiveness, spiraling higher and higher until our brains short-circuited and we abruptly stopped, not speaking for another few weeks, until the depression set in again.

'I'm coming for you, Michael…' It's the first time I mentally call him by his first name, which immediately sets my face aglow, as though I had done something wrong. I do acknowledge that stalking Pennington may pose a challenge, for now that he opted to alert me to his existence and presence on the periphery of my life, it is likely he'll purposely alter his habits as much as possible in order to prevent me from being able to get a read on him.

Now, if there's one thing I know about the human brain, it is that it has its limitations. The brain is not a natural deceiver, which means it strains to uncover untruths. Creating, maintaining and building upon untruths poses an even greater challenge. Likewise, the brain is at all times scrambling to identify and create patterns, familiarity, a routine.

Regardless of how skilled a deceiver Pennington may be, the fact that his slave master – his brain – is destined to create a new reliable pattern for him to live by, showing me how he misleads and entraps, what and whom he lies about, will aid me.

There are different stages and elements to this endeavor, which may not be rushed. I see the term "lack of impulse control" misapplied whenever people so brazenly comment on serial murder. In reality, though, organized killing takes quite a bit of patience. And patience only ever almost eludes me when I have already secured a victim. This is when the painkillers and alcohol come into play.

But no, patience does not only ensure that I keep evading law enforcement for another few decades, but it's a luscious brand of masochism. I refer to it as self-sadism, only because I abhor the thought of thinking of myself as a masochist or submissive in any way. But yes, it is a way to prolong and savor the anticipation.

I fondly recall the era pre-cell phones, CCTV and traffic cameras. The golden era of serial killing that so abruptly came to an end in the mid to late nineties. Half of my prep work involves working with and familiarizing myself with new technology, which – for the record – I loathe with a passion, as well as deliberating how not to get caught using or even just trying to bypass it.

In ye olden days, I would have simply gone to a payphone to call Isobel Cutter's workplace and/or her home in order to ascertain her whereabouts, but there aren't many left, and most of them are in places that are heavily monitored. Instead, I brought a brand new burner phone with me, and I park my car a good bit into the woods on the outskirts of town. There are no hiking trails near here, but of course that doesn't mean that there may not be humans around. This bit is unfortunately one of the riskier parts of what I do.

I grab the bag from the trunk, meandering into the lush greenness, behind a tree with a wide trunk, to change. I am a missionary today, because no one will take a second look at a female wandering alongside the interstate into town if she's a missionary, complete with a Book of Mormon under her arm and a name tag announcing that she's "Sister Sarah," one of the most generic and hence forgettable Biblical names in existence. My shoes are two sizes too large, padded with foam inserts to make walking in them less uncomfortable. Regardless, I know my feet will be sore after I return home.

I pull out the sheet of paper from the front pouch of my backpack, on which I scribbled down all relevant phone numbers I plan on dialing today, and try the front desk of the local hospital first.
"Hi, this is Dani calling for Isobel Cutter in Management of Emergency Services," I chirp into the phone. "Could you patch me through, please?"
"Last name?"
"Rolling," I lie. Neither does anyone usually understand these little serial killer-related jokes, but I also can never share with anyone my hilariousness, which occasionally frustrates me.
"What is this regarding?" the female voice on the other end asks, managing to sound both bored and authoritative at the same time.
"I'm not sure, I was told to call her back?"
"Please hold."
"Sure, thank you!" I say brightly, but the receptionist is already gone.
"Hello, this is Isobel Cutter speaking, how may I help you?" Miss Cutter's lower-pitched voice is gentler than expected. I also notice the complete absence of panic, grief or any other type of negative human emotion in it.
"Oh, hello? Can you hear me? This connection is really bad, but I just wanted…" I hang up.
I may not understand motherhood or familial loyalty, but I at least know that no mother on earth would sound this composed if she had just been informed about the disappearance or death of her daughter. Unless she is like me, and Pennington, that is. If I have some sort of bizarre Fred and Rose West triangulation scenario on my hands, I'd be at a loss about how to even approach this dilemma. The Wests had been among Britain's most hated serial murderers who'd buried the body of one of their own children in their backyard.
Elysia must have only just moved out after graduating high school, so unless there's history I haven't yet uncovered, and

which would be a reason for Cutter and her daughter not to regularly communicate, I will have mere days to establish the basics of the Pennington case, as well as my stalking routine, before this area will be under constant police surveillance.

I cannot be certain whether this was Pennington's first murder, but it was all too neatly, too cleverly perpetrated for it to be so. In which case he will also be aware of how much danger he put himself – and potentially me – in, because he will be investigated either way, regardless of his status as a law enforcement officer.

I deliberate whether to call the police department to ask for Detective Pennington. He may smell a rat and stop by at home after my anonymous call, in which case I'll have to abort my mission. In fact, it may even be his day off, and I'm not yet clued in on what rotating schedule the local police department uses, as they typically don't announce it publicly. Smaller departments often use four days on, three off or vice versa, with twelve-, ten- or eight-hour shifts.

I opt against calling the police department at this present time, dialing his home number instead, though that might be just as unwise. But no one answers. Satisfied, I close the Book of Mormon and continue on my way towards town.

An hour and a half later, I have reached my destination, and naturally, not one of the occasional drivers passing me bothered to stop to ask whether they could give me a ride. This is the magic of Bundyland, combined with my garb. People are already hesitant to offer anyone a ride because the Pacific Northwest is nationally known as serial killer central, but to have someone in your car blathering on about the angel Moroni and John Smith is even more unwelcome than a murderous maniac.

You may wonder then, why I chose this persona today, as at first glance it might appear unwise to you, considering I wanted access to Pennington's neighbors. Although Mormon conversion attempts were rarely successful, they usually had something else to offer that hardly anyone ever refused, in my experience, and we will get to what that is shortly.

Pennington's home is located at the end of a cul-de-sac, with two more homes on the left and two more on the right side of his. It's 10 A.M. when I knock on the door of the first house on the right. I already know that elderly Mrs. Virginia Blackwell lives at this address, and ought to be home, hypothetically. After about a minute, I ring the doorbell for a second time. Nothing.

I decide to make my way around the house, into the backyard, and immediately lay eyes on a figure further in the distance, raking leaves.

"Excuse me!" I shout in a slightly altered voice, waving at whom I presume to be Mrs. Blackwell. "Hi!"

She stops working, leaning on the rake while simultaneously shielding her eyes against the morning sun with her hand.

"Oh hello," she calls over, then slowly sets into motion, squinting at me once she stops about six feet short of me.

"I apologize for interrupting you, Ma'am," I say obsequiously. "I see now that you are busy, but I'm with the Church of Latter Day Saints, and wondered if I would be allowed to share with you the restored Gospel on this beautiful day?"

Mrs. Blackwell coughs, wipes her mouth with the back of a jittery hand, before running a finger up the bridge of her nose.

"Oh!" She cries. "My glasses!" Then she buries her head in her left hand, chuckling. "I left them inside. See, they're a little loose and I'm always afraid I might lose them during gardening or yard work. Pardon me."

The older people got, the more they threw spaghetti at the wall in terms of an overabundance of recounting in minute detail their day's events. It is as though they were covertly fighting their own glaring insignificance by overemphasizing anything and everything happening to them throughout what remains of their lives.

I respond with high-pitched bell-like laughter. "No worries, Ma'am."

I have killed at least one person from every demographic but the old ones are more often in the habit of leaving so gracefully. There is no real regret, not the same intensity of fear. They already lived their lives, and in this economy, I surmise that most of them are quite content dying after all. Which renders the entire affair of killing them futile, as it did not adequately feed the Rider.

"Well," she offers hesitantly, "You're with the Mormons? I already go to a church of a different denomination here in town, to be perfectly honest."

I give her my most genuine smile. "I understand, Ma'am. I'm not here to save anyone who's already been saved by our Lord, Jesus Christ. But now that I am here, I'd feel bad leaving without offering to help you with your yard work. Please let me assist you?"

There you have it. My ruse. Latter Day Saints are well known for offering such altruistic services not only to members of their church, but to anyone, regardless of whether they believed they could convert them.

"Well," she repeats, and by the tone of her voice I know she's about to send me away, so I cut in, quoting, "For thou, Lord, hast made me glad through thy work: I will triumph in the works of thy hands."

Mrs. Blackwell simply looks at me, until, with a shy giggle, I add, "Psalm 92:4. That's from the Bible, not the Book of Mormon."

"Oh. Right. Okay, but I can't pay you, dear."

"This is strictly a good deed without any strings attached, Ma'am," I retort, beaming even more widely. "If you like, you could sit down in one of the lawn chairs and keep me company while I rake the rest of your leaves, though."

"The rest of my leaves? Honey, that's going to be another few hours!" she laughs. "I doubt you'll be wanting to do the entire yard."

Of course I do. I want to do the entire yard, want to learn about her hobbies, what she collects, whether she has friends and is close with her family, who her neighbors are and which annoying habits they have, whether she likes or is in regular contact with any of them, and if not for what reason. I want everything Mrs. Blackwell has to offer. And fast, since I'm running out of time.

Half an hour later, I'm already well informed about key components of Mrs. Blackwell's unexceptional schedule and life. An hour into raking, she asks me to call her Virginia, which finally allows me to point to my overpriced silver name tag to reveal, "I'm Sister Sarah."

Well, it would have been overpriced had I bought it online. I killed Sister Sarah years ago, holding on to her name tag, glasses and Book of Mormon, just in case. You may make the common mistake of identifying these items as souvenirs, trophies. I kill liberally enough that I have no use for such items. I do always require props, ensembles, and gadgets of any kind, however.

Another hour later, Virginia offers me a can of soda but as I am a Latter Day Saint today, I decline, asking for a glass of tap water instead. I will rinse and wipe my fingerprints off of the glass later on, counting on her to invite me in after this strenuous task. I'm not particularly worried about fingerprints on the rake, as it will be easy enough to wipe them off on the hem of my dress.

Once I finished bagging all the leaves on her property, Virginia asks whether I'd like to join her for a sandwich and fruit salad inside.

While she works on our snack, squinting at an orange she is fileting at the kitchen island, she drones on about her excruciatingly stale life. Suddenly, I spot her glasses right behind her on the counter next to the stove.

I move to stand next to her, feigning interest in her fruit salad recipe, then casually lean back against the counter, and shove them up my sleeve, before moving back towards the open living room space, trying to spy on Pennington's home through the tall glass doors leading to the back patio. As quietly as possible, I let the glasses disappear in the gargantuan potted plant sitting in front of the doors, pressing them into the humid earth and rearranging the leaves to cover them.

"Don't open the patio doors, Sister," Virginia chuckles, "those raccoons are little scoundrels. Back at the old house, my husband always said not to feed them but after we divorced, they became like pet companions to me."

"I understand," I coo, as I turn back around to face her. "God's creatures offer incomparable comfort to us humans, don't they?"

"They sure do, but their appetite puts a real strain on my budget," Virginia quips, and I deliver the most emotive fake giggle I can muster.

"It must be nice to live in a cul-de-sac," I slowly deliberate. "It's quiet, I would think, and there aren't many neighbors around to bother you during the day. Well, on the other hand, it might get a little bit scary out here at night."

"I've gotten so used to the song of the woods out back, I cannot recall a time I was ever scared in this home since I moved in around eleven years ago." Virginia rinses off the knife in the sink, then stops. "I guess it could also be because one of my neighbors is a cop. Lovely man; the entire family is."

She carries both our plates to the couch and asks me to sit down with her. When she grabs a triangle of her sandwich, I ask, "Would you mind if I said grace?" In my mind, the word is capitalized, for everything I do is always connected to Grace, and I enjoy these little inside jokes between me and the Rider, who existed solely due to her. I picture him neatly folding his claws together, an impish grin illuminating his usually smoky features as he repeats after me, "Bless us, Lord, for these your gifts that we're about to receive from your bounty through Christ our Savior, Amen."

"Amen," Virginia quietly says a split second before stuffing half a sandwich into her mouth.

While chewing, she inquires, "I always thought Mormon missionaries were younger, no offense."

"That's mostly true," I reply, "I spent eighteen months doing the Lord's work in Sweden right after community college, and got married at twenty-three, after a two-week engagement." I sigh. "I cannot conceive, so I decided to do the Christian thing and set him free. Since I am childless, I am at liberty to share the restored Gospel with others despite my age, according to current divine revelations."

I hope to change the subject again soon, as Virginia had only just started telling me about the neighbor I came here for.

"I'm Swedish on my mother's side." Virginia's gaze is suddenly turned inward, yet thousands of miles away. "We used to spend our summers there at my uncle's until I was fourteen. Pratar du svenska då?"

"Det gör jag visst, men du snacker ju som en infödd!" I exclaim with genuine surprise, my heart beating twice as fast as it did before Virginia's revelation. Alas, I never do come unprepared, and this reminds me of why that is.

Though I had never been a missionary in Sweden, I'd completed an exchange year during high school, just North of Stockholm. My extracurricular activities included getting involved with a group of second wave Black Metal musicians whom I occasionally desecrated cemeteries with, and accidentally helping found a quasi-Pagan chaos-gnostic cult heavily promoting salvation through suicide. It was still active, both gaining, hence losing, members regularly. And the irony of it pleases me greatly.

Virginia's voice tears through my teenage memories. "Oh, you're really good. I have no idea what you said. I just remember this one phrase and a few individual words."

Before she can continue indulging in her banal childhood recollections, I open my mouth to speak, but the ring of the doorbell interrupts me.

"Oh! Excuse me a moment. You know, I think that may be my neighbor, the nice policeman. He wanted to help me dispose of the leaves you raked earlier."

The limp sandwich triangle I'd been holding between my fingers falls back onto the plate as my eyes widen. But Virginia has already risen, thankfully unaware of my panic-stricken reaction.

Whether Pennington will come traipsing through the living room to get to the back yard, or move around back, he will spot me sitting on his neighbor's couch through the massive window front either way. He hadn't picked up his landline when I'd called earlier, so he must only have returned home from work within the last few hours.

"Virginia!" I call after her. "Could I use your restroom, please? Is it upstairs?"

"Just a moment, dear, I don't want to keep Michael waiting."

For the blink of an eye, my mind goes blank, only to head right into overdrive. There go all my carefully crafted plans! – One day to acquaint myself with the neighbors and layout of their properties. Another one to pay the Colonial Revival style hospital building Miss Cutter works at a visit. I'd already laid out my cancer cap for the occasion. The day after, I would have finally focused on Pennington himself.

The Rider keeps expelling frantic thoughts that bounce around in my skull without direction or purpose, until my focus lands on one particular mental image: Me in handcuffs, at the mercy of a deranged butcher who, oh, who absolutely wanted to frame me for the murder of his stepdaughter! How could I have ever been so idiotic to believe otherwise?!

Thoughtlessly, I shoot up from the couch, throwing the porcelain plate onto the couch table where it angrily rattles back and forth before settling down. Running down the hallway as quietly as I can in an attempt to stop Virginia in some way, I reach for her shoulder as she already reaches for the door knob.

It's too late.

The Rider, for once fully grasping the severity of the situation, is too aghast to mock me in a tough love sort of attempt of motivating me into action, and unceremoniously catapults himself out of the pit, mounting me.

Chapter 9
Good Faith

Pennington's naturally authoritative visage appears in the doorway. He opens his mouth to return his neighbor's chipper greeting, yet freezes midway through as he lays eyes on us. Virginia follows his gaze, turning around and doing a little jump when she realizes we're standing directly behind her.
"Heavens, you scared me, Sister!" she exhales, clutching both fists to her chest. "I'm so very sorry, Virginia," we smoothly reply. "That wasn't my intention. I didn't want to be impolite, so I followed to greet the policeman friend you'd mentioned."
"Didn't you say you needed to pee, dear? The upstairs bathroom is right down the hall, last door on the right," she croaks.
We blink at her, and even Pennington visibly struggles to regain his composure after her remark. As soon as our eyes meet, he looks away, absorbing our ensemble instead. The thick glasses obscuring our eyes, dark brown wig with its hair parted in the middle, two unruly looking strands of outgrown bangs falling into our face. His eyes remain on our name tag longer than necessary. Suddenly, his posture changes, he leans forward ever so slightly, as though he were about to bow, until he dynamically bounces back on his heels, simply stating, "I'm here to collect your garden waste, Virginia. Furthermore, I will gladly return Sister Sarah back home or wherever she'd like to go."
There's a finality to his words that vexes us, but the Rider part of us is a wiser animal than Emily is, and thus we remain silent. Virginia looks back and forth between Pennington and us, as though sensing some tension, squinting in order to read our facial expressions, but ultimately relenting. "Oh, alright," she bleats shrilly. "That is very nice of you, Michael. But oh –! Our snacks! Would you like to come in and have a sandwich and some fruit salad with us?"

"I appreciate your kind gesture, Virginia, but I must be on my way. Now, Sister, would you be so kind as to help me carry the trash bags?"

It's even more infuriating that he doesn't want to leave us out of his sight, as though we were some unbridled beast, and so we pettily retort, "Of course, *Officer*," prompting Pennington's eyebrow to twitch once, though he does not correct us.

"Sister, would you like me to bag your sandwich for you?" Virginia addresses us while leading the way through the living room and out the side door to the backyard.

"That would be lovely. And while you do that, please let me wash our plates and my glass real quick, Ma'am." I stress the words *plates* and *glass* while looking over my shoulder at Pennington, who curtly nods, adding, "Yes, that would be the polite thing to do, Sister."

Virginia is palpably confused about being overruled in her own house in such a direct manner, but all she offers is a feeble, "Oh. Well, that's not necessary, but alright, I suppose." She walks over to the sliding doors, looking back at Pennington. "Michael? Did – did you want to pick up the bags now?"

Not taking his eyes off of us as we saunter past him with our glass and plate in hand, he responds, "I shall aid Sister Sarah in washing the dishes first, but then, naturally, Virginia, as promised, the garden waste."

Virginia doesn't look too happy about the response but is too polite to insist, muttering, "Looks like there's nothing for me to do around here today but sit down." Thus she resumes her spot on the sofa, listlessly picking at her fruit salad with the fork.

Meanwhile, Pennington doesn't say even one word to us as he picks up the glass from our hands, careful to wipe off our prints with the dish towel in the process. The fact he caught our hint and acted on it, further suggests he meant us no harm. His silence feels like punishment, and we are once more bewildered by the fact it causes us any grief at all.

Minutes later, he has set the plate back onto its designated shelf, but while we start moving around the kitchen isle, ready to take on the trash bags, we notice he isn't quite finished yet, quietly wiping down the counters, faucet and sink. For the first time, his face is relaxed, his mouth not set in a rigid line. It's endearing to watch his oversized hands squeeze the towel between the faucet and its handles to reach even the tiniest water spot. His voice is unexpectedly loud, giving us a jolt, as he calls over to his neighbor, "Virginia, would you be able to produce some vinegar and baking soda for me?"

Is he kidding? He looks right past us at his neighbor, who starts rising from the couch, "What's that, baking soda? I'm not sure I still have any, what is it for?"

Pennington waits until she is by his side, then points, "The lime is back. You may want to soak it in some vinegar and baking soda for ten minutes, then wipe it off with microfiber cloth. Should you have any, I could do it for you right now, before we depart."

Apparently, he's not kidding. It ought not to have surprised us, given that we've never read about an organized killer who didn't fulfill several criteria of obsessive-compulsive disorder. We do, too.

"Let me see," Virginia brays while rifling through the contents of her kitchen cabinet, "no baking soda, but I still have some hydrogen peroxide and vinegar in the garage, would that work?" Pennington holds up a finger as though he were a schoolmaster scolding a disorderly student. "Never," he says, "ever mix hydrogen peroxide and vinegar. The two will form a chemical compound called peracetic acid, which is highly toxic as well as corrosive to any surface applied to. As well, the fumes will cause severe respiratory issues and chemical burns to the eyes."

We're starting to get bored and retract into ourself for a private conversation, as Virginia and Pennington discuss how to resolve the catastrophic threat some grimy crust on her sink seemingly poses.

Now, Pennington's unexpected presence puts us at an even greater disadvantage than before. He was effectively made aware of our actively being on his case. The question is how he will react to our presence at his neighbor's. Will he decide we are too dangerous to keep alive? Once we are in his car, we will have to remain wholly alert, even if he attempts to distract us with small talk. In case he locks the doors, we should have our answer. Next on the list of questions to answer, does he have weapons in his car, and does he carry when not on the job? This will be more difficult to determine. One swift motion with a heavy object and we'd be incapacitated. We have a handsome little firesteel knife holstered to our thigh, which we obviously cannot inconspicuously keep at the ready, so we'll have to rely on the gun in the front pouch of the backpack to aid us in case of need. And hope that we're agile enough within the confines of the vehicle to defend ourself. Our one advantage is that we'll come at him with the combined powers of Emily and Rider.

We wince when we feel the slight touch of a hand on our shoulder. "I think he wants you to help him with the garbage bags now," Virginia informs us. "If you're still up for it, that is, dear. I just realize I've been hogging your time, and you probably wanted to visit a few other houses in the neighborhood."

"It's my pleasure, I can always come back," we respond in Sarah's nasal Alto while glancing at Pennington, who gives us a look of cold fury that could cut through bone more effectively than my high quality German WMF Kineo chopping knife could.

Ten minutes later, the last of the garden waste is neatly tucked away on the backseat of Pennington's silver Nissan Altima. Virginia has retracted into her abode, but not before offering us a dollar for all our hard work. We had just been about to refuse when Pennington cut in, declining the dollar for us. Before the Rider part of us even stood a chance to grip the reins even harder, Emily surfaced for just long enough to slight Pennington once more, humbly replying, "With your permission, I will donate it to our parish's genealogy project," after which the Rider forcibly reintegrated her back into our shared persona, though not without shock, as this incident happened to be a novum.

Pennington had been careful to take every single bag from our hands, rather than permitting us to place it inside the trunk and on the backseat ourself. He'd also been smart enough to relieve us of our backpack and lock it inside the trunk. We had politely objected, but when he insisted, it had appeared wiser to obey, being that Virginia had accompanied us to the car and followed our tense exchanges with visible interest, before waddling back inside.

Finally, Pennington unlocks the front doors one last time, snarling, "Get in," but as we reach for the door handle, the locks click again and we pull out the latch in vain.

"I told you to get in." His voice is low and dangerous, it's the voice we use with our victims. He activates the lock once more, then deactivates it again as we reach for latch a second time. We look at him over the top of his Nissan with the same expressionless face he wears, exactly aware of what he is doing. Asserting dominance, attempting to confuse us enough to submit inside. After a good long while of his eyes boring into ours, he unlocks the car and positions himself behind the wheel.

After opening the passenger door, we have mere seconds of pulling up our long dress enough to reach underneath it, pull the knife out of the sheath attached to our thigh and slip it into our sleeve. Long skirt bunched in our left hand, we take our seat next to Pennington, and shut the door.

Without so much as glancing at us, he smoothly backs out of Virginia's driveway and onto the road. We decide not to grant him the satisfaction of speaking first, but minutes later, we appreciate that he is at least as stubborn as we are, continually working the muscles in his jaw with covert anger, rather than breaking the silence, which becomes increasingly unnerving.

Lastly, finally, we have reached the city limit, and, surrounded by slim conifers on either side of the road, we glide ever forward. A circumstance that ought to worry us, as Pennington will now have no witnesses present for whatever he may have in store for us. Without a doubt, the reverse is true as well, fortunately. However sanguine this encounter may turn and conclude, we stand a far better chance out here, where no prying eyes follow our every defensive or deadly move.
He shifts in his seat, provoking us into fishing for the edges of the knife, but he keeps both hands on the wheel.
"Today's bold excursion of yours, I trust you know, may end perilously for the both of us," he announces. "Explain yourself."
Imbued with the acumen and intellectual contortionism of the Rider, we coolly counter. "Hadn't you yourself stated, Detective, that you would like for me to get to know you better?"
He grimaces in response. "I am incapable of determining whether you are making an attempt at being cute or whether it is even humanly feasible for anyone to concoct a plan this inane."
The reply does more than enrage us, it genuinely stings.
"You mean as inane as disposing of your deceased stepdaughter in my basement and putting yourself in a position where – very soon – you and your every prior and future move will be under scrutiny by your community's best and brightest?"
He scoffs, "That isn't going to happen. In fact, I had been anticipating to share with you the specifics of my elaborate

enterprise, but…" He stops himself, finishes with a murmur, "I don't know. Clearly, I made a mistake here."

While the notion of an elaborate plan piques our interest, his admission of believing we cannot be trusted is oddly mortifying. "I, too, had a plan, Detective," we say quietly, still unsure as to how much of it we are willing and able to reveal to him. "Perhaps we ought to speak candidly now? It would appear that you have me at a disadvantage, evidently knowing so much about me, whereas I am yet straining to comprehend the impetus of you approaching me."

He does not respond for a while, but even though we refuse to look at him, we can tell there's a war raging behind his eyes. "Agreed," he ultimately concedes. Though we are still oblivious as to where we are headed, we contend ourself to shifting our torso just enough to watch Pennington's reflection in the car window. His black woolen Eagles football hat reaches down to his eyebrows, the anthracite zipped sweater looks worn and is a fairly tight fit, suggesting that he may have put on a good amount of weight over the last few years.

When his head unexpectedly spins in our direction, his body shifts and his hand reaches towards us, we pull out the knife and lean as far back against the passenger door as possible.

Pennington freezes, then – eyes darting back and forth between the road ahead of us, the knife, and his hand – he pulls the latter back, revealing that he'd been reaching for his vape pen.

The corners of his mouth twitch as he settles back into his seat and says, "Why, Miss Sand, I should have frisked you before inviting you into my vehicle." He glances at me and winks. "Maybe I still should. What else may you hide under that chaste-looking garb of yours? A gun? – A bazooka?" He chuckles, quietly at first, then his chuckle turns into a natural laugh so splendidly infectious it's bursting with joie de vivre. The sound both startles and entrances us, and, tentatively, we giggle, then relax our posture to laugh right along with him until our shoulders shake.

Though we lost our surprise moment, we do not slide the knife back into its sheath, instead pushing it back up our sleeve.

We are just past Tumwater on I-5 when we feel comfortable enough to announce, "You still have Mrs. Blackwell's garden waste in your car."

"I'm well aware," he responds. "I will tend to it later. Now that I happen to have you all to myself, there's something I would like to show you. Your actions and earlier reply established that my expectations were exaggerated."

We're not sure we like the sounding of that. As though he had read our mind, he continues, "My communication with you could, perhaps, have been more advantageous. I vow to do my utmost to remain forthcoming with you from hereon out, should you not run for the hills, considering where I am taking you, that is."

"And where *are* you taking me, Detective?" we inquire.

"My own kill room."

His reply has our heart miss a beat, though we say in the same even voice, "And where is that?"

"Enumclaw, currently. Right outside of Enumclaw."

"Nice. Woodsy." We wonder what he means with the word *currently*, but refrain from asking.

"Isn't everything in Washington?" he shrugs.

With our firearm neatly tucked away in a trunk we have no access to, our knife already discovered by this potential mortal enemy of ours who had only just disclosed he thought of us as mentally impaired, our heart rate accelerates considerably, as we strive to form somewhat of a viable escape plan.

"I must disclose, "Pennington adds, "that this room, as you may anticipate, is filled with instruments of torture and an exclusive assortment of weaponry. And that I also am carrying weapons currently. Now," he says matter-of-factly, as though proposing an

ordinary business deal, "I would like to offer you my gun before we enter my cabin. To show…" he looks over at me, "good faith." His uniquely blue eyes stop our heart for a fraction longer than his following proposal ever could have. "I want to trust you, Miss Sand. I will start laying the foundation of this trust by laying my life in your hands. In return, I have a request that, should you decline it, will not affect my decision to deliver my gun to you."
"Alright," we say. "What is your request, Detective?"
"For you to grant me permission to call you Emily. For you to call me Michael."
For the first time, the lunacy of this entire scenario strikes us full force. We are a sadistic – physically – female serial killer with what psychiatrists would consider moderate other specified dissociative disorder, sitting in a car with a serial killer cop who's taking us to his secret murder palace, in which he does heaven knows what to his victims, and may very well do the same with us.
Well, it's not as though there weren't a myriad of killer cops, soldiers or even killer couples, both romantic and platonic, out there. In fact, law enforcement and the military are high on the list of those occupations antisocial personalities take an interest in pursuing. Entire books, podcasts, documentary series solely focus on this exact subject.
As so many of us in my online group, we'd so often pondered whether a serial killer had ever murdered another serial killer, be it deliberately or indeliberately. Moreover, we had discussed how several of the aforementioned murderous duos had met. In cases such as Roy Norris' and Lawrence Bittaker, it came as no surprise that two violent offenders who'd met in prison, would team up after their release to wreak more havoc on the world.
In case of Henry Lee Lucas and Ottis Toole, the fact that they'd found each other at a soup kitchen, and eventually divulged to each other the fantasies of rape and murder they both harbored, invited more questions. Who had first sensed in the other the same

wildness that lurked inside him? Dared probe further as to how committed the other was about possibly breathing life into these fantasies together?

As for the murderers in romantic relationships, it appeared there was conventionally one instigator, often a factor one psychopath, and one more unstable partner, a factor two psychopath – previously known as a sociopath - or a limerent borderline personality, to give just two examples.

Jason Teale, better known as Paul Bernardo, had terrified the Scarborough neighborhood of his native Ontario for years before meeting his future wife Leanne Teale, also known as Karla Homolka. Her teenage diaries revealed fantasies of rape and violence, and shortly after meeting her, Jason graduated to murder. Furthermore, forensics indicated that Leanne had carried out at least one of the murders on her own, without Jason's presence. She was the dominant partner in their relationship. Who, we wonder, would we be in this equation, if Pennington's intentions were of a romantic nature after all?

"Miss Sand?" The Detective's voice is a quiet, hoarse hum. He's nervous. And, uncomfortably enough, the Emily side of us is, too. Once more, she rears up as the reins slip from the Rider's grasp. It is entirely her voice that responds, "Yes. Michael. You may call me Emily."

Chapter 10
To That End, You May Do Whatever You Please

It's mid-afternoon when, after navigating across uneven terrain and more or less hidden trails, Michael parks in front of a surprisingly shabby travel trailer deep within a part of the forest so thick with trees and underbrush, that just a smidgen of daylight filters through the wide treetops.
Once we'd left Enumclaw behind us, we had been effectively lost as to where we were headed, as Michael had meandered through the impenetrable green without any landmarks so prominent we could be sure to recognize again, other than one tall beech tree whose trunk began to show signs of rot.
"Kindly remain seated," Michael requests, but although his tone is polite, it is, as per usual, decisive. Two fingers on the tip of the blade, we obey, eying him closely as he steps around the car to open the passenger door for us.
"Please," he says, offering us his hand.
His hyperbolic courteousness doesn't quite seem to suit his casual outfit. In fact, we have trouble marrying the concept of Michael's demeanor and vernacular with being a law enforcement officer at all, whose sentences are conventionally clipped, direct, and whose interactions with us in the Bundy group mostly consist of phrases: *It is what it is. So there's that. Can confirm.* The inmates I converse with via government-approved and monitored websites and email services have largely adopted this manner of speaking.
Releasing our hold on the blade, we take Michael's hand and exit the car. He doesn't take a step back, and so we remain for a while – our body inches from his, looking up into his smooth face.
"What are you feeling right now?" he probes, a question that may have prompted Emily's breath to quicken, had she been on her own.
"Nothing."

With an impish grin, Michael softly says, "And if I placed my hand above your heart, would it betray you?"

Now our heart does begin to hammer too frantically in our chest to formulate a witty reply in our head, and eventually, he lets go of our hand.

"Follow me, Emily, into one of the embodiments of my ruinous soul pavillion. I will now reach for my weapons in order to relinquish them to you. Withal I shall do something no sane officer of the law would ever do."

He overemphasizes the word *officer* in a way that insinuates it's a direct response to our referring to him as an Officer rather than a Detective earlier, and that it still bothered him.

"I will turn my back to you and stay ahead of you at all times during our joint expedition today. Does that sound fair?"

When we merely hold out our hand in reply, Michael reaches inside the back of his pants to produce a shabby looking leather sheath. Pulling on the horn handle of the knife it contains, we find ourself face to face with an especially heinous looking little blade, sharpened so many times that half of it has been filed off over what must have been years, if not decades. It looks closer to a fish or boning knife by now.

Next, Michael unzips his sweater, and we take a step back to give him some space, but he misinterprets our gesture, instead holding up both hands as if to assuage us. "I'm wearing a shoulder holster, Emily. However, I trust you are familiar with how to handle a firearm." He puts both hands behind his back. "You have my permission to take it from me. All that I ask is for you not to shoot me with it, should today's revelations have the adverse effect I had been hoping they would have."

We raise an eyebrow at him.

"That would hurt my feelings," Michael says, and we cannot decide whether he's being facetious or not. Paradoxically, there is a strange aura of both danger and vulnerability around him that –

even in our Rider persona – renders us incapable of responding coherently.

We'd immediately taken notice that the grass around the edges of the trailer's wheels still looked freshly flattened. Michael must have been telling us the truth. This was merely his current kill site, and he was smart enough to move the trailer around on a regular basis, probably boondocking on public land. But a travel trailer would still be registered somewhere, and depending on whether he turned out to be friend or foe, this fact might aid us.
It is momentarily dark inside, until we hear the flick of a light switch. The trailer is paneled with wood on the inside. There's a seating area with faded looking 70's upholstery, a stove that has seen better days despite being as squeaky clean as everything else in here. The door on the far right end likely leads to the restroom, the one straight ahead, we presume, to the bedroom.
"I shan't open them so as not to spook you, but stowed inside these wall cabinets are my weapons. I prefer to keep them in alphabetical order to save time. Would you like to take a look?"
"I believe you," we merely say.
A tad deflated, he nods, turns, opens his mouth as though to speak, then thinks better of it, and struts towards the door in the back, ceremonially swinging it open.

There's no bed inside the rear room, whose floor is lined with layers of robust dark green tarp. Just a folded up cot in the corner. It takes a few seconds for us to identify the reticent stench which appears to stem from the twelve large blue plastic bins evenly spaced apart in a half circle across from us. It's earthen, humid, with an underlying but distinct note of rottenness.
"What is this," we slowly say. "I don't understand. Are you marinating your victims in these bins?"

Michael laughs a bright belly laugh. "Marinating my victims," he repeats, shaking his head. "No. This is where I am currently vermicomposting the remains of your last two victims."

"Vermy-what now?"

"Vermicompost. Red wiggler worms? Black soldier flies? Maggots? Well, the maggots are kept separately. They don't play well with other puppies."

"Ah," we reply cluelessly. "That sounds nice."

Michael reaches towards us, yet stops a few inches short of grabbing our hand. "Step inside. Careful, the tarp is a bit slippery."

We look at his outstretched hand. "Michael. How did you get access to my cabin?"

He drops his hand and there's a passing hint of chagrin on his face before he calmly replies, "Emily, I am showing you how to trust me. I am letting you into my world. That part, however, requires trust on your part. I promise you, we will get to any and all things. For now, please feel free to verify that I am telling you the truth about the remains of your last victims."

He waddles towards one of the bins, crouches down and opens its lid. The stench that hits our nostrils makes us gasp. We turn towards the door, coughing, instinctively trying to breathe through our mouth. He's inhaling through his nostrils, without a care in the world. I am well aware of the medical observation that psychopaths have an impaired sense of smell. Alas, that sets me apart from my breed.

"Have you ever heard of a freezer?" we finally ask.

Michael's voice comes from directly behind us, startling us so much we raise the gun while spinning around. He keeps an eye on it, but doesn't take a step back.

"Don't worry. I am not going to touch you unless you expressly grant me permission to," he says. "Are you alright?"

"Yes," we breathe, attempting not to gag. Our watering eyes fall upon the wiggling mess inside the bin behind him, and we instinctively reach for him to steady us.

His hand on our elbow is firm yet gentle. "Emily," he says, almost despondent. "I didn't mean to… I thought…"

"I'm fine," we breathe, another wave of nausea hitting us. "It's the wiggling. It's just…the wiggling isn't good."

He leads us out towards the seated area, helps us sit down and takes his place at the table across from us, watching us struggling to breathe.

With as much feigned affective empathy we can imbue our voice with under the circumstances, we eventually coo, "I appreciate your willingness to build trust between us, and for this purpose, I would like for us to be upfront with each other. I wonder why you would help me dispose of the bodies of my victims, how you found me, and what your interest in me learning about who you are is?"

He frowns, though not unkindly. "I happened to spot you one night, Emily, as you were parking your vehicle deep inside the woods Southest of Port Orchard. It appeared you were handling," he pauses for a moment, "cargo." He is evidently lost in a vivid memory from months ago that I only vaguely recall. "You tripped over your own feet and said, "Shoot," which has stuck with me ever since, as you were on your own, and yet you didn't cuss. You seemed…" His eyes focus on me again, "I don't know," he admits, running a thumb across his lower lip. "There was something about you."

"What then?"

"Well, I dug up your grave. As you may be able to imagine, it didn't take long for me to verify you had attempted to dispose of part of a human torso. But before that, I followed you through the woods and back to your car. There was a moment during which I thought you had become aware of my presence, as I had carelessly stepped on a twig that snapped under my foot. Your head swiveled around, and you reached for your gun."

We actually remembered that moment now. Just as 6'9 tall serial murderer Edmund Kemper had once noted in an interview, it truly was scary going out into the woods alone to dispose of a body. Being that we were stuck in a female body, there were always other concerns rather than just capture. What if we ran into a human creature far more ferocious than us?

Michael continues, "I recall that although your face and entire posture were temporarily timid, something inside you appeared to lift you up. You were entirely an apex predator despite the impenetrable blackness staring back at you." He clasps his hand in front of him and lays them both on the table, inches from mine. "You awed me, as it were."

It may have impressed him less had he known that it was but the Rider who had whispered to Emily to have courage, back in those woods. That without him, she was nothing.

"And you have been following me ever since?" we inquire, still wondering how he managed to do so without our noticing it.

"Yes. Sporadically. I have withal not solely subjected you to surveillance, I pledged to protect you."

Something about his tone irks us. There is an arrogance about his self-assurance that we would just love to punish him for.

"And what makes you think I need protection?"

He shrugs. "I would surmise anyone needs protection every once in a while. My resources, I daresay, are nothing to be disdained. And it is entirely my pleasure to share any and all of them with you, Emily Sand."

I ask the question I always mocked my victims for asking me. "Why? Why me? You work in homicide, you must have arrested hundreds of offenders over the years, some of them, without question, female. Why take such an exceptional interest in me personally?"

Michael's eyes wander to the tips of his own fingers, stretching them just a tad further until they almost touch ours. "Because," he says, "at first I believed you to be a mirror image of me. Watching you over the past few months, I have recently come to realize, however, that you are a part of me, of what I am, who I am. The part that was missing. You belong with me in the most fantastically cruel and genuine of ways. I have killed on my own, been on my own, for decades, always secretly yearning to find someone to share with who I truly am inside. And stumbling across you, my dear, in those lonesome woods, I finally found the one person I believe may not just understand but fully appreciate me. All of me."

We let the words sink in.

His gun is in our hand, the clip fully loaded, the safety off. And this man, this odd-looking but strangely beautiful man, with his most peculiar way of speaking, and his lively ocean eyes, is offering us all that we had secretly dreamed of. A companion to rely on, to plot with, someone to share in all our perversity and depravity, a partner in crime quite literally.

But our vis-á-vis would have to accept that we were a package deal. "Michael, are you alone in your body?"

The question catches him off guard. "Pardon? I'm afraid I don't understand?"

"What I mean is, what *we* mean is," we gulp, taking a few seconds to mull over how to proceed. "We are more than just Emily. When we get into a certain mindset, our shadow self merges with Emily."

Michael leans back in his seat, his hands, previously so close to ours, vanish underneath the table. It's an indeliberate gesture of pulling away from us, but the implied rejection hurts us far more than we care to admit.

"Hm," he simply states, but we are not convinced he understands.

"All that Ted Bundy attempted to explain to Dr. Dorothy Otnow Lewis about his Entity, that which she misinterpreted as dissociative identity disorder, that is what the Rider is. Dennis Rader's Batter demon, Son of Sam's Harvey, Danny Rolling's Gemini and Ennad."

As a law enforcement officer, Michael would undoubtedly be familiar with all these names of infamous offenders.

His chest rises and falls with slow, steady breaths. He doesn't seem as perturbed as we would have anticipated after this our most sensitive, and perhaps slightly psychotic, announcement.

"I had never considered giving a name to my Id," he finally admits. "I can cognitively relate to what you speak of, however."

We search his eyes for a hint of irony, for the obvious lie. For how could anyone ever understand what it was like to be ridden? Then again, we are not conversing with any random, average person but with someone who just presented to us his maggot farm happily chowing away at Grace and her plastic-breasted friend.

We incline our head. "So your intentions towards Emily, or us, are…"

"Amorous," Michael simply declares.

"Is Miss Cutter aware of this?" we shoot back, searching his face for a reaction, but it reveals neither surprise nor shock.

"Isobel and I have been separated for almost a year."

"And yet you live together under one roof."

He shrugs noncommittally. "Finances. In part. Primarily, however – and I shall only ever concede this to you – I wanted to watch up close her delectable, indelible anguish once she learns of her daughter's fate."

We awkwardly cross our legs, trying to breathe steadily. This certainly isn't the right time to get aroused.

"Right. You mentioned earlier that you had a plan in place, and we are curious as to what it entails."

"I have the wherewithal to ensure a young man will take the fall for Elysia's murder. A crook, and conveniently, her boyfriend."
We don't respond, keep looking at our vis-á-vis expectantly.
"Very well," Michael sighs. "I want to confide in you about my life, all of it, so you will understand how I arrived at the decisions I, and my own Id," he winks, "have in recent weeks. I had hoped for this to occur in a more –" he looks around the trailer, "romantic setting. So for now, with your permission, I shall relay to you in brief the following. My stepdaughter, young as she may have been, insouciant as she may have seemed, was a deeply disturbed person out to ruin my reputation. Trust that you made the right decision in targeting her, but just as well, trust that I had to act before you could. She was mine to kill."
"Seems to be a strange coincidence that we targeted someone you are indirectly related to," we say, distrust building inside us once more, until we recall how we had even decided to set our sights on her. "Oh. You placed the flyer inside our mailbox, didn't you? The one announcing the opening of the store she worked at?"
"Why, you truly are a woman of unparalleled intellect," Michael smiles. "I was yet unaware of whether you would…bite, but I'd hoped in case you did, this would provide the adequate framework for me to introduce myself to you."
"You deprived me of my torture and kill experience. I had plans for the one you took from me and killed. You stole from me. You left me the clean-up."
"I'm cleaning up for you, too," he nods towards the back door.
"This appeared to me to be a fair trade."
"So this entire wild plan of yours was a serial killer meet-cute." we uncertainly conclude.
"I surmise that is a way to put it." Without missing a beat, Michael adds, "Do you trust me?"
And oh, how we wanted to. We yearned to trust someone with our wanton secrets, to be inspired by their own unapologetic,

unrestrained wildness. More than that, we wanted to trust Michael specifically, though it was yet a mystery as to why. Perhaps it was just as simple as he had said, admitting to us there had been something about us that attracted him. Did attraction work like this? We wouldn't know. We'd never been truly attracted to anyone we'd feigned to have relationships with, our human toys merely means of satisfying baser urges, and to signal to our environment that we were "normal."

"I think we can," we say, not entirely without surprise. "We want to…"

"Then let go," Michael urges us. "Lose it with me. Be with me. Kill with me. Love me, hate me, fuck me, save me."

Well. That was quite the proposal. One that once more prompted us to uncomfortably shift in our seat in an attempt to keep in check the growing pulse between our legs.

His hands are back on the table, palms turned upward in an invitation of taking a hold of them. And then, we simply do. Michael's eyes glitter with impish elation, and we find ourself unable to look away; our head spinning, a million questions forming in our mind, a million hopes bursting forth from the old bottomless pit. Worse still, from an even more vile place, our rootkit, that human part of us we had crammed into the far corners of our being.

Our hands have touched innumerable humans over the years. Shaken hands, dismembered others, run our fingers over the bare chests of our boyfriends as well as lifeless victims. No living person has ever been able to elicit any type of sincere response from us. Remarkably enough, none of what we experienced with and for our freshly deceased victims compares to this alarming sensation now. Once our hands feel the softness of Michael's own, it's as if they meld with ours, become ours. We cannot tell where we end and he begins. And we do not do what we usually do, we do not "experience" something, we…feel, for the second time in just a little over a day, after decades of having settled into a comfortable sort of emotional stupor.

Michael is first to break the silence. "It is with profound regret I must inform you I will have to return, shortly. However, I want to see you again. Will you? See me?"

"Yes," we say in a husky voice, straining to remain in full control of ourself, adding, "Well, the past twenty-four hours have been a wild ride from start to finish."

Michael squeezes our hands, "The first of many wild rides…and to that end, you may do whatever you please!"

Like a schoolgirl, we blush, straining not to giggle. Michael leans towards us, assuring us with a most alluring voice, a strange chorus of low and scratchy, soft and determined, "I'm not kidding. Flirting? Yes. But not kidding. And get ready because things are about to get dark in our story."

Chapter 11
Violent Love, Pure Rage

After we had disclosed to Michael the location of our vehicle, he had returned us to it, insisting on waiting for us to change back into our regular clothes behind a tree, as dusk was upon us by then. He is well aware we can take care of ourself, but the Victorian sentiment is endearing, and what is more, oddly appreciated.

Immediately before the drive back to Seattle, the Rider had quietly disentangled himself from me, now lazily lounging in his cave so we can each tend to our own obsessive thoughts about today's events.

Around bedtime, I receive a brief text message that reads, "Will place a call tomorrow around noon." Insomnia plagues me at night; I am delirious and reliving the kill experience, until, eventually, I decide to relent and start my day by catching up with my landlady and Bundy group duties.

When my phone finally buzzes around 4 P.M., and the words, "You around?" appear on the screen, I do not reply at once, finishing my conversation with an elderly lady intending to rent one of my cabins. Fifteen minutes later, another text message comes in.

"Clearly, you are at home, choosing to ignore me. If your intention is to play immature games with me, Emily, believing they would impress upon me your womanly mysteriousness and independence, I will have you know that all you are doing is turning me *off* and away."

I gape at the message, noticing my chin quite literally dropped. While I type out a polite and placating response, more text messages appear on the screen in quick succession. One an emoji of a broken heart, then a crying one, and lastly a knife, before Michael resumes to avail himself of human speech again.

"I had been so certain you were the one... I cannot fathom your rejection of me, taking into account all the commonalities we share. You are, I realize, not ready for a relationship."

I can't tell whether he is being facetious or not, still staring at the messages on the screen, my mind reeling as to how to reply. But when he writes, "Very well, I shall honor your wish of never being contacted by me again," I hit the call button, only for Michael to let it ring, until I am being redirected to his mailbox. I leave a message, but call back again several more times, eager to allay his perplexing misinterpretations of my not having answered him without delay.

'These are the first stages of trauma-binding you to him, you fool,' the Rider whispers in agitation. 'I was willing to consider his proposal, for both our sake, but now that he is using his own abandonment issues to create a fear of abandonment in you, there is no doubt he was love-bombing us yesterday.'

Hours later, after I had sent two more text messages, assuring Michael all this had been but a misunderstanding, he replies, "Understood. I intend to call within the next five minutes. I would appreciate if you would a) pick up and b) we could agree to forget our miscommunication."

My relief weighs harder than my confusion, thus I agree. In a way, his eagerness was flattering, his impulsiveness a show of how invested he already was in me.

"Hey," he greets me coolly. "How are you two today?"

I chuckle in response. "It's just me now. But I am well, thank you."

"Should you be free tonight, I'd like to take you out."

"Is it wise for us to be seen together in public at this present time?" I frown.

"No. You had better recall that fact in case you intend to pay any further visits to my neighbors. As for myself, I shall take you on a trolling date."

A faint gasp escapes my lips.

"Are you excited?"

Am I ever. "Yes," I smile, ignoring the Rider's faint whisper that it could be a trap.

"Good. Wear something inconspicuous, a black hoodie and pants, boots. I will text you the coordinates of where to pick me up at 9 P.M. sharp." He adds, "And Emily?"

"Yes?"

"Sharp."

I'd had an inkling about whom we'd be stalking on this cool summer night, and Michael confirms my suspicion.

Washington has always had a tremendous homeless problem; the whereabouts of the less fortunate being recorded on different national park websites, so as to aid regular visitors, campers and boondockers to avoid coming anywhere near them.

Though the majority remains in the cities at night, enough of them retreat to the woods. I myself had stumbled across trees with makeshift hammocks attached to nine inch nails, on occasion. Over the years, I'd learned to avoid specific areas inside the Washington woods, yet more encampments sprouted up anywhere, anytime, posing yet another infuriating challenge for me. The homeless make for less ideal victims than one would anticipate. For they are usually filthy, and with filth comes disease.

"Are you armed?" Michael inquires once we step out of his car.

"I thought this was a trolling date."

His grin is menace embodied, and so excruciatingly seductive to me that my heart stumbles before settling into a hectic rhythm.

"Surprise," he simply states.

And with that, despite his earlier reservations, the Rider bursts forth to fill me with his glorious rage, too curious and greedy a beast to resist a kill. With an equally fiendish grin on our face, we produce a large knife we had strapped to our back.

"We trust our outdoorsy soiree will not pose an issue once the investigation into your stepdaughter's disappearance is underway?"

Michael stares at us, blinks. "So this is what it looks like. When your Id overtakes you," he tonelessly announces, adding, after a moment of silence, "It looks absolutely beautiful, Emily. But then, everything about you is aggressively exquisite."

We choose not to reply to his flattery, though it does appear genuine.

In response to my earlier question, Michael sighs, "No. Thankfully, Isobel's drinking habit facilitated the administration of a mild tranquilizer; she will not wake for many hours. As you may have estimated, my car is parked in the driveway for all neighbors to behold. I shall make my way back to the house the same way I escaped – through the woods adjacent to our backyard."

Satisfied with his elaboration, we nod. "Very well, then."

Michael lowers his head conspiratorially. "Within the last two weeks, I have observed a young man repeatedly set up camp near here. Follow me, and keep your eyes trained on our left, I shall keep eyes on our right, just in case."

Though the moon is almost full, casting a cold haunting light over the darkly idyllic scenery, we advance at a glacial pace, so as to avoid making a sound that would announce our presence. Ultimately, Michael raises his hand, bidding us to come to a halt. "You see him?" he whispers.

We nod. We had already smelled the smoke of the inexpert campfire minutes ago. In its soothing orange glow squats a gaunt man, aluminum tarp loosely wrapped around his shoulders.

"You go around the left in a quarter circle," Michael murmurs. "I will go around the right. Once you see me step into the clearing, follow suit. Yes?"

"Yes."

Eyes and ears alert, we inch forward ever so quietly, but, impressively enough, so does Michael, despite his weight. As soon as his tall dark figure steps out of the shadow of the conifers, we do the same, yet sheath the knife again when realizing our companion opted to approach our prey empty-handed.

The homeless man's mimic reveals unease as his head swivels around, first to Michael, and then to us. He rises from the ground, body tense and alert.

"Hey, this is my spot," he yelps defiantly, the high pitch of his voice disclosing the degree of his insecurity. He hasn't been homeless for long. His haircut and relatively clean clothes speak to it. He exhibits none of the natural predation hardened homeless people who have spent years of their lives on the street do.

"Relax," we gently say. "We were just looking for a campfire to warm our bones, someone to share some stories with. I'm Michaela, what's your name?"

Eyes wide, he is still distrustful of us. We are thrilled when Michael appears to have caught our drift, introducing himself with, "I'm Emerson. May we sit with you a while?"

Truthfully, there is no reason not to reveal our true name to the homeless man, and we cannot reliably say why we assumed Michael's name as our own. Perhaps we did because we remember so vividly the sensation of Michael's hands in ours, the frenzied yearning for oneness it had brought on, as well as the despair of the realization that we could never truly melt into him, *become* him as Emily could with the Rider. There was something else we understood in that moment. That inserting fingers into our victims' wounds, digging around in these strangers with our bare hands, sullying ourself with their blood and forcing our juices into their mouths, was a perverted attempt at facilitating this oneness with someone.

Michael must have felt it too, though, for he assumed our name as his, referring to himself as Emerson.

"Aight." The young man looks back and forth between us. "Caden. I ain't got any food to share, though, just that fire."

Having been granted permission to approach, we sweetly smile at him, instinctively coordinating our steps with Michael's wide strides. As soon as we are within reach, we extend our hand, and Caden, chuckling nervously, reaches for it. Grabbing him by the wrist, we pull him close while swiftly drawing the knife out of its holster, holding it to his throat. Michael's movements are elegant, a cruel, murderous dance, as he slips behind our victim, and slings his right arm around Caden's neck.

"Don't move." There it is again, that enticing chorus of low-pitched authoritativeness and hoarse melancholy.

Caden cusses, whimpers, "I told you, I ain't got nothing!"

Michael laughs in response. "Oh, but you do possess everything we could ever desire."

"What's that?" our victim asks.

"Your life," we say tonelessly, cocking our head.

It's time. This will be over quickly, we can tell, because this isn't as much about the murder, as it is about bonding with, and building trust between, Michael and us.

Before the human sow can even squeal a plea, our knife slashes across Caden's throat so viciously that its tip momentarily gets lodged inside. Michael releases his hold of our victim and stabs him in the lung, prompting a colorful response from Caden, who gurgles up blood bubbles that burst on his lips, only to slowly drip down from his chin. He stumbles, perhaps not even feeling the pain just yet thanks to the shock of our sudden onslaught. He falls slowly, fighting it, although his trembling hands now clutch at the massive wound on his neck, in an attempt not to – literally – lose his head. We had sliced it half off within one swift circular motion. Once Caden staggers to his knees, we cannot resist the sweet sight, the tender vulnerability of the moment. The knife slips from our grasp, and we dip our hands into the gushing red sea of life, only to smear it across our cheeks, all the way down our neck. Delirious with triumphant lust, we barely acknowledge Michael's own labored breath, his low groans, as he loses himself in the moment with us.

And right then and there, while Caden is twitching on the ground, struggling for air but only ever inhaling blood, it happens. Eyebrow raised, Michael's darkened eyes bore into ours. The longing in that moment is so overwhelming, we begin trembling uncontrollably. Michael hooks a finger into the rim of our pants to pull us closer. And in that storm, we find our calm. Everything inside us that was torn apart within the last two days, floating disorganized inside us, that had us question ourself, is reconfigured in unforeseen and dramatic ways.

Michael's lips are surprisingly soft on ours. We can tell that he is yet holding back, drawing out this delicious first moment of uncoordinated passion between us. How do our bodies respond to each other, where do we let our hands wander first, how fast or slow do we go?

But as soon as Michael makes a small incision in his hand, only to trace his blood-stained finger across our lips, as soon as he leans in to share himself with us in a kiss, there are no deliberations anymore. No preposterous human anxieties about being desirable enough in the nude. There is only instinct.

Ripping at each other's clothes with increasing fervor, Michael starts pulling us down on the ground.

"Michael… Wait."

He gives us a hungry look when we point to the body on the ground.

"You want me to take you on his corpse?"
We nod, and faster than we can blink, we are thrown onto the heap of rapidly cooling human flesh, skin, and coagulating blood. Interesting, for one, because we'd never fancied ourself submissive in the slightest.
We have no time to think, or speak, for that matter. All we are capable of doing is to stare into Michael's eyes glowing dark blue in the dim light of the campfire. All we feel is… everything, everything. The physical sensations, but most of all, something we'd never known yet instinctively knew as human intimacy. It wasn't the intimacy we shared with our victims, it was a new high entirely. A violent love, a pure rage, a beauty and truth beyond what was accepted or even comprehended by human cattle.
There is not even a second of hesitation on our part when Michael wraps his hand around our throat and leans in to whisper, "You're mine." And after another extended kiss, he adds, "And I am yours, Emily. I need to be yours. I want you to own me. Will you? Own me?"
But we can only sigh in response, wrap our arms around his neck, and our legs around his midsection to pull him in deeper.
Whereas the kill was swift, the rest of Michael's and our time together certainly was not. We cannot count how many embraces we shared in these late night hours, or at what point – and how – we even decided to dance around our victim's campfire naked, howling like madmen to a rabid tune only we were capable of hearing. Truly, his embrace was a potent medicine for an illness we hadn't even been aware we suffered from.
Once we manage to break free from this our most perverse rapture, the Rider does the same, granting me the privacy to enjoy this new-found bliss with Michael as just Emily.
My head is bedded on his chest, and we are covered only by Caden's aluminum blanket. Michael, suddenly looking oddly

glum, stares into the flame of the campfire. "Who was your first kill?"

I had anticipated anything but this question, having no previous experience with fellow serial killing paramours, and because his body tenses up, I know my hesitation to reply vexes him.

"She…" I slowly begin, still reluctant to lay open this most vulnerable of secrets. "She was loosely affiliated with my family."

"How?"

Now it is my turn to look sullen. I am not ready. Particularly since there are still so many questions he has not yet answered.

"Well," I continue in an attempt to stall. "It's been such a long time. She was at our house a lot, I surmise."

"You surmise?"

"Yes."

"She was a tenant? A family member?"

"She was never a family member," I decidedly state. "She was my father's nurse, tending to him while he lay dying."

Michael does not respond, and for some reason, he appears even more apprehensive than before. His body feels unforgivingly solid, as though he were attempting to repel me. There's, perhaps not a rift, but a tiny crack in the foundation of our budding relationship, it appears. I cannot make sense of his reaction. Perhaps it was all in my mind? It must simply be the paranoia of divulging information this sensitive to another living creature.

Before I can address the issue, however, Michael speaks again.

"Who was your favorite kill?"

Now, this one was easy. "The first one."

"I see," he says.

"And yours?"

"Tonight, of course." With this, he turns back to me, running his thumb across my lips.

"Oh, tonight is a new favorite, an event I am still doing my best to thoroughly process," I offer stupidly. Suddenly, I understand

Michael's reaction. He'd baited me, perhaps not intentionally, but he'd hoped my response would be the same as his, strengthening our bond in the process.

The Rider teases my mind with a smoky tendril. 'Careful. Something about this isn't right."

'You're paranoid!' I cannot contain my chagrin. 'Or jealous.'

The moment is ruined, and so I focus on a more practical issue at hand. I nod at Caden. "Michael, how are we going to dispose of him?"

His beam is bright, long vertical dimples parting his cheeks. For some reason that is a sight I never want to miss again in my life. "I've got that covered. Get dressed."

I ought to have anticipated that despite its small size, the bag Michael had carried when I had picked him up at the side of the road would contain hacksaws and tarp. We won't have to concern ourselves with the blood left behind, the critters and insects will do our dirty work for us.

Michael hadn't lied, his resources, inside knowledge of city procedures and building projects will be an asset to me as well. Apparently, his method of disposing of bodies by insects is just one of many.

Around 2 A.M. we find ourselves back in his hometown, parking the car as closely to the construction site as possible. The concrete will be poured tomorrow, and Caden's body parts will be in a shallow grave beneath it.

Michael's last words to me are seared into my brain, my heart, my soul, reverberating through me. "Admit it. I reached a place in you tonight that would be very difficult to go back from. I know I did. And you have done the same to me. If you need to feed again, you know how to reach me. I am *your* pleasure. Whenever you need me. I live but to serve you in pleasure and pain, Emily Sand."

Perhaps it is the narcissist in me, but I like how he always uses my full name to give his words more impact. I know this to be a manipulation tactic, one I have often used in the past, but if this is an attempt of manipulating me into falling for him, I don't even mind.

At home, I drop down onto my bed fully clothed, type a last text message to Michael, and fall fast asleep.

Whereas the physical exhaustion of the past few days was something I could have handled, the exhaustion that came with being opened up to a world of emotions was not. How did the human animals do this, day in, day out? And what did it say about me, that I was now willingly indulging in the same type of chaos?

Chapter 12
Run

A day passes without a response from Michael. And then another. Against my better knowledge, I text again. Nothing.

Concern gives way to panic, then bewilderment and hurt, with a steaming side dish of fury. I have kept up to date on my news media stalking, and it appears as though Elysia has not yet been reported missing, which is why I cannot fathom the complete lack of contact – or interest? – on behalf of Michael's.

I roam from room to room in an attempt to find something to occupy myself with, settling on watching a fly struggling to free itself from a cobweb behind the fruit basket in my kitchen. Its little wings were propelling madly, an angry sound emanating from them; a battle cry, or perhaps a violently defiant death song. 'Just like me,' I think. I got trapped in a repulsively syrupy web of love and terror. I am not afraid of losing Michael, I feel *terror* at the mere thought of it. I had never known this feeling other than having irrational nightmares about running out of lives to extinguish.

As with any kill, memory fragments intertwine as they replay in my head, but what is usually a climactic experience leaving me in a blissful stupor, has now become tainted. Images of Michael's face hardening, the memory of how his body had grown stiff, and the anxiety of no contact merge with the pleasant ones. It doesn't help that the Rider rattles around in his pit, demanding to be heard on this. I don't want to entertain his theories, all revolving around this entire Michael debacle being part of a long con. How do you even feign what we had shared? It was impossible. Right? It was, right? It was too exclusive to be feigned or replicated.

'You think Gerald Gallego, Fred West, Jason Teale, David Parker Ray and consorts didn't keep side pieces?' the Rider chuckles hollowly.

'Not ones they could share their homicidal selves with, no,' I shoot back irately. 'They mate for life, it appears.'

'They were apprehended before they could discard their mates for a new one,' replies he.

On day three, I have fully succumbed to depression. A sensation I only ever experience after weeks of bathing in the recollections of a kill, leaving them without potency. Was this revenge for me not having picked up the phone when he had called on the day of Caden's murder?

I decide to combat my despondency by driving to Enumclaw to find my way back to Michael's vermicomposting trailer. If he was indeed playing some type of game with me, I had better destroy any evidence of my previous solo kill, and any DNA left behind during my visit to his trailer. As a policeman, he'd always find ways to justify the presence of his own DNA at the scene, a luxury I couldn't claim for myself. Or he could simply dispose of his, leaving mine behind.

Additionally, the Rider had made a mental list of all the dump sites Michael may have followed me to after he'd stumbled across me in the forest all those weeks ago. The prospect of having to rebury several dozen body parts is outright nauseating.

Hours of searching later, just when I had decided to drive back home, I hit the brakes of one of my delivery vehicles when I spot a tree I distinctly remember Michael had passed on the afternoon he'd caught me at his neighbor's. Its color is slightly off, the bottom trunk displaying a hint of beginning rot.

After one more hour of driving back and forth, I finally sneak up on the trailer, a watchful eye on the periphery. Despite – or perhaps due to – its age, I struggle to get access to it, and sigh a sigh of relief when the lock finally clicks.

Loading the heavy crates into my vehicle is no easy task, and it doesn't take long until I am shaking, drenched in sweat; in part thanks to the uncomfortable forensics suit and hood I donned for this project. Lastly, I clean the trailer top to bottom to eradicate any trace of my previous visit.

I meticulously work through the day, the Rider, not smoky now but ablaze, giving me the stamina to carry on. My resolve only falters momentarily, once it is time to dispose of the wiggling, rotting contents in the vats. Despite my current activities, I still childishly check my phone for a possible message from Michael's every once in a while.

I will have to continue phase two tomorrow, however. There are not enough hours in a day to do all I did *and* rebury the other body parts. Naturally, I keep coded lists of all my dumpsites, written in a code only Kate could hypothetically decipher because we both created it. Risky, but also fun. I kept the list in order not to bury two body parts in the same location, or too closely to one another, for one, but also as a reminder of precisely what is at stake should I ever make a grave mistake – no pun intended.

Around 3 A.M., I am woken up by the continuous buzzing of my phone. It's Michael. I deliberate whether I should answer at all, but when he simply keeps calling, I relent.

"Michael," we greet him.

His booming voice shakes with enmity. "So tell me, Emily, are you just completely stupid, or insane, or what exactly is your endgame here? What did you do with the vats in my trailer?"

"Risk factor elimination. I hadn't heard from you. Were you being investigated? Had you been arrested? How would I know? So you are most welcome for me erasing all that could have led to you, hence me, being connected to any murders."

After steadying his breath for a few seconds, Michael snidely responds, "You glorious martyr. Thank you. For your sacrifice. – I

will have you know, I'm always eager to find someone who models language removing martyrdom from the equation, and as of this moment, you are not presenting yourself in an ideal light."
I choose to ignore the insult, though I can feel the Rider rear his head; he isn't going to let that one slide. "Where were you these last few days?"
"Not that it's any of your concern, but I must, as you know, mask as both an officer of the law as well as a dependable fiancé."
The word is like a knife to our ego. "Congratulations. Did you propose within the last three days? Because you had impressed upon me that you and Miss Cutter were no longer romantically affiliated."
The conversation derails from there, prompting Michael to hang up. And I? Am forlorn. However I lost myself so quickly is beyond me.

In the morning, another text message arrives while I am brewing coffee in the kitchen. It reads, "Emily. I beg of you to understand this. – Last night wasn't anger. Last night was fear. It scares me how much I already need you. The thought of losing you… of you distrusting me… is all but insufferable. I shudder to think what I would do should you ever leave me. I would have to die by my own hand to end my grief. Forever yours, -M."
The Rider's pulsating features appear at the rim of my consciousness. 'Permission to approach,' he smirks.
'Granted.'
'You need therapy.'
I roll my eyes as I take my first sip of coffee, then pause midway through. Verily, the Rider spoke the truth. With my carefully crafted internal order cast into disarray, it was now that I ran the risk of making crucial mistakes as it pertained to my secret life. I wondered how I would even broach the subject to a therapist. Obviously, I couldn't just admit to being a serial killer, as

confidentiality had its limitations, regrettably. Rewriting the narrative in a way that still showcased my current issues would pose a challenge. But I was, in my own way, a writer, sans a pen and inkwell, having created an entire faux life for others to read and never once doubt. I was an unreliable, albeit convincing narrator, as you will have to agree by now.
The Rider growls his next suggestion loudly enough inside me that his voice ricochets from every corner of my mind.
'Why, that I could do,' I smile slyly in response.

Well aware of the games lovers are in the habit of playing with each other, I still can't contain myself enough not to hasten to reply to Michael's message. He swears that the engagement is for show only, that he and Cutter had agreed to take a break without officially ending their engagement. And that he needed her and his colleagues to believe it while he was building up to exacting his revenge on her. Had it been anyone else, just another human man, I would not have bought one word of it. But… it was the only person I had ever met who was my equal. He could never have with her what he could have with me. He had verbalized exactly how I felt as well – I needed him just as much as he did me, now that I knew he existed.
Our next phone conversation starts out with cautious politeness. He states that, in order to keep building trust on both sides, he wouldn't have to learn where the vats were. He only requested to know if I was certain they would never be found. This I confirm to him. After a while, the conversation veers off into another direction, becoming more casual.
We exchange information about where we went to school, how we first realized we were a breed apart from the humans, speak about our favorite movies, literature, his rock climbing hobby, and our most awkward kill experience. Michael's previous relationships had all been turbulent, and though I am uncomfortable listening to

him detailing them for me, I listen, as it appeared to be a cathartic experience for him. I also learn how Michael gained access to my cabin, and that his decision to join the force was not solely inspired by the desire to learn how to stay under the radar. A family member, he tells me, was murdered when he was a juvenile, forever annihilating his sense of justice and security.

To hear him share with me tidbits of every aspect of his life, and in turn speak about mine, without reservation and hesitation, excites me so much my cheeks and forehead flush. It is a different type of bonding we do this night, but, I feel, just as much of a significant one.

At the end of the call, Michael vows once more to learn to do better about keeping me in the loop.

'You should still rebury the body parts," the Rider whispers to me afterwards.

'Duly noted,' I inform him, displeased that he would ruin this sentimental moment for me.

Alas, my renewed exhilaration is cut short, and my face falls the second I lay eyes on the message Michael sends to me in the afternoon.

"It's on. Do NOT try to make contact in any way, shape or form as I now have eyes on me 24/7."

One may think that the most impulsive thing I do is to be a serial killer. But, as you may have gathered by now, I am guarded and meticulous. The most impulsive thing I have ever done was to open the rootkit for a complete stranger, just because he was also a serial killer. Which reminds me of one of the main reasons I had always, always kept my human interactions shallow. The more someone knows you, the more of a powerful enemy they could become. "Friends are the enemies you don't yet know you have," my friend Kate always says. Ironically, I don't think Kate would even bat an eyelash should she ever find out who I really am. She is a Kayser Soze in her own right, a pro-social Machiavellian mastermind, who, without question, could outsmart me in a heartbeat. I know I'll need to distract myself within the next few days, until I'm ready to face the consequences of everything that had transpired with Michael, so I send her a brief text to see if she'd like to hang out. There's someone in her general area I needed to see anyway.

I mainly turn on the news and browse the news pages on my phone so as to occupy myself. That's why it doesn't immediately compute when the reporter says, "…female human head found in what appears to be a partial grave."

Slowly, I raise my head, more *wanting* to believe than actually believing it to be a coincidence. Where's the remote control?! When I find it, I turn up the volume and take in every word. Yes. Tiger Mountain. They found Elysia's head.

'Run.' The Rider utters but this one word.

I am too perplexed to run, let alone move a single muscle. This is my worst nightmare come true. I need answers, need to hear from Michael himself that, or if, he set me up. If I called him, and he was innocent on the charges of framing me, I might inadvertently connect him to the murder, should his burner phone be detected. If I don't contact him, I was essentially sitting ducks. What do I do?! What, just what?!

The Rider bangs both palms on the walls of his pit in an attempt to shake me up enough to spin into action. 'RUN! NOW!'

And then I do.

Chapter 13
Always

I'm somewhere in Oregon, halfway to my house outside of Sacramento, when the phone buzzes next to me on the passenger's seat of my car. Picking it up bears a certain risk, but I cannot help myself. I need answers.

"Did you set me up?" Michael asks, the tone of his voice more aggrieved than furious.

"No! Did you?"

"I would sooner die than betray you. I had anticipated you to know and believe it by now."

When I don't respond, Michael asks, "Where are you? You're on a highway? Yes?"

"I...am out for a drive," I say evasively.

"Good. Leave Washington – I have a feeling that is what you are currently doing anyway. Do not tell me where you are going, and stay under the radar. I want you to learn to trust me, and clearly, in order for you to do so, it will require a level of abnormal patience and trust from me. It is my joy and pleasure to provide both to you. Now," Michael's voice grows stern, "for the hard part. This number will be trashed within the next few minutes. Whether or how often I'll get to make contact with a new random number, I do not yet know. My main focus will be on working towards protecting you, and us. I need my wit about me to facilitate this, meaning the less contact we have, the less emotional I am, and the lesser the chance of me making a mistake."

The rootkit part of me wants to scream and beg for him not to leave me, but the Rider already has a hand pressed over her mouth.

"Alright," I breathe shakily.

"I will see you again, Emily. I live and breathe for the day of our reunion. I must go, but will send that last message I had alluded to, after hanging up. Something to hold on to, perhaps?"

As soon as we said our goodbyes, I steer the car towards the side of the road, nervously anticipating Michael's message. He sends it in several installments, and it reads,

"Emily. Our time together has only just begun. Please trust that, despite this fact, you are the very fabric and fiber of who I am. I am lost without you, torn up without you, sad beyond words without you, broken without you.

I am not only in love with you, I am addicted to you, that love, mind, face, voice, eyes, passion, rage, tenderness. You keep me whole.

I have never felt less alone. That's just how you are. That's just what you do.

I will hold you, kiss you, pleasure you, love you, kill with you, and for you. I belong to you. I will always belong to you. I hope you know that. I hope you really understand what that means.

You are the best part of not only who I am but who I want to become. I would happily give you anything that was mine to give, and more than a few things that are not. I would sooner die than to betray or hurt you. I would sooner live alone than to *ever* lie to you. I have never *really* been in love. Not like this. Never like this. Madly, insanely, passionately in love.

You own me, my love. Without question, reservation or the power to revoke. My heart, your life, your love, sharp knife…

I have to have you. Be mine. Be mine. Be mine. All mine.

Love me. That's all I need and want. I'm forever yours, Emily Sand. Forever yours.

Always."

Having been prohibited from replying, I still pen a note that I will never send, something to cherish, to remember all the emotions his letter evoked in me. Should I, for some reason, lose the ability to feel all I feel now, I want to at least have visible proof that none of this was a strange fever dream but reality. Time would tell whether this was a fond or embarrassing memory.

My isolated California abode, about forty-five minutes away from Sacramento, lies undisturbed, its flaking paint giving the impression of poverty and privation. My California costumes, and the persona – Zadie Shore - I have created for my time here, reinforce this impression. A way to throw off law enforcement, should anyone ever start to connect the California murders with the ones in Washington, mostly, but also a wonderful way to broaden the range of my acting skills.

After a quick sweep of the grounds and house, ascertaining that all cameras and locks work flawlessly and are undisturbed, I sit down in the upstairs kitchen to prepare my next abduction.

And pardon me for laughing maniacally, for you do not yet know what the Rider had suggested to me earlier, now, do you?

I have a particular fondness for malls, in case that hasn't become obvious by now. Not only do they supply me with prime meat almost without fail, but abducting victims from such a place also increases the brain thrill. Much like Ted Bundy did during his Lake Sammamish kidnappings, I count on the face-blindness of people in crowds. Humans easily let down their guard in such settings due to believing there's safety in numbers.

Any successful abduction ensures that I have done more than strike terror in the heart of one person, and their family. It is a declaration of dominance for all within the community to bear witness to and tremble at. The Rider and I am the creature that wrecks their sense of security and certitude. Their faux superiority of 'This could never happen to me and my own as we do not walk the streets after dark, do not belong to this demographic, don't indulge in that lifestyle' becomes 'This could have been me, although I live the life of a law-abiding citizen, undeserving of punishment,', or alternately 'This could just as easily happen to my daughter, son, mother, father.'

I must, however, concede that such spontaneous kidnappings have their downside. See, I have in the past had to just swiftly execute those who, upon closer inspection, didn't provide me with the brain thrill. They revealed themselves to be without flavor, either physiologically or psychologically. It is, perhaps, akin to consuming a lavish, delicious meal as opposed to eating junk just to sustain yourself. In case of the latter, there's an integral part missing from the culinary experience, and the craving for the *right* kind of food will only ever increase. This I also have in common with Ted Bundy, who, dissatisfied with the Ott girl, returned to Lake Sam to lure with him another victim he could take his time with. Of course, today, no actual chance abduction will take place. I know exactly who I am after.

I'm wearing a wig with long auburn hair, light gray ¾ leggings underneath a wide brown hoodie, and my usual baseball cap. I'd been following him from his home to the mall and back outside. Swaying a little, I breathe, "Excuse me," and reach for the nearest car roof as though looking to steady myself. "I'm so sorry, but I need help?"

I see the way he looks me over, evaluating me. Who am I, a tweaker? A mentally ill person? Or really just a woman in need of medical attention?

I bend over, clutching at my lower abdomen. "Please help me."

He cannot help himself. Occupational hazard. "Are you alright?" With my eyes closed, I only hear him set down his shopping bags on the concrete, and a second later he's jogged around his shabby family car, pulling me up by the elbow. I like his touch. It's gentle yet firm. A healing touch of sorts.

"Do you need to sit down for a spell?" Although he's doing his best to hide it, his voice still has a faint Southern twang.

"Again, I apologize," I gulp. "I recently had my appendix removed? And I think something's not right. I came here with my friend but it appears she left."

He rubs my arm in a gesture of comfort. "Why don't we call your friend together? Do you have a phone?"

"She was watching my things, phone included, when I went to the restroom. When I came out she was gone. I had the mall call her out over speaker and waited for almost an hour."

He frowns. "That doesn't seem very nice for you. Did she know you are sick?" He's good. He prioritizes my feelings, validating my experience, all the while making no assumptive statements regarding my non-existent friend's wrongdoing. He is *asking* questions, trying to understand, not judging.

His fingers reach inside the back pocket of his cool-dad jeans. I know what he's going to ask next in order to solve the issue and get on with his boring suburban life, so I quickly add, "I don't know her number by heart."

Here it comes.

The lip biting, the inner turmoil.

"I know you will have other plans than helping some strange girl from the parking lot today but…I honestly think I need to go to a hospital?" I moan. "I'll reimburse you for the gas."

"Once you have your purse back?" he inquires. Smart. I cannot abide by a lazy mind, and I will need him to challenge me plenty later on. "No, really, don't worry about gas or anything. But yeah, I could probably give you a ride. Can you stand on your own or would you like my help?"

When I reach for his arm again, he steps in, pulling me towards him by the waist before he slowly guides me towards his vehicle. I make sure to keep my head down so the cameras installed on the lot won't get more than my cap and lower side profile. It's also a good way to avoid smartphone cameras. The sheer nonsense people film themselves doing never ceases to confound me. They'll film their food, their new ghetto-goth girl nails, themselves slurping slushies in their car outside the mall. Only God knows how many crimes and criminals have made it onto tape that no one even has the faintest idea about.

As he helps lower me into the passenger seat I remark, "The next hospital in town won't do me any good since I have no ID with me, but my hospital is right outside of town, if that's alright with you? They know me there."

I see something about this doesn't sit quite right with him, but to my relief, he nods without further comment. He gracefully jogs back to get his shopping bags, throws them in the back, hectically fumbles the key into the ignition, and right before he starts the motor, he turns towards me to offer a few more reassuring words. I don't hear them, just watch the expression on his face. The quaint blend of empathy and professional distance. He really is beautiful. Not my type actually, but the way he carries himself, his entire being glowing with purpose, sparks my curiosity.

When his hand reaches for the stick shift, his naked skin briefly brushes against mine, prompting me to let out a surprised sigh of platonic pleasure.

"Try not to worry, Ma'am," he says, taking my sigh for one of pain. "You'll be taken good care of. I would like to think everything will turn out just fine in the end."

It appears to be nothing more than a platitude, but I can tell he chose each word with care. He doesn't say, 'Don't worry' but suggests to 'try.' Reminding me that the staff at the hospital will know what to do. He doesn't say 'I know you'll be fine' but that 'he would like to think things would eventually be.'

Nothing he says is a promise, everything is but a cautious suggestion.

A gust of wind blows a strand of his short wavy hair my way through the open window. The scent of his shampoo hits my nostrils. Its smell accelerates my heartrate so much I have to cross

my arms in front of my chest. The urge to grab him by the back of his neck and reel him in close enough for me to bury my face in his hair is strong.
Pulling out of the parking lot, he starts activating his GPS.
"Where's your hospital?"
No, no. That's not how we'll play it, Sir.
"Oh, if you don't mind I'll just tell you which way to go. Good way of distracting myself from the pain, concentrating on something else, right?" I ask meekly and though there's that micro expression of dislike again, he nods curtly, switching it off.
"I understand. Pardon, what was your name?"
"Zadie. Zadie Shore."

Naturally, I have a good idea about which streets to avoid, know where the traffic cameras are located in this area, know the streets police cars frequently patrol. I've trolled down here so many times, I have lost count.
One glance at him, his clothes, the interior of his car and I have him all figured out. Dangling from the mirror inside the vehicle is a Christian fish symbol with Darwinist legs. He's an atheist, which comes as no surprise, considering. It's a humorous stab at the religiously delusional who believe this perversion of totemism would grant them safety from harm. It's a counter-statement. A challenge.
All his belongings speak of exquisite taste – likely his wife's – but are nevertheless worn. Having children really does put a damper on one's quality of life, it appears.
After he introduces himself to me as Nick Yeoman, I make a few attempts at small talk, lest he focus too much on where we're going and how we're getting there. His replies are monosyllabic at first, but eventually I take a stab at a topic I know he won't be able to resist.

"A girl in my psychology class used to have the same pendant you have hanging on your mirror," I say. "She introduced me to Richard Dawkins' work. Are you familiar with him?"

His posture becomes more alert as he delves into an anecdote about his time in college, devouring atheist literature. He's excited. Takes pride in his views.

A nostalgic smile illuminates the perfect symmetry of his face as these memories draw him further back in time. He starts talking about summers spent fly fishing in Georgia – of all places – as a boy, and something something connotation to the walking fish pendant.

We have left civilization behind us. There are no more cars in sight in either direction of the road, and at some point I interrupt him, "Hey. There's a short cut to the hospital, if you turn right where the large boulder is in the distance. See it?"

He frowns. "A short cut? Are you sure? I think this'll lead us someplace further into No Man's Land. I had better get the GPS going," he adds, more to himself than to me.

I chuckle. "Trust me, no one was more surprised than I was upon discovering it's a short cut. We can drive around if you prefer, but it's a good extra half an hour. This way would be..." I bend over again, faking another onslaught of pain, "faster..."

He eyes me with a mixture of concern and skepticism. "Well...if you're sure. We can turn around in a minute or so if it looks to be the wrong way, I guess."

"Oh, I am quite sure," I smile through gritted teeth. "Unless, you know, you're uncomfortable being alone in a car with me in the middle of nowhere. I get it, technically I could be a serial killer."

He giggles a carefree belly giggle that shakes his shoulders. I have to grit my teeth as I wrestle with the Rider leaping forward to reach for me. Not. Yet.

We're approximately a mile away from my house with its expansive downstairs dungeon now. Thick trees and impenetrable shrubbery encircle us, concealing the lush green fields and plains farther ahead.

I jump up in my seat and cry out, topple over, holding on to my midsection. "Stop the car, stop the car!" I moan, and he shouts, "What is it? What's happening?"

"Just…please. Stop the car," I repeat, my face contorted in agony, "Please…"

He does as asked and faster than he can blink, I reach over and pull the key out of the ignition, only to produce the tranquilizer gun previously hidden in the front pouch of my hoodie.

"What are you doing!" he yells, nevertheless holding up his hands in a defensive gesture. His own mask – one of professionalism – is back on his face just mere seconds later however. His voice is restrained as he offers, "I will gladly give you my wallet and car – anything you like. I don't mind trekking back home to my wife and children."

I cock my head as I listen to the undertone of panic in the driver's voice, trying to reason his way out of the situation, thinking that mentioning his family will make me relent. But he already knows. The shift in our eyes, the mydriasis, informs him that no mortal verbiage is capable of changing my mind.

He does not scream for help, but scream he does. I blink as his hands form into claws and he roars at me like a wild animal.

Why, no one's ever had that reaction, though it would make sense for him as someone who's flitted back and forth between studying neuroscience, evolutionary psychology and forensic psychology, only to end up becoming a psychological psychotherapist. And he may have been correct that anyone other than me would have been perturbed by his socially inacceptable outburst.

"Doctor, your imitation of a teddy bear is endearing, but would you be so kind as to cease your tomfoolery this instant – if you'd like to live, that is."

His arms drop into his lap. "What do you want? Whatever it is we can work on this together."

"Splendid. Then work with me on this," I say, lifting the gun a few inches higher, shooting him point blank.

"Ow!" he whines in surprise, staring at the dart protruding from his chest in horror, then starting to sway back and forth. "Wh-what is th..." He mumbles something incoherent, then, as his brain is going haywire, he asks, "Will you take care of me?"

"Always," I promise, a second before he collapses in his seat. Horse tranquilizer will do that to you.

Chapter 14
This Is Why, And This Is How

There are yet so many things you do not know about me, and I am hard-pressed to fit them all inside this story laid out before you. One of these aforementioned secrets entails my time spent in a BDSM group in Tacoma. The High House was, in reality, just a group with multiple bases across the US, as far as I was aware anyway, at which society's upper echelons engaged in pompous rituals with pseudo-occult connotations. It was half community and half commune, which provided some additional training to me as it pertained to torture, and provided me with short-lived brain thrills.

My time there was cut short, and I was quietly dismissed. A fact that still confounds me, considering I ended up biting off the nose of the CEO of a multinational conglomerate when he dared use a whip on me during one of the High House's soirees. It has since been reattached, I'm told. But to this day, I believe I owe the fact I was allowed to escape unscathed to my acquaintance Mr. Robert Bryce, who was also the one who had to be torn off of the CEO's throat after I'd been restrained. He appeared to take rules more seriously than I had anticipated.

Rob had overseen my training, not officially, but he had certainly taken me under his wing in a way. Personal friendships were discouraged, and we certainly weren't friends, but we'd often spent time together after our individual scenes and sessions, me smoking and him scowling at my habit, while telling me about his day life and job, his family and upbringing, his artistic hobbies. It had taken a few years for me to realize how much I actually knew about him. He was a smart and careful, perhaps even a cunning man, who hid these facts behind an exterior of humor, so acting this unwisely had, in hindsight, astounded me about him, who was otherwise known as "the unknowable" at the High House.

It is, as mentioned earlier, also Rob's gang that aids me in the disposal of my victims' vehicles across the Pacific Northwest. He knows better than to ask questions, and I know better than to tell. Rob remains among the few individuals whom I, despite my level of awareness about his habits and life, yet fail to fully figure out, which is just one thing about him that excites me. A chiropractor and acupressurist, his torture methods manage to frighten as much as repulse even me. That anyone would volunteer to be maimed in this manner, and experience any semblance of an erotic sensation, is beyond my comprehension. What is more, his victims pay him for his services. I have never seen him in anything but a chipper mood, even while temporarily paralyzing his clients or hitting pressure points to cause intense physical pain, and something tells me I also never want to.

It is Rob's number I dial now, aware that breaking the good doctor will require special reinforcements. See, my parting gift to Rob was my kitty, which he tended to while I was in Washington.

I knew I could trust Rob, to a degree at least. He hadn't even flinched, had accepted our preposterous claim that the kitty had agreed to its ordeal. Whether he did believe it or not, we didn't know.

So. Knowing so well the orderly world of mental health professionals, neither violence nor speaking with a silver tongue would deconstruct it. Only something incomprehensibly bizarre could. This is where the kitty came in.

Early in the evening, the doorbell has me scramble to my feet so unexpectedly I almost knock over the couch table. The ominous dream sequences involving Michael had intermittently roused me from my sleep throughout the day, leaving me in the same sorry state I have been in for the past week.

Rob has come alone, as he mostly does when it's me he visits. He has a good body and devilishly handsome face, and is completely aware of the effect his charming smile and self-assuredness have on women, is hence a jovial sort of flirt, and no female is safe from his advances. I don't think anyone's ever resisted either, and he usually has several girlfriends at the same time, on top of being married.

For some reason, despite our undeniable attraction to one another, his flirting with me has always been more cautious, even before the nose incident.

His crazed blue eyes shimmer even more insanely the second I open the door. "Hi," he winks at me. "Aren't you a sight for sore eyes."

"Did you bring my kitty?"

"All work and no play makes Emily a dull girl," he pouts. "Not even a handshake? Tongue kiss?"

I laugh. "Sure, come get it."

"You come get it," he grins, but immediately turns around again. "Come on out, it's still out back in the truck."

Thus concludes our little flirt, as it always does. This time around, it doesn't put me in the same deviously lighthearted mood that our banter usually does, however. Michael's face appears before my inner eye, and won't leave.

I frown as I listen inside, trying to discern what it is that is happening down there. It's a rootkit emotion, this I grasp, but it's been too long I recall the word for it, or what it means. Having no time to dwell on the issue, I jog down the porch steps and take the leash from Rob's hand.

I tug on its leash, and it follows. A flabby old creature who once used to be a man, and who is now a thing that doesn't remember its name.

It had tried to break me once, while it was still a man, because I had bruised his ego by dismissing him from our relationship. I didn't mind liars, per se, but the man's megalomania hadn't sat right with me. He'd claimed to have been a navy SEAL, which initially had roused no suspicions, until he began sharing stories with me that were so absurd one needn't even bother researching whether they had merit. During his BUD/S training his hands were purportedly tied behind his back, before he was tossed into a pool with a shark. Further exploits of his involved breaking into a Turkish prison underwater to spring free a fellow SEAL Team Six member, being employed as a governmental assassin, as well as sailing around the world in a pop-bottle boat.

I neither speak of it to anyone, nor do I think of the events that had unfolded often, not even when the creature is around.

After the man had humiliated the body I inhabit, the Rider had taken me into the pit to sleep for a few months. He was the one who knew how to handle such situations, and so I stayed unconscious, trusting the process of his miracle work. I don't recall more than what seems like strange dream sequences from that time, but of course I eventually came to acknowledge that my body, commanded by the Rider, had gone into a kill frenzy, and when it was safe to wake up, the Rider had gone on one last quest with me, before resting awhile. We had hunted the man down, and made him a kitty.

Whenever the Rider and I open its cage to feed it, we enjoy seeing it hiss and growl in confused terror, then relax and gratefully accept the bowl of food of whatever leftovers we couldn't finish. It used to bite, so I had one of Rob's associates remove its teeth, and Rob had broken him to an extent it could only walk on all fours now, its spine bent and its joints crooked. Watching it suck on its food, swallowing it with considerable difficulty, spitting and coughing, is rather amusing, even almost a decade later. Whenever we are in the trolling stage in California, around the time we get bored or too anxious before a strike, we will visit its cage. Poke at it with metal rods and laugh at its frightened, yet vicious reactions. We poke at it until it bleeds, until it whimpers and curls up, too exhausted to fight.

Another business partner of Rob's is a tattoo artist who also specializes in body modifications, so kitty looks like a kitty now, too. It's amazing the things you can do if you have both the funds as well as a voiceless creature to abuse.

Currently, its tattooed face is looking up at me, meowing softly, its modified cat mouth, complete with whiskers, trembling while hobbling down the stairs into the dungeon. As soon as I have locked the creature into the Western room, the yellow room, I stroll into the blue room on the Eastern wall.

Dr. Yeoman is still stretched out on the narrow bed, soft snores escaping his lips. I drag the chair across the floor, sit down, and wait for him to wake up, while the Rider dances in his pit, thrilled I took his advice, though mainly, I'm certain, because he loves the prospect of receiving more attention by way of therapy.

It takes the good doctor almost twenty more minutes to become lucid again and shake off the after-effects of the Ketamine. I keep looking down at my hands to offer him what little privacy I can in order for him to get accustomed to his new situation and adjust to his new home.

Eventually, I hear the chain rattle, as he's moving towards the edge of the bed, holding out his cuffed hands to me.

"What's the meaning of this, Miss Shore?"

"I require psychiatric monitoring and treatment, Dr. Y."

He frowns, evidently not enjoying his new moniker. I found it to be a particularly humorous one, as that was exactly the question I had for him – *'Doctor, why? Why is this happening to me.'*

His voice is calm. "You could have booked an appointment through my office for that." He pauses. "You still can. I'm willing to work with you, provided you'll let me go."

I laugh. "Stop. We're both too smart for this, and if you degrade yourself any further, I'll begin to hold you in contempt. That isn't a dynamic that works for therapy. Therapy is the only thing I desire from you, and the only reason not to dispose of you. It'll serve you well to listen very closely now." I point towards the camera up above his bed. "Our sessions will be taped, and I will provide you with the tapes so you can rewatch them for proper analysis. I will be honest with you, but I am more prone to lying because in the wild, I have to. I may not realize I'm masking while I'm doing it, and I need you to pay attention and point out my inconsistencies." I hold up a hand, impatiently closing my eyes for a moment, when I see his mouth open. "I instructed you to listen. You may speak when I tell you to. Now is not that time. Consider this our introductory session, during which I will tell you how I came to be a serial killer."

The doctor's jaw drops. "A serial killer."

I lean back in my chair, casually fishing a cigarette out of my pack. "You'll regret having spoken again, unasked."

"Miss Shore, if you expect me to counsel you, I have to interject to ask questions."

From all I'd read and seen of and about him, I'd hoped he'd remain rooted in reason and reality, rather than to try and keep bargaining with me, or worse, beg. I enjoy being right. I cannot stand when I'm wrong, and would never admit to it either. He doesn't look away when my eyes drill into him. His gaze is neutral but open, and interestingly, it's me who looks away first.

"Alright. That seems fair enough. So, yes. I am a serial killer. I have many names, and though I introduced myself to you as Zadie Shore, my core persona now is that of Emily Sand, though I was born with a different name. A name I do not speak anymore because the Rider renamed me after he was born. In any case, the day this body was born was a cold day, when the mountain was yet out in Seattle."

"Poetic. And to establish the basics, you are seeking help because you want to stop being a serial killer?"

"No. I've recently developed – or reconnected with? – some… strange human emotions and impulsivities I am unsure about how to master. These could also put me at risk as it pertains to discovery."
He lets that sink in. "Maybe we can talk more about how that happened. Was there an event that sparked these emotions?"
"Yes, and I'll get to that," I sigh, "but first things first."
I recount the basics of my childhood and family life, patiently answering all follow-up questions. Dr. Y had asked for a pen and paper in order to take notes, so I stop intermittently whenever I see him scribbling down something on his notepad. His submission is but a small thrill, but a triumphant one nevertheless. Of course, I'm aware that he solely wants to take notes in the hope that there will be a way to escape, and that he'll manage to take them with him, in order to surrender them to law enforcement and prison psychologists.
Once it's time to delve into the hospital story, my fingers start to tremble. I hold them up to the doctor's face, "This is what I mean. This is a genuine physiological reaction stemming from emotions I yet never actually felt before. Now I do. Ever since I met this man, my entire system has been in uproar."
He nods, scribbles something again, doesn't even look up when I leave the room to get a glass and the bottle of whiskey for myself.

"When I was nine years old, I climbed an apple tree in the orchard behind the home."
"The home? Not your home?"
"It was my home until that day. It was the home this body lived in after that. My home is in the pit."
He frowns but I give him no time to inquire. "I fell from rather high up in the tree, and while unconscious, was rushed to the hospital, where it was concluded I had broken my hip and pelvis. The night nurse…her name was Grace. Grace C. Walker. Though

delirium may occur due to the mechanism of such a fracture, the operation, and anesthetic…" I swallow, "In retrospect, I think she gave me something during the nights. It never showed up on blood tests, or they weren't screening for whatever it was. The children's ward was in the basement of the hospital. I'd heard the staff talking about it – they called it the pit – and I remember it scared me because I had this vision of a dark hole I would never be able to emerge from. I thought I would die down there. And I did, in a way."

I take a large sip from the glass. The doctor looks displeased but appears to sense it's best not to object.

"She woke me up. She wanted me awake. The headboard wasn't against the wall anymore, she stood behind the bed, holding down my arms above my head. She was strong.

It was dark, but everything was so colorful and bright and strange at the same time. I thought I was still dreaming, at first. There were others there, in the room with us. One was outside, a young man, I believe. I could only make out his slender frame in the doorway, except I could also sort of see his eyes because they were such a bright shade of blue, always a glitter in them. I just kept looking at them, I had to."

I pause to refill my glass and light another cigarette.

"Take your time," the doctor reassures me quietly, all the while not making direct eye contact in order to be respectful.

"The first man in the room climbed on top of the bed, straddling me. The pain in my hip was unbearable. But he skidded upward until his groin was right in front of my face."

I break off again, look inside and find the Rider's outstretched hand. He grips it tightly, whispering words of violently vengeful comfort.

"They never raped me, you know, conventionally, though when one of them climbed on top of me on one occasion, he re-fractured my pelvis. Grace said it was because I had fallen out of bed. And I wasn't quite sure what was real and what wasn't. The mother didn't believe me, she said I was envious of all the attention my daddy was getting because he'd been diagnosed with cancer, so I was fabricating this story.

Anyway, I stayed intact until I was in my twenties, and people increasingly wondered why I didn't have boyfriends. I had to get their focus off of me to stay inconspicuous. But yeah," I take another drag from the cigarette, "I don't remember these nights in a clearly linear timeline either. – The drugs maybe? But in between and afterwards, they would laugh and scream in my face, to confuse me, probably. They kept telling me I was dreaming, but at the same time threatened no one would believe me if I told, that I would be committed to the crazy ward where they kill people who can't get better."

"First of all, I'm very sorry this happened to you," the doctor says gently. "I hope you can be benign with yourself. Do you struggle with blaming yourself?"

I cannot help but smirk. I'd known what I was in for with therapy, but his words still amuse me. "No. Never."

He coughs when I light another cigarette and blow the smoke in his general direction.

"You mentioned something about the young man standing in the doorway. That you felt you had to keep looking into his eyes. Did this happen on more than this one occasion?"

"It happened every time. There was something in his eyes, something I could hold on to, and he never looked away, he always looked right into my eyes. I've thoroughly educated myself on all aspects of sexual child abuse, Doctor, so I understand now, in hindsight, why I did it, what that anchor point meant. I am also of the mind it's correlated to how the Rider was born. I'm curious whether you agree."

"You, you mentioned that word before. The – what, rider?"

I twirl the bottle around on the console next to me. Two thirds still remain, and I know I'll need them later.

"During the day, a different array of nurses cared for me, though occasionally, Grace had a day shift as well. She was friendly during the day, kind even. The mother came to visit after the first night, apologizing to Grace that she hadn't been able to come sooner, explaining about my father's condition. Well, that was her excuse anyway. Grace and the mother appeared to bond immediately. But that will be a story for another session."

I sigh. "Either way. One night, the young man in the doorway was gone. I had nowhere to hold on to, and I felt myself slipping inside… I can't really explain it… I saw a vision of the ward, the room, as an actual dark pit inside me. I hung off of the edge of it, struggling to gain footing. I knew I was dying. I felt, I sensed… a hand, like a smoky tendril rising out of the bottomless blackness. And there was a voice coming from down below, it was the Rider's. The voice said, "Take my hand, Emily." I did. And he saved me. – So," I conclude. "This is why, and this is how."

I smile, remembering the long hours spent talking to him as a child, the way he'd played little games with me so as to exercise and drill me in survival. Sometimes cruelly, but never without care. His was a honey badger-mother sort of nurture, as I still shy away from calling it love. It was brutal, but it never lied, and always had the best intentions at heart.

Despite my young age, I'd always known, on some level, that I had created the Rider, that he wasn't real, or rather, he was me, the only part of me that I could accept because it fought to survive, no matter the price. On another level, I also knew I couldn't exist without him, and still wondered if at some point he may have become real, if that was even possible. Perhaps the doctor knew, though I wasn't sure I was ready to hear his professional opinion on this issue just yet.

"It's interesting that you identify the pit – the hospital room where the molestation took place – as your home. I'd like to talk about this more during our next session." The doctor clears his throat. "You mentioned that you intend to continue therapy tomorrow, but Miss Sand, be mindful of the after-effects of it. I wouldn't recommend therapy for more than twice a week."

"I appreciate your professional gnosis, Doctor," I reply. "Therapy must occur daily, though, as time is of the essence. I assure you, I can handle it, and the Rider is dying to meet you as well." I point towards the mini fridge serving as his nightstand. "Your supper is in there. Please have it now, so I can do the dishes in a few minutes."

I realize that a neurotypical person would experience guilt at having spiked his food with a potent hallucinogenic, after only just having relayed to him the fact her rapists did the same to her. I experience no guilt about it in the slightest, yet this is when I realize that when I had flirted with Rob earlier, and Michael's face had appeared before my inner eye, the feeling accompanying it had, indeed, been guilt.

As soon as the word enters my mind, I hear the Rider roar in outrage, and what's worse, pain, that I would betray him, my savior and only ally, like this.

We both know no rootkit emotion has the power to hinder, maybe even kill, him but guilt.

Chapter 15
A Fierce Cacophony Of Contrary Forces

Rob is still upstairs, sitting at the round beech kitchen table, one hand on his narrow hip, looking down at the sports section of the newspaper spread out before him. He glances up briefly when I walk in and take a swig from the bottle of beer he took from my fridge.

"Rob?"

He looks up. "Yeah?"

"Why have you never tried to have sex with me?"

He raises his eyebrows, blinks and snorts. "Come on. Something happen down there?"

If there's one thing my overinflated ego cannot bear, it's getting snubbed, which fortunately is a rare occurrence. I usually don't get uncomfortable, I get rage, though I'd never show it, but with the rootkit having spilled into me, I feel the awkwardness quite deeply, nevertheless determined not to let it affect my behavior. I place the bottle back on the table and snicker, "You should have seen your face."

In response, he laughs insecurely; obviously attempting to discern whether I was pulling his leg or lied when he rejected my advances. But he expertly overplays the situation, as per usual. "So you need me downstairs, or what? I gotta leave in an hour, my son is coming home from college and Jill needs me to pick up groceries from the store."

"He's ingesting the drug as we speak. It will be another twenty minutes, roughly."

"Oh, okay." He shrugs and lowers his head to continue reading the paper. But the combination of whiskey and fear of the Rider's rage if I do not handle the guilt issue as soon as possible, embolden me.

"Rob."

"Christ, lady, what." He swats his hand at me in mock irritation. "If you ever change your mind, let me know."
He gives me a piercing stare for a few seconds, pupils dilating slightly, but of course his phone rings right when he bites his lip and raises an eyebrow at me. Instinctively, he looks down at it, smiles. "It's my wife."
Rob disappears into the living room, leaving me to all my guilt and confusion. Once Rob's phone call has ended, it's well past the twenty minute mark.
Quietly, the two of us walk down into the dungeon side by side, where he takes seat in the control room while I get the kitty. Rob always asks if I "need" him downstairs, but in reality, he wants to be down here as much as I do.
Evidently, the doctor is already tripping out of his wits, and he frantically rubs his eyes as soon as he lays eyes on the creature that just entered his cell.
There's only one chair in the control room, so I resort to leaning against the wall behind Rob, watching the chaos unfurl. My eyes keep darting to the back of his head, wondering how he could commit long term, to having a family he evidently loved, while still torturing people on the side. Did these two aspects of his life ever bleed into one another? I sense that I can't ask him about it, however, and force myself to pay attention.

Kitty examines the room carefully, alertly, sniffing the floor, the corners of the room, and ultimately the edges of the bed. Dr. Y is still simply staring at it, likely not believing his eyes, or at least silently praying that this creature was a hallucination.
The kitty settles in front of the white steel frame of the bed, curiously looking up at the man on it, a soft, quivering meow escaping its malformed snout. Shyly, it puts its front paws on the bed, cocks its head.
Rob's chuckle is dry and toneless when Dr. Y moans, "Oh my

God," shrinking back from the thing moving to climb into bed with him. Despite the overdose we administered, his professionalism remains yet intact. "What's your name?" he asks the kitty, who stupidly returns his gaze without blinking.

"The kitty doesn't understand human language, doctor," we advise via intercom.

A fleeting look of utter disgust and contempt crosses the doctor's face. "Sir, please get off the bed," he politely asks. "Why don't you take that chair over there so we can talk?"

Rob and I simultaneously burst into laughter.

The kitty advances on Dr. Y and bumps his head into him, purring. He hoists himself up from the bed and pounds his fists on the mirror. "What have you done to him?! What is this?!"

But the creature is decidedly aroused, and the more vigorously Dr. Y rejects its advances, the wilder it gets, chasing him around the room. Eventually, both fall to the floor in a tangled heap, withal the kitty proceeds to rub his head between the good doctor's legs. With terror in his eyes, he knocks its head away with one knee.

See, I neglected to mention one thing. I had conditioned the thing to mistake rejection for an invitation, and to remain relentless in the pursuit for sexual affection. Affection it would never be able to enjoy or even consummate again, as I had had more than just its teeth removed.

The good doctor almost seems to go through the five stages of grief, as he's reaching a decision on how to proceed.

First, there is shock and denial in light of his grotesque ordeal. Second comes pain and guilt. It is visible on his smooth face, burning lines of sorrow into it that, I know, will never go away again. The guilt, I surmise, is due to not being able to help this man. Likely playing into it is the general sense of guilt humans feel when the fact that we are all interconnected hits, and what that actually means, for it is no beautiful feeling of unity. It is a fierce cacophony of contrary forces clashing together and fighting for dominance each; all the secret and inhumanly human things that lurk within.

I'm impressed with the doctor's resolve. He's palpably fighting to enter the anger stage. Finally, though, it overtakes him, and he punches the creature in the face as vigorously as he can. There it lies on the floor, little kitty lips and toothless gums bleeding, its entire body shaking from violent sobs, clawing at its own head in despair. What did it do wrong? It doesn't understand. Why is it being punished so cruelly for wanting some love?

Perhaps Dr. Y would have retracted to the bed to trip out in peace, had the kitty not dared reach for the doctor's ankles once more. It is then that his face turns red with panic-stricken rage, prompting him to wrap his chain around the pathetic thing's neck. He doesn't even stop strangling when its tongue is already lolling out of its mouth, eyes rolling back in their sockets. After it goes limp and slouches to the ground unconsciously, the doctor crawls back onto his bed, crying, screaming mostly incoherent words of regret and apology.

Rob swivels around on his chair to face me. "This is still all consensual, right?"

It's questions like these that always confuse me about him. I was never fully on the ins and outs of the aforementioned community we met in, yet had always suspected things weren't at all times as consensual as they'd been sold to me as. Not to mention, Rob's gang had disposed of dozens of cars for me, and he'd come to pick up the good doctor's vehicle today, too. What was he playing at? But I resort to calmly counter, "You know very well how extreme some people like it, Rob."

Not a direct lie, just a general statement that he will, hopefully, interpret as intended. He gives me a long probing look, before replying. "We better get it back into the other room. I have to hit the road now."

My next three weeks are spent spiraling further into the valley of depression and near-suicidal ideation. Here and there, during these episodes, tears ran down my face and my body was shaken by sobs, but at the same token, I was but a curious observer of the spectacle, not emotionally involved in any of it.

This time is different. I feel everything, each emotion is a wound to my unpracticed heart. Every morning, I wake to more building blocks added to the guilt wall. So tall is it by now, that I can hardly see or hear the Rider anymore.

I am either hungover or already intoxicated whenever I feed the pets their meals and the doctor his hallucinogens, after which I condition and indoctrinate him for a spell. I take both my guests to the little hidden shower room that connects their cells behind the control room, wash the doctor's and my clothes, resume therapy and fall asleep on the floral couch, rather than in the upstairs bed, simply because I lack the energy and motivation to ascend the stairs at the end of the day.

Whenever I am seconds away from praising myself for not having thought of Michael for an extended period of time, my eyes wander to the clock, realizing it's been less than an hour at most. I regularly check my phone, and restart it, but there are no messages from him, and the news report only sparsely about Elysia's murder case.

Doctor Y believes I suffer from limerence – love obsession – prompted by the fact that I'd never hoped to find a serial killing mate and believed Michael to be my only chance at romance. I suspect that he doesn't dare directly address the fact he doubts someone like me could even unselfishly love, and that my addiction to brain thrills, my paraphilias and misinterpretation of pain as love would always invite disaster. But I read between the lines rather well.

Our sessions are, for the most part, a reconnaissance of my earlier life, as well as an attempt to control the rootkit, which, even the doctor has to concede, poses a considerable threat to me.

Though I cannot help speculate that his main concern, particularly as it pertains to my heavy alcohol consumption, is that his presence might slip my mind, resulting in his accidental starvation.

He only brought up his family once more, and grew silent the moment I reminded him that to let him go meant to have to make his disappearance permanent.

I also show him the newspaper clippings about his perplexing disappearance. I had not known about his and his wife's altercation before his departure to the mall, and law enforcement alluded to the possibility no foul play was involved. A euphemism to suggest he'd either gone on a bender or indefinitely shirked his familial responsibilities. Primarily, I admire the doctor's ability to focus on my case in the face of a personal crisis.

At the start of the fourth week, Kate, who resides in Santa Cruz, finally replies to my message. She has stayed at both my main Pacific Northwest abodes, never asking questions, though of course I caught her looking at the name "Shore" on the mailbox. I agree to her proposal of a visit, as it will grant me the opportunity to sober up and work my way back into a brain thrill stage.

I spend the day prior to her arrival strictly abstaining from alcohol, one of the worst days of my life in that I just have to bear all the ambivalent emotions.

The next day, July 24th, I oversleep, then hectically clean the house as best I can, tearing open all doors and windows to air out the stench of alcohol, sweat, depression, and smoke.

Although I've been sober for over a day, I still feel removed from reality, as though I were viewing everything through a transparent curtain. I'm just about to fluff the pillows on the couch when I hear it.

A noise emanating from behind the door that leads down to the dungeon.

And then another, far too close for comfort.

I feel all blood drain from my cheeks.

I know it to be impossible, for obviously I always locked up the cells after feeding my pets. I even remember doing it drunk or high as it has become part of my muscle memory; the Rider having drilled the importance of always staying on top of things, even if not fully conscious, into me since early childhood.

Still, I must investigate. At least Kate is scheduled to arrive no sooner than in half an hour, which alleviates the pressure.

My hand hovers above the door knob, but I cannot detect any further sounds coming from the dungeon. Perhaps due to the frantic beating of my own heart, prompting the blood to rush through my ears.

I yank the door open, which, despite being made of steel, visibly trembles as it bangs against the banister.

The cell doors on the other end of the vast staging and kill area are closed, and hopefully locked. I look around the room from the top stair, but it's impossible to tell if anything is out of place, any item missing from the wall shelves.

Is someone cowering beneath the landing? Waiting to trip me? I tighten my grip around the gun, gripping the banister with my left to cautiously descend the concrete staircase.

When someone gets a hold of my ankle, I tumble down the steps and the Rider growls across the guilt wall, 'Hold on to the gun!'

But as soon as I land on the hard ground, gasping for breath, there's a flurry of movement and the doctor's foot stomps onto my wrist. I exhale sharply but do not cry out in pain, alas, I involuntarily let go of my weapon. When he kicks it away from me, I spin around on the ground and wedge my legs between his, bringing him down. He falls onto the kitty, which he must have freed as well, though I have no time to think about how he achieved it. It whines in pain and agitation, hobbling back and forth between myself and the doctor, who, regrettably, lets the chain leash slip from his fingers as he frantically kicks at my legs while attempting to stand up.

Then, from somewhere overhead, Kate's voice calls to me.

"Yo, girlfriend, where you at!"

In its confusion, the kitty hops over me, dashing up the stairs. But although I hear Kate's horrified screeching only moments later, and indefinable commotion, there's nothing I can do to come to my friend's aid, for the doctor is straddling me, both hands clamped firmly around my throat. His face is out of reach, and each time I attempt to force my arms upward to break his hold, he smartly shifts his arms and body weight.

'Help me! Come into me!' I implore the Rider, whom I cannot see, other than for his smoky tail billowing up behind him. Although he screams in reply, I hear his words as barely a whisper. 'I can't. The guilt barrier is too strong.'

'If I die so will you! Ride me already!'

He slams headfirst into the wall, to no avail. I start convulsing, a million pin pricks appearing before my eyes. And yet, the doctor doesn't let up.

Just when I close my eyes to accept my much deserved fate, I hear him shout, "No, don't!" And then the air rushes back into my lungs so suddenly that I start coughing.

"Oh my God! Oh my God, are you okay?!" Kate keeps asking over and over. My eyes are tearing up so much I cannot see more than a blurry female shape hovering over me, one arm stretched out and pointed at the doctor, who is pleading with her to listen to him, rushing through an explanation of how I had kidnapped him. The sound of the discharge and bullet hitting the ceiling is deafening and makes me wince. Kate must have picked up my gun from the floor. Why the doctor had not done the same, strangling me instead, eludes me at this point. Had he solely wanted to render me unconscious, rather than kill me?

I roll on to my side and try to steady my breath, swallowing as much saliva as possible to ease the raw burn in my still swelling throat. Minutes pass and finally, my breath steadies somewhat, allowing me to sit up. Kate's eyes are still on the doctor, an iron expression in them. She doesn't so much as glance at me when she repeats, "Are you alright?"

"Yeah, yes," I croak. "Kate, where is…the other one?"

"Upstairs. Whatever that was tried to attack me. I –" she pauses. "I knocked it out. Okay, I don't know what's going on here."

"Miss," the doctor tries again, "Listen to me."

She ignores his pleas. "Next bullet goes right into your head, Bozo. You leave my friend alone." She's good. Quick-witted. She didn't know which name the doctor knew me by, likely remembering the fake name on the mailbox, hence resorting to referring to me as her friend.

I am at a loss for words regarding how to reason my way out of why I have two strange men – one stranger than the other, surely – in my basement. I realize I cannot simply return the doctor to his cell either, until I have figured out exactly how he managed to get loose. I don't dare request back the gun from Kate at this point, and instead suggest we all head upstairs.

The creature that was once a man is lying on the ground, its head sticking to a pool of its own wine red blood.

"Oh, shoot," I murmur when my eyes fall on the vase Kate used to render it unconscious. "Kate, that's crystal." I rush to the creature's side and feel for a pulse, then turn around to gaze up at both her and the doctor. "You killed it."

Kate doesn't blink, her large gray eyes expressionless. "Okay," she merely states.

Is she in shock, or more like me than I had even anticipated? I cannot tell. I give her a few seconds, then address her with her full first name, for impact. "Katherine."

"Hm?"

"Do you understand what I said to you?"

"Yeah no, I…" Finally, she blinks, curses. "My head is a mess. What are we going to do now?! I can't go to prison, but it was self-defense, right? But like, who is this guy in the first place, did he break in?! And who are *you*?!" she shrilly inquires, with a nod directed at the doctor.

"I'm –" the doctor starts, but I cut him off, the ache in my throat nearly unbearable when I raise my voice.

"If you do not hold your tongue, so help me, you will be lying on the ground next to that," I point at the kitty, "within mere seconds."

Kate stares off into space. "I brought Polish grapefruit vodka. Not sure how to pronounce it, but I bought it because it had a funny sounding name, you know? And my son said you don't get a hangover from it."

Definitely shock.

"That sounds lovely," I reply gently. "Why don't you sit down on the couch, both of you, and I'll get glasses for the," I glance at the bottle on the couch table, "Lubelska?"

And this is how Kate became my best friend.

Chapter 16
Kate

The blood is still rushing in my ears, every limb in my body hurts from the fall, my previously fractured pelvis and hip are both on fire as well as throbbing dully, and my head is feeling as though it were embedded in cotton. I can't think straight, and yet I'm distressingly aware that I must contrive an at least moderately believable story, as well as convince Kate that going to the police was not an option.

I deliberate excusing myself to go downstairs and retrieve some more drugs to blend into my guests' drinks. But on top of appearing extremely suspicious, I can hardly stand anymore, and the stairs seem like an insurmountable challenge.

Besides, I cannot exactly hold Kate hostage downstairs, because there's a cyber-trail of our communication, and she will immediately be reported missing by her extensive family whom she's very close to.

When I return from the kitchen, I notice that one of my guests covered the kitty's body with the blanket from the couch. They're both sat on opposite sides of the couch, with Kate resting the gun on her thigh. Her golden brown hair is in disarray, her usually artfully arranged bun atop her head hangs limply off to the side, a few loose strands of hair framing her flushed face.

"Could you pour the drinks, Kate?" I ask, easing myself into a chair across the sofa. "This guy here just tripped me on the stairs, and you know what he did to me next, so I'm a little shaky right now."

"Oh. Yeah, I can do that," she says almost absent-mindedly.

"I can hold on to the gun for you for a bit, if you're worried about him," I gesture towards the doctor. Without speaking, she obliges – a good sign, indicating she still trusts me. Thus we sit, quietly sipping our drinks for a while.

'What should we do?' I ask the Rider in my mind.

'We've both sensed there may be more to her,' he replies, peering through the hole his head had punched into the guilt barrier. 'Tell her the truth. If we're wrong and she becomes frustrating, find a permanent solution.'

'I can't kill her, I'll be arrested immediately.'

'Liar. You would know how to spin it. Just you kept her inside the rootkit, although she even told you 'Friends are the enemies you don't yet know you have.''

The doctor clears his throat, prompting me to look up and scowl at him for interrupting our private conversation. I can tell from the expression in his eyes that he knows what I was doing, attempting to snap me out of it. I can't risk for him to share any more with Kate, but at the same time, my hazy brain remains mystified on how to work her. And then, be it the rootkit, or me – the shell – or the Rider, I crumble.

"Kate." Her eyes meet mine. "We've known each other ten years."

"Yes."

"You have, on occasion, supplied me with archival information when I asked you to, and I know you. You erased all traces of you having done so. You also never asked me for what purpose I required that information."

"Correct."

"You have also seen that the name on my mailbox here isn't Sand. You've looked me up as well. Whatever you found, and I'm curious what precisely that may be, you never told anyone about it." Mentally, I add, 'Because I'm still free.'

She twirls the glass around in her hands. "I'm a professional researcher. So yeah. I looked into you. I… have theories, but I was never sure."

I contemplate what aspect of the conversation to focus on for a few seconds. "What are your theories?" I finally dare ask.

"Well. You know how I told you about the Murder Accountability Project webpage?"
Oh God. I feel the Rider push against the guilt wall again, determined to break through.
She swallows. "I thought, okay, this is crazy, don't go Liz Kloepfer on her." She turns to the doctor. "That was Ted Bundy's fiancée? The one who turned him in? But anyway, I digress, uh. So after I saw your Shore mailbox, I looked up property records, and I thought, well, this is what Bundy did, right? Use fake names, and talking to Detective Keppel about how he wished he'd had a crematorium. I mean, you don't have a crematorium, but a nice car park, different homes in different states, that seems convenient. I tried to sneak a few Minnesota Multiple Personality Inventory questions into our messages, or steered the conversation to a topic related to one of the questions, to determine if you were a psychopath." She sighs. "And ultimately, I researched unsolved homicides of the past ten years on that Murder Accountability website, and well, I thought maybe you're a serial killer."
That wretched Ted Bundy and my association to his case had done me in at last. And I had let my guard down around Kate to the extent it had not occurred to me I was being asked personality inventory questions.
She must have had suspicions about me for at least seven years, when we started our online trolling projects together, three years after running into each other in an astrology group, discovering we were both also interested in True Crime. I had converted her to Ted Bundy, and she had converted me to Danny Rolling.
"But you didn't go to the police, told no one else," I state more than I ask.
"No."
"Why?"
"I'm not sure," she sniffles. "It's not like I thought you'd kill me or mine."

This is not the answer of a neurotypical person with the average amount of affective empathy. I can tell from her tone of voice and the expression in her eyes that she's being truthful. Perhaps she just needed a little push, now that she had already killed someone? On the other hand, it is a distinct possibility that my recent binges and today's lack of oxygen to my brain had left me actually and medically retarded.

"I may have found physically permanent and final solutions for people," I cautiously begin.

And then, she just laughs. It's a throaty yet elven sound; she never liked it, but I always found it infectious, no matter what dreary mood I had been in before. Another component of her laugh is that she can't fake it, no matter how hard she may try.

"You're a serial killer running a serial killer group online," she snickers. "I have so many questions. Do you kill for fun, gain, what? Give me the stats, victimology, modus operandi, everything!" Her face falls. "Please don't kill me, though, now that I know," she requests.

The Rider's constant howling about her cunningly playing me until she has an opportunity to alert the authorities, weigh on me while I listen to Kate bombarding me with questions and speculations, intermittently laughing her bell-like laughter.

The doctor has shrunken farther away from her throughout the conversation, gawking at her as though she had begun to sprout horns.

"So," she sighs. "Let's start with what happened here. Who, what, huh?!"

Now it's my turn to chuckle. "Alright, that is fair. This is Nick," I gesture towards the doctor, "my therapist. I did invite him to permanently reside at my abode, but don't intend to kill him, unless he seeks to escape or murder me a second time."

I scowl at him, whom I will never address as Dr. Yeoman, or more playfully as Dr. Y, again, before fixing my gaze on her again. "The creature you killed used to be my ex-boyfriend, many years ago, when he was still a man."

I swallow, searching for my smoky protector's solace. I could never utter the word before; too humiliating was it, even though the Rider had kept the experience safe and stowed away. I have since used the term in therapy several times, and conclude that it was time for exposure therapy. "He raped me. And this is what I did to him. I kept him alive like this, as a kitty, for punishment. It appears that somehow Nick managed to free himself as well as the kitty."

"So you are a pro-social serial killer!" she exclaims excitedly. "You're like a vigilante?"

This is the Kate I know. Enthusiastic, not terribly empathic in that she doesn't even offer any words of comfort about the assault, but that level honesty is also what I admire about her. She's practical, a thrill junkie, and feelings just get in the way of that. Perhaps it's still more politic to let her believe her vigilante theory for now, though if she researched homicides, linking them to me via the Murder Accountability Project site, she ought to at least have considered by now that this is not so.

"Hm," I nonchalantly offer in return.

"And why the therapy?"

I grab the pack of cigarettes from the couch table, pour us another round of drinks, and tell her a version of the truth. I leave out Michael for now, and allude only to "life circumstances" that convinced me I required professional help, citing my childhood trauma as the real reason.

"I'm glad you at least killed Grace," she growls once I finished.

I shift in my chair, wincing when pain stabs through my hip. The fall made the usually dull throbbing almost unbearable.

"Kate, we have to talk about how to go about," I pause for dramatic effect, "the kitty issue."

She blinks, quickly gulps down some more of the pink colored liquid. "Yeah. I know." She looks at me expectantly.

"We can't involve the authorities in this, you know that, right? We're in this together now," I stress, "just like with our other projects. Some of those could land us both in prison, and added murder and abduction charges are nothing any of us or your family needs."

She does not object, posits that in order to build trust between us, she would leave me the vase with her finger prints on it, would even give me something in writing about her being responsible for the creature's death. Is her offer prompted by fear, and she playing the long con? The lack of jitters, the absence of a nervous breakdown, any degree of self-blame, her carefree laughter, all convince me that the Rider and I may have been right about her all along.

"You seem very calm for someone who just took someone's life." I look at her chest, "What's going on in there right now?"

Her eyes glaze over for a moment, a slight frown on her face, as she appears to search inside herself to answer my question.

Finally, her eyes meet mine again. "Not as much as I thought it would whenever I wondered what it'd be like to kill someone. There's some fear, because I don't want my son to have to face the consequences if I'm caught." Interestingly, she does not mention her husband.

Then, she says one last thing. "I want you to know, this, with us, isn't just tit for tat for me. I know I'm aloof, we both are, but," she gulps, "you're sort of my best friend."

And with all these human emotions swirling around freely inside me, one particular feeling washes over me, its name eludes me, but it is a type of emotional warmth.

"You are my best friend as well, Kate," I reply with a genuine smile. "Now let's go, we need to clean up and put Nick back in his cell."

Kate is my strength on this day, as she has been many times before. I could never feel the gratitude before, and the mental acknowledgment hadn't carried the same weight.

My muscles have tensed up so drastically I can barely move, thus mostly delegate tasks. Both Kate and Nick bandage the kitty's head wound with Seran wrap before hauling it onto a steel slab downstairs, then return to remove the mess in the hallway. I will need a new floor, which meant another phone call to Rob who'd have to safely dispose of the old one.

Luminol, which is not as commonly used as crime shows would have anyone believe, reacted to the iron in rust, coffee and to bleach, but newer techniques have made it more difficult to conceal blood residue, and I was not the biggest risk taker as it pertained to forensic evidence.

I am not at all concerned about Nick's reaction, but wonder how on earth I should broach the subject of dismemberment to Kate. I could always stow the kitty in one of my freezers whole until I was physically back up to speed enough to dismember it myself, though I wasn't fond of the idea. I wanted her in on this every step of the way to irrevocably tether her to me, lest she betray me.

But Kate surprises me once more, asking me with glowing eyes about disposal methods and whether *we* should wait until after dark to rid ourselves of the body. Nick is vomiting all over the floor, and repeatedly so, yet Kate wordlessly hands him a bucket, sending him to a far corner of the dungeon to keep the stench at bay. When she leashes him to the wall, she keeps the chain too short for him to reach any of the shelves, though there's hardly anything he could use as a weapon. Still, I am, once more, impressed by her foresight.

When she hesitantly cuts into the cold flesh of the kitty after listening to my instructions, she exclaims, "Oh!" but doesn't gag, doesn't flinch.

"I guess deep down I always knew I had it in me, but when I met you, I felt like…" Kate stops cutting, vivaciously gesturing around to find the best way to phrase it. "Like we had more in common than we both let on. We basically already killed together. We murdered reputations, businesses and drove people to commit themselves to a psych ward." She laughs at the memories, then hangs her head. "Am I a psychopath? I can't be a psychopath, I do love my son. I cheat on Jack occasionally, sure, but who can eat chocolate ice-cream every day? The excitement wears off quickly." We'd never talked much about personal things. In fact, she hadn't even revealed her husband's name to me until two years into our friendship, and her cheating admission throws me.

"There's no external reason, no trauma or head injury that would explain my flat affects. I just never felt particularly guilty about anything except for not feeling guilty, ironically."

"Did you ever take the MMPI yourself? At least after you had sneaked questions of it into our conversations?"

She sighs. "No. I knew a professional would have to evaluate my answers to give a conclusive statement about my mental health, and I was afraid they'd recommend for CPS to take Will away from me, but now that he's of age and in college…"

I nod. "We have a therapist at our disposal, feel free to browse through the personality inventories Nick went through with me later; they're printed out in a file in his cell."

I help Kate bag the individual body parts, and force the doctor to do the same, who flinches and, as there's nothing left in his stomach to throw up, dry-gags each time his hands touches an extremity.

Kate offers to make us all sandwiches after the bag and tag phase, providing her with enough time to take a cursory glance at the questionnaires. Nick is chained to the bed, gaping at his sandwich as though it were yet another limb. I had Kate blend some hallucinogens into his drink, so he ought to loosen up again soon. Kate and I are sitting next to each other at the narrow console desk on the Eastern wall of the room, the file between us. All the while, her fingers keep absentmindedly stroking the upper corners of the pages we go through, and then I see it.

The imprint. It's from the large paper clip I suddenly recall I forgot to remove from the pages after therapy, in my drunken stupor. I'd been exhausted, feeling vulnerable and irate at the same time, stomping out of the room without even looking back.

"Nick," I address him, turning around to face him. "Where is the paperclip you used to uncuff yourself and unlock the door?"

"I don't have a paperclip." His denial catapults me into a murderous rage. Perhaps he wanted to die based on all I have done to him, though for my standards, I had put him through nothing really dramatic. Yet.

I stride over to the bed and backhand him. "Do not lie to me again. I know you have it."

Kudos to him, even though I had drugged him up daily, using the kitty and my own skills to brainwash him, he still hadn't broken down just yet.

"Give it to me, Nick."

Reluctantly, he reaches into his sock, producing the paperclip. He had smartly bent both ends out of shape, one to unlock handcuffs, and both ends to open door locks. It appears his record may not be as spotless as anticipated, which I will interrogate him about at a later date.

As I meditate on whether I should string him up in the middle of the dungeon by his feet for punishment, my phone buzzes.

I do not recognize the phone number, but I would recognize the jargon anywhere.

It's Michael.

Chapter 17
A Welcomed Distraction

Michael! It's Michael! Michael... My head is spinning, the adrenaline pumping through my body so abruptly that I must sit down on the edge of the bed next to Nick, to try and control my labored breath.

Michael's message reads, "Good afternoon, Emily Sand... my love, my one and only love. I would appreciate a brief chat with you on the phone, if I may, and if you so desire, that is."

Without thinking twice, I hit the call button, my heart skipping a beat when I hear his voice.

He chuckles warmly, "Why, that was fast. Am I to interpret your eagerness as you having missed me each second of every day as well?"

"Yes!" I yell far too loudly, hurting my still swollen throat. I can feel my cheeks glow, eyes grow wide, and my heart...oh, that wretched, murderous heart of mine feels so tender now that he finally reached out to me.

Kate looks at me with mock concern, followed by an expression that informs me she won't stop asking me about whom I could ever possibly get this excited about.

Michael laughs, a sound that sends little shockwaves through my whole body, and when he starts speaking, I close my eyes, so I can soak up his every word, to crawl into his strangely irresistible voice and stay safe in there.

"Good. I wish this were entirely a social call, but before we get down to business, I must know how you have fared, wherever you are. And remember, wherever you are, I'm always there with you in spirit. I hope I will be there in body as soon as possible, however."

When I rise from the bed to leave the blue room for some privacy, the connection goes bad, and after some moving back and forth, I decide to stay where I am, lest I lose Michael and cannot reach him again. I know our time is cut short today, and don't want to waste precious minutes. Of course, this means that Kate will learn, in part, what the ominous "life circumstances" I had alluded to involved.

When I finally get to replying to Michael's earlier question, I glance over at Kate, then at Nick, undecided about whether I should reveal to Michael what had happened. I didn't want him to believe I was being careless.

"My days have been mostly filled with activities – chores around the house," I report, unable to lie to him, but also unable to be completely truthful.

"What is wrong with your voice? Are you ill? I can tell that there is something you are not telling me. Emily," he sighs shakily, "you must tell me the truth. Uncertainty is nothing I can bear as it pertains to you and me."

He listens quietly as I relay to him the events of the last few weeks, only gasps when I get to the part where Nick attacked me. I choose my words with great care, and the intermittent pauses I require to sort my thoughts on how to leave out Kate entirely, Michael fortunately reads as me trying to spare my sore throat. Although I am hopelessly in love with him, I must acknowledge I feel too protective of Kate for Michael to view her as a possible threat – and act on it. Particularly now that I had found in her more of an ally I had ever foreseen.

"How did this – kitty? – of yours survive without you being present at your current abode?" He finally asks.

I swallow. "Stocks of food and water," I say, hanging my head in guilt and shame. I hadn't felt anything when concealing Kate's existence, but all this added lying appeared to patch up the guilt wall. I couldn't concede that the stocks of food and water had been provided by Rob in a secret basement room at one of his offices. Nick and the kitty were already two wild cards I had had to admit to, which, perhaps, is enough for one day. I could tell Michael was displeased by my revelation, resulting in me thinking back to when he'd called me inane, questioning my reliability.

"Understood. Now, here's an update on the investigation. If you want it?" Michael asks.

"Of course." I had begun neglecting to peruse the news media on a daily basis while drunkenly working with Nick.

And then Michael shares with me his laborious efforts of steering the investigation towards Elysia's tweaker boyfriend, never directly getting involved or pointing to any leads so as not to arouse the suspicion of his colleagues who were equally attempting to clear him and Cutter, alongside other family and friends. A hammer with the boyfriend's fingerprints and Elysia's blood residue on it was located at his apartment, along with compromising printouts and maps, as well as other suspicious computer activity, which all sealed his fate.

The head had recently been released to be cremated; they'd never found the rest of her body parts.

Michael was pretending to tend to Cutter, while gaslighting her into starting altercations with him and ramping up her alcohol intake to a degree she had been found drunk at work and suspended for two weeks.

"Once I have successfully driven her into irrevocable dependency, and lunacy, I will be able to dismiss her from our farce of a relationship without anyone, particularly law enforcement, considering my behavior dubious, or probing once more into my possible involvement with my stepdaughter's death. It is then I intend to reunite with you. If you'll still have me. Will you? Have me?"

"I will always have you, Michael, no matter how long it takes," I blurt out before I can stop myself, uncomfortably aware I just gave Kate a name. Her face remains even, but I see her eyebrow briefly twitch, knowing the name registered and she would eventually want to launch her own investigation to determine who he was, though fortunately she won't get far without a last name. For now. "I want you to know that I'm in California, Southeast of Sacramento, near Cosumnes River. I live here as Zadie Shore," I tell Michael, and he sighs a deep, quivering sigh of relief and elation.

"Thank you. I appreciate that trusting anyone, even me, poses a challenge for you, and you have now given me a gift I shall always hold close to my heart. I will protect your faith in me with my life."

After a few more minutes of conversation, he advises that he'll need to leave, and that this number, too, will be disconnected, but that he will do his best to stay in touch with me.

When the call ends, I stare at the phone, and fear, longing as well as a strange sense of loss roll into one, ripping at my heart, though I'm fully aware that feelings aren't stored in the heart, not felt by the heart. But it's difficult for me, in my current predicament, not to at least take into consideration that our bond is more than a chemical cocktail in my brain, an organic drug-high duping me.

"So, who's Michael?" Kate asks, still chewing on the last few bites of her sandwich.

I ignore the question. "We'll need to wrap up Operation Kitty-Cat. It's time for you to learn how to dispose of a body."

She laughs. "You say that as if you know I already developed a taste for killing, leaving bodies all over Northern California. Well. You do it, and I think very highly of you, which makes it easier to justify, I guess. And there are so many people! Who deserve killing! Did you know that?! Really, really sick people…we should talk about that somet- or, actually…" she pulls out her phone and starts typing. I eye her nervously, without yet commenting. But without my even asking, she shows me the phone, and there's nothing in her message to her husband that sounds like a code

word for 'Send help.' She only informed him she'd be staying the night at my place to help me get over a breakup.
Nick makes a startled little sound in the back of his throat, shaking his head in a way that suggests he was stimming – self-soothing. Only then do I realize how insane this entire day with all of its surprise events has been. Michael is back. I have a best friend. And she is talking to me about wanting to kill even more people, asking for my counsel. My life could not get any better at this point in time.

It poses a certain risk to take Nick, who is still moderately tripping, with us in the wee morning hours, in order to bury the kitty's individual body parts across Northern California. The fact Nick had freed himself, despite my knowing how, is still a cause for concern and future paranoia. I'll have to increase the terror and his involvement in my criminal activities to draw him onto my side. The events surrounding Kate had been a blessing in disguise, reinforcing in his drug-addled brain the impression that no one he'd reach out to, be it Rob, Kate or Michael, was safe. The more people refused to save him, the more Nick would begin to question his own sanity, would develop Stockholm Syndrome, I hoped.

Hours later, we have returned to the house. I give Kate the bed, and resume my position on the old velvet couch, though I am unable to fall asleep for a long time. Michael is on my mind far more than today's events even, and I catch myself spinning a joint blissful future in my mind. Us living together, having Sunday brunch, murdering together – just living the good life.
Kate stays another night, leaving on a Sunday evening after the doctor had done a rudimentary assessment of her via the personality inventories she'd filled out.

Most pedestrians believe Robert D. Hare's checklist and the MMPI to be the be-all, end-all in terms of determining whether someone qualified for antisocial personality disorder. And we're not even talking Michael Stone's ridiculously unscientific "scale of evil." Indeed, there were two more tests that clinicians availed themselves of which had never seen the light of day, had never been posted online for the simple-minded to misread and self-diagnose.

Moreover, it took far more to assess someone reliably, and gage whether the answers they had given on the test reflected reality or were a miscalculation on behalf of the test taker. Particularly trauma survivors often engaged in artificial mimicry, misrepresenting themselves to feel in control again, to a degree that they scored astoundingly high on so-called dark triad traits in tests, stemming from unhealthy coping mechanisms adopted while being abused by family, a lover, or even a co-worker.

Kate will have to retake the tests every three months and report back about her current life circumstances. Her sessions with Nick are, of course, going to remain confidential, other than what she chooses to share with me.

Her parting words to me include an attempt to elicit a promise of helping her kill one of the women online she considers an enemy. Kate very cleverly stays clear of any type of argument or interactions with those she loathes. I know the woman she speaks of. And know she lives in the Midwest. This endeavor would certainly be a welcomed distraction to ban my obsessive thoughts about Michael to the back of my mind.

'I could take a detour and visit Rob on the way there.' It's a split second thought coming out of nowhere, and I have to shake my head to ban the urgency of it from my mind, wondering where on earth it came from. There's no reason for me to visit with Rob. I don't even know his schedule and whether he'd be at home, as he's mostly traveling back and forth due to work. His is a home I could never go to because I have no way of explaining my presence to his wife, and the thought of meeting her made me strangely uncomfortable.

I'd never had grounds to summon Rob for personal reasons either, particularly now that I had Michael.

'Did you do this?' I ask the Rider. 'Did you put that thought in my head?'

'No. But if you reinforce that guilt wall, I will desert you next time someone is at your throat,' the Rider warns me. Without replying, I reach through the narrow hole in the wall to push him off of the edge of the pit in retaliation. I don't believe him. Most of all, I don't believe it wasn't him who put that thought in my mind, and his lie angers me.

Another eight weeks pass, without even just one message from Michael, during which Kate visits every weekend to be treated by Nick and share with me more about the woman she intends to kill. She's serious about her endeavor, I can tell.

As well, she is serious about sharing with me more about her personal life. She gives me full accounts of her favorite fictional serial killers and how they had inspired her in real life, shows me dozens of videos of her dog Nacho, her family members' birthday parties, and her house. Being that she is Northern German, she also explains to me how to cook the perfect champagne-sauerkraut with bacon, and we waste half a day exchanging recipes, though I begin to enjoy these social interactions, so perhaps the word waste was relative.

But we do also stalk Kate's enemy together, learning her habits, routines, whom she interacts with, what social media pages she frequents, and everything her real life as well as online friends and family do.

I know the woman, Bianca Sabo, from some of Kate's longer voice notes over the last few years. By all accounts, she is more than just your average bully and stalker, concocting wild tales about those she targets being neo-Nazis, or alternatively pedophiles, along with other undesirables. She had cost people their jobs, homes, friends, going as far as calling CPS on those who had children. She's ugly inside out, hence uninteresting to the Rider, thus I am relieved I shall exclusively aid in her abduction and stand by as Kate transports her hideous soul on over to the next plane of existence.

But truth be told, I crave all these distractions, particularly now that I limit myself to one drink before bedtime. Michael's absence is physically painful, and so is Nick's verdict on my case.

For some reason, and I can only speculate that the hallucinogens are at play here, he has deluded himself into considering me possessing factor two psychopathic traits only. Factor two's, previously labeled sociopaths, were reactive, created by circumstance, trauma. Celebrity psychologists such as Drs. Martha Stout and Ramani Durvasula posited they could hypothetically still be re-educated to an extent and possessed a weak conscience. Nick is of the opinion that my main problem lies with my alleged complex post-traumatic stress disorder, that my numbness was a result of the sexual abuse, in combination with the mother's neglect and overall histrionic behavior, as well as the loss of the only stable force in my life, my daddy.

When Nick brought up other specified dissociative disorder, and suggested the Rider's disintegration, in order to heal me from my trauma-induced murderous exploits, we had flown into a rage, stringing Nick up by the feet in the middle of the dungeon, leaving him in this position for an hour. He would have deserved to hang there longer, but temporary loss of vision and asphyxiation are real possibilities in this position, as I had learned the hard way while in my early twenties.

Though it had taken a copious amount of time, Kate and I had been able to convince Nick that it had been him who'd killed the

kitty, and that we were the ones protecting him from being arrested. Whenever I beat him, Kate cried out, asking him why he would strike her. A bizarre tactic I'd borrowed from a documentary on torture and interrogation methods.
Once Nick had broken down, sobbing at my feet, holding onto and kissing them while vowing to never ever hurt us again, thanking us for our mercy and patience, I knew we had him. The rest would be easy days.

It's September 18th when Kate returns to my house, complete with her own kill kit in hand. She'd already owned most of the items in it, and paid for the rest in cash, wearing a wig whilst keeping her face away from any of the stores' cameras. She's come a long way fast, unsurprisingly, as her knowledge about all things True Crime have certainly sped along her hands-on education.
As per usual, we are hard-pressed for time. Kate's several day long absence must go unnoticed, and can only occur because she suggested her husband and son spend a little quality time camping.
The rest of her family, who occasionally stop by unannounced, were made aware of her requiring some alone time to redecorate the basement. I had already redecorated the basement with her one recent afternoon while she was home alone. Her husband fortunately never went down there as it was Kate's domain, and would, if ever asked by authorities, unwittingly lie about when the work had taken place, delivering her a somewhat reliable alibi.
The way Kate kills is swift and inelegant. She stands before the lifeless body of the woman she had so despised while alive, a ponderous expression on her pale face.
"She deserved it," Kate declares. "But it feels different this time. I don't know how to explain. I'm not upset but there's something that feels off."

"Your first kill was self-defense. You can't justify this kill to yourself in the same way," I gingerly counter.

But since the Rider teases at the edges, always whispering that she, and anyone, might sell me out at any given moment, I add, "You may even believe to experience remorse, but I found it's just anxiety over getting caught in disguise. Just recall your family's faces whenever you have negative feelings about today, they'll give you strength."

The implication is clear. Don't mess this up. Don't ruin both our lives, as well as your family's lives, by turning yourself in or making careless mistakes.

Kate nods cautiously, holding up her blood-stained hands, turning them over to gaze at them with a mix of reverence and bewilderment. "I really did it."

She still appears withdrawn on the way back to California, and I know better than to pry. Whenever she disappears for weeks at a time, and leaves my messages on read, it means she is processing something or other, and I respect her needs. I have already said all I could to her about all the physical and metaphysical mechanisms and machinations of homicide. It is for her to combine theory and practice now. And should anything go awry, I still have the vase with her fingerprints on it.

Twilight enshrouds me as I steer my car through the narrow pathway in the woods to reach my house. As soon as I reach the edge of the clearing, I spot someone sitting atop my front porch steps. When I draw closer, the man brings a hand to his face, and a cloud of thick smoke rises above his head. Vape. It's Michael.

My finger pulls the latch before I even stop the car, and I accidentally step on the gas rather than the brake at first. I jump out, not bothering to close the door, running, running towards him.

He stands up to smooth out his pants, and walks a few steps towards me, his arms already open to welcome me into them. And as we stand, embracing each other, I start crying, trembling pathetically, but Michael strokes my hair and whispers words of solace and love into my ear.

"Michael…" I can only repeat his name, over and over, because anything else, any type of human speech, pales in comparison to his name, to what it – and he – means to me.

Chapter 18
Back Into The Rider's Den

Michael seats himself at the kitchen table while I grab the whiskey, complete with two glasses, from the wall cabinets. When he sees my fingers tremble as I am about to fill up our glasses, he takes the bottle from my hand and sets it down. His fingers find mine and hold them to his cheek. His eyes remain trained on mine. His face his calm, though not as austere as usual, but his eyes are smiling, their blue spilling over and flooding my soul, washing away all the uncertainty, rage and agony of the previous months.

Once I sit down, he updates me about the events of the past two months, closing with the fact that Cutter had had a nervous breakdown, after which she committed herself to a psychosocial hospital.

Michael would keep the house, as only his name was on the lease, and Cutter's parents had retrieved all of her furniture and possessions to lock them inside a storage unit for the time being. Elysia's boyfriend had proved to be more than a convenient fall guy. He had instantaneously gotten on the wrong side of the wrong people behind bars, while awaiting trial, and had not survived.

And now Michael was free. Free to be with me. Covertly, as it wouldn't be wise to be seen together by his colleagues or anyone else, in his view. And although he explains his reasoning for it thoroughly, and logically, it still doesn't sit right with me. I cannot tell exactly why, but I also don't want Michael to believe I'm starting a fight with him, too happy am I that he has returned to me.

Michael had requested some time off, still careful to avoid leaving a paper trail in the form of credit card charges on his drive here, and now we would have several blissful weeks together.

There's an awkward silence once all is said and done, during which we both nervously look back and forth between our hands we'd wrapped around our glasses, and each other, until he confesses, "I haven't been able to think about anything but our night together. Whenever I closed my eyes, I could still taste your lips on mine, and feel your devotion to me as you gave yourself over to me, body, mind and soul. The knowledge that you are mine helped carry me through my days."

And with this, we hastily rise from our chairs and fly into each other's arms. We're both all raw instinct, and I cannot even tell how or when we made it upstairs. Afterwards, we lie on the bed entangled, panting and sweating, too delirious about our reunion to think or speak, until he falls asleep. I'm exhausted but can't sleep in the presence of a man since the kitty, so I snooze, jerking up each time Michael moves in his sleep.

In the morning, Michael rolls over to face me and cups my cheek with his hand. I gaze into his eyes, still marveling at the fact we were finally together.

At last, he clears his throat, asking, "Whenever I thought of you, all of you, including your Rider, I began wondering why he is male."

"Oh," I say in surprise, for not even Nick had asked me this question, particularly after I'd strung him up for wanting to disintegrate the Rider. The question makes me uncomfortable, and I do my best to be vague. "He was just there one day, fully formed, and he's never changed, neither in spirit nor in appearance or gender."

Michael's fingers lazily stroke my back after I nestled up to him, bedding my head on his chest. "Is it because something happened to you that made you feel powerless as a female?"

I freeze, inhaling sharply, unable to look at him. "Why would you think something happened to me, Michael?"

"If that were the case, I would have to know. I have a powerful need to protect you. And that night –" he pauses. "That night by the fire, you mentioned your first kill. I sense there is more to it. Is that true?"

Why had it been easier to confide in Kate about this issue, though there was no one else in the world I craved to share everything with as much as with Michael? Maybe because I wanted him to always look at me the way he always did, with the cautious reverence one would have for an apex predator, his equal, not a pitiably frail prey animal.

I would have been incapable of admitting it to myself prior to therapy, yet deep down I knew that was precisely how I viewed myself, as weak. And that the creation of the Rider, a strong male to protect me from all harm, had been the result of my self-hatred for being physically inferior, as a child at first, and then as a female, when I understood what that meant.

The Rider had shown me that abuse was strength. To have been abused meant to see the world in a way, in a light, that no one else could understand. You were either the cattle or the butcher. That was the only strength there was to be had in this world. And with my carefully honed powers as a temptress, a seductress and a liar, and the Rider's volatility, we made an invincible team of butchers.

"Emily," Michael nudges me. "Talk to me."

I cave and confess; slowly, shyly, at first, aware of my nudity, the physical representation of my inner vulnerability. Halfway through my account, he sits up to reach for his phone and starts swiping through it, prompting me to go silent. After about a minute, he looks down on me. "Oh, keep going, sweetheart, I'm listening."

'Don't tell him any more,' the Rider hisses. 'This is a ploy.'

"I…" I start up again, confused by his demeanor. "I, where was I? Well…" I continue in my story, while Michael slides down on his back, staring at the ceiling as if he were a million miles away, in his own thoughts.

Kate's lack of empathy hadn't bothered me, why did Michael's? I tell myself I am overreacting, a byproduct of not having reintegrated the rootkit emotions into all their originally designated places. But when Michael finally closes his eyes, and, minutes later, begins snoring softly, I cannot help but feel hurt. And betrayed.

Of course, he had been driving without even taking a break, just to reunite with me. His fatigue was more than understandable. He'd done all he had in order for us to be together, and here I was, laying out before him my entire complex and traumatizing life history.

'You cannot see clearly,' the Rider advises. 'Your rootkit makes you a fool, and you are putting yourself at risk bringing all these people in on our secrets.' He adds a whispered warning. 'No one will ever protect you but me,' His smoky fingers are playing with the ends of my hair, the way I had wished, as a girl, the mother would have.

'That's not true,' I retort. 'Kate is protecting my secret. Nick will, eventually. And Rob has protected me in the past. Stop trying to isolate me.'

He hisses again, his wispy tongue lighting up to lick across my cheek like hot fire, searing me. A mental branding of sorts, and though I know no trace of it will show on my flesh, I still physically feel the intensity of the pain.

With this, he wafts back into the deep black den down below, leaving me with his subtle warning.

Still in shock, I watch Michael continue to snore, his heavy chest rising and falling, and decide to visit Nick in his cell.

"Emily!" Nick looks up from his book to greet me with a delighted smile. Every time his broken parts were reassembled a tad more, and by now he was doing the reassembling himself for the most part, as a gift and evidence of his by now swiftly advancing fealty to me, he received a little present. His favorite food, music, a book. Creature comforts to bond over. So far the most poignant one had been unchaining him from the bed.

"Are you enjoying your read, Nick?"

"I am. I appreciate Eagleman's work." Unsurprisingly, I'd known that, due to his mentioning the neuroscientist in one of his lectures that had found their way onto YouTube. Something I hadn't mentioned to him, as it was integral to his training he believed me to be intuitive and in tune with him. A person who understood him like nobody else on this planet could.

"Nick, we have company, and I would like to speak with you about it."

"Oh?" He briefly glances at the page number and lays the book down on the bed next to his knees.

"Michael has come for me. To be with me. He is asleep upstairs, but I –" I struggle for words, for how to begin. "The Rider doesn't like him. He blames him for opening the rootkit and building the guilt barrier, and I believe he's deliberately impairing my judgment, so that I will increasingly find fault with Michael and leave him."

Nick's eye noticeably twitches now that I had brought up the Rider. But before he can even form a mitigating reply in his mind or open his mouth to reply, the dungeon alarm goes off, notifying me that someone is at the front door. The alarm will sound upstairs, too.

I jump up from the chair so suddenly I knock it over, already racing up the stairs when I realize I forgot to close, let alone lock, the door to Nick's room.

Praying the alarm didn't rouse Michael from his sleep, I rush across the front room, already recognizing the shape through the old-fashioned lace curtains covering the glass-paneled front door.

"Rob!" I breathe, turning around to nervously glance at the staircase. "How can I help you?"

He doesn't reply at first, merely peers at me with eyes looking even more fiercely crazed than usual, his pupils tiny black dots reminiscent of laser points. Then he throws back his head, chortling once. Another typical gesture of his I had never learned to read.

"I still had all these supplies for your kitty, they're out back on the pickup. I thought you might need them, since it's been a while I heard from you, and I'll be in Washington this weekend."

I blink at him a few times, then remember that I had, indeed, neglected to fill Rob in on the fact the kitty was deceased.

"Right," I finally say, scratching my eyebrow. "That's very thoughtful of you, thank you. There's been a development."

"Want to tell me about it inside?" He takes one step closer but then his eyes leave mine, looking at something in the distance.

I turn, and certainly enough, Michael, now fully dressed save for his bare feet, descends the staircase, coming to a halt next to me. Rob looks at me, then fixes his gaze back up at Michael.

The silence is awkward, though I'm confounded as to why. Why does no one speak? Why can't I? The – however rudimentary – emotions I had allowed to spill into me appear to have impaired this previously coldly calculated genius of mine, as well as my ability to swiftly read social cues and situations. I simply hadn't even thought of any way to explain Rob's existence to Michael, because I'd been careless enough not to anticipate they would ever meet.

Finally, Rob's usual smirk returns to his face and he extends a hand towards Michael. "Do you know what a polar bear weighs?" But Michael's only reaction is to arrogantly raise an eyebrow at him. "Enough to break the ice. Hi, I'm Rob." He winks at me and smiles in radiant contentment when I burst into laughter right on the spot. A laughter that subsides the moment I lay eyes on Michael's facial expression.

"Anyways," Rob concludes, finally retracting his hand and becoming serious again. "I gotta blaze again, but if you change your mind about the firewood, my wife will bring it over since I won't be back until Monday." His eyes are intense, as though there were a secret message in his words but I'm too flustered to understand it.

Nevertheless, I coo, "Why, certainly," my voice far too high-pitched to sound credible to my own ears. I wondered how Rob handled his own rootkit, still being able to fabricate a lie so easily without even having to think twice, and without blushing.

As soon as I close the door, Michael cocks his head at me questioningly. Based on what Rob had implied, I respond, "Rob's a neighbor. He and his wife occasionally supply me with free firewood."

It's dangerous to lie to a law enforcement officer whose research would easily reveal who my next neighbors – miles away from my own house – actually are, but even more dangerous is that I experience no guilt about telling Michael an untruth, but relief. A circumstance that immediately has the Rider rambunctiously dance from one end of his cave to the other, howling so wildly the guilt wall trembles, but it still won't crumble. A fact that worries me, as there must be something else at play I'm incapable of grasping and acknowledging.

"Hm." Michael gives me a glance over from head to toe, as though he were reading more than just my voice and face but my body language, detecting the obvious deception oozing from my entire being.

But then his own posture relaxes, and he places both of his hands firmly on each side of my shoulders.

"You and I," he demonically grins, "must kill again. Have you recently stilled your urges, or would you be up for a joint murder expedition, my love?"

Though I had anticipated his proposal, I am taken aback by its timing, not only because it had occurred so shortly after our reunion, but in part because I had secretly hoped he would address what I had confessed to him regarding my childhood and the reasons I had become what I am. As well, I had looked forward to asking him the same question, for our only lengthy phone conversation from months ago had led us to cover many personal topics, without yet delving too deeply into our fatal perversities. Instead, I lie some more. "Sure, Michael. And no, I haven't had the opportunity to kill. We'll need to go troll later tod–"

He cuts me off. "I have someone in mind."

I swallow dryly, "Is it another family member? I'd prefer not to have to spend another few months without you."

He smiles his dimply smile in response. "No. Not a family member, and no one either of us is acquainted with on a personal level. His name is Paul Whithurst, a felon who successfully evaded the law based on a technicality. I happen to have researched him to a degree I know where he will be tonight."

This sounded like someone Kate would be interested in slaying, but naturally, I don't say so. Thus, I am reminded of the fact that there is one introduction to be made today, however. But Michael is averse to meeting Nick, stating that he'd prefer there be no living witnesses to his existence, unnecessarily citing the time the doctor had almost murdered me during his escape attempt.

I reflect on whether to bring up my current obstacle of not being able to unite with the Rider. Would Michael get mad again? But without the Rider, I am pitifully weak. Michael must, I decide, learn of it in order to better protect himself, as well as me. My disclosure doesn't appear to faze him, in fact, he acts rather dismissively about it.

Hence I return to the dungeon on my own, finding the door to the blue room still wide open. As soon as I am close enough to spy the edge of the bed, I spot the doctor's feet, jiggling either with nervousness or to a tune on the Walkman I gave him. And certainly enough, he still has his nose buried in David Eagleman's book while faint sounds of Orff's Carmina Burana echo from his headphones. This had been his unscheduled litmus test, and he passed with flying colors.

After yet locking him back up, I return to Michael, who had retrieved Whithurst's file from his rental vehicle that was parked behind the house. Once we have adequately prepared ourselves, the rest of the day is filled with awkward silences that dismay me to a point of near anxiety. I make several futile attempts at conversation, wanting to learn more about his own kill philosophy, and offering mine, but he remains monosyllabic, appearing preoccupied.

How could there be so little to say to each other after so many months spent apart? Was Michael being shy, did he need time to process my hospital story, could he simply not focus on anything that might take attention away from tonight? Or was the only thing we really did have in common the fact we were both killers?

After dark, we make our way to Sacramento in one of my vehicles, both of us in disguise, then hop on different buses, never together, meeting up a few blocks away from the bus stops in order to walk the rest of the stretch. The tavern Whithurst supposedly frequents every weekend is located in Del Paso Heights, one of the worst neighborhoods of the city. Across from it is another similar establishment, and it is here, by the window, Michael and I settle, so as to keep an eye on the comings and goings at the tavern across the street.

Hours pass, unsurprisingly without much conversation. We order drinks to amplify the effect of the painkillers we both had popped, until, right around closing time, Whithurst finally stumbles out of the narrow tavern door.

His greasy blackish hair is slicked back, revealing a flat pancake face with hauntingly empty eyes so light and strange that it's impossible to tell the color from a distance.

Immediately, Michael throws some cash on the table, barking, "Let's go," and so we do. We follow Whithurst at a safe distance. Michael's job is to watch him at all times, mine is to watch our surroundings and whether anyone was paying us too much attention. I'm trying to break through the guilt wall, to coax the Rider into jumping it, but he's just standing there, at the edge of the pit, beating his tail. Can he really not come into me or won't he, in part, perhaps, due to our last hostile interaction? I can't tell. All I know is I will have to do this one as just Emily. But at least I will have Michael with me.

It happens in an alleyway, which we had anticipated might be the case, though we had played through different scenarios of how and where to kill Whithurst, one being in his own apartment. Whithurst turns right to disappear behind a dumpster, and soon enough we smell and hear the splashing of urine hitting the pavement. We advance upon him, me in front of Michael, for I am supposed to wrap the wire around Whithurst's throat and bring him to his knees. But right after I pull the wire out of the pocket of my black hoodie, Michael shouts "Watch out!" at Whithurst, who turns around, and faster than I can follow, grabs a hold of both my wrists.

We wrestle for a split second until his fist connects with my mouth. And he keeps punching, and punching. Then, once I am lying on the ground, he starts kicking at me. I shield my stomach and ribs with my hands, afraid that his kicks will break my fingers, leaving me completely defenseless.

The last thing I see before I fade away, back into the Rider's den, crashing hard through the guilt wall and taking every last bit down with me, is Michael standing at a safe distance, watching on.

Chapter 19
Awake, Dreaming, Or Dead

I'm not certain whether I'm awake, dreaming, or dead, until I feel him carefully, gently, slide into me. He's never done it this way, as his approach is always swift and violent. But it is the Rider, and now we are finally reunited, his strength and determination opening our eyes, tearing a few eyelashes off in the process. It's blood. Crusted blood that sealed our eyes shut. We cannot see much, but we can tell that we are in the back of someone's car. We manage to perk up our aching head long enough to look at the driver, our hip exploding in sheer agony, to a degree we have to clamp our hand over our mouth so as not to scream.
It is Michael. Where did he get the car? Where is he taking us? But Emily is slipping, and although the Rider cries, 'Don't!' I fall back into the pit, disentangled from him, and all he can do is follow to wrap me in his arms until his power transfers onto and reinvigorates me.

When I open my eyes, I have no concept of time. How long have I been asleep, and where am I? My eyes are swollen; I can hardly open them, but they feel clean of blood. I cautiously probe with my tongue, and certainly enough, my lip is split in three places. And the smell, the smell is all my childhood terror prompting my eyes to fly open with a start. I'm at a hospital.
'Don't react now,' the Rider whispers. 'Just breathe, use our six senses to acclimate yourself.' The sixth sense, of course, being him. 'I will give you this because I know you need it,' he says softly, reaching inside my heart to place something there. I cry, silently, crying even more because the salty liquid bites into my wounds, and he holds me through it. He forgives me for deserting him for my insane rootkit obsession, and I forgive him for his reluctance to try, letting the emotions swirl around inside unfettered, dangerous

creatures that needed riding as much as I did.

My smoky protector pulls me down into the far corners of the pit, where I find all these strange human emotions pulsing, glowing, in the old chest that he had kept locked for decades before Michael came along. But now the Rider had chased down and returned each emotion to the rootkit, yet leaving it ajar, unwilling to deprive me of anything I could ever desire or crave. And now, he informs me, each feeling will be filtered through him, so it can do no harm to me, and us.

After a while, the tears subside, bit by bit, little aftershocks shaking my shoulders every now and then, until I'm fully calm, and the Rider pulls the sadness out to place it back inside the chest.

'Now,' he murmurs. 'You must know that Michael took you to a hospital in Washington. He laid you down on the ground right in front of the entrance and left.'

I shake my head. I don't understand? Why would he sabotage our operation, watch me being battered, and then drive me to a hospital? Why a Washington hospital and not the nearest one in Sacramento? Because Zadie Shore was a ghost, and if law enforcement were called, my cover would be blown? This confuses me even more, because I wouldn't have found myself in this current predicament without Michael letting Whithurst almost beat me to death.

'I can't tell you. If I knew I would,' the Rider sighs. 'I only know some of what was being said and that occurred. You need to disappear before law enforcement is being called. No one knows who you are yet, and we need to keep it that way.'

Trying my best not to moan, not to scream from the level of pain I'm in, I slowly peel myself out of bed, opening the narrow locker across the room, and find my phone. It has only 10% left, but appears to work.

Kate is too far away, though I acknowledge I will have to contact her about Nick during my absence. When I dial Rob's number, he picks up after the second ring.

"Rob, I'm at a hospital in Washington. Could one of your boys pick me up."

He inhales sharply. "Which one?"

I rummage through the leaflets and flyers laid out on my nightstand, and have to hold on to the metal bedframe to steady myself when I lay eyes on the name. It's my childhood hospital, the original pit just lurking several levels below me… But I pull myself together enough to give Rob the name.

"Half an hour. Be out front." The line goes dead.

It takes me over twenty minutes to get dressed, realizing that my fat suit and wig are gone. Michael must have removed them before dropping me off here, which adds to my confusion, because it insinuates he had done so in order to protect me.

It's no easy task to sneak out of the hospital, particularly after I had looked into the bathroom mirror to assess the damage to my body. The clothes will conceal the various bruises and abrasions on my body, but the state of my face is a different question entirely. I pull the hood of my hoodie as far down as I can, keeping my head down and the hair in my face, stuffing the clipboard hanging at the foot of my bed that lists me as "Jane Doe" into the back of my pants, before I leave.

It's not one of Rob's men who is out front but Rob himself, hands in his pockets, when I finally exit the hospital. And now I understand his remark and the way his eyes had bored into mine. He had wanted to let me know if I needed him in Sacramento, he wouldn't be able to personally help; almost as if he had sensed something off about Michael.

He inhales and exhales audibly when he lays eyes on me, bringing his fist to his mouth, its knuckles as white as his face. "Who did this to you?" And when I look into his eyes, so filled with rage and pain and care, the Rider pulls out a feeling, small as a mustard seed, and lets me feel it.

The guilt, the guilt towards Michael had been because I had kept Rob in the rootkit. I hadn't known, and I also couldn't have felt it in any way because no feeling that arose ever touched me, or my heart, being born into the burial chest of the rootkit.

It was Rob who had always protected me, and who had always been a friend to me, despite our rare face to face interactions. Rob had shielded me just like my daddy always had, before he had deteriorated and died.

I probably hadn't felt guilty lying to Michael about Kate because I had known Rob longer, so the lie was more impactful. Is that how it worked? I wasn't sure, but I can't explain it otherwise.

Rob asks again, "Who did this? Was it the guy I saw at your place? Because if it was, I'm going to rip him to shreds and scatter his remains to all four corners of the winds."

My smile feels so debilitating I almost faint from the physical pain, and all I am capable of replying is, "Take me home, Rob."

Even sitting upright in his car proves too much of a challenge, and soon my head lolls back and forth, my face sweaty and flushed, while I'm groaning in delirium.

Once we are inside my building, Rob props me up against the wall, holding me in place with his knee that he wedged between my legs. But there is nothing ambiguous about it, nor is there about him fishing the keys out of the front pocket of my jeans. After he gently eases me onto the bed, the last thing I feel, until I fade back into the Rider's arms, is Rob rolling me onto my side, pulling the clipboard out of my pants and seating himself next to me on the bed, his warm hand atop my own.

It is the doorbell that wakes me, as well as Rob jumping up from the bed, jogging towards the front door. I'm too groggy to open my eyes more than half an inch, but shortly thereafter, another man enters the bedroom, an old-fashioned black leather bag in hand. He's about a head taller than Rob, wearing his salt and pepper-colored hair slicked back. His eyes are an icy shade of turquoise, a friendly, empathic twinkle in them. The man takes the clipboard from Rob's hand, listening to Rob's muttered explanations as he gestures back and forth between the medical notes and me. The other man keeps nodding while reading through my file, then addresses me.

"Ma'am, I am Dr. Hershel McClurg. I'm going to examine you now. I need you to sit up, please, can you do that?" Looking back at Rob he says, "Rob, I'm going to need you to wait outside."

Rob shakes his head. "Nah. Uh-uh. No way in hell. I'll turn around."

Once McClurg has examined me, he writes something down on his notepad, tears it off to hand to Rob, informing him, "Nothing appears to be broken. Have her take one of these every morning for ten days, and those," he points to the bottom of the prescription "as needed. And if her temperature rises above 104°, call me again."

He thinks it's a fever. But it's really just the Rider burning to keep me alive.

At the end of the first day, the Rider has granted me enough strength to be able to call Kate. I tell her where the spare key is hidden on my property, and she vows to supply Nick with enough groceries for a week.

Later that night, Rob carries a tray with a bowl of soup into the bedroom, placing it next to him on the bed and insisting on spoon-feeding me once he sees my hands and arms shake and my cheeks flush furiously with overexertion. Rob, I know, is not someone to take anyone's no for an answer, yet the way he exerts his willpower with me is surprisingly gentle, albeit firm.

He guides me towards the shower and closes his eyes while undressing me, since I am unable to lift my arms above my head or bend down enough to remove my pants, after which he begins to remove his own clothes.

"What are you doing?!" I cry out.

"Your hair is greasy and there's still some blood residue in it. You can't wash it yourself. I'm not going to look, don't worry."

Afterwards, Rob dries me off, dresses me, then opens his eyes and leads me back to bed. I am once more about to fade from overexhaustion, but appreciate I will have to warn him, as Michael had previously gained access to both my apartment as well as my Idylwood cabin. I stammer, closing my eyes in between, uncertain if I can stay lucid, but eventually, Rob knows all that is relevant for him to know at this point.

On day three I can at least sit up by myself to suck on mashed potatoes and other pureed food. Rob wears my frilly apron when serving the meals he prepares for me, and his eyes light up each time I burst into laughter at the sight of him, though my ribs hurt so much I have to hold onto them seconds later, my laughter turning into hollow coughs.

The day after, I am awakened by voices coming from the living room, Rob's and another female's. I listen to their conversation, but it's so soft I only hear a few isolated words and giggles, which tells me it's one of his girlfriends. I had wondered how he was able to stay past the weekend, how he had justified it to his wife. Likely with a work emergency at his Washington practice.

Eventually, I hear footsteps approaching, and when Rob swings open the bedroom door, he states, "You're awake! Okay, so I have to head back home, but Amber will stay with you."

Of course her name is Amber, and of course she's an empty-eyed twenty-something goth model type girl with platinum blonde hair, piercings obscuring her face. They'd likely met at the High House as well.

He looks at her, and she giggles again. Oh my Lord. "Give us a minute, Amber?" Rob murmurs, winking.

She demurely casts down her eyes and turns around to leave, her heels clicking on – probably ruining – my antique hardwood floor. Rob closes the door and sits down on the edge of the bed, one knee propped up on it, his fingers impatiently drumming a hectic rhythm on the blanket. "Two things," he starts. "I know his name is Michael Pennington because when I was at your house, I returned the same night to check out the plates of the rental car he'd parked out back. And after all you told me, I had my associates work a little of their magic. I also know he's a cop." He shakes his head. "What on earth were you thinking getting involved with someone like that?"

I disappreciate his condescension, though I acknowledge the validity of his concerns. I still have trouble being able to tell which of my memories of the last half a week were reality as opposed to fever dreams, but I do recall Rob threatening to kill Michael for hurting me.

"You can't go after him, Rob," I reply tonelessly. "Please promise me you won't."

He does his odd head-shrugging chortle again. "Emily…"

"You don't understand what he is. I can't tell you any more, Rob, please just stay away from him. I will take care of it."

He gives me a long probing look before speaking again. "Did you ever believe that all of what happens at The High House is voluntary?" he asks, making my jaw drop, not because I hadn't secretly anticipated as much, but because I didn't think he'd ever relay this type of secret to me, particularly over a decade and a half later.

He continues, "And did you ever believe that I didn't know the kitty didn't agree to its ordeal? All those cars you keep bringing to us to repaint or dispose of… We both know you're not a carjacker." Again, he shakes his head.

"What are you saying?" I respond, not ready to share with yet another person my exploits of being a serial killer, considering the recent betrayal I had suffered. His eyes bore into mine. "Don't bullshit a bullshitter, Emily." It's what I had, over the years, often said to him. Always laughing while doing so, but I had, for some reason, always needed him to understand that I knew what he was, that despite my enjoying our flirting, he could never get to me the way he did with all the other girls.

He proceeds, "We've both had to lie by omission, and with the truth, but we've known each other too long to directly lie to each other."

I nod, and leave it at that, for the most part due to not wanting to get into the topic before I felt back up to speed and had conferred with the Rider in detail about how to clean up the mess I had already made.

"Secondly," he says, his tone less harsh now. "Amber is a good friend who – "

"Don't bullshit a bullshitter," I interject, without having planned to do so this vehemently, and without understanding why his obvious euphemism even bothered me.

He frowns, but then his face relaxes and he grins, almost a tad too triumphantly, the crow's feet around his eyes deepening while doing so. "Amber is armed and here to protect you. She will also tend to your every need. I have to go. For now. Oh, before I forget," he reaches inside the pocket of his flannel shirt, "these are your new keys. You have new locks of the kind he won't be able to get into, the windows have bars, both have alarms…" he scratches his beard. "I guess that's it." He clicks his tongue at me twice and winks, prompting me to give him a broad smirk. I knew he was aware I had always had a thing for his sleazy tongue clicks. As well as the fact he reserved them for me only.

Another week passes, during which I spend an exorbitant amount of time tending to the Bundy group online, interspersed by occasional updates from Kate about my therapist pet. I catch up on work, writing email after email to my employees and assistants, going through the bookings on our website, checking my bank accounts.

I keep as busy as possible, and yet, my thoughts obsessively return to Michael, and all the questions surrounding his intentions, and our time together.

We hurt the ones we love, they say. I could live with that. Far worse though, the ones we love hurt us. That I cannot abide by. When I reach out to the Rider, he nods in agreement, 'He has to die.'

And then Michael calls.

Chapter 20
All Ducks In A Row, All Eggs In One Basket

I don't answer the first three times around but he appears undeterred, until I finally pick up.

"What do you want?"

Michael's voice trembles. "Emily, are you at home now? I have been so worried about you."

His response unsettles me to the extent my mind goes blank for a moment, leaving me to frantically blink, unable to process whether he is merely a bold liar, considering me so mentally inept that I was incapable of discerning the obvious manipulation attempt, or if I had possibly overreacted, misremembering his involvement in Whithurst's attack. In the course of my Bundy studies, I had familiarized myself with the basics of Elizabeth Loftus' work on human memory and the malleability of it. He sounded so…sincere. I find myself incapable of replying, and after the seconds tick away, he asks, "Are you still there?"

"Hm," I reply, angling for time to gather my thoughts. "I'm still alive, despite your attempt of getting me killed."

Michael's response is swift, aggressive and loud. "That's an interesting rendition of history, at which you have proven yourself to be an expert in the past, if only it serves your purpose of being viewed as a martyred victim of circumstances you yourself created. If you recall, I am the one who drove you to a hospital, calling each day to ask how you were holding up."

I can't help but huff. "There are no missed calls in my log."

"Are you calling me a liar?" he asks, even more loudly. "On the first day, my calls wouldn't go through, likely due to the hospital's fire protection ceiling. Instead, I called the hospital's landline, and kept calling, though they would not relent, refusing to provide me with information about you, due to data protection laws. I did not identify myself as an officer of the law, naturally, and so I had no

grounds to learn anything about your state or whereabouts."
When I see the Rider's hand emerge from the pit, carrying a bulb glowing coldly, I inform him, 'I don't need to feel it, my mind is already distrustful enough of him.' He shrugs, retracting into the blackness, though, I notice, not without an air of satisfactory glee about him.

Returning my focus to the conversation with Michael, I inquire, "For what reason did you alert Whithurst to my presence, and watch as he pummeled me, rather than intervene?"

Michael's stammered explanation confuses me even more. "I spotted him holding what I believed to be a knife in his other hand, and panicked, concerned for your safety. I did not call out to Whithurst, Emily, I called out to you to watch out. When he began attacking you, I froze, momentarily. Can you truly fault me for my feelings for you? And that the events, which all happened in quick succession, if you remember, paralyzed me?"

"And could you elaborate on the reason you took me all the way back to a hospital in Washington?"

"I didn't think it wise for the name Zadie Shore to appear in an official police report, or for Emily Sand to turn up in California where she has no business of being. And due to the severity of your injuries, the medical staff would have had to alert law enforcement as soon as you had woken up. I thought you would stand a better chance at home, on your own turf. I knew you would have to make a run for it, yet had no way of knowing how well you knew your way around Sacramento."

Could it be that he was telling the truth after all? He'd also ingested more painkillers and alcohol than I had, perhaps they had skewed his vision, slowed his senses. It made no sense he would put me in danger, only to save my life and protect my identity. Then again, by protecting my identity, he was protecting his own as well. I can tell the Rider's discontent as he reads my every thought and deliberation, but opt to ignore him until I had elicited more information from Michael.

As our conversation progresses, he inquires whether I'm at my Seattle apartment, and without hesitation, I state, "No, I'm not. I enjoyed talking to you today, Michael, but I have an appointment to get to. I will speak with you soon?"

I can tell the level of his disappointment at my not revealing my exact location to him, but he at least quietly accepts it.

Several minutes after hanging up, he messages me.

"Thank you for permitting me to communicate with you today. That courage will never be forgotten. Ever. If it's true (and it is) that anger and hurt can tear down and destroy, then it's equally true that love and trust can rebuild. That's now what we did. We rebuilt.

I am so sorry I let you down. I am so sorry I left you feeling betrayed. I am sorry for missing the mark and for not following through. I am sorry for being loud and making you feel afraid earlier. I am sorry, I am just so very sorry. For every part I played in all that went wrong. I will own my parts by becoming better at this. I will not take for granted what we have."

'Lies,' the Rider yawns. 'You have a terrible hand at choosing men, you know? Why don't you give Rob a call, maybe you can add him to your harem of men to mentally, physically or sexually wreck you, since you appear to like it.'

'Don't be a...' I reply scathingly, startled at my almost using bad language. 'Leave Rob out of this. He didn't have to take care of me, and yet he did.'

He laughs. 'Of course he did. You've been an elusive hole for the better of fifteen years, and this is his way of finally getting to fill it.'

I ignore him to pen a note back to Michael. It's partly true, though I leave out the fact that the Rider and I had conferred about killing him for what I'd perceived as his disloyalty.

"When I believed you had abandoned and betrayed me, I felt as though a limb was missing, and I wasn't quite certain whether I was metaphorically or literally dying."

Seconds later, he writes back, "That turns me on. That makes me so insanely hard."

I stare at the words, and despite my own ghoulish emotional predilections, they strike me as so utterly wrong, that my entire body tenses up, sending throbbing waves of pain through my hip. But I wouldn't know how to phrase my concerns anyway, and have no time to do so, as the doorbell rings, and Amber barges in just seconds later, gun in hand, asking, "Are you awake? Armed? Good." She disappears again, her whore heels further ruining my precious floor. I identify the voice coming from the hallway as Kate's, and call out, "Let her in, Amber!"

But it isn't merely Kate who saunters into my bedroom. It's Nick, too.

Kate immediately holds up her hands in a conciliatory gesture. "I know what you're thinking. But Nick wanted to see you. And after spending all this one on one time with him, it seemed," she shoots him a sideways glance, "like it would work well enough at this point?"

Nick is already by my side, wringing his hands. "What happened to you, Emily? We should resume therapy at once."

"Maybe Kate should stay for this session," I meekly suggest, realizing how much I had missed my regular appointments, slash confessionals, with him. It may be time to bring Kate in on all things Michael to get a fresh, unbiased perspective.

Once I have recounted in minute detail all there was to know about Michael, from his occupation, kill trailer, background and habits, Kate is already spinning various scenarios in which we could trick Michael to test his loyalties, presenting revenge ideas for each of them, should he fail them.

It isn't until Nick unanticipatedly chimes in that Kate's and my jaw drop, however. "What if we abducted Isobel Cutter? She has valuable information about Michael, and in case we need it, she is leverage." When he sees the expressions on our faces, he adds, "What? Not a good idea?"

I clear my throat. "This, no, this is an excellent idea, actually."

I look at Kate for confirmation and she nods, then gives us this to deliberate, "What about cameras at the hospital though? And the fact that you, Nick, vanished from the face of the earth. How do you suggest we work around that?"

"Oh," he replies jovially, "I thought that much was obvious. My hair's already grown out, and we'll just dye it brown. I'll grow a beard, for some reason my beard was always brown, though my hair isn't. If Emily has property in the name of Zadie Shore, she will have a way of obtaining a fake ID for me. I will make an appointment to visit with Isobel, convince her to give a 72-hour notice for a discharge waiver. You mentioned she had committed herself, so unless she acted violently at the ward or let the staff come to the conclusion that she might pose a threat to herself or others, or that she wouldn't be able to care for herself once released, there will be an assessment, after which we can pick her up. No further paperwork needed. Another plus is the fact she's at a state mental hospital. Awful places in terms of security, overcrowded, understaffed… they'll be happy to get her off their hands."

"She doesn't know you though," Kate says. "How do you propose to get her to agree to see you, without alerting the staff to the fact you are a complete stranger to her? And once you do get to see her, how will you convince her to go with you?"

Nick shrugs his shoulders. "We should bring her in on what Michael did to her."

"That's insane!" Kate cries out. "She'd immediately call for security, or worse, for the police. And when people realize who you are, it'll be an FBI case because two states are involved, which will put all of us at risk."

Nick scowls at her, obviously dissatisfied with her outburst. "I'm a psychologist, Kate," he retorts, inclining his head a tad too arrogantly. "I read people rather well. I'll know how to present our case to her so that she'll understand it's in her best interest to play along." He pauses, his eyes turning inward. "I could always claim that I'm an undercover cop. That we need her help…"

Kate's laughter is harsh, absent its usual elven-like quality. "An undercover cop-psychologist. Okay. Sure."

"Oh, so you have a better idea? Let's hear it then," he says, leaning back and defensively folding his arms across his chest.

'Look at these two bickering like reluctant turtle doves.' I blink the Rider away. I have no time to entertain his whiles. More importantly, I'm yet too paranoid to fully trust Nick. He had certainly done well over the last few weeks, but trusting him enough to let him out of our sight, step into a mental hospital, his turf, where he could very easily alert anyone to Kate's and my existence, was a risk I wasn't sure I could yet take in good conscience. Even if one of us went with him, he could so easily make a mistake to alert the staff to the fact something wasn't quite right, and neither Kate nor I would know what precisely that was until the trap snapped shut.

As always in my life, either nothing happened for days or weeks at a time, or everything happened at once. I tense up as soon as I hear someone unlock the front door, followed by Amber's tender coo, "Ohhh! Baby!"

I roll my eyes, as soon as I hear the frantic lip-smacking, followed by her happily sighing and muttering under her breath.

Both Kate's and Nick's eyes are trained on the door, and as soon as it opens and Rob steps into the bedroom, I realize the full extent of the predicament I'm in.

Everything the Rider had always warned me about, every bout of what I had identified as paranoia, was now reality. I was in a room with everyone, save for Michael, who knew, or in Rob's case, suspected, what I was. I had all my ducks in a row, but also all my eggs in one basket, which, if you are a serial killer, is unfortunate.
"Uh, hi," Rob says in his usual upbeat tone of voice, a crooked grin on his face. His greeting earns him but a hesitant mumbled response from Kate and Nick. I can tell whenever Rob's stressed because his voice has just an ever so slightly higher pitch. Everyone thinks he's just this funny guy, a social butterfly without depth, but he's not a big talker unless he's with me, and doesn't like people in general, particularly not if he doesn't know whether they posed a threat to him and his business. I look around the crowded room, and have no idea how to even begin making introductions.
Each person in here serves a purpose in my life and is embedded in the rootkit, yet every one of them also has the power and wherewithal to deconstruct me to the point of annihilation. On the other hand, I hold the same power. It's a cold war situation we are in, which, I realize, may make for the best and most loyal friendships after all.
Rob's voice jerks me out of my silent musings. "It's like I just walked in on a secret gathering," he jokes. "And you are all thinking 'Should we kill this guy or bring him in on what we're doing?'"
I clear my throat. "Well, you always have been an eerily intuitive man, though I assure you, I would never touch even just one hair on your head."
"Oh, really," he grins. "Well, I don't have hair on my head but you're very welcome to touch the rest of me in whatever way you like."
I laugh. "These are my friends, Kate and Nick. They will help me take care of the Michael Pennington situation."

Rob doesn't miss a beat when responding, "What's our plan?"
"Uh," Kate says, holding up a hand. "Who are you?"
"That's Rob. I told you he picked me up from the hospital to take me back here," I inform her.
"And how much does he know about what we do?" Nick slowly asks, his chin resting in his hand and a look of grave concern on his face. I look at him, impressed with what expert brainwashers Kate and I were. He does seem fully on board with everything, though I know the one thing to break his resolve is his bond to his children. Maybe I should just kill them, despite my usual hesitancy to create underage victims. But I realize how desperately I need and want him in the Rider's and my life.
"I'm not concerned about what you guys usually do or don't do. Pennington has to go," comes Rob's vehement answer.
"I know you can handle yourself but I don't want anything to happen to you if this goes sideways," I start, but he cuts me off.
"I'm going to be in on this one way or another."
I know better than to argue with Rob, and so we brief him on what Kate had immediately dubbed Operation Asylum, until I ask Kate and Nick to give me a minute alone with Rob.
"We've trained Nick well," I say, inclining my head in the hope that he will understand. "Perhaps, though, it would be wise if he didn't go in alone." Before I can voice my concerns, Rob interrupts me again.
"I can go with him. I know my way around hospitals and medical lingo in general, and can also provide lab coats, name tags, what have you," he offers.
"Naturally, I will reimburse you, including for the time you spent here caring for me."
He scoffs, not angrily, though perhaps a bit disappointedly. "We have our deal for the cars and the rest. This isn't business, there will be no payment."
"Why are you doing all of this for me?"

He scratches the top of his baseball cap. "Stop overthinking things."

It's not an answer to my question, but I know I won't get any more out of him for now, or ever, and so I press my lips together, until I decide to accept. "Alright. We make an appointment to see Isobel tomorrow. I believe Kate will have to take Nick back by tonight, and depending on when the visitation may take place, are you sure you can return to Washington on short notice?"

"Oh, I'm not leaving," Rob says. "Amber is going home, I'll be staying with you."

The notion stirs something in me. Not upset, at all, perhaps mental agitation was a better word, though I can't pinpoint why. I had lived with Rob for several days just recently, but now that I neither am nor feel close to death, something about it triggers me.

The Rider remains silent, no helpful hand reaching up to let me feel why I have these reservations towards Rob.

I shrug, and say, "Say thank you to Amber for me. She did her best, I guess."

I'm not sure why I'm lying. She had done absolutely wonderfully, caring for me day and night. Perhaps I'm just picking up my old habit of staying a practiced liar, and in control?

Chapter 21
Anything You Can Do, I Can Do Better

As it turned out, my estimate of carrying out this operation within a week had been far too optimistic. As cell phone use was even prohibited on low level wards, for fear one patient could snap a photo of another and make it public, breaching HIPAA laws in the process, the only way to contact Cutter was to call the ward she was on to ask to speak to her. This posed yet more issues, as phone calls were recorded, though Nick assured us they were at least not indefinitely stored. According to Google, he was telling the truth. Kate experienced some scheduling conflicts due to a birthday in her family on the first weekend after we'd loosely begun working on our abduction plan, whereas Rob refused to leave my side, and I refused to let any of his boys enter my California abode without supervision. One of them still managed to briefly meet with Kate, who supplied him with new, passport style photos of Nick, whose hair is now brown, beard long enough to obscure half his face. The fake ID, diplomas and assorted other documents should be ready within next week. We may not need them now, but they would come in handy eventually, and they would prove an asset in the continued separation of Nick from his old self and life.

In other news, my stress level is increasing exponentially with each passing day, albeit not due to our team's impending enterprise, but because of living with Rob. He sleeps on the couch, as he previously had, cooks and cleans and entertains me, though at the end of the next week I feel well enough to join him in doing little tasks.

I occasionally hear him argue with his wife over the phone, who evidently cannot fathom his long absence. Part of me wants to convince him to leave to smooth things over with Jill, but the stronger part of me keeps quiet, covertly reveling in their marital issues. I mean, of course it would. I haven't been able to kill for quite some time now. Operation Asylum and Rob's marital drama provide the only nourishment for my destructive urges at present time.

He so casually climbs into my bed to lean back against the headboard, stretching out his slim long legs before switching on the TV to watch his sports games, or an old movie, that it's as if he's always been here, with me. Because he always seems comfortable in his own skin, never a worry on his mind, I myself feel comfortable in the moment. Until I remember that he shouldn't be here, and that at some point, he won't be.

Whenever Michael calls, I put him on loudspeaker because Rob insisted on standing by to type out a note in his cell phone on how best to stall, how to placate him. I wouldn't actually need Rob's expertise, though I would never admit it to him. I like the way his sky blue eyes smile at me, and how he takes pleasure in helping me, nodding at me in encouragement whenever I follow his lead. "Michael, is Paul Whithurst still alive? He saw both our faces, how should we go about this issue?" I had asked several days ago. And Michael had offered a vague reply, stating that there was nothing to worry about any longer. Kate had immediately entered Whithurst's name into the plethora of databases she had access to at work, and shared with Rob and me the disappointing news that Whithurst was, indeed, alive. This cast even more doubt on Michael's motives, though I still wanted there to be a good explanation, in fact, I believed there to be one because I needed it. I found no enjoyment in playing Michael, though I knew it to be necessary.

Three weeks later, our team has reassembled. Kate obtained blueprints of the hospital, along with detailed street maps, having highlighted which possible routes to take in case we ran into trouble and had to make a quick getaway.

We hand Nick a new burner phone and gather around him on the bed as though we were about to do a prank phone call at a teenage sleepover, which, in a sense, isn't too far off.

Kate had practiced with Nick until he seemed secure enough in his faux identity, Dr. Nick David. There were hundreds of Dr. Nick Davidses across the country, several in Washington, so that name had seemed like a relatively safe option. The videos Kate had sent me of how she'd trained Nick were as hilarious as they were concerning, for their banter and mock fighting increasingly gave the impression that there was something else brooding underneath the surface. If Kate developed genuine feelings for the doctor, it could work to my disadvantage, depending on where her loyalties would fall. If they lay with me, it could further separate Nick from his old life, however.

I watch Kate watch Nick, the hint of a smile bending the corners of her lips, as his eyes are turned inward while waiting for someone at the ward to pick up his call.

Once that happens, he elegantly but briefly states his case. He claims to be a trauma specialist who'd taken an interest in Isobel Cutter's case after learning about it through the media, offering his help pro bono. It still sounds like a transparent and unoriginal ruse to me, but after a few minutes of back and forth with what I presume to be the receptionist, she agrees to take his number, promising that Cutter, if interested, would call him back during patient call hours.

But Cutter doesn't call back that day, and Kate has to leave for California again. Obviously, we cannot leave the phone with Nick in his cell just yet, though none of us utters these words. Ultimately, it is decided that Nick will stay with Rob and me. There's a brief power struggle over sleeping arrangements, as neither man wants to sleep in one bed together, and Rob doesn't trust Nick enough to let him sleep next to me either. I see where this is going, and certainly enough, Rob decides he would sleep in bed with me to let Nick have the couch. I blush, likely a quasi-post-traumatic stress reaction to my waking up to being raped by the man I had made a kitty, after which I had never slept in the presence of any man ever again. Thus I remain mute, too perplexed to object.

But once Rob pulls me aside into the next room, he leans in and murmurs, "We're gonna take turns sleeping while Nick is awake. Let's let him think he's the one keeping watch. But even if we restrain him, we can't leave him out of our sight, with hypothetical access to the front door and kitchen, locked or not, and your weapons stashed everywhere –" he stops when my eyes widen, grinning, "Oh yes, I know all about those. Did you think I wouldn't find them when I secured the apartment for you? Anyways..." He shuffles his feet, and does his little backwards head shrugging chortle again before putting his hands in his pockets. He looks as nervous as I feel, though I hadn't even realized the Rider giving me access to that emotion.

'Of course we would be nervous, it's because of Nick,' I scoff at the Rider, handing back the emotion, certain I don't have to feel through to the bottom of it.

It's almost mid-October, at which point Rob and I have almost reached our breaking point due to sleep deprivation. Every time he gently wakes me to take my shift, I am surprised I was capable of sleeping in his presence at all, and I wonder if I would have ever been able to learn to sleep next to Michael.

At long last, after another two calls to the ward, Nick's burner phone rings one afternoon.

"Oh my God!" Nick shouts, almost a tad too excited, before rushing to it, and, after taking a deep breath to calm his nerves, answering it.

"Yes, hello, this is Isobel Cutter speaking," the woman on the other end says. Her voice sounds weary, as though it were a much older version of her, which, I am aware without yet comprehending it, is a byproduct of human grief.

She proceeds, "I apologize for the delay in returning your call, though part of this delay has been intentional. To be frank, I initially didn't intend to respond to your atypical contact request. However," she inhales shakily, "I'm willing to listen to your proposal. Something regarding a new type of trauma therapy?"

'She has adopted Michael's vernacular,' the Rider quietly notes. 'Maybe you'll end up being one happy, dysfunctional, polyamorous patchwork family, trading pompous words on a daily basis.'

'Shh!' I chide him, 'I'm trying to listen!'

Nick's voice is smooth and empathetic when he replies, sharing with Cutter how he became aware of her case and that he had found conventional therapies such as EMDR and Cognitive Behavioral Therapy might temporarily alleviate traumatic memories and feelings, without yet ever completely dissolving them, especially in cases as severe as hers. Consequentially, Nick claims to have developed his own type of therapy. There is a brief moment during which I fear she will hang up, as she accuses him of wanting to use her as a human guinea pig. To his credit, Nick isn't thrown by her response. He has worked with paranoid individuals before, acutely aware of which mental pressure points to activate or avoid in order to coax the desired reaction out of his patients. Not that Cutter was actually even paranoid enough, considering that there existed no new revolutionary therapy at all.

"To allay your understandable fears, Miss Cutter, my team and I have worked with over a hundred clients over the last few years, and our success rate remains steady at 97%, with a temporary recidivism rate of 5%."

"I have no place to stay," Cutter says, the dejection in her voice palpable. "I don't want to stay at my parents' place if I were to leave this facility."

And then I see a glint in Nick's eyes that briefly stops my heart. It's the same glint I see in the mirror each time I check my costume before departing to lure a victim to certain death.

"We have worked with inpatients before. You would have all necessities, food, shelter and medication."

"Why are you doing this for people? Pro bono, I mean? Why would you do this for me?"

Nick pauses for a moment; he had not anticipated the question. Before either Rob, Kate or I can finish typing out response suggestions in our phones for him, he chuckles, retorting, "I'm an Aquarius?"

Cutter's laughter is a genuine one. Nick was a wonderful combination of professional, sly and charming. He had listened to Kate's and my endless ravings about astrology for months, working it to his advantage now.

"What, pray tell, is the protocol now? How do I get out of here? Please advise."

Nick coaches her on the assessment, snapping his fingers at Rob and myself to hand him the clipboard with the upcoming questions she would face. He asks about her behavior on the ward, recommending what keywords to use, how to carry herself, to make eye contact. Strangely enough, Cutter doesn't question him on the ethics of what he is doing. Perhaps her yearning to at least *feel* free again overshadows her common sense.

A little over a week later, during one of the worst snows Seattle had ever seen, it is time to pick up Isobel Cutter. She would occupy the cell next to Nick's.

Rob has a field day with his costume. After retracting to my bedroom to don it, he comes out with the wig and mustache on, but instead of wearing the clothes we had picked out for him, he wears the butterfly sundress that I purchased at the store Elysia had worked at. He strikes a little pose and bends over laughing at our reactions. It's then I notice that I haven't had to clutch my ribs while laughing for at least a week now. My bruises are almost all healed up. A few minutes after Rob returns to the bedroom, I follow, knocking on the door. "Rob?"

"Yeah!" He calls, his voice as insouciant as always.

When I enter, I see he's wearing pants but no shirt. "Oh," I say, blushing. "I'm sorry, I thought you were decent."

"I've never been decent a day in my life," he smirks, and I smile in response, before becoming serious again.

"Once Kate, Nick and I return to California with Cutter, I want you to go back home to Jill. I heard you on the phone with her a few times. I don't want..." I strain to find the right words. No. That's a lie. I know all the right words, I just don't want to speak them.

"I know," he simply states, focusing intently on his fingers as he unbuttons the dress shirt he snatched up from the bed. "I'll go. Keep me updated though."

Kate and I wait in the car while Rob and Nick walk into the building together. Despite wearing disguises, both men instinctively keep their heads down as soon as they approach the entrance.

About fifteen minutes later, they re-emerge, without Isobel Cutter in tow. Kate and I look at each other, perplexed, and as soon as Rob and Nick climb into the backseat, we turn around to unanimously cry out, "What happened?!"

"She wasn't there," Nick says. "The person we spoke to at the ward told us she had checked out, but either had none, or refused to offer up information other than that. She started becoming suspicious, and we thought it best to leave, saying there must have been a communication error on our part, and that Cutter had likely gone to meet our associate."

Kate shakes her head. "That doesn't make sense. Where would she even go? She said she didn't want to go to her parents' place."
I start the car. "We need a new plan. Most assuredly, we must get to the bottom of what any of this means, and find her as soon as possible."

Back in my apartment, we gather around the couch table, each of us holding a glass of whiskey in our hand. We exchange hesitant glances but no one knows quite what to say.
"Where do her parents live? Maybe we should stake out the place, see if she changed her mind about –"
I don't hear the rest of what Rob suggests because my phone buzzes. I don't recognize the number, but the text says, "Anything you can do, I can do better. I can do anything better than you." It's a line from an old Irving Berlin tune. I stare at the message, too paralyzed to understand, to think, to speak.
Then it hits me.
Michael has the apartment bugged, or my phone, or both. He'd spent some time in here alone while I was in the shower, saving his number to my phone. He certainly could have done it then. He may even have visited my apartment any time before or after our first official encounter. For after we had reconnected via phone months earlier, he had shared with me his secret of how he gained access to almost any and all buildings he desired – with a skeleton key. Moreover, he had bragged about his lock picking skills. He certainly could enter any of my dwellings, save for the California one which had always been secured with automatic locks. This explained why he had waited for me on the porch steps when seeking me out there. But any of the buildings I owned were open to him at any given time.
Truth be told, I couldn't determine why I hadn't considered the possibility before, particularly taking into account his occupation. Perhaps because I had struggled with rootkit emotions

uncontrolled, too preoccupied to put my usual paranoia to good use. And because of my disability of feeling my feelings rather than to abort them into the rootkit, I had delivered all of my friends to Michael on a silver platter. Anything spoken in this apartment had been known to him for weeks, for months. I remember the time he had feigned believing that I was ignoring him when I had not been able to pick up his call, and how he had responded with emotional hostage-taking. It had always been a game. Always.

I abruptly rise from my chair and put a finger to my lips, point at my phone and put it on the table, motioning for everyone else to do the same. Once they do, I wordlessly wave for our team to follow me outside.

We gather in a circle in the backyard of the building, each of us shivering in the freezing cold. I am being met with everyone's expectant stares.

"Michael has her," I say tonelessly, relaying to them the contents of the text message and my suspicions about being bugged.

Rob's face is ashen. "I always have one or two of my boys keep eyes on Jill but I have to go home. Now." He glances at me, then down, and turns to leave without further ado. And though I want to, I don't stop him.

Kate shakes her head. "This bald-headed freak. I'll have to leave, too, but not before we find the bug. I doubt he's going to do anything now anyway. He's just reveling in his little triumph, but it will be short-lived, trust me. Are you sure it couldn't be cameras? What about the California home? And all the others, all the buildings you rent out?" She keeps peppering me with questions, and I answer as best I can, despite remaining monosyllabic about it all. Too shocked am I to yet fully comprehend what had happened. And that Michael had done this. To *me*. I turn to Nick.

"Why would Michael do all he has done thus far? What is his motivation, you think? We need your psychological expertise now, so don't you clam up, Nick."

"Well," his tone is cautious, "I'm a psychologist, a therapist, not a mind reader, but if I were to venture a guess, his behavior speaks to ulterior motives. His actions indicate he may not have your best interests at heart. As a serial killer," he looks at me hesitantly, "he will suffer from some type of disorder. Or multiple disorders."

"That tells me absolutely nothing," I say angrily.

"Emily," Nick holds up his hands, "Without a formal assessment, I cannot exactly tell you anything more concrete here. From what you shared with me, it sounds he ticks off several criteria for borderline personality disorder, but I can't diagnose him without having spoken to him, I'm sorry. CPTSD and BPD present similarly and are often conflated with each other, resulting in misdiagnoses, so it's not surprising you two would immediately form this type of intense bond." He sighs. "Well, since he knows all of our identities except mine, and has the resources he has, it's time to maybe… bring him in. I offer to condition him the way you attempted to do with me."

Abduct Michael?!

"Let's shelf this conversation and any further plans until we have found the bugs, or cameras, or whatever he used to keep tabs on us, alright?" Kate breathes, massaging the root of her nose with two fingers.

We agree that each of us should search every room individually, twice, and that we needed to remove the batteries and SIM cards from our phones until we had acquired new ones, as they might still be tracked if merely turned off.

Six hours later, we have discovered all bugs; one had been hidden in each room. We flush them down the toilet, and sit down to reconvene, ordering bug detection devices for both Kate and myself.

Kate, all mom, intends to call Will home from college to move him back into her and Jack's place. Too afraid is she that Michael may exact revenge on her by harming her family, despite my interjection that Michael hadn't made a move on any of my friends, or their families, in weeks, if not longer.
Nick and I will dismantle my Washington cabins one by one, disposing of all evidence as to what usually occurred in their secret basements, then return to California together.

Kate leaves late at night, and right after I shut the front door behind her, I turn around. "Nick."
"Yes?" he asks, his face as smooth and open as ever.
"How long ago did you break through the brainwashing?"
The muscles in his cheeks twitch as he grinds his teeth. "So you do know. How did you figure it out?"
"I wasn't quite certain actually, until you just admitted it to me. I saw an expression in your eyes when you called Isobel Cutter a while ago, that I know all too well. And earlier you offered to brainwash Michael in the same way we had "attempted" to do with you."
He walks over to the green velvet sofa, sitting down. "I thought you might catch that as soon as I'd said it."
"You could have easily overpowered Kate. You could have easily flagged down any cop on the drives here and back on multiple occasions."
He leans forward, placing his elbows on his knees. "The truth is…" I can tell how difficult it is for him to force out the confession. "I like this. So maybe your brainwashing did have kind of an effect on me." Almost pleadingly, he looks up at me. "I'm not a cruel person, Emily. I like helping people. But you have to understand that as a young neuroscience student, we did experiments with rodents."

"Rodents," I stupidly reply. "Okay." I have no idea what he's trying to say.

"When you spoke about 'the humans' the way you did, it reminded me of how I had viewed the lab rats and mice. And that we had watched them with more than just clinical interest after a while. Numbness turned to cruelty when we started betting on them. We would laugh at their failures, too. And when they died, when we killed them…"

"I understand," I huskily reply.

"Do you? Because I know I should have done anything in my power to reunite with my family and turn you in. But… I don't miss them as much as I should. I know they'll be fine without me. And I know I will be fine without them.

You don't know what it's like, ordinary life, family life. It's boring, Emily. Everything I ever did as a young man was relegated to memory, memories ever shrinking with each passing year. I used to do work and travel, I backpacked through Australia while Ivan Milat was active. I did so many crazy, adventurous, dangerous things!"

"Is that when you learned how to pick locks with paperclips?" I ask.

He nods. "My friend who traveled with me for a while, he taught me how to get access to motels and hostels that way. A back door, an open window, any room we wanted, and disappear in the morning before the maids did their rounds."

He runs a hand through his unruly hair before finishing his original thought. "Anyway. Then one day you wake up, you have kids your wife insisted on having, and pets who hate you as much as you hate them, and every day is the same. The only excitement you get is from watching crime and thriller movies, always wondering, what would it be like? Not to kill, but just to be this free? To not always be as bored as you are boring."

I can't determine how much of this was still the brainwashing, or how much of it was calculation. I shouldn't, and yet I ask, "Where do you see this going, Nick? Where do you see yourself a year from now? Five years from now?"

He leans back on the couch, his face excited. "Well, I always wanted to be a writer. I had wondered if I couldn't perhaps write about us."

"Excuse me?!"

His voice is intent when he continues, "Think about it. I could turn your story, our story, into a book series. Novels, obviously. With crucial elements changed so no one would be able to connect us to our crimes."

I acknowledge I had to provide him with more than just room and board, and a few added perks.

"These novels could encourage other offenders, and those on the verge of offending, to seek help," he adds.

"You want to inspire other serial killers to abduct therapists all over the world?" I ask incredulously.

"Obviously not," he huffs. "But with my psychological expertise added to these novels, I could give pointers on how to present their cases to a therapist without admitting to any crimes, which, as you know, we have to report. I could also subversively vie for the public to change their views on disordered individuals, and violent offenders in general. I don't believe it's conducive the way you lot are being spoken of. It's easier to admit to having a problem when being encouraged, rather than condemned. Condemnation only leads to cultivating one's compulsions further."

My impulse is to instantly reject his proposition, alas, two challenges am I facing now. For one, his idea strokes my narcissistic ego, and secondly, it would prove interesting to see whether his alleged aspiration to become a novelist was a ploy to sneak distress calls into his writings. It could be a means to both keep him occupied as well as further test his loyalties.

After briefly conferring with the Rider, who, to my surprise, agrees with me, Nick and I shake on it.

And then we rest, him locked into my bedroom, and me on the couch, before we begin our strenuous task of dismantling decades worth of the Rider's and my shared life – my cabins.

Chapter 22
Ocean Shores

Nick and I work morning to night in the course of the following weeks. We switch all cabins to automatic locks, rendering Michael's skeleton key useless.

Of course I never turn my back towards Nick. Likewise, I don't trust him around kitchen utensils or boiling water just yet, hence I'm the one who cooks and cleans, falling into a dreamless sleep each night before 10 P.M. We only start speaking once certain we discovered all bugs in any cabin. It is disadvantageous enough that Michael had already gleaned insight into our team's operations and knew we were onto him after we had irately flushed the Seattle apartment listening devices.

I'm yet strangely calm, perhaps in part due to my progress with therapy, perhaps because I know Michael wouldn't go the official law enforcement route to take me down; this much becomes clear the more time passes without a S.W.A.T. team storming in to arrest me and free Nick. If taking me down was even what Michael intended to do.

I had not responded to him after his snarky little message, and he certainly hadn't reached out again either. I would have loved to have someone keep an eye on him, but Rob had not answered to my two text messages updating him about current events, likely blaming me for what had happened, as well as himself for offering to aid me on a personal, rather than a business level.

And Kate, being such a new killer, wasn't someone I was comfortable pitting against an animal like Michael, not that she would have left her family's side anyway.

Redoing the cabins costs me an arm and a leg, no pun intended, and although Nick can still not help dry-gagging intermittently, he seems to slowly get accustomed to the task of digging up bodies to dissolve them once and for all. The majority of the remains are skeletonized by now anyway. I had mostly grown out of the compulsion to keep my victims' remains close in my late twenties. But running my hands across the brittle bones, twining my finger through what remains of their hair, reminds me of what an efficient killer I am, and my heart swells with pride. And my loins itch, recalling all the tender moments had shared with my spirit lovers. Unfortunately, I also grow painfully aware of how much time has passed since I've had time to take on a lover.

The Rider keeps banging his palms against the black rock walls of his pit, roaring, whining, curling up writhing in agony, only to hop up again and claw his way to the edges of the pit, ripping at my mind with his claws.

One sleepless night, after tossing and turning, trying to ignore *the discontent,* the Rider's agonizing is simply too much to bear. I jump out of bed and decide to troll for a victim. I dress and retrieve my kill kit from the bedroom closet of my Ocean Shores home. I'd never planned on actually killing here, as it is a small town and the median age of citizens remains consistent at sixty-two. But of course I always kept my kill kit close anyway. It was a security blanket. And right now it proves to be my salvation. The fact that Ocean Shores was also a tourist town was certainly convenient, though I'd still have to be very careful of the prying eyes of elderly busybody insomniacs with no life.

Compelled to check on Nick, I descend the stairs and unlock the basement door. Despite my treading lightly, Nick wakes, sleepily rubbing his eyes after switching on the little lamp I left him next to his mattress.

"What are you doing?" he asks, his eyes falling onto the bag in my hand. "Oh. Emily…"

Sweat trickles from my brow, my neck and chest, running down my back to settle between my buttocks, though I keep all my dwellings at a steady 63.5 degrees. It's the kill urge, the coals of it burning hot.

"I can't stop it," I reply to Nick. "I have to."
He looks at me without blinking for a very long time, then nods and switches off the light again. Before I close the door behind me, he mumbles, "Let's talk about this in therapy tomorrow."

I start driving, listening to music and pondering Ted Bundy's time in Utah. Whether it was true, no one but him knew, yet he had stated to investigator Dennis Couch that he'd made an honest attempt at not killing upon moving to the Beehive State, "only" planning on raping his first victim there. He'd claimed she began screaming and he had been forced to murder her. I wondered now, would it be possible to unlearn killing? And what would happen to the Rider in that case? Would he die as well, or learn to adapt? Nick's plan to write a book had triggered these musings, along with his insistence that I did not have to possess affective empathy to learn to do the right thing. Perhaps I could regress to rape, then to trolling, to writing, which, essentially, equated to fantasizing? Unsurprisingly, the Rider was averse to the idea, throwing temper tantrums in the below and tormenting me with random childhood memories. 'Remember how it felt…to be that powerless…'
'What if we did what Kate does? Remove individuals who are deserving of a more permanent solution.'
He had laughed his hollow laugh then, shaking his head. 'You know as well as I do that you are a lust murderer. That kill experience with Kate provided no sustenance to us. Why, you didn't even get wet. Best of luck finding someone who "deserves" it that you are actually attracted to. You kill what you love, what you can't be or have, what you envy.'
'I neither loved nor envied the homeless man I murdered with Michael," I shoot back.
'Because it wasn't about the victim but about bonding with Michael, as we both well know,' he reminds me, not without exasperation.

'You're missing the point entirely, as per usual,' I inform him, an air of arrogance about me, mimicking his. 'Erotic arousal could be replaced with righteousness and purpose, whilst you'd still get to slaughter as freely and as often as you require.'
Our conversation replays in my mind while I park my vehicle a block away from the first Inn, creeping towards the beach on which I hope to catch a midnight snack.
It is a Friday night, and tourist couples occasionally enjoyed lighting campfires on the beach on the weekend, spending long hours just staring into the flames. Apparently this was considered romantic by the general population. They didn't even burn anyone in the flames for entertainment; they just sat there, quietly, side by side. It utterly transfixed me how anyone could think of this as anything but dull.
Certainly enough, there is someone at the beach. A lone straggler, removed from its pack of humans. He's not sitting at a fire, but I see the light of his cigarette whenever he takes a drag. Sneaking along the shore, hidden by the tall grass, I circle around him, towards the cliff, to watch him from a safer spot that will conceal me from anyone staring out over the ocean from the Inn.
My phone vibrates, and annoyed, I pull it out of my coat pocket. "Can't sleep?"
It's yet another unlisted number, which can only mean one thing. It's Michael. The Rider immediately slithers towards the rootkit chest, a hand at the ready. I hit the call button, and Michael picks up at once.
"One would think that working as hard as you and Nick do, insomnia weren't as much of an issue as it appears to be," he greets me, the irony dripping from his every word.
"I am indeed tired, Michael," I reply. "Of your games. So you have my vehicles bugged as well? At least a wiretap would be difficult to petition the attorney general and DOJ official for without compromising yourself. Shall I keep taking guesses at what

precisely your endgame is, or would you prefer to meet face to face to do, or try to do, whatever it is you have in store for me?"
I hear him sucking on his vape pen on the other end of the phone a few times. "No bug, just a GPS tracker," he mumbles and sighs. I can hear him scratch his goatee, the vape pen he's holding in the same hand clinking against his phone. "Emily," he finally says. "Do you recall what I had relayed to you at my trailer?"
I don't respond, and so he provides the answer for me. "That I would do all it took to protect you, as I had been afforded convenient resources due to my job to do so."
I laugh bitterly, "Your euphemisms are endearing, but let's call a spade a spade; you spied on me."
"And you sabotage your own happiness, happiness I had eagerly anticipated to share with you, by continually distrusting me. You stalked my neighborhood, you disposed of my vats when I could not respond to you in a timely fashion, you confided in complete strangers about who I was and then planned to abduct Isobel to elicit from her information about me for the purpose of blackmail or worse." His voice is a tender embrace of all the broken parts inside me, holding them together at that moment. Letting his words sink in, I slouch down against the hard, humid rock of the cliff. His vape pen clicks again.
'He's gaslighting you,' the Rider says, impatiently drumming his fingers on the lid of the rootkit.
Instead of responding to him, I reply to Michael. "I know that Paul Whithurst isn't dead."
"Yes," he sighs. "And in your weakened state I could not risk you going on another impulsive mission to carry out a potentially unsuccessful strike against him. With all that was going on, including my return to Washington after our brief California reunion, I have not had a chance to correct the fact he is, as of this moment, still alive. I know where he is and what he does at all times."

"You're just bugging everyone, aren't you?" I state incredulously, aware of the double entendre. Then add, "Maybe you're right. You're right... Did you make sure they'll never connect you to Isobel's disappearance?"

Michael scoffs. "Neither will I be connected to anything I have done, nor will anyone connect you to anything you have done, or learn all that we have done together. And, I might add, I would never harm your friends."

"Why?"

"Because I love you," he simply declares. "And I would like for you and I to see each other again. I will not give up on us unless you outright dismiss me."

The Rider claws at his own head, stomping his feet on the ground as though he were Rumpelstiltskin, eager to sink into the ground, never to be seen again, for he knows already that my mind is made up.

'I need closure, I need to understand what he is, and what his endgame is,' I tell him.

But the Rider merely shakes his head and drops his shoulders, eyes closed. 'You can lie to me, but at least don't lie to your conscious self. It'll get both of us killed.'

Returning to the conversation with Michael, I slowly say, "I would welcome it if we were to meet in a setting that puts both of us at ease. One suggestion could be a more public place that does yet not allow for prying eyes."

The way he breathes tells me that he is upset, and when he replies, it is through clenched teeth. "Well. If it takes that to provide you with a sense of security, then I will abide by it. Wait in your vehicle at the Inn. It will be close enough for anyone to hear you scream should I attack you, which, for the record, I have no intention of doing."

I laugh. "I cannot wait two and a half hours in my car for you to arrive from Seattle."

"I am not *in* Seattle." His voice has that strangely musical, that lulling quality again. "After the events surrounding our regrettable separation in relation to the Paul Whithurst debacle, I found myself incapable of not being in your immediate vicinity, in case…you needed me." He clears his throat. "I don't trust that Nick person."

Ignoring his latter admission, I breathe, "I don't understand, what about work?"

"On my days off, wherever you and Nick venture, I follow. I depart again once I must perform my occupational duties," he informs me matter-of-factly. "But I must disclose I have taken sick days, and overtime, too. I find myself unable of combating the need to be close to you, even if you weren't aware of my presence."

Am I flattered by his commitment or distrustful of his motives? But he could have very easily gone after each of my friends, as well as me, and yet he had not.

"I shall wait for you in my car then. How soon will you be here?"

"I won't be long. I'm outside of Ocean Shores as I was unable to book a room within town limits," he replies, a smile in his voice.

And so I wait. I wait with bated breath, attempting to steady my nerves, checking the clock every few minutes, obsessively replaying all that had occurred between Michael and me over the last few months in my mind. After half an hour, I look at all the inns, bed & breakfasts and motels close to Ocean Shores, chiding myself for not insisting Michael provide me with a more accurate estimate than 'soon.'

After an hour, I text him, but he does not reply. A little while later, I call, but he does not answer.

I spy into the pit, my eyes adjusting to the inner darkness, but the Rider appears as clueless as I am. We brainstorm for a few seconds, until I freeze mid-sentence, and the Rider growls, 'Nick!'

Without thinking, I start the car, racing towards my idyllic little cabin, immersed in conversation with the Rider.
'He said he doesn't trust Nick, does that mean he wants to protect me?!'
'You have to stop being an idiot, Emily. He's picking you off one by one, now that you're on to him. He was biding his time, banking on us having to eventually leave Nick to satisfy our kill urge.'
My response is a growl that swells to an extended low-pitched scream of anger and frustration with myself.
When I arrive at the cabin, I find the door wide ajar. Still, I rush towards the basement, gun drawn, ready to fire, but the house is empty.

Scrolling through my phonebook, I stop at Rob's name, my finger hovering above the call button. But I don't know where Rob is, and since he had not answered any of my messages, I was averse to making myself any more vulnerable by begging for his help.
I scroll back up, and like an automaton call Kate, though I know full well she won't be of any help, being as far away as she is. But I realize that my mind is not only disquieted, it is panicked, and craves a familiar voice other than the Rider's. Nick was more important to me than I had realized.
I sigh a sigh of relief when Kate picks up, her voice sleepy. "It is late," she coos, drawing out each word. "What's up?"
I rush through my explanation of what had happened, shamefully admitting to the fact I had intended to see Michael on my own, and as soon as I mention Nick's abduction, I hear her bed creak and her bare feet on the floor. She hobbles down two staircases until she is in the basement, shout-whispering into the phone, "You listen to me, Emily, you find Nick and you bring him back home. Give me a minute, I'm going to send you the exact coordinates of where Michael is headed."

Stumped, I reply, "How would *you* know?!"

"You told me about his kill trailer, didn't you? I know a little bit about how to write algorithms, so at first I tried to search for whether he'd bought park tickets, went to campsites. When that didn't happen..." She pauses. "Okay, don't get mad but after the whole bugging incident, I put a GPS tracker on his trailer and car."

"We'll talk about you going on dangerous missions by yourself without alerting me to the fact later," I reply through clenched teeth. "But well done, I will concede that without the GPS tracker we'd be utterly lost right now."

I had known Kate had taken a handful of computer classes in college, but I had never listened or asked about them, in part due to believing I knew enough about the surface web to retrieve all information crucial to my murderous endeavors, plus her archival databases had delivered to me those tidbits of information I myself hadn't been able to come by on my own. I hadn't known she knew how to write algorithms, though, and this fact once more reminds me that as soon as this whole Michael business had come to a conclusion, we would need to reconvene and learn to communicate more efficiently.

Should I survive tonight, there were more schemes to weave and enemies to slay, hopefully together, and hopefully with Nick by our side. For now, I just impatiently stand by, as I hear her frantically typing on the keyboard of her laptop.

"He's parked the trailer close to a known hotspot for homeless activity near Snoqualmie Valley. Texting you coordinates right now."

"That is over three hours away, why wouldn't he just park the trailer at a homeless hotspot on the Southwestern outskirts of Olympic National Forest?" I wonder out loud, then shrug and add, "If you don't hear from me in four hours, know that Michael will come after you and Rob as well. I can't...I don't have time to text Rob, you have to do it. And you have to finish Michael, should I fail."

I hear but don't absorb Kate's agitated reply because Rob's face appears before my inner eye. I catch a glimpse of one of the orbs rattling in the rootkit, but the Rider's claw firmly keeps it in place. I am too proud to degrade myself further. He'd made his choice. Silence spoke louder than words.

"Emily," Kate addresses me. "Did you hear what I said?"

"No. I was looking at street signs, apologies."

"I said you *will* kill this man. You will come back to me. And you will bring Nick back to me. I will stand by, phone in hand, laptop in hand, and you will voice clip me every fifteen minutes so I know what's going on."

I ignore her plea to return Nick to her. It appears the Rider had been correct about their budding feelings for each other.

I merely reply, "Understood. On my way, keep me posted on his car's location."

I crawl underneath the car with a flashlight, and less than a minute later, I spot the GPS tracker Michael had attached to it. I rip it off and angrily toss it away from me. If Michael, as I strongly suspect, keeps eyes on it, he will believe that I was still at the cabin, rather than chasing after him and Nick.

I am hard-pressed for time, I'm aware, and race through the night like a maniac, sending silent prayers to the heavens that no traffic cop will stop me. It would end badly for them. I'm an animal cornered, too rabid not to run on anything but instinct, too unbothered to even care how many bodies I would leave in my wake to save Nick.

Chapter 23
Georgia

Eventually, Kate calls, rather than to voice clip, a strain in her voice. "He's not going to Snoqualmie, he turned North on 108. I think he's going home?"

"What on earth is he doing," I mumble. "Stay on line with me, I need to know each of his movements as they occur."

Although Michael had had a head start of about half an hour, I managed to catch up to him to a point where only twenty minutes separate us. Once he is past Kamilche, there is no doubt he is going home.

And certainly enough, his vehicle stops moving the moment he is back at his cul-de-sac. Yet not in front of his own home, rather, in front of Virginia Blackwell's.

"What is going on?!" I shout into the phone. "What does his elderly neighbor have to do with any of this?!"

But Kate doesn't respond to my question, instead stating with surprise, "He's on the move again. Hang on." Less than a minute goes by when she advises that Michael's car now remains parked at his own address.

None of it makes any sense to me, and neither, I can tell, does it to Kate. She has begun frantically typing away on her laptop again, sending me screenshots of both homes' floor plans.

"Listen," she yawns, "I need both hands and full concentration. I'll try to find out who Virginia Blackwell is to Michael."

"Please do. I presume Michael unloaded Nick at her home, then parked his car in front of his own home so as not to rouse any neighbor's suspicion." I inhale deeply. "Michael had told me, months ago, that he would take me to his *current* kill site. I had believed that to mean he was moving the trailer around, not that he may have other – stationary – kill rooms. What if," I slowly deliberate, "Blackwell is a snowbird, and he tends to her home while she's away? Maybe she spends the winter months in Florida, as so many Washingtonian seniors do?"

"Alright," she responds. "I'll keep that in mind. I'll call or text if I find anything of use to us."

The universe had once more aligned in my favor. I had not been stopped for speeding, and, killing the headlights, approach the cul-de-sac less than twenty minutes after Michael did. I park my vehicle about 150 feet away and off to the side of his street. Lastly, I send one last whispered voice message to Kate, asking her to only text until further notice, then turn off the ringer and vibrate feature, setting the screen to light up only very dimly whenever a text message came in.

Before silently sneaking towards my target, I close my eyes and invite the Rider to merge. I shudder as he overwhelms me, a bliss that can never be dulled, not even three decades after the first merging. He is pure dopamine whenever he rides me.

It's sometime after 2 A.M., the homes are all dark. Everyone appears to be asleep. It's a split-second decision that I wouldn't attempt to break and enter Michael's home first, but to immediately focus on Virginia's instead. There's no alarm sign anywhere on her property, there are no cameras, prop or otherwise, no cameras, mysterious cords that would give the impression she uses more than a door to keep herself safe from the creatures who stalked through the night with ill intent. She had, after all, admitted to Emily that she always felt safe here due to her neighborhood cop friend, which at least puts us at a small advantage. Picking her lock, it doesn't take long for us to detect the familiar click, swiftly and silently squeezing through the door before closing it behind us.

We lean forward in the dark and prick up our ears, yet hearing nothing but the blood rush through our own. Carefully, we test the first two steps of the staircase. Top to bottom is how to efficiently search a house. The stairs creak, though, and we decide we cannot risk it.

Like most newer Washington homes, Virginia's does not have a basement, but if Nick were anywhere in this house, it would likely be in the garage. The door underneath the stairs was the one that led to the garage off to the side of the building that faced the woods. With some added insulation, no one would hear a victim's screams, or any commotion, even during the quietest hours of night when, thanks to a psychoacoustic effect, all sounds appeared amplified.

The bottom step creaks once more when we take our foot off of it. A female voice, Virginia's, calls downstairs from somewhere up above, "Michael?" And then, as so often in our life, everything happens at once.

Our phone lights up in our front jeans pocket. We reach for it, reading Kate's message, which temporarily immobilizes us. "Virginia Blackwell's real name is Grace Walker! She's Michael's birth mother, GET OUT OF THERE NOW! Sending the cavalry!!!" Whoever the cavalry was is beyond our grasp. Hopefully not law enforcement, as we would rather die than be incarcerated, and there was simply no way around it if police stormed the place. It is just as beyond our comprehension how Grace could even be alive. We had killed her. We had murdered the monster almost thirty years ago. She had always been the monster, not underneath but behind our bed, the hospital bed, holding down our arms as Emily's body had been violated. And we had stupidly believed there had never been an inquiry because we had disposed of her cleverly enough for no one to connect us to her disappearance, despite her working at Emily's childhood home at the time. No one had ever checked the well behind our house, but then again, neither had we. We'd come back to the house each March 16th, standing before it silently, stoically, and reminiscing in the kill whilst renewing the faith in our marvelous capabilities.

Grace's face appears at the top of the stairs, seconds before we hear the door to the garage open. We raise our arm and aim the gun at the torso of the unarmed woman, keeping our eyes trained on the man who appears in the doorway straight ahead.

The doorway. The man in the doorway. It was him. His eyes that had been our anchor point.

An image flashes before our eyes, as we recall the phone conversation with Michael, during which he had shared with us that he became a policeman due to the murder of one of his family members.

Only, she had not stayed dead.

The dim garage light illuminates half of Michael's face, and we hardly even notice the upward motion of his arm when he draws his own gun to point it at us. When we look into his ocean blue eyes, anguish pierces our chest, spreading all throughout our body.

"It's you," we croak. "You are the orderly at the hospital who looked at me each time I was being raped."

"Drop it," Michael's tone is pure menace. "I will put you down if you don't."

Grace jumps out of sight, and all we hear are her footsteps somewhere up above, hobbling away. We lost our advantage, and begrudgingly acknowledge that if we dared move our arm towards Michael, we would immediately lose our life.

"Drop it now, and drop the phone," Michael repeats, his voice predatorily low, his eyes overcome with cruel exultation. We do as asked, standing before him naked – in other words, unarmed – and helpless.

Grace's fragile frame reappears, making her way down the stairs with her hand clamped around an impressively large gun.

"Start walking towards him," she commands, calling us an expletive we know we will make her pay for later. There's no doubt in our mind whenever we are merged, that we will make it, and the fact that neither Michael nor Grace hadn't shot us yet meant that they have worse planned for us. We will have a fighting chance somewhere down the road.

Michael beckons us to walk through the door, and as soon as we do, we spot Nick, who is sitting on a chair, bloodied and bruised, hands cuffed behind his back around a wooden support beam in the middle of the garage. He's gagged, his eyes growing wide as soon as he spots us, making frantic seal noises while trying to speak through the gag.

Humans.

Michael pulls up another chair from the long work bench on the Southern wall, forcing us down on it. While his smug visage looks down on us, Grace removes the rock climbing rope from Nick's ankles to tie our hands behind the beam. Her touch sends shockwaves through our entire body, flashbacks to the hospital flickering across our inner eye, though united we keep our composure.

As we carefully strain against our tightly wound fetters, we notice they yet feel elastic. They're made of dynamic rope, which absorbs the energy of a fallen climber, rather than static rope, traditionally used to anchor a climber. She would likely not be aware of the difference, on the contrary to Michael, an avid rock climber. But though his hands are steady, his entire posture is stiff, eyes narrowed and trained on Grace. He's attempting to conceal his nervousness, appearing not to pay attention to detail, instead relying on his mother.

"Michael," we address him, and his lip curls up as though he were a snarling animal trying to keep us at bay, despite our posing no viable threat to him in our current state.

We proceed, undeterred, "Obviously, you won." Though we doubt our words will assuage him, we let them sink in, hoping for the best. And indeed, hesitantly but steadily, his body and mimic somewhat relax. We speak with our Emily voice, not the low hum of our combined self, for Michael still believes the Rider to be trapped behind a wall.

"I wondered whether you'd satisfy my curiosity on how you outsmarted me."

"Do you," he states tonelessly, his eyes darting back over to his mother. We can feel his yearning to confess, as if he were a mediocre Disney villain. It is entirely due to Grace's presence that he hesitates, we realize. She calls the shots, and it is her we have to attempt to get to talk before Michael would even entertain the idea.

"So Grace," we giggle, "you look rather well for a nearly thirty year old corpse. How did you get out of that well?" And as soon as the word escapes our lips, our skin erupts in goosebumps again. The well, the black well in the backyard of our childhood home had served as inspiration for her last name, Blackwell.

Grace rises, looking down on us. We still cannot recall her face. Nothing about her seems familiar, other than her frame, now that we know who she is, which, after all these years, is far frailer than it used to be.

"You were always an insufferable brat, Georgia," she huffs. The fact she calls us by our birth name unsettles us so much we close our eyes, slowly inhaling and exhaling in an attempt to steady us. She observes our reaction with cruel satisfaction.

"Your fearlessness never made up for the fact you aren't the sharpest tool in the shed. It was unfortunate that your mother overheard me speaking with Michael on the phone, otherwise I would have never had to induce her heart attack. I was just there for an extra paycheck after my rotten ex-husband had left me reeling financially, and to make sure you'd keep your mouth shut. I wasn't a killer before you came along, that's all *your* doing."

She sighs and licks her lips before finally answering our question. "I woke up in that well, not knowing how long I had been out after you stabbed me. I slipped several times when steadying my back against the wall to push myself up with my legs, inch by inch. Did you really believe a child could outsmart a grown woman? You should have chained the lid to that well."

We sure should have, yet being that Emily's body had been a mere ten years old when perpetrating her first – evidently botched - murderous attack, and the Rider had been even younger, who could blame us, really?

"Did you know who I was when I first came to visit you last fall?" we ask, instead of addressing her plight of climbing out of the well, gravely injured.

"I would have recognized you had you not hidden my glasses from me, you deceitful wench. They were ruined when you placed them in my Ficus. I had to get new ones but you can pay for that later."

We can't help but laugh at the pettiness of her comment, but she shakes her head, her face a mask of faux pity. "I know all about how you stalked Michael after you'd located him. You spied on the neighborhood, going house to house to learn his and Isobel's routine so you could abduct and murder her."

What on earth was she talking about. Was she gaslighting or solely repeating lies her son had fed her? In either case, she wasn't particularly good with timelines, it appeared. We search Michael's eyes, whose facial expression gives nothing away.

"It's over, mother," he sagely announces. "We got her."

We chortle, "So I stalked *you* is how you spun the story for your mother? And why would you not have killed me the second you discovered me at your mother's house last fall? Why not drive me off into the woods to kill and bury me there?"

Grace makes an impatient little sound. "How would he have known who you were? He had never seen you before in his life. It was not until you murdered Isobel he learned about it." She clears her throat, and for the first time we notice she speaks with the same melancholically melodic yet raucous voice as her son. "You are not a rational person, Georgia. You spent the entirety of your life in pursuit of revenge for a vexing rape fantasy your psychotic mind was compelled to translate into a delusion of assault that never occurred, for the sole reason that you experienced guilt about your sexual deviancy."

We glance back and forth between the mother and son duo, half impressed with the extent and quick-wittedness of the bizarre, elaborate gaslighting.

We return our attention to Michael. We have to catch him by his pride as a man, we know, or lose. "Your mother is speaking to me. Are you man enough to speak to me, Michael, or are you just a mentally destitute momma's boy clinging to her apron strings?"

He raises an eyebrow, leaning back his head in a show of superiority. And although, once we had realized who he was, we hated him, instantaneously and irrevocably, as well as the fact he had been inside us, not only physically but emotionally, he is still one of the most beautiful creatures we had ever beheld.

Blue eyes. All our boyfriends had had them. We had always sought them out among a crowd. They had always been our solace anchor point because of him.

Michael turns to Grace. "Leave."

She shakes her head, "That is not a good idea, Michael."

"Leave!" he shouts, and, with begrudging obsequiousness, she obeys, closing the garage door behind her.

"I recall the way you looked at me," Michael admits, his voice breaking on the last syllables. He clears his throat. "I fell in love with your quiet defiance. The way you didn't close your eyes like the other girls and boys did, even when the men were inside your mouth. The drugs and brainwashing didn't have the same effect on you. Whenever your eyes bored into mine, I knew *you*, Georgia Underwood, were mine, and that throughout it all, you had also fantasized about it being me being inside you."

We keep our face even, although the way he spoke our old name, evidently tasting each syllable, each letter, on his tongue, is nauseating. We are, once more, grateful for the fact Emily did not have to bear his vileness alone. These revelations would have broken her far more than the sexual assault ever could have. He had constructed for Emily a Phantom Prince to love. The only person to match our darkness but, ironically, tragically, also the one to bring the light into our life. How was it remotely possible he could feign being the perfect person for us when he was yet incapable of being, or becoming, it? We gape at his forehead, wondering what it would require to untangle the faulty wiring in his brain. He was…just his illness. He was disease in human form.

"Michael," we start again. "Do you remember when you told me how you had first discovered me in the forest, as I was burying the torso of one of my victims? That wasn't true, though. It was not the first time."

He grimaces, his mouth twitching as though confused about whether to smile while recalling the memory, or not.

"I remember," he concedes quietly, his eyes momentarily flaring up, like deep blue waves crashing onto the sandy shore, before he veers off into a long, confessional rant.

"Mother said to leave you be after she had escaped. Craving a fresh start, she transformed herself into Virginia Blackwell, and for a long time, I trustingly followed her lead. However, when the kill compulsion rose to a crescendo inside me, and I took my first victim, my thoughts wandered back to you. I sought you out after this incident, and your presence restored my peace. For a while. Until the addiction reared its head again. I watched over you, and unknowingly, you over me, for so many years… I did follow you that night, into the woods, and upon determining you were like me… It did something to me. I knew I had made you, I had created the perfect companion for me without even being aware of it through these long lonely years."

His eyes return to focus on us rather than on what appeared to be fond memories for him. Extending his arm, his dry, smooth palm cups our cheek. It takes everything in our power to lean into it, eyes inviting, a faint smile on our lips. We could not wait to dismember this predator's hands. We now had our answer as to whether we would ever be capable of slaughtering a fellow serial killer, an animal like ourself. But in the end, he was nothing like us. He was the fiend we had always believed ourself to be.

Michael carries on, "Had you not traipsed right into mother's home, our relationship would have remained a secret, Georgia, but you forced my hand. You got too close."

Amazing blame-shifting.

He stops himself, withdrawing his hand from our face, his cheeks twitching until the vertical dimples reappear, reminding us of how much we had loved the sight of them until just moments ago.

He crouches down on the floor, his face so close to ours we have to squint to see his eyes, and, instinctively, we lean back past the wooden beam. The back of our head bumps into Nick's, who makes a startled little sound, reminding us of the fact he was not only present, but conscious and listening. Nick had suggested Michael might be a borderline personality. This gave us an idea on what to say.

"Why did Grace abandon you?" we inquire, our voice gentle and empathic.

He flinches. "Her husband compelled her to do so. I am the product of an affair, and despite Mr. Walker's best attempts at raising a bastard, he ultimately determined he was incapable of doing so. At one and a half years, I entered the foster care system. I have no memory of it, but my foster mother, it is said, sexually abused the younger infants in her care. Those who had no speech yet. One of the older ones observed her taking me into the bath tub with her, and..." he grows quiet. "She appears to have had a penchant for intermittently drowning the babes while pleasuring herself."

Yes. Violence begets reprisal, always by loss instilled. Michael had not broken the cycle. And neither had we.

"After being removed from my foster mother, I was adopted by the Penningtons." He scratches his nose. "They were kind people," he says, not without disdain, we note. "I never had any sense of belonging with them. At eighteen years old, I sought out my birth mother, and –" he bites his lower lip, "every question I had ever had about who I am was answered in full. Intellectually, mentally, I had returned home, though I still never truly felt I knew who I was. All I understood was that to be a predator is my genetic inheritance, my birthright, my destiny."

"Mr. Walker accepted you once you reconnected with Grace?" we ask.

He snorts. "She chose me," he says triumphantly, an insane flicker in his eyes. "She divorced him to be with me. She helped me curb my prescription drug addiction, nursed me back into who I should always have been. There was none like us."

"Except for me," we coax. "Michael… I still love you. I can see now that we are bonded, and that you turned me into who I am. How could I not be eternally indebted to you for this gift borne of true love?"

He nods his head, then shakes it, evidently torn. "I can't trust you anymore after all you did to me."

Well. As he'd said to me on other occasions, this certainly was an interesting rendition of history.

"You know, Georgia Underwood," he breathes, leaning his forehead against ours. "Truth be told, I ought to have ended you as soon as you communicated to me, back at the campfire, that the murder of my mother was your fondest memory. After which, though I loved you, I also hated you."

It dawns on us that his intermittent reinforcement had not been entirely voluntary, but that it had, instead, stemmed from his being legitimately alternating between extreme emotions.

"Is this why you unburied Elysia's head so it would be discovered, and watched as Whitmore battered me? Your hatred for me? But your love for me yet resulted in you driving me to the hospital."

"Yes."

With this, he rises and elegantly spins around to retrieve the duct tape from the work bench.

The fact he had no questions for us, did not raise the issue of how we had known he would be here, or that Grace was his mother, meant the hatred had won. And that we were not supposed to survive.

Chapter 24
The Cavalry

In preparation of being gagged, we'd produced as much saliva as possible within the brief timeframe afforded to us, parting our lips ever so slightly as soon as Michael had moved to put the duct tape in place.
We do our best to push more and more saliva through our lips and against the tape, loosening it until we start wildly moving our lower facial muscles in a circular motion. We feel like we're unhinging our own jaw in the process but keep at it with persistence. Minutes pass, and we try to count the seconds, lose track in between about how much time has passed. Twenty minutes? More?
There! We grip part of the tape with our teeth and start chewing, ripping at it. Spitting it out, it still clings to the left side of our cheek, but at least now we can speak freely. We'll have to hurry, too, as Grace cut off the circulation in our hands.
"Nick, listen to us. We can get the rope off, but not without your help. Try to hook a finger or two into it, and we will attempt to squeeze out of it loop by loop."
He makes a noise behind his gag that we take for agreement, and moments later his fingers are on the rope. But either his fingers keep slipping, or we get stuck, and our hands bump into each other uncoordinatedly. We work until both of us are panting, and our fingers are sore and trembling. Eventually, after what feels like a good hour, we find an in. Once the first loop is off, the rest is fairly easy.
We scramble to our feet, ripping off Nick's gag and whisper, "Where's the key to the handcuffs?"
"Michael has it on him."
Of course he did. The garage door leading to the street is chained, the door to the house is locked, as are the drawers of the

workbench. We lower our chin onto our chest, close our eyes to deeply in- and exhale, then systematically go through each shelf in the garage, but there's nothing that would serve as a weapon, only cleaning products neatly and alphabetically lined up in flat vats. Just as we are about to succumb and sink to the floor in despair, our eyes fall onto a dark bottle on the last shelf, whose label identifies it as vinegar. We recall the day we had visited Grace's home, when Michael had told her about how to keep her sink clean of lime. What had he said, what was it… something created a toxic compound when mixed with vinegar. We start back up at the first shelf again, carefully reading each label to see if it jogs our memory. Hydrogen peroxide! It was hydrogen peroxide.

As quietly as possible, we remove all the bottles from one of the vats, placing them on the floor. After pouring half of the contents of the vinegar into the emptied vat, we rush towards Nick, quickly filling him in on our plan.

"Okay, we don't know how strong the fumes will be. So we're going to take off our pants now."

"I don't… what?!" he whispers, taken aback. "You want to sit on my face?!"

We grimace. "Don't be gross. There's nothing else to use in here to protect you with, other than wrapping our pants around your head. And," we mumble, more to ourself than to him, "we'll have to use our shirt on ourself."

Once these tasks had been completed and we moved the vat towards the door, we scramble to come up with the best way to get our captors' attention. Banging on the door was a bad idea, as it would alert them to the fact we had freed ourselves from our fetters. The garage is insulated, likely soundproof, at least to a degree, so screaming may be futile. We shall still give it a go, however.

We feel a bit silly shouting for help through the keyhole at the top of our lungs, but there you go. Swiftly, we add the hydrogen peroxide to the vinegar, and lift the vat up to our chest, the fumes yet burning our lungs as well as the one eye we had to leave uncovered.

And soon enough, we hear a key being turned in the lock. The door swings open, revealing Grace's furious visage, which we forcefully toss the peracetic acid at. She stumbles sideways into the door, which loudly bangs against the wall, and drops the gun. A high-pitched strangled sound escapes her lungs. We pull her inside by the arm, yanking out the key from the outside of the door and slam the latter shut just as Michael starts racing towards us from the living room. We lock the door with fleeting fingers, feeling it shudder as he rams his massive body against it, praying that if he had access to a spare key, the cylinder would prohibit him from opening the door with another key already inserted. Grace clutches at her eyes with both hands now, coughing and wailing like a banshee. We pick up the gun and remove the shirt from our face. Our eyes are tearing up, lungs stinging, but even if it cost us our health or even our own life, we would watch Grace die without anything obscuring our vision.

It would likely be wiser to use her as leverage, but we are overcome with a quaint mixture of righteous anger and rage, determined to end it. Since our captors had heard us screaming through the keyhole, we dare not shoot her, lest we rouse the neighborhood. Good. We craved a more intimate kill method in her case anyway.

Michael had fortunately given up on attempting to break down the door, thus we hastily retrieve the dynamic rope, tying Grace's hands behind her back as tightly as we can muster.

With slow, celebratory deliberation, we straddle her, wrapping our hands around her throat, our fingers expertly feeling for her carotid arteries.

We had always counted our blessings as it pertained to memorable kill experiences, relishing in what, over the years, became fewer and fewer novelties. Slaughtering the creature whom we despised most on earth for a second time certainly was a novum.

The blood-shot eyes of the woman who had murdered our mother, and Georgia, bulge out of their sockets, purplish swelling tongue lolling out of her mouth as we keep strangling, our fingernails viciously digging into the wrinkly skin of her neck. When she starts convulsing, we realize that although this was undeniably the most exhilarating kill of our life, it yet does not sexually excite us. This was an execution. Closure.

It does not take long for Grace to go limp, but although we cannot detect a pulse anymore, we keep our hands wrapped around her throat, knowing it could take up to five more minutes for exitus to occur. Our fingers and palms are burning up and itching, so strong is the toxic compound of the peracetic acid, but we will not relent. While counting down the seconds, Michael is back at the door. We hear it break and splinter and crane back our neck to see it being pried apart in the middle, at the lock. He must be using a crowbar, and if he is, he'll be through the door within moments.

No. No! Grace must die. And then so did Michael.

We keep our eyes trained on the gun, listening intently to the noise at the door while counting down the last minute. But before the time is up, there's a loud crash and the door bursts open. We immediately pick up the gun, jump up and point it at our opponent.

But it isn't Michael who stands before us, crowbar in hand, it is the cavalry Kate had alluded to in her last text message to me.

It's Rob.

Chapter 25
Rob

Behind an apprehensive looking Rob, two more men file into the room, guns in hand, and now that the door is ajar, we hear more feet overhead, hastily tripping back downstairs.

We recognize one of the men in the garage as the head of security from the place Rob and us had met at fifteen years prior. We had never seen Dimitri out of his black military style clothes, and though his hair is now gray, he still wears the same grim expression on his face. We nod at him but he ignores the greeting. Our eyes wander back to Rob. We have no words. We simply stand and stare at him, incapable of moving.

"Don't shoot the help," he says, before his facial expression relaxes and he gives us his usual side grin, winking at us.

We instinctively lower the gun when the Rider releases the reins, creeping back towards the pit. The sensation makes me shiver, and I am perplexed he would not want to soak up the triumph of having defeated one of our enemies in our united form.

Mistaking my trembling and heavy breathing for agitation, Rob takes a few large strides towards me, his eyes intense and his face a mask of genuine concern. "Are you ok?" he asks.

However, as soon as I open my mouth to speak, the Rider plunges his claw into my chest, leaving an orb of emotion in there too large for me to bear. I gasp, leaning forward in shock. I recognize aspects of the feeling from when Rob had picked me up at the hospital, though it had been small as a mustard seed then. It had blossomed into something unanticipated by now.

Oh.

I had feelings for Rob.

Which, I am well aware, was beyond rhyme or reason, considering his overall…life circumstances.

I'm taken aback at how versatile this strange emotion was, how many different threads it consisted of. Friendship. Loyalty. Support. Lightheartedness. Humor. And quite a few things more. The way I felt for Rob was not akin to the roller coaster passion-obsession I had experienced for Michael; in fact, it was strange in that it was absent of any trace of rage. The way to, perhaps, best describe it was a playful flavor of peaceful.

'Why are you giving me this now?!' I ask the Rider, who merely shrugs.

'Took up too much space in the rootkit, and it comes unfiltered. For now. Keep it a while. If you want. Maybe I was wrong about him, and about keeping it from you.'

I have an inkling that there's more to it than he's ready to confess at this present time, and that his "gift" may be related to Michael's revolting admissions to and speculations about me. Time would tell if the wounds Michael had slain could be healed, or whether Rob was just a band aid on a fatal wound.

Rob holsters his gun, laying both hands on the sides of my shoulders, and the way his touch makes my heart stutter in my chest is rather unsettling, albeit in a pleasant way. I suddenly become acutely aware of the fact I am wearing nothing but a bra and panties.

"You need to sit down?" he asks, keeping his crazed blue eyes firmly trained on my face. I'd like to think that he does so because he's being respectful, but maybe I'd deluded myself all these years and he's simply not attracted to me. The prospect alone is disheartening.

"Excuse me," a muffled voice in the background interrupts, "but could someone take the pants off of my face?" It's Nick. I cannot help but laugh and awkwardly rub my forehead.

Rob gives Dimitri a curt nod and the latter instantly spins into action, while one of the other men get to work on Nick's handcuffs.

Rob unbuttons his black military style jacket to gently wrap it around me, eyes still averted as he buttons it back up for me. He leads me back to the other chair and holds on to my waist to steady me as I sit down, knees evidently shaking. Although his touch is merely caring, my body responds in a very non-caring – carnal – way. It doesn't help that once he snatched up my pants from the floor, he lifts my leg by the calf to help me back into them. Every time his hands touch my naked skin, I clench my teeth, so strong is the desire to fall upon him.

But Rob is all business now, and as I zip up my skinny jeans, he scratches his beard, stating, "Michael is gone. He came back out of his house, axe in hand, just as we arrived, but disappeared out back into the woods when he saw us."

A single tear runs down my cheek, and Rob blinks in surprise, assuring me, "We'll get him eventually."

"No," I reply, not without embarrassment, "that's just because of the peracetic acid fumes. I should probably get my eyes and lungs checked out. And Nick's, too."

On the drive back to my Seattle apartment, Nick and I sit side by side in the back of the dark van. Two men had stayed behind at the house, cleaning the crime scene and disposing of any evidence that could trace back to any of us.

One of Rob's men had silently handed me back my phone and taken my car keys in exchange. I watch him drive behind us as we exit the cul-de-sac, his face a mask of vacant dutifulness.

I immediately voice clip Kate, relaying to her the details of everything that had happened, and thanking her profusely for calling Rob. If he had not been in Tacoma, if he had been in Seattle, or even farther away, Nick and I may not have survived.

I'm too tired for a direct phone call, and let Kate know I'd speak to her live tomorrow, which, thankfully, she accepts without further ado, though she asks about Nick three times during our brief exchange.

I'm too flustered to absorb the following events of the night. Once I lie in bed, staring at the ceiling, all I still recall is that Rob had informed me Dr. McClurg, the same physician who had examined me after I had fled the hospital weeks prior, would visit with me the next day.

I'm disappointed Rob had had to leave with the other men, as they were officially on business for The High House, but am also in no state to attempt a seduction.

I am startled awake for no particular reason, disheveled and disoriented, a few short hours later, almost tripping over my own feet when rushing out the bedroom door so as to verify Nick's whereabouts. I discover him still locked inside the bathroom. Rob's men had tossed my razor – and for some reason my plunger – out in the hallway. Anything that could make for a weapon, I surmise. Nick is curled up on a thin woolen blanket on the cold floor, his head bedded on a furry decorative pillow from my Chippendale couch. How thoughtful.

He rises as soon as he opens his eyes, an all too radiant smirk stretched across his face, eyes aglow, inquiring about how I am and offering to prepare breakfast for the both of us. His facial bruises had now turned a dark shade of blue and green, but he speaks and laughs without even flinching.

I take the risk. The hot shower helps loosen up the tension in my muscles, my hip, as well as the ache in my fingers. I make a mental note to acquire a finger exercising tool, recalling that the BTK killer Dennis Rader had used one when realizing what daunting a task strangulation turned out to be.

I listen intently for the door alarm, as I had deliberately left the key in the front door, but Nick makes no escape attempt.

When I shuffle into the kitchen, he is just about to shovel scrambled eggs and bacon onto two plates. I'm not particularly hungry, listlessly pushing around the food on my plate while he almost obsessively recounts last night's events, giggling frantically like a hobbit, and mentioning, I notice, Kate and her brilliance in every other sentence. Then he says something that I had deliberately not brought up during our conversation in the backyard the day we had first discovered Michael's bugs. I thought he might lie about it, in case he had not yet developed a type of Stockholm Syndrome.

"I appreciate all you've done for me, but I hope you understand that when I spent all this one-on-one time with Kate while you were injured, she helped me like none other. She alleviated my fears of being sentenced to death if I was ever caught for the murder of your kitty. She...gave me myself back when I realized I could never go back to the family again."

The family. Not *his* family. He's ready.

"Nick," I say quietly, after having conferred with the Rider for a few minutes. "Then I believe it's time to give you something as well. I will give you Kate."

The confusion on his face is palpable. "You will give me Kate? What does that mean, to kill? Oh, I am never going to kill again, and I would never kill someone I l...ike." Nice save. We give him an ironic look.

"Kate is a dear friend," Nick stresses, his usual composed psychologist self again.

I lean back in my chair, crossing my arms.

"Alright," he ultimately concedes. "Perhaps we feel about each other the way you and Rob do."

The smug grin disappears from my face as abruptly as though someone had flicked off a light switch. He raises his eyebrows a tad too arrogantly for my taste, pointedly asking, "Is anyone still aware of the fact I *am* a psychologist? I know all."

But all matters of skewed brain chemistry aside, we both are acutely aware of having more urgent matters to tend to. Thus we conference-call Kate, briefly filling her in on my plan on how to alert law enforcement to Michael's murder of Elysia without implicating myself.

We shelved trying to locate Isobel Cutter's remains for now, as there's more urgent matters to tend to, such as dismantling another three cabins, two further down South in California and an abandoned one in Oregon, close to where Rob resides with his wife.

With Michael on the loose, we'll have to move fast in also unearthing all remaining body parts and dispose of them as well as the prop-"trophies" I'd kept.

Fortunately, I had killed relatively few people as an adolescent, less than one a year, whom I had left out in the open, save for Grace. My blitz attack victims of old had been discovered almost immediately despite never having been linked to me.

During my college years, I'd had even fewer victims, thus I had not begun ramping up numbers until entering my mid-twenties. We were looking at close to fifty bodies in total, and a little less than four-hundred body parts, most of which Nick and I had already rid ourselves of. But these numbers certainly serve to once more leave me utterly enmeshed with myself.

Our team also considers to which degree we should involve Rob, offering him and his men a lucrative deal in the process. The lucrative deal notion stemmed from Kate, who appears oblivious to my feelings for Rob, as she's already coming up with plans on how to ensnare and even blackmail him, should he be averse to the idea. I appreciate her unawareness all the more, as it indicates Nick had adhered to the standards of confidentiality while treating me.

Later in the day, Dr. McClurg stops by. Fortunately, Nick had been too far away for the fumes to have done any damage to him; his lungs and eyes are clear, though the same cannot be said about me. McClurg estimates it may take up to three weeks for me to heal, recommending I avoid physically exhausting activities and cigarettes.
I do smoke like a chimney on the drive to see Rob, though, who had shared with me he would remain in Tacoma for another three days.
It is with interest I note, the more I dig through its contents, that the orb in my chest holds not only outright positive emotions, but also genuine concern, worry, nervousness and other feelings I have yet to identify.
The nervousness forces me to keep my fingers busy, as well as occupy my mind with loud music while the wind is blowing through the open car windows, messing up my caramel blonde hair.
I had put Nick on a bus to California, where Kate will pick him up to sneak him into the basement of here home until both of them decided anything further. I had been hesitant about her plan, although I knew Jack never set foot down there, but I knew she enjoyed these little games, and the danger of the secrecy.

It's late at night when I exit my car, taking in the sight of the seedy motel Rob always chose to frequent. He could easily stay at the High House, but he was a man obsessed with privacy. Which is what the motel offers, and both the owner and guests avoid each other, having too much to lose in case they did otherwise.
I could have texted Rob, or called, requesting for him to share with me his room number; I could even do it now, but for reasons unknown I have a strong need to see his face when I surprise him. Twelve doors to go. But I expect to find him behind the last one on

the right, with only one neighboring room and the reception on the far other end of the building.

Seconds after I knock, the door opens, and as soon as I look into Rob's eyes, I am, once more, reminded of how much he meant to me. Seeing him in his usual attire, a flannel and t-shirt of his favorite home state's sports team, complete with a baseball cap, feels like coming home, conjuring a genuine smile onto my lips. The expression in his eyes changes from friendly indifference to surprise, to what could be concern.

"What are you doing here, what's going on?"

But I find myself at a loss for words. Instead, I take a step towards him, lingering on the threshold. He's maybe two inches taller than I am, I consciously realize for the first time in fifteen years. I look at his lips, and then back into his eyes.

And then he knows.

There's a split second of indecision during which it almost seems he's struggling with a guilty conscience, though he's far too proud a person to ever admit it, and I'm probably too in love – and aroused – to discern whether the guilt had anything to do with his wife, other girlfriends, or he was hesitant because he thought he was taking advantage of me after having gone through all I recently had. But I am delighted that his want for me is stronger than any possible reservations when he grabs me by the waist and pulls me into him, his tongue already in my mouth, hands cupping my face, as he kicks the shabby motel door shut.

It's almost scandalous how quickly we both relieve each other of our clothes, and we never make it to the bed. Not for round one anyway.

As we stand in the entrance way in a naked embrace, I lick and kiss my way up his neck, only to surprise myself when whispering into his ear, "Make me yours."

He smiles at me, his eyes smile at me, in a way that both revives and melts my heart at the same time. It doesn't even come close to his usual coprophagous grin, and, instead, he appears relieved, as though he had secretly anticipated this moment as much as I had over the years, despite my immediately banning any awareness of it into the rootkit.

When I get up from my knees, I wince, and Rob places a hand on my hip, rubbing it gently. He doesn't know, but he knows I have some type of old injury. I take his hand and lead him towards the bed, but before we even get to it, he wraps his arms around me from behind and starts kissing my neck, sighing into my ear. The two-seater couch is nearest to us, and it is there we end up next.

I may be a serial killer living what to outsiders may appear adventurously, deliciously even, yet must disclose that my intimate relations had for the most part been somewhat dull, if not even sterile. I'd had ulterior goals. With boyfriends I had engaged because their presence in my life was requisite to appearing normal, and in case of corrupting men and women in relationships, my motive had been a short-lived, albeit potent, brain thrill.

Thus I am delighted by Rob's versatility and how convenient the shape and form of a couch could be for the purpose of getting creative. He's a quaint blend of rough and sensual; as well, his stamina is impressive, though he is well over a decade older than I am. I have no trouble seeing why he is as popular as he is with the ladies, but I want more than just his body. All in due time, perhaps?

We move from the couch to the bed over an hour after my arrival.

"I want it rough." My voice is husky. "And filthy."

There it is again, his old devious smirk.

I'd never thought I would enjoy any of this as much as I do with Rob, or come the way I do with him, no holds barred. His domination is gentle and makes me feel protected, cared for. He's paternal in a non-incestuous way.

I already know I need more of this, of him, in my life. He was my antidepressant, removing the heaviness from my life, the bitterness over what I was.

Afterwards, he leans up against the headboard, long legs stretched out across the mattress. The stiff white sheet covers his lap and thighs. I'm wearing nothing but his unbuttoned flannel, my head resting on his thighs, as we're watching TV. He lazily strokes my hair with his slim, graceful fingers, and eventually says, "Hey. Remember when I came by the day that guy was at your place in California?"

"Yeah?"

"Did you ever wonder why I did?"

I turn around and re-bed my head to look up at him. "You said you wanted to return the kitty's items to me."

He does his little backwards head flip, chortling, "You had said to me before that, 'If you ever change your mind, let me know.' This was me having changed my mind."

My face falls. "You had come to…" I stop, not knowing how to finish that thought. "And then you saw Michael coming down the stairs. Rob, I'm sorry."

He shakes his head, running his fingers across my temple down to my chin, the crazed gleam in his eyes ever present, although his smile is tender. "It's okay."

And all of a sudden, I understood, too, why the tension between the two men had cost me the ability to speak then.

When I wake next to Rob in the morning, I deliberate whether to wake him, but knowing how little sleep he always got, I cannot bring myself to do so. I decide to quietly leave and focus on my scheduled meeting with Nick and Kate. By the time I slip out the door, the sun lazily creeps over the horizon.

I had been apprehensive about Rob's men retrieving the rest of Elysia's body parts, not because I feared Michael would have removed them to do what I intended to do to him now, but because I was nothing if not a control freak. No. I could not be sure, but doubted he would do anything that would jeopardize he would get to kill me himself, particularly bearing in mind I had executed his mother. Twice.

Still, it would be unwise to have an enemy as powerful as Michael possibly know my every dump site and definitely know the locations of my cabins. Now that an APB would be issued on him, thanks to my placing Elysia's teeth in his trailer and making a brief, untraceable call to his work place, he would likely act even more unpredictably and ruthlessly. If he were to be apprehended by police, he might try to cut a deal and give me up, or even attempt to spin another insane story about me having stalked, entrapped, framed or blackmailed him, just as he had told Grace.

My Michael side quest completed, I leave to reunite with Nick and Kate.

About nine hours later, I stop at a motel right outside of Medford, Oregon, to wash up and nap for a spell. I hear the text come in while I'm in the shower, since I'd not dared take one in Rob's motel room for fear I would wake him. Well, I shan't lie, in part I had wanted him on and inside me a little while longer, too.

The message is from Rob. "I just realized it was your birthday." Just as I'm typing a reply, a voice clip comes through.

"Happy birthday, babygirl. Or should I call you my sexy little slut? I'd love to give you a fuck and a suck for each candle on your cake." He ends his message with my favorite – two sleazy tongue clicks – which go straight between my legs, but also result in me giggling maniacally. However Rob steadily manages to be funny and sexy at the same time remains another mystery to me.

Another voice message appears on the screen. Rob sighs, pauses, only to softly say, "You do something to me, and I love that feeling, Just know that you captured my heart and –" he laughs nervously, "don't drop it."

I sink down onto the edge of the bed. I hadn't expected this, though all he had ever done for me proved the verity of his statement. I can mentally see my brain light up like a Christmas tree his message makes me so giddy.

Rob sends a video. He looks so sincere...I wondered if he looked the same with his other girlfriends when they were in private. "So anyways. After I stayed with you at your place... I missed you. That is why I never answered your texts. I miss you when we don't talk. You were on my mind every day, all day. And I tried... I know I shouldn't feel this way, so... But I always have fun with you, and I never want that fun to end. And I'll always, I'll always be there for you, and I know you'll always be there for me." Before I realize what I'm doing, or if I actually mean it, I had already responded to the sentiment in his last voice clip, "You can hold love for more than one person in your heart, Rob."

At last, the conversation turns to business. Rob's men had successfully recovered Elysia's remains and were in the process of unearthing and then cremating all other victims' limbs.

Rob and I settle on meeting up in California on his trip down to San Diego in two days' time. I don't stay awake all night, obsessing over Rob, the way I had over Michael. In fact, I sleep as well as I likely hadn't in years.

Chapter 26
We Owe Loyalty To No Man

Since neither Jack nor Will were supposed to know my identity and face, and definitely not Rob's, Kate had agreed to take Nick back to my Sacramento home for the day to devise a battle plan. Although our team had been made aware I was to arrive within the hour, I ring the doorbell to my own California home, rather than let myself in, lest there were some uncomfortable surprises involving nudity awaiting me. Young passion and all that. I just hoped they had changed the sheets in case they had been overcome by carnal desires.

Kate practically attack-hugs me, clinging to me while excitedly chattering into my ear, before I even had a chance to utter a single word of greeting, though I squeeze in a quick question about whether they had searched the house for bugs, which Kate confirms – there had been none, as expected – before peppering me with more disjointed information and impressions of hers. Nick remains in the background, hands in brand new khaki pants, which definitely did not come from the limited wardrobe I had bought for him and stored in the little cupboard in his former cell. He appears a tad awkward, whipping back and forth on his feet and nodding at me encouragingly whenever I glance over at him. Once Kate lets go of me, I understand why. He isn't sure about how to greet me, approaching only hesitantly, hand extended at first, then withdrawing it, only to give me a brief, one-armed hug.

"Happy belated birthday, by the way," he beams.

Kate looks back and forth between us. "When was your birthday?" I never saw a point in celebrating it, as it was but this body's birthday, and the Rider and I celebrated our own on the day he was born, and I was reborn.

It's adorable though, that Kate, my friend of ten years, had never thought of the fact that at some point during the year, it would have been my birthday.

"Yesterday," I reply.

"Of course you would be a Sagittarius," she retorts, "just like Ted Bundy."

I laugh and mindlessly take off my scarf. "We do have a few things in common, I believe."

Kate's eyes widen, "What on earth is that?! Are those hickeys? I don't understand," her eyes narrow, "are those from Michael!?" She looks over at Nick, who simply shakes his head in response. I know I won't get out of this one, and indeed, before I can object, she grabs me by the wrist and pulls me towards the kitchen, calling over her shoulder for Nick to wait upstairs. He obeys, either because he wouldn't want to be part of this type of conversation, or because he is a good pet.

Kate pushes me down on a chair before grabbing two glasses and the leftover grapefruit Lubelska from the cabinets above the sink. "Talk. Now." She commands, after taking a large gulp from her glass, the fingers of her other hand drumming an impatient staccato rhythm on the table.

Reminding her that this one ought to be a brief conversation, as Operation Michael certainly took precedence, I yet reveal to her the recent developments between Rob and myself, feeling my cheeks flush in the process.

Kate's facial expression is a mixture of concern and skepticism; she's always been unnervingly intuitive. "You're in love with him. Emily... Don't be loyal to Rob. He will never be loyal to you. No man is, but especially not Rob. We owe loyalty to no man. Take yourself five slutty men and keep them on a rotation schedule to avoid catching feelings. Whenever things get too personal, whenever one of them doesn't have time for you or acts up, you move on over to the next one for a while. He should be there for

you to use whenever you need to, not the other way around."
Kate's gaze is hypnotic. I know it all too well. It's the same psychopathic stare I employ when attempting to be impactful with the humans.

"And don't believe his lies about how he feels about you. Everything he says to you, he says to all the other girls." She leans forward, repeating, "Don't believe him. Remember Michael."

"He's not Michael," I interject, doing my utmost best to conceal my irritation, though mostly because I have a need to bask in the positives of this new infatuation, rather than the negatives; all the heartache, paranoia and what-ifs.

I recall all the times I had laughingly called Rob a bullshitter to his face, when he had denied to me he was cheating because he had been on a different time zone, where the deed had either not yet occurred, or he had found other ways of either justifying and rendering his moral transgressions nil and void in his mind.

I was a murderess. Was his cheating something that bothered me? I search inside. No. It wasn't the fact he gave his body away so freely, it had always been the hesitation about him perhaps giving away more than just that. I was able to share his heart with Rob's wife because I was the intruder. Anyone intruding on what was mine, splitting his focus and the part of him that belonged to me, that I intended to own completely, even further, would not survive.

The memory of when I had first laid eyes on him back in Tacoma, and the way he had taken my breath away, makes me blush.

He'd arrived at the High House sitting in the back of a battered old Volkswagen driven by a spent looking milf, one arm casually slung around the shoulder of a platinum haired girl whose vacant eyes screamed heroin rather than heroin chic. I had chalked up my quaint reaction to his work clothes; the black dress pants and white shirt that revealed a few inches of his chest, along with a sleazy man-necklace. Sleeves rolled up over slender but muscular arms. He so casually commanded respect, radiating the warmth and brilliance of the sun itself.

I had always accepted that he was not only an easy-going, happy guy, but a happy cheater, too, who yet deeply loved his wife. Merely, he sporadically grew bored of her, restless, one flavor woman never enough for him, just as his practices hadn't been enough. He kept them mostly for appearances, having strategically acquired them in cities The High House operated in.

I had subconsciously grasped that this was the only way I could have him, only ever temporarily, only half of him, if even that, and never the piece that I wanted. As it were, I would only ever be relegated to the shadows, a delectable secret, perhaps, but a secret nevertheless.

Just as I was Kate's secret. Just as I had been Michael's secret. And just as I would remain Nick's secret.

The cognition pains me, and terribly so. It pierced more than just my narcissistic ego that none of the people I was closest to could stand by me out in the open.

Suddenly I understand why I had had to occasionally share with Rob that I knew what he was by calling him a bullshitter, reminding him that he would never have me. It was a protective measure, a way to convince myself as well as him to stay away.

The orb flies from the rootkit into my chest before the Rider has a chance to intercept it. Right now, in this moment, I hate the Rider because I understood his endgame. He wanted this to crush me, to incinerate any trace of whatever love I could potentially feel. Self-sabotage with a twist.

Attachment hunger stemming from unhealed childhood trauma was a volatile beast. We choose partners who resemble, in spirit, our primary caregivers in order to heal ourselves as well as the relationship with said caregiver, hoping to finally receive what had been denied to us as children – unconditional love.

I had chosen Michael because he had resembled the Rider, a dark father figure. And I had chosen Rob, someone who would always neglect me in favor of his family, just as the mother had neglected me in favor of my daddy. And Grace. Perhaps I had even chosen my much older human boyfriends, and Kate, because they were substitute mother and father figures.

Whatever I was, however many people I had killed, I wasn't in the slightest immune to romance, and to always secretly searching for a love that would accept all of who I was. A love that would heal the wounds of all the abuse and neglect, rather than to utilize them, weaponize them, compelling me to act as monstrously as my abusers had, so as to experience a sense of control, as if I had overcome being just the girl down in the Rider's pit.

And that kind of love would always pose a threat to the Rider, for it was not only guilt that could disintegrate him, I now acknowledge. I do not even bother looking down into the pit to confront him. I knew he was lounging down there, gloating.

The back of the chair creaks softly when Kate leans against it, yanking me out of my silent meditations.

As though she had listened in on them, she offers her wisdom to me, unasked. "Strangle your love for Rob and keep its corpse in a display case in your heart, as a constant reminder of how love goes. Because it will. Go that way. This way you'll at least get to exert some control."

"Wow!" I exclaim, not without shock, the laughter I force out ringing all too fake in my own ears. "Is that how you feel about your husband? Or me?"

She waves her hand in dismissal. "I have love for my son, but he is also mine, he belongs to me. The way I love him is the same way I love you, like a dog who protects and defends its property. Love is an overemotional word for loyalty. There's no loyalty when it comes to romantic or sexual impulses, not even if you create a cold war situation."

This made sense to me. I raise my glass to her, "Bottoms up, and then we have work to do."

Nick stands off to the side of the white board in the middle of the dungeon, his chin resting on his right hand, taking in all of the information we had gathered. Kate was adding a few final notes with black marker, while I was pinning the last handful of sheets of our Michael file to a pin board.
Some of the questions revolve around what had happened to Isobel Cutter's remains, for the new vermicomposting vats in Michael's trailer had been empty, and whether Paul Whithurst and Michael were working together or not. Michael could have simply stolen a vehicle to drive me back to Washington, though. It wouldn't necessarily have been Paul's.
For now, we focus on the battle plan at hand, starting with the dismantlement of this as well as the remaining homes. Having to rip apart this particular home depressed me somewhat, as I had always been particularly fond of it. I had bought it off an elderly couple, never replacing the antiquated furniture and decorations because it reminded me of my paternal grandparents' home in which I had always felt safe, even after the hospital.
Rob had only two men to spare for the cabin project, the rest were already tending to my victims' remains. Not only do I now understand that Rob is part of a whole army, but that he must, by default, have a far higher position at The High House than I'd ever known. What Rob doesn't disclose himself I know better than to inquire about, however. I focus on my gratitude for his willingness to help. Even if I was paying his men, I was not paying him a dime. He had refused, as always.

When Rob joins us, he lingers on the porch, not awkwardly, merely, he winks at me, then looks me up and down, one eyebrow raised. Still always the flirt.

Finally, he plants a lip-smacking kiss on my mouth that has me laugh out loud, pulling me into his arms, before grabbing my hand and strutting into the front room to beam at Kate and Nick, who, despite their best attempts, cannot entirely conceal their awkward smirks.

Once we get to discussing each of our roles in this operation, I am enthralled that Rob refers to the four of us as "our team."

Rob and I would seek out Whithurst at his place and question him about his possible affiliations to Michael, after which Whithurst would be permanently taken care of.

Whereas Nick would join Rob's man in Oregon, Kate would return home to guard her family. Rob had kindly spared a man to help keep an eye on them while here.

I sigh and look at Rob. "And you?"

"Jill's taken care of. Family always comes first."

It shouldn't, and yet his words sting. Of course I was not, and would never be, family in any official capacity. And yet, he had, with one offhand remark made very clear the position I would have in his life. I wanted to say, "Look around you, Rob, friends *are* family. And what is someone you claim you keep in your heart?" Instead, I sternly nod.

"Alright," I conclude, "let's get to it then. I created a group chat for us, let's use it. No more single ventures, projects and unanticipated news. Whatever either of us do, it concerns everyone in this room equally. We check in every hour until further notice, in particular as it pertains to any Michael news."

Rob and I sneak up the creaky, carpeted stairs to Paul Whithurst's apartment in El Paso Heights, Sacramento. The walls are thin, ambient noise from televisions, music, conversations and altercations filling the hallways.

Guns at the ready, we take our positions on either side of the door. If Whithurst looked through the peephole, he wouldn't be able to

see us, though if impulsive enough, he may shoot through the door. As agreed, Rob is the one who knocks.
Silence.
Then, a female voice coyly asks, "Who is it?"
We exchange a surprised glance, as we knew Whithurst lived alone, but Rob is already replying in a low, raspy hum, "It's me." One by one, locks click, and then we find ourselves face to face with Isobel Cutter.

Chapter 27
Anything You Can Dig, I Can Dig Deeper

With a confused, slightly dazed, smile on her face, she looks at Rob, then at me, which is when she moves to slam the door shut, but we are quicker. I lean the weight of my entire body into the door as silently as possible, and Rob lodges his foot between the door and its frame, lunging forward to grab Cutter by the throat. A strangled, "Help!" escapes her lips, but Rob murmurs into her ear, "Don't make a sound. Are you alone?"
Before she can even reply, the floorboards creak, and a male voice asks, "What are you doing at the door?"
A man steps into the front room from off to the left. As soon as he lays eyes on us, he dashes towards the only open window behind the couch and across the front door.
I would recognize Paul's flat pancake face with its empty light green eyes anywhere, and the Rider does not wait another second, elegantly exiting the den and overtaking me gloriously.
Whithurst is a scrawny man, and with one jump he is out the window, starting down the fire escape, Rob on his tail.
But as soon as Rob leans outside the window, he sharply pulls back again.
"I'll shoot you if you come after me!" Whithurst roars, adding a particularly heinous expletive in the middle of his sentence.
The fact he screamed loudly enough for the entire street to hear is already alarming enough. We couldn't risk a public shootout, no matter how unlikely it seemed that anyone would call the authorities, watch or film us. The steel of the fire escape rattles one last time before the last thing we hear is Paul's feet hitting the pavement, sprinting down the alley.
After locking the front door, we walk Cutter to the chair juxtaposed to the couch, and Rob searches the rest of the apartment. We hadn't expected Michael, or anyone else, to be here

after Whithurst's boisterous escape, but better safe than sorry. The place is confined and filthy, its bottle green walls letting it appear even dinkier than it already was.

There's what could be considered a kitchen unit on the right side of the front room. Its counters are overgrown with moldy and greasy pots, plates and other kitchen utensils. The trash can is overflowing, its smell nauseating.

Someone had made a home on the couch, and from the men's slippers and grimy pillow carelessly flung onto a discarded pizza carton right next to it, it looks to have been Whithurst.

After a few minutes, Rob returns from the bedroom, a bathrobe belt in hand and sheet casually slung over his arm, from which he starts cutting two equally long strips. Binding material.

"Make it three," we suggest, and though we see the confusion on his face, Rob obliges. We motion for Cutter to sit down on the wooden chair.

"Tie them as far apart as you can. Each hand to another strut," we advise Rob, and now he understands. After our time spent at Grace's garage, we would never again bind anyone's hands together to give them a chance to escape.

"What do you want?" the once black-haired woman asks eventually. It's uncanny how much she looks like a Mediterranean version of ourself, or rather, she used to. For now her hair is the same color as ours, and she appears to be wearing blue contact lenses. When first spying her photo online, we had wondered whether Michael had chosen us because our likeness had consciously or subconsciously registered with him. Of course, after the revelations in Grace's garage, we had had to ponder if it had been exactly the other way around.

"First of all, where is Michael?" we ask Cutter.

She giggles and smacks her lips. "Can't tell. Also don't know." Doubtful.

We lower our voice. "You realize that should you keep resisting, you will experience unspeakable physical pain?"

"Pain is a queen," she giggles, then leans back her head and laughs.

We grab her chin and look at her eyes. Her pupils are dilated, her forehead coated with a thin film of sweat, although it was uncomfortably cold in the apartment.

"She's high," we sigh. "I surmise Michael took my conditioning Nick as inspiration when listening in on me talking to you and Kate about it."

Rob scowls. "We have to get going. We can't risk staying, not knowing what Whithurst will do or if he'll come back with Michael in tow."

"Agreed," we curtly nod. "Isobel," we address her again. "Would you like for me to take you to Michael?"

"Michael!" She happily exclaims, but then frowns. "Who's Isobel?"

Rob looks at me, inclining his head. "This, this is the right woman… right?"

We ignore him, struck with a terrible foreboding.

"What's your name?" we ask her.

"It's Georgia," she beams.

Her response stops our heart. We had anticipated for her to reply that she was Emily.

Georgia.

The child we once were.

That was what Michael wanted, the child – the raped child, his victim – not Emily, the grown woman, the survivor.

"Who's Georgia?" Rob asks, perplexed.

"I don't know," we firmly reply.

"Well," Rob mumbles, "anyways. Let's roll. Now."

We yet cannot help ourself and tear a small piece of paper off of a dusty, sandy notepad on the ground, scribbling on it, "Anything you can dig, I can dig deeper. I can dig anything deeper than you."

We know Michael will understand the reference. And hopefully the implication of us planning on burying Cutter would make him emotional enough to result in inattentiveness and mistakes, as it had at Grace's garage. Picking up a crusty knife from the kitchen counter with our sleeve, to avoid leaving fingerprints, we ram it through the note into the inner side of the front door before leaving.

With no further potential danger present, the Rider had swiftly retracted to his cave again. He's pacing up and down impatiently, licking his wispy charcoal black lips, deeply aroused by the prospect of finally, finally, being able to torture again. His pleas echo through the below, ricocheting off of the walls and reverberating through my conscious mind. 'We need to kill her. We need to rip at her flesh, and burn and destroy her.'

Cutter is blaring a happy song about her love for Michael, and her love for us, in the backseat next to Rob, as I steer the car back towards the house.

Rob is trying to drown out her shrill Manson girl-esque chants by shouting questions at me. "Why the hell would Michael do this to her?"

"Because he's insane?" I shrug. "Good grief, Rob, can't you just gag her?"

"With what! I sure won't take off my pants and wrap them around her head like you did with the doctor!" He yells.

We had removed Cutter's restraints for the purpose of walking her out the front door and down the alley to my vehicle, where we had bound her hands in the front with the bathrobe belt, but not thought to take the cut up strings of sheet with us.

I look into the rearview mirror, yelping, "Hey Georgia!" Speaking the name again after all these decades makes me physically ill.

She looks at me with wide, frantic eyes, but stops singing, for the moment.

"If you keep very quiet now, and listen inside, you can hear Michael's voice calling to you. The nearer we get to where he is, the louder you'll be able to hear him. But you have to be very quiet. Okay?"

"Okay," she agrees, cocking her head and turning her eyes inward. Rob sighs a sigh of relief, swallows and softly says, "Hey."

I look at him in the rear mirror. I know what's coming.

"I have to go back home. I hope you understand…" He stops, evidently struggling with words.

"I do understand, Rob," I respond calmly, far calmer than I feel. "Now that I have not only killed Grace but taken Isobel, Michael will do anything in his power to get leverage. I'll be fine, he's not going to come for me just yet."

I train my eyes back on the road, and he does not respond. There was nothing else to add.

About forty-five minutes later, we are back at the house. Nick and Kate are gone, and Rob beckons me to follow him to his car so he can say goodbye. I lean into him and gaze into his eyes, drink in the sight of his alluring crow's feet, testimony to a life spent laughing and smiling for as often as he could, and rest my palms on his chest.

"You had better not forget me," I say playfully.

He laughs. "How could I, babygirl? You're my favorite slut."

My veneer does not betray me as I chuckle, "Well, I *have* always appreciated your honesty," but his words cut deep. I didn't mind being his slut as much as he was mine, but I didn't take well to being placed in the same category as his vacuous living sex dolls that he referred to as good, trusted and loyal friends. I wanted to be more than just his stupid friend.

I disentangle from him and pull my cardigan tight around me, crossing my arms, and feigning a smile. "Go. Drive safely."

Oblivious to the blow he had just dealt me, he winks, puckers his lips as though to send me an invisible kiss, and enters his car to leave.

'Take it away,' I ask the Rider. 'Stow that pain in the rootkit. Please.'

'I can't,' he replies matter-of-factly. 'It's part of the package. I can either remove it all, which include your feelings for him, or you will have to bear it.'

Annoyed, I make a rude hand gesture at him and return to the world.

Fortunately Cutter is very agreeable when I lead her down into the dungeon. Quietly, she seats herself on the bed in the yellow room on the left. She watches me with interest as I shackle her, still being under the impression that she is soon to meet Michael.

She doesn't seem to comprehend that she has been drugged, can hence not supply me with information on which drug I'm looking for, and how long it will take to wear off. I suspect it's an MDMA, Ecstasy perhaps, due to the overabundance of love statements and songs she had thrown at Rob and me in the car. But I will have to wait to speak with her to assess the level of brainwashing she is under after her artificial high wore off, and leave her with a jug of water, instructing her to have a glass ever half an hour.

I text the group chat, sharing with them the latest events.

Four hours later, I unlock Cutter's door to find her lying on her side. A fearful expression enters her eyes as she sits up on the mattress, which is immediately replaced with a mask of superiority. It's like looking in a mirror, utterly disconcerting.

"I would like for you to understand this," Cutter begins, clearing her throat. "I am going to kill you."

"Why is that, pray tell?" I ask, pulling up the chair from the narrow console desk, crossing my legs once seated.

"Simple," she concludes. "I am a serial killer."

"Georgia Underwood, the serial killer," I nod. "And who do you believe I am?"

"The woman posing as me. The woman who murdered Michael's mother. It is because of you we had to flee and live at this rat-infested dirt hole!"

"I'd like for you to tell me about your life, from your earliest memories onward," I gently encourage her.

"I shall do no such thing," Cutter huffs.

"Then I will string you up out there in the staging area, and torture you until you comply." I move to stand up, and though her face remains even, I see the flicker of fear in her eyes.

"Why would you want for me to tell you about my life?" she asks, leaning back on her hands, the chains rattling melodically as she does.

"I'd like to understand who you are. I have no intention of killing you," I assure her.

"Lies," she spits. "You also swore you would take me to see Michael when you abducted me."

I smile. "So you do still remember that. Can you also explain your mental state last night? Because you came with us rather willingly. Singing joyous tunes in the car. Why do you think that is?"

She frantically blinks. She knows something isn't quite right but can't put her finger on it.

"That's alright," I say. "We'll get to that later. Now. Please. Humor me."

And when Cutter launches into her alleged childhood memories, my mind immediately wanders to the journals I kept at my Seattle apartment. Michael must have read them. I had never told him about how I'd spent my summers, my first day at school, or mentioned Mitzi, the cat my daddy had gifted me on my fifth birthday. But it is not until she delves into the orchard story leading up to the hospital that my blood freezes. I watch her starting to hiccup, her cheeks flushed, trying to hold back the tears as she recounts what is not hers to recount.

Relieved the Rider stands guard at the rootkit, her reactions still make me physically ill. What Michael had partaken in, and what he had done to me himself, was frightful enough, but that he would implant this kind of trauma into someone else's mind all but repulsed me.

Had the hospital not happened, who knows what I could have been? Would I have ever killed? Would the Rider have formed at all? But if I had not been violated and forever altered, I also would have never met Kate. Rob. Nick.

If I were able to move backwards in time, preventing my fall from the apple tree – would I? What weighed harder, the possibility of a normal life, or the loyalty to my friends?

And I realize for the first time that I was grateful. That I all but loved the life of danger and violence and excitement as much as I loved my friends, and that meant by default I had to embrace the trauma, my creator.

I had hardly heard a word that Cutter had said during my silent musings, and focus back on her as she drones on about her time in high school. No mentions of murder. I had never jotted them down in any of my journals. In fact, back then I had begun lying about my activities and whereabouts in my diaries, should they ever fall into the hands of law enforcement.

Once Cutter finishes her faux life story with, "And now we are here, you and I," I rise from the chair, wincing when the pain shoots through my hip. It will be a long few days with sleep deprivation and ultimately reprogramming for Cutter. Starting tomorrow, I will finally interview her about who Whithurst was. Though of course I anticipated Michael would eventually come for me, or rather the other Georgia, meaning I faced at least as much sleep deprivation as my unwilling guest.

I spend the rest of the day reinforcing the house; barring the windows and front door shut with old floorboards from the shed, hiding weapons everywhere, until I finally collapse on the couch to tend to my Ted Bundy group for relaxation.

Of course, I do not stay awake, being as exhausted as I am, and am roused from my nap by a loud clang, followed by an odd rolling noise. My eyes follow the source, and there is a ball of fire rolling towards me, stopped in its motion by the couch. It left a trace of fire along its way, and I smell the gasoline immediately, although I yet have trouble fathoming what is going on and where the ball came from.

Then, a second ball is dropped down the chimney, leaving yet another trace of fire and gasoline everywhere. I see the fluid leaking out of holes punched all across it, and now half my carpet is already on fire.

Someone was up on the roof, trying to smoke me out.

Chapter 28
Rage, Pristine & Simple, Healing & Merciful

Still drunk with sleep, I hastily rip the charger out of my phone and stagger over the back of the couch, watching as the flames begin licking up at it, coughing from the smoke that fills the room. A third ball is being dropped down the chimney, and immediately after, a fourth.

A fire extinguisher won't help me at this rate, and so I sprint towards the dungeon door, calling for the Rider, who, for a second time within mere hours, catapults himself into me with such force we collapse against the cold steel door. We yank it open and hurry down the staircase. We have mere seconds to decide whether to take Cutter with us, and what events to fabricate so she will follow willingly, or shoot her point blank instead.

With fleeting fingers, we unlock her door, hit the light switch, and vigorously shake her by the shoulders before reaching for our keychain to unlock her shackles. "Wake up! The house is on fire, we need to get out. And don't try anything, for your own good, this is an emergency and I am trying to save both our lives."

She squints, trying to adjust to the bright overhead light. Her voice is thick with sleep. "Why is the house on fire?"

"I fell asleep. I placed a candle too close to the curtains. They caught on fire."

Skeptically, she inclines her head, but says nothing as we instruct her to walk into the control room. We cannot risk turning our back to her, hence tell her to crawl underneath the narrow cot in the back and feel for the latch, quickly grabbing an oversized hoodie from the closet to keep warm in the low 40s weather. When we hear the mechanical click, we draw our gun, crouch down and tell her to crawl into the tunnel leading outside, trying to keep enough distance between us that any attempts at kicking us in the face to escape will be unsuccessful. We had an exit tunnel, or something akin to it, in almost every home, in case a S.W.A.T. team ever stormed in to arrest us. The Rider's idea, of course.

However there are so many spider webs down in the tunnel, and things, either living or dead, landing in our hair, worming their way down the back of our shirt, is beyond us, but we keep moving forward, upward, on our knees and elbows until we hit the outer wall.

"Feel for the latch," we advise at the same time we already hear the click, and then we are outside. From the outside, the lid of the tunnel exit is masked as a junction box.

"Towards the woods," we whisper, "run as silently as you can, watch your step."

But our triumph of having fled the burning house is short-lived because as soon as we step outside the shadow of the house, we hear someone yell from high above, "Georgia!"

Cutter, feeling addressed and recognizing the voice, stops and turns to look up at Paul Whithurst, standing up on the roof. Michael must be near, but we cannot yet spy him anywhere. We gruffly grab Cutter by the hair and position an arm around her neck, holding the gun to her head.

"Paul, I will shoot her if you make an attempt at shooting me from up there. Toss your gun down and sit down with your back turned towards us!" we shout back at him. But Paul does no such thing. Instead, he ducks and hobbles out of sight, and we hear the rattling of what we presume to be the ladder from the shed built into the back of the house. We had mere seconds until he would come running at us, guns blazing.

"Move!" we agitatedly whisper, pushing Cutter forward, and reluctantly, she obeys.

We look back over our shoulder every few seconds and thankfully enter the woods just as Whithurst charges into the open space leading up to the tree line, firing his first shot.

We hurry through the woods blindly, Whithurst on our tail.

Although it is winter, and the trees bare, the moon is but a sickle, not bright enough to illuminate our path, but fortunately also not strong enough to facilitate Paul and Michael detecting our movement amidst the trees. We do our best to breathe in through our nose, but our teeth are already chattering despicably in Northern California's chilly December weather. The crispy leaves betray us, the crunching sound of our steps echoing through the woods, leading Whithurst directly towards us. We grab Cutter's arm, mouthing, "Stop," and listen intently.

What was that rustling to our right Whithurst moving away from us? Or was it Michael closing in on us from the side? Our thought process is interrupted when Cutter inhales deeply and screams at the top of her lungs, "Michael!" which is immediately followed by footsteps swiftly approaching.

One set of footsteps, we note as we punch Cutter in the side of her head, prompting her to stagger sideways, moaning. But whoever it was, he had been closer than anticipated, and now he was stepping out from behind a tree. We reach for Cutter's hair to pull her towards us, using her as a shield as we back away a nearby tree.

Whithurst casually trudges towards us, coming to a halt once he is close enough to make out the gun we are holding to Cutter's temple. And then. He starts laughing a dirty, unmelodic laugh. "You know I can easily shoot fake Georgia and take you instead, right?" he snarls, his voice dripping with a mixture of sarcasm and resentment. Who on earth was this guy to Michael?! We had to find out.

"Yes!" Cutter exclaims, misinterpreting his words. "Shoot her! It's me, Paul! It's me, shoot her!"

We press the nozzle of the gun harder into her temple to shut her up, but if we had believed Charity's breast leaking silicone to be the most bizarre thing we would ever witness, we were about to be disproven. For Cutter unanticipatedly begins shuddering, groaning, as though in physical distress, mumbling, "Yes, come into me."

After learning Michael had implanted her with Emily's childhood trauma, it ought to have come as no surprise that he had also implanted a Rider in her, but the notion alone offends us. The Rider, and our shared persona, could never be replicated. The mere suggestion equaled sacrilege, the attempt warranting the death penalty, via extensive torture.

"Quiet," we murmur into Cutter's ear, tightening our chokehold before addressing the man in front of us. There was no point in pretending we were just one, obviously.

"Paul, if you would like for Isobel to live, we advise you to answer our questions. First of all, where is Michael? Call him to you now." Whithurst theatrically hangs his head, two greasy streaks of black hair falling into his face. He scratches his nose as if deliberating, then looks back up again, chuckling, "Michael ain't here."

Was he saying that he was acting on his own or that he had instructions from Michael? At this pace, we wouldn't be getting anywhere within the next few hours.

"Who are you to Michael, how did you meet, why are you helping him?" we inquire further.

Whether Whithurst would have responded to our questions satisfactorily, we would never learn. For, seemingly out of nowhere, we hear rustling footsteps, twigs being snapped in half. Someone was swiftly advancing upon us from somewhere off to the right. We glance back and forth between Whithurst's all too casually self-assured posture, and the direction the commotion was emanating from.

We cannot believe our eyes when we recognize the man striding towards us. Our heart, previously hammering in our chest, is now dancing to a light-footed steady beat, accompanied only by the exuberant ringing of triumph in our ears.

Rob.

Rob had come for us. Again.

But the moment a rapturous smile lights up our face and eyes, Rob raises his weapon, aiming it at us. "Drop the gun, Emily."

We listen to Whithurst's renewed frantic laughter, not yet comprehending the meaning behind it, or Rob's words. We feel the breeze on our face and the air entering and exiting our lungs as though in slow motion. Everything was so terribly real, almost too real for it to be real. And then… rage. Rage, pristine and simple, healing and merciful, flowing into our chest, squeezing into the orb, extinguishing its light, poisoning, paralyzing, each and every emotion in it, so we could see, could understand.

Rob… had betrayed us.

"Let her go, Emily, and drop the gun," Rob reiterates, pronouncing each word as slowly and distinctly as though it were its own sentence.

Whithurst turns to Rob to address him. "We should just –" and that is when we take the gun off of Cutter's temple and fire three times into Whithurst's chest in quick succession. Well, twice, to be fair, because he was already slumping to the ground after the first two shots, so the third one hit him in the face instead. Serendipity, we suppose.

Without delay, we withdraw our arm to reposition the gun and shoot Cutter in the head. Firing the gun so close to our own ears was certainly one of our worse ideas. Our ears ring, our vision is blurred. The woman collapses just as Whithurst had, like a spider struck with a fly swatter. No graceful fall, back arched, arms swaying back and forth. No dramatic music. This is how people in the real world died when shot. They simply fell to the ground like the heavy meat sacks they were, remaining unanimated because of a tiny two inch piece of a lead-core bullet.

"No!" Rob desperately shouts, stumbling forward, "No… You just killed yourself!"

We train our weapon on him. "I advise you not to come closer and to relinquish your firearm to me," we say, our face a mask of nothingness. Because nothing was all that was left. We felt nothing for him any longer.

"Wait!" he croaks, "Listen to me. Please!" But we notice that he is still holding the gun, though it is no longer directly pointed at us. "Emily, you don't understand."

"I understand. You betrayed me. You are working with Michael." We are too proud to pathetically ask as to why. It doesn't matter anymore. All that mattered was that we would murder him. Slowly.

"Please!" he pleads. "Please hear me out." And without missing a beat, he continues, "Michael has Jill."

Family always comes first.

Our face falls. And for some odd reason, all the memories come rushing back in so forcefully that it bucks off the Rider. The time Rob had first spoken to me, the way he had smelled then. The time he had come to me when I had to have intestinal surgery, confiding in me about his own health issues, and then, just leaving again, never using any of his kindness, or my weakness, to his advantage. The way he always touched his neck when nervous, followed by "Anyways," grammatically incorrect but always still so endearing to me. How he had, on occasion, looked me over while living with me, but never tried anything regardless. Us sitting cross-legged on the bed eating candy and imitating different international accents, until he had fallen sideways onto the bed, roaring with laughter because he had mistaken my Indian accent for Irish. The times he'd shown me his magic tricks, smiling each time I'd grabbed his hands and pried apart his fingers because I could not figure out how he made objects disappear within the blink of an eye. Our night together, and the way he had whispered "I love you" when he thought I had fallen asleep in his arms. All these little human things I had partaken in. Everything I had felt instead of just "experienced" like my robotic fake self. Because whatever I was, murderer, sadist, monster, ghoul, alien, I was at the core, I realize, still quite human. Perhaps not a good person. But a person nevertheless.

A person whose narcissism, the need to be revered for her deceptive and violent skills, was a defense mechanism for wanting to be loved for all the things she was too scared to show, for fear of being rejected, and, in some form or another, raped again. Had I not loved, and trusted, I would still have been betrayed, though I would not have felt the impact, the full meaning of it. But I would have betrayed myself far more, never knowing what all I could be and feel.

I hadn't realized I'd dropped my arm, the Glock lying loosely in my hand. Rob activates the trigger of his weapon, and I wince once I am hit.

I would have thought a bullet would sting more. I would have anticipated I'd slump down to the ground as Whithurst and Cutter had. I feel rather strange.

And when dropping my chin onto my chest, feeling rather slow and heavy all of a sudden, the last thing I notice is that I was not hit by a bullet, but with a little arrow protruding from my chest. Then. Nothing.

Chapter 29
Razor Sharp Tongue

It is the Rider who wakes me, his claw tenderly caressing my cheek in the impenetrable darkness.

'Where are we?' I whisper to him, but he merely shrugs. I am lying on my side, hands bound in the back. The shoulder I am lying on hurts, suggesting I have been unconscious and in this unfavorable position for a while. Even more than this, my chest hurts, and, foolishly, I first believe it to be the sting of betrayal, until I become more lucid and realize that it is the wound where the arrow struck me. As I move to stretch out my legs, I inadvertently kick against something solid, plastic.

Wherever I am, I am being moved, and then I understand what the steady, humming, rushing sound represented. I was in a car, more specifically, in the trunk of one, likely Rob's.

Knowing my tranquilizers, I had probably been out for about an hour. I am still groggy, my mind sluggish, though aware that the after-effects of whatever tranquilizer had been used on me could last up to three hours on average.

But the Rider would not be the Rider if he were not pure magic. A psychologically explicable magic perhaps, but magic nevertheless. And so my dark subconscious pulls me into him, into a deep meditative state, in which he nourishes me, and fits together puzzle pieces of plans, one, then two, then a few more. I cannot yet make sense of the words, but they are there, waiting, ready for me to comprehend them once the slowness has subsided.

He'd only pulled me into him like this once, after the man who had been the kitty, Stuart, had raped me. And the Rider had sucked it all out, the disgust, the self-pity, the self-hatred, the frantic suicidal ideation. He had then bedded me, a grateful husk, on a bed of oblivion in the lowest corners of the den, to rest a while.

Consciously, I begin to count the seconds, to keep track of time. Though I make mistakes, eventually an hour has passed, meaning we may have been on the road for about two to two and a half hours. If Michael had Jill, I doubted he would keep her at the Bryce's home on Peacock Lane, Portland, Oregon, roughly nine hours away from my California hideout. Too risky. Michael was a patient animal, but Rob in his situation certainly was not. Knowing him, he'd likely have pressed Michael to meet somewhere halfway.

I had to get Rob's attention somehow, and force him to open the trunk. Chances of escape were rather slim, but perhaps I could strike up a conversation with him, eliciting valuable information to aid me later on, once alone with Michael.

I also wonder if Rob was still updating our group chat from both his and my phone to have Kate think everything was going according to plan. She hadn't checked Michael's trailer location after it had appeared at the police compound. And so, approximately half an hour later, almost back to form, the Rider sets me free, though his hand remains in mine, squeezing it encouragingly.

I begin kicking so viciously at the inner plastic covering of the trunk, that I hurt my feet, my knees, wearing myself out. Perhaps five minutes go by, until I feel the vehicle slowing down, and with a soft screech, it comes to a halt completely.

Footsteps.

A gun being cocked.

And then the click of the trunk being opened. It is still dark outside, and by my estimate it must be around 3 A.M. If I had counted the seconds and hours somewhat correctly, and was right about Rob taking me to Oregon, we'd have to be somewhere around Redding by now.

Rob looks down at me, the rear lights casting his face in an unearthly glow.

I have never seen him like this before.
Cold.
Serious.
Not even the hint of a smile in his eyes, with the crow's feet giving away his lighthearted mood. There had always been this excited light in his eyes when he had looked into mine. And that light had gone out.

He appears disheveled, as though he were fighting off some type of illness, and I know the sickening worry is not because of or for me, but his wife.

He looks at me as though I were a stranger. And in a way, I am. Now. And I will stay that way, until I kill him. His wife. His son. His men. Leaving no trace of his ever having existed behind. This I know with a degree of certitude that transcends both narcissistic ego and actual hurt feelings. And I am reminded, in this moment that I am looking up into another face of a person that I used to love, and who betrayed me, of who I am. Have to be. If I want to survive. I am ABOUT RAGE.

"Where are you going to meet up with Michael?" I ask in as neutral a voice as I can muster under the circumstances.

I hear faint laughter, and only then realize that Rob is holding a phone in his other hand. It's Michael's laughter.

"I can't help you, Emily," Rob says. I want to believe that he is sorry about that fact, but he is too composed for me to truly believe it.

"May I speak with Michael?" I press him further. "I'd like to –"

"Stop," he interrupts me, wiping away some anxiety-induced sweat from his forehead, phone still in hand. "Just stop. Stop kicking, stop fighting, stop everything. I mean it. Or I'll have to tranq you again."

He slams the lid shut with such force that the entire car shakes.

'Michael has been forcing him to video chat with him so he cannot alert our team or his men to aid you,' the Rider whispers.

'Hm,' I reply, loathing the fact that the suggestion lights a spark of hope inside my mind, because it meant coming for him later would be a bothersome experience, to say the least. 'Why are you defending him?'

'Maybe you were wrong about me and my plans in relation to Rob,' he ominously states, but I have no time to contemplate what he could mean.

Michael must have gotten to him after he had departed my driveway. Several hours later, in fact, prompting Rob to turn around and then aid Whithurst in the attack on me.

I do heed Rob's words, struggling against my fetters as silently as possible, despite panting and sweating mere minutes in, swallowing air, gulping it down and starting to hiccup pathetically. But whatever I do, advised by my good self, the Rider, I do not manage to free myself. Not when he merges with me, no, not even until the last minute when the car comes to its final halt.

The Rider slips a smoky tendril into me, but, uncertain as to why, I beg, 'Not yet. Not until Rob is gone.'

He nods, his smoky shape billowing around me in quiet anticipation.

When Rob opens the trunk, he entirely avoids looking into my eyes, wordlessly pulling me up by one arm and carefully setting me down on the ground. The tender, thoughtful gesture is ludicrous, considering he was delivering me to the man who intended to commit double homicide of the Rider and me.

I look around me, and catch Michael standing at the entrance of a different trailer in the periphery of my eye. We are in the middle of a forest, and by my estimate, we'd be somewhat close to where I had sat in a cheap motel just days ago, listening to Rob's birthday message to me. Kate's words echo in my ears, as well as my reply. "He's not Michael." A little raped girl's tragically stupid dream of salvation.

The Rider nudges me in the ribs, requesting for me to whisper to Rob to give me a fighting chance, to coax him into changing his mind by sharing with him that I had been awake when he had whispered "I love you" into my ear, and lying about feeling the same way.

Never. Never would I degrade myself like this again.

"Where is she," Rob growls at Michael, but the latter simply laughs his bright, impish belly laughter. Rob draws his gun and holds it to my temple.

"She's inside. In the back," Michael snarls.

"Then you bring her out," Rob demands curtly.

Both men engage in a brief staring contest, before Michael ultimately takes a few steps back, never turning his back to Rob, vanishing inside the trailer.

I hear her muffled hyperventilating and attempts to scream through what I presume was a gag, before I see her. She's wearing dirty mom jeans that are ripped, revealing scraped and bloodied knees. I am relieved that she is wearing a hood over her head. I don't want to see her face. I don't even want to see her face once I will kill her in front of Rob. Perhaps I could turn Rob into my next kitty. The idea excites and invigorates me, though the Rider, I note, remains quiet.

"Send her to me, slide both your and her phone into her back pocket, and I will send you the piece of meat you call a wife," Michael says, all too calmly. Rob obeys, then gives me a slight push that yet sends me stumbling forward.

"Jill, walk slowly, follow my voice," Rob calls over my shoulder. When I pass her, I deliberate for a split second whether I should simply attack her and try to break her neck, but it would be too quick a death, for one, and secondly, I'm in the line of fire of both men.

Jill must have walked faster than I was, despite being unable to see, because I hear her sobbing and screeching through the gag, as

Rob murmurs words of reassurance, love and apology. I cannot help it. I don't want to, and yet I turn around. I have to see it. I need this image, need it to imprint in my brain, must feed the visual to the Rider so we would turn it into the resolve we required to fight Michael with everything we had, just so we could return to Rob and destroy him.

The way Rob looks at Jill, as he removes the hood from her head, gently tugging at the duct tape that had been wound around her head and hair, and the way he consoles her, breaks me. Because I know right then and there I will never have this. Never. And never made life seem very long. Endless, in fact.

Maybe I should just kill everyone. Kate. Nick. Their families. Everyone. Go back to my old ways. My life had been quiet before all this.

Without warning, my legs grow weak and I stumble, falling to my knees as soon as I hear Rob close the passenger side of the door, then, seconds later, the one on the driver's side. Stubbornly, I rise again, although Michael is already by my side, hooking his arm underneath my elbow to pull me up and forward.

Just as I am dragged up the steep steps into the trailer, I hear the car door open again, only for Rob to shout, "Wait!"

I do not want to, but automatically turn sideways to look at him just in time to hear Jill screech, "What are you doing!"

Rob ignores her, and holds up both of his hands, his gun dangling from his thumb. "Michael, let me say goodbye to her."

Michael barks an abrupt, curt laughter, shaking his head. "Absolutely not."

"I've known her fifteen years. I will put my gun on the ground. Just let me say goodbye," Rob argues.

I cannot believe the gall of this man. Or did he really know me so little that he was not anticipating I would not in the very least spit in his face once he was within spitting distance? I could even bite off his treacherous nose. Poetic justice, and a throwback to High

House times.

Michael chuckles, "You knew her fifteen years and yet so easily betrayed her. I would not risk it were I in your stead. She's a feisty one."

Rob's eyes meet mine. "Remember how you kept saying to me over the years how you'd always loved my razor sharp tongue? Then let me kiss you goodbye with it."

Jill appears too shocked to speak, let alone scream at her husband, her greasy, dirt- and tear-stained face a mask of utter disbelief.

I stare back at Rob in bewilderment. I had never once uttered these words to him. Was he confusing me with one of his other girlfriends, at the worst possible moment at that!?

But something in his eyes stops me from retorting with a snide remark. There's an urgency in them that raises my curiosity. I dare not call it hope at least, though it almost appeared as though his words were carrying a secret message to me.

'What is he referring to!' I bellow at the Rider, but he is as clueless as I am.

In reply to Rob, I nod, and Michael chortles in derision, commanding, "Gun and jacket on the ground, lift up your shirt, turn around in a circle for me, then roll up your pant legs."

Without missing a beat, Rob obliges, still holding up his hands as he cautiously approaches.

"Just so we are clear," Michael continues, "try anything, anything at all, and I will rape your wife to death in front of you, and then force you to rape Emily to death, lest you'd like to keep that male appendage between your manwhoring legs, that is."

I can tell the threat prompted Rob to have second thoughts, for he stops in his tracks, giving Michael a death stare with eyes as fierce and cold as steel. In order to shift his attention away from Michael, I breathe, "Rob," and indeed, he fixes his gaze on me instead, taking another few step towards me.

His hands reach up to pull down my face towards his, and he kisses me, slowly, lovingly. A lie of a kiss. His fingers slide through my long, messy hair, down the front of my body, and then I feel it. A slight pressure when one of the fingers of his right hand slides into the tiny watch pocket of my jeans, just as Michael barks from behind me, "Hands where I can see them!"

Rob pulls back, holding out his empty hands to Michael, but when I crane back my neck, I see the suspicion on Michael's face so clearly, eyes narrowed, looking back and forth between Rob and me, that I know I will have to do something. And I do.

My hands are still tied behind my back, but I headbutt Rob with all my might, so brutally, in fact, that he staggers backwards and falls to the ground, blood pouring from a small gash in his eyebrow. In the distance, Jill is wailing like a wounded animal. Silly human cow. It didn't say the best about Rob he'd bound himself to such a weakling.

My own head feels as if it were exploding, and though I do not cry out, I sharply suck in the air through my teeth, blinking away the tears.

Michael laughs happily, clapping his hands together once, before grabbing me by the nape of my neck and pulling me backwards into the trailer.

"Go back home, Rob," Michael spits at him, who is scrambling back to his feet, "and I advise you one last time not to send any of your men or so-called "team" – your and Emily's friends – after me once you have access to communication devices again. You are aware how the two men fared that were to guard Jill at all times. Should you pursue me in the future, I shall also take your son next time around. And oh, all the deviant entertainment I would have you engage in with each other. I'm sure you are capable of imagining it, Rob, for did you not call yourself a dog and a pervert when squatting at Emily's apartment?"

He closes the door and directs me towards the back of the trailer where he gruffly pats me down for weapons. When he reaches inside the right front pocket of my jeans, I clench my teeth, imploring any possible deity or benevolent higher entity to prevent him from checking the watch pocket, although with my hands bound in the back, I am yet clueless on how to reach it. Providentially, he does not, and pushes me down onto a metal chair that is surrounded by fresh blue plastic vats. The mental image of creatures squirming around inside turns my stomach.
I move my feet as inconspicuously as possible to try and determine if the chair is made from steel, too heavy to tip over, but then see that it's been anchored into the ground with large screws and chains. There is no getting away for me. I'm trapped.
When Michael pulls out a large carving knife from behind his back, he rests the side of the blade on his lips, then taps his teeth with it in a bizarre gesture of attempted intimidation, while looking at me with an ironic expression on his face. "Recognize that knife?"
I don't.
"It's the kitchen knife you availed yourself of in order to stab my mother, twenty-nine years ago," he volunteers.
I had not removed the knife when stabbing Grace because she had at once plunged backwards into the well, whose outer rim had perhaps reached up to her groin. Daddy had always warned me about not stepping too closely, although we usually kept an old wooden lid on it. I had occasionally removed it, late at night after sneaking out of the house while the mother was arguing with my daddy, or whenever they were not at home, to try and spy the movement of the mice that had gotten trapped down there. They had been desperately paddling around, scratching at the walls in an attempt to climb back up. I had dropped rope into the well, hoping they'd climb up on it, saving themselves, but they never

did. Suddenly I understand why the squirming of the vermin in Michael's vats had affected me the way it had.

It had been smart of Grace to leave the knife, essentially a plug, in place in lieu of pulling it out of her gut, otherwise she would have swiftly bled out, the cold well water doing its part in speeding along her demise. As a nurse, she would of course have known as much.

Michael moves to stand behind me, placing a hand on my back to push me forward and lift up my fettered hands a little higher. I feel the cold hardness of the blade when he slips it in between my hands and begins cutting away at the rope Rob had bound me with.

The Rider beats his tail so wildly I can hear it crack like a whip. 'Let me come into you,' he growls. 'Rob is gone, why are you denying me? We have to pounce on Michael as soon as our hands are free!'

'Michael is armed, taller and stronger. And he can tell when you enter me. He thinks you are still trapped behind a wall. We don't want him to change his mind and kill us quickly, on the spot, for fear we could come loose and fight back, united,' I reply. 'He will drive off with us soon, have patience.'

I hear the sound of handcuffs behind me, and certainly enough, Michael cuffs each of my hands to the armrests of the chair. The universe had once more synchronized to my needs, for had he cuffed me in the back, I would not be able to reach inside the tiny watch pocket to uncover what Rob had left me with.

But perhaps I had spoken too soon, as Michael briefly leaves the room, only to return with a roll of heavy duty duct tape to secure my ankles to the legs of the chair as well.

"Now, I would duct tape your filthy whore mouth shut," he says, his eyes glimmering ferociously, "but a part of me hopes to hear you scream and beg on our drive to your final destination."

In other words, he'd be driving through isolated terrain where he would not have to be concerned about my screams. Which, of course, he will never hear.

"It will, in a way, be your final destination, too, Michael," I respond. "You turned Isobel into a version of me because it is me you crave. You will erase not only thirty years of history, your history, our history, but a part of yourself that you will never be able to retrieve. I believe you know that, deep down."

"You murdered my mother!" he roars, his face flushing red, cheeks trembling.

"And your mother murdered my mother," I quietly state.

I see the inner war that is raging inside him reflected in his eyes, but he still keeps shaking his head. "You murdered Isobel. You murdered Paul. And you made me listen to it."

So he had kept Rob on the phone the entire time, not solely while I was in the trunk of his car. I clear my throat, throwing the first thing at him that comes to mind. "Well. If you must kill me, who loves you more than I even love killing, then would you at least share with me who Paul was to you?" I ask. "His passing upsets you, I can tell, but of course you do know that all you ever shared with me was that he was a crook you intended to kill together with me."

There's a faint flicker of realization in Michael's eyes, as though he suddenly remembered that fact.

"He was my foster brother," he murmurs huskily. "He was the boy who saved me from my sadistic pedophile rapist of a foster mother."

My whole body erupts in goosebumps when the words sink in. I had killed the man whom he regarded as his savior, likely far more than Grace even. I think back to his confession of having alternated between his love and hate for me. I wondered how Whithurst had reacted after Michael had stepped in, disallowing him to kill me after setting up the stunt. He'd used him because he had not been ready to kill me himself at that point in time.

"Michael, you refer to her as your sadistic pedophile rapist, and call Paul your savior, yet you proudly told me, the night you held me at your mother's garage, that it had been your destiny to be a serial murderer. How do you marry these two concepts?" I probe.

"If you love who you are, then you must love your history. As well as where it has taken you – to me. Maybe you had outgrown your mother and brother. Maybe everything was supposed to happen like this so we could be together without any brittle family ties holding us back."

His eye twitches. Had he ever even thought about the cognitive dissonance? I am not smart, but can be cryptic enough to pass for it. Could I confuse him so that he would doubt himself enough to fall for my nonsensical psycho-babble?

"I –" he starts, his eyes darting around the room. But he never finishes his thought, instead pursing his lips, inhaling sharply and dropping his chin onto his chest, eyes closed.

The last thing Michael says before abruptly turning to close the door behind him and driving off with me is, "I'm going to enjoy face-fucking you the way they did. I'll fuck the Rider right out of you, and I'll use a knife to do it. You'll pay for your crimes."

I surmise that was the problem with serial killers. We always found a way to justify our behavior with our own victim status. We had all been victims to different combinations of neurodiversities, neglect, abuse, isolation, head injuries, fantasies spinning out of control, before we had slain our first victim – ourselves – the second we had either made the active choice or been overwhelmed by our ill belief that to kill was to live, and to live was to die.

I acknowledge my own cognitive dissonance, having called Michael nothing but his disease, just because I myself had different standards as to whom and how to rape and kill. Just as Edmund Kemper had spoken derisively of Herbert Mullin's victimology and motivations, as Charles Manson had labeled Ted Bundy a "poop butt," and Ian Brady had psychoanalyzed a myriad of fellow population control specialists in his book on serial homicide.

I hear the sound of the motor being started, and the vehicle, along with the travel trailer, is set into motion, jerking back and forth, left to right on the uneven terrain.

Chapter 30
The Heart Is Deceitful Above All Things

'Now,' I whisper to the Rider, and he flies into me, limbs already outstretched for a quick taking. Without delay, we lift our hips off of the seat, bringing them as close to the fingers of our right hand as possible, in order to reach inside the watch pocket.

The trailer sharply jerks to the side, and we are thrown back hard onto the steel seat of the chair, our hip, pelvis and injured head exploding in pain. If we reach inside the pocket now and then lose grip of whatever is inside with the trailer rocking side to side uncontrollably, we'd lose our only possible advantage. How long would Michael be driving to ascertain no one would find us? Would Rob even bother sending anyone after us? We doubted it, remembering his face when Michael had threatened him.

Once Michael stopped the vehicle, would we have enough time to pry out the item and make use of it? Was it a handcuff key? And if so, would it even fit? We decide to stop our endless train of questions and thoughts, and try again, bringing our hips to our right hand. The duct tape our feet is taped to the chair legs with holds us back, but we wiggle and stretch until finally, our index finger slips inside the watch pocket, touching what appears to be a piece of paper.

This had to be a joke. What good would paper do us!? Had Rob left us with a cheesy and utterly useless love note!? But as we feel alongside the edges of the paper, we notice it feels too solid, and gripping it with our thumb, carefully sliding it an inch out of our jeans, we see it is a razor blade.

His razor sharp tongue. So Rob really *had* given us a clue. And a weapon.

Not yet attempting to unwrap the blade, we keep it tightly clutched between our fingers, playing out different scenarios in our head about how and when to best attack Michael with it. We doubted he'd kill us in the trailer, instead wanting more room to move around, more access to our body parts, front and back, to slice and stab at us, more daylight to drink in with his eyes the pain he was inflicting. Or at least we hoped so, because if he didn't uncuff us from the chair, Rob's putting himself in danger to leave us with the razor blade would have been a pointless endeavor. Michael drives. And drives. And drives. Half insane with hip and coccyx pain from the hard surface of the steel seat, we do our best to shift our weight from our right to our left, keeping straight our back, and remaining calm while counting out the seconds, minutes, hours. Around four hours later, the trailer starts slowing down. We could be anywhere from Northern or Western Oregon to Northern California or close to the Eastern Idaho border, but wherever we are, it will be isolated.

The paper wrapper that holds the blade is sticking to our sweaty palms and fingers by now, but we work as swiftly, albeit gingerly, as humanly possible. Careful not to drop the wrapper, we fold it up to push it back inside the watch pocket. The razor rests between our index and middle finger when Michael re-enters the backroom, gun in one hand, a bunch of keys in his other.

Neither of us speaks as he uncuffs our left, and then our right wrist from the chair, only to restrain us again behind our back with one set of handcuffs, ultimately poking us in the back with the nozzle of his firearm in an indication to stand up and walk outside.

We will have to wait until we exited the trailer for an opportunity to attack. For one, the trailer is too narrow for us to abruptly turn and smack away his gun hand aimed at us, and secondly, when we half turn our head to look where he is in proximity to us in the periphery of our eye, we see that Michael smartly keeps his distance.

The dark, naked tree branches reach up into the whitish-gray cloudy morning sky as though invoking it in a silent ritual to witness and celebrate what is to occur. The air is humid and chilly, the ground yet dry. We walk down the steps onto a carpet of leaves; the golden brown-reddish carpet leading towards both glory as well as death.

We need not ask where to head to, we already spotted the long, thick chain dangling from the tree branch about thirty-five feet away which Michael must have prepared for us at some point in the recent few days. We know we cannot let him string us up by it. Would he cuff us in the front to do it, or do it the way we were, dislocating our shoulders and elbows in the process? It's a distinct possibility, as his prerogative was to inflict as much pain as possible.

What, what could we possibly use against him that would prompt him to feel the need to re-cuff us in the front?

His mother. Grace. He had bonded with her over their shared depravity, even though she had sold the underage patients to sexual predators so as to sustain herself financially, whereas Michael had discovered he enjoyed the annihilation of another human being.

What we are about to do is dangerous, we know. We begin snickering until it grows into a loud and hearty laughter, and, stopping in our tracks, we bend over, our shoulders shaking. Michael's crunching footsteps on the withered leaves come to a halt.

"And what, pray tell, is the cause of your frivolous mirth, or is it merely a sign of hysteria, prompted by the cognition that you, Georgia Underwood, are about to die a very prolonged death?"

"You know, they say that your life passes in front of your eyes before you die. And I am just recalling –" We howl with laughter, then start up again. "You should have seen the expression on your mother's face, and the way the blood vessels in her eyes burst while I was strangling her to death," we chortle, distressingly aware of the fact of our helplessness. Hands bound, back turned towards him. But we do not turn around, and conjure up different images in our mind to help us laugh as convincingly as possible. Some are of our victims, some are about how we had duped people at church, destroyed relationships, a few memories are of Kate and us laughing about her dog's antics, yet others are of Rob and his shenanigans.

We have almost given up hope, when, finally, Michael roars. He sounds like a wounded predator, outraged that another, stronger, predator had dealt him a mortal wound.

And then. He pounces on us. A brutal kick to our lumbar spine sends us staggering forward, and though we try to turn our torso so we'd land on our left shoulder, our face still crashes onto the frozen surface of the ground. We hardly feel it, as our hip and pelvis are on fire, and we inhale sharply, determined not to cry out.

The point of trying to land on our left shoulder was that we wanted to avoid losing the razor, or for it to slice through the tender flesh between our fingers, the resulting blood tipping off Michael.

"Is that all you are capable of doing?" we cough. "Watch as little girls are being raped and torture those you rendered help- as well as defenseless? Are you a man or a mouse?" We laugh again, but not long enough for him to reply, spitting at him, "You would never stand a chance against me if my hands were free. You wouldn't even dare face me if you had a knife and my hands were free, though weaponless. You are a bastard baby coward, Michael Walker."

Either Michael would fly into a rage and kill us quickly, or he'd want to take us up on our offer to fight him unarmed because we'd questioned his virility and mocked his mother. We hoped we knew him well enough that our inkling was correct and the perverted cat and mouse game appealed to him.

We hear him breathe behind us like a shuffling tank and stay down.

The seconds tick by.

Seven.

Then fourteen.

At fourteen, the leaves rustle underneath his heavy footsteps. We close our eyes, trying to steel our every muscle in case he would stab us in the back – literally this time – despite knowing that no muscle would be able to stop a carving knife.

Then, the tinkling of his key chain. His knee lands hard on our back, and this time, we gasp in pain. Clutching the razor even more tightly between our fingers, our frantic thoughts are zigzagging through our mind. If he does not uncuff us, how would we be able to attack him most effectively with our back turned, razor in hand, where could we cut to inflict the most damage? His crotch? Or his femoral artery?

Michael leans towards us, snarling, "You think you can take me on? *Me*?! I am smarter than you. I am a man. I am better trained than you. And your Rider has deserted you. Anything you may have deluded yourself into believing you can do to me, I will see coming from a mile away because I know you inside out." He sniffles, perhaps from the cold. "But alright," he adds coolly. "I concede you brought to my awareness the fact that watching you pitifully fight back until I have overpowered you, so I may revel in my conquest deservedly, does sound more exhilarating."

Maybe there was a God after all. That he would aid us probably didn't say the best about him though. He'd merely chosen one predator over another. Perhaps God was a Darwinist.

Michael inserts the key into the first cuff, our left, weak and unarmed, hand again, and then finally the right one. As soon as the pressure of his knee increases due to gathering enough momentum to rise, we ready ourselves. When his knee comes off of our bones and flesh, we push ourselves up with our left arm, spiral around and aim for his throat. The blade sears through the massive softness of skin, fat and flesh, but wide-eyed, he withdraws before we can get to the carotid artery in time. Instinctively, he stabs at us and our old kitchen knife lodges itself inside our left forearm as we defensively hold it up to protect our torso. Roaring in angry pain, we yank our arm to the side, deepening the wound but also tearing it out of our opponent's hand. Our skin erupts in goosebumps when we hear the wet tear of the flesh and witness our injured arm cry a stream of red blood-tears that steadily drip down onto the forest ground.

We forget where we'd heard the quote, but we had always lived by it. "Always attack. Even in defense, attack." Thus we jump to our feet, imbued with the near-supernatural strength and stamina of adrenaline, courtesy of the Rider, and haul ourselves at the enemy, who had taken a knee, swaying back and forth, one hand tightly pressed onto the gaping wound in his neck. It had been a botched but still somewhat effective cut, in that he was bleeding heavily.

We cannot risk the knife slipping out of our wound, so refrain from punching him in the head with our left, instead slamming the right side of our body into his, crashing down to the ground. But as his fingers leave his throat, they find ours. We had had no chance to properly inhale, meaning it will take mere seconds until we will begin convulsing uncontrollably.

Although the angle is not ideal, his arms blocking our way towards his throat, we gather our last strength and reach around them to trace the razor across his neck once more. And then back again. His arms fall to the side and it is then we cut his throat from ear to ear, so brutally, so deeply, that the blade rips into our own fingers.

We stand up and stagger backwards, leaning back our head to howl at the sky, screaming an outright shocking expletive, over and over, until the sharpness of the pain subsides, instead giving way to a dull throbbing.

Finally, we have ourselves under control enough that we look down at the person who was our victim and perpetrator rolled into one. He's lying flat on his back, hectically blinking at the dirty white sky, eyes still conveying very clearly the disbelief over the fact he was, without the shadow of a doubt, dying.
"Michael."
He looks at us, the blood pouring more and more slowly out of his shredded throat now. However, all of a sudden, we have no words. Our mind is a blank notebook, our thoughts a pen without ink.
And then we do something, something so strange and so unlike us, that we ourselves blink in surprise. For we kneel down beside Michael, careful to keep the arm with the kitchen knife still stuck inside away from his grasp, and we reach for his hand, holding it in ours, our thumb stroking the root of his while looking into his eyes.
It is almost as though all the excess rage he and his mother had injected, had seeded us with, was now draining back into him. We feel no rage for him anymore. Rather, we are overcome with a strange sense of melancholic understanding and peace. We sense forgiveness in it, too. For him, for his mother, for whoever or whatever turned her into what she was, for all who came before her, every survivor turned predator. And for all who came before us, having created fertile ground for our twisted genetics and behavioral development due to trauma.
At some point we come to acknowledge that Michael is dead. The blood flow had come to an end. He does not blink anymore, his chest remains still, no more breath is left in him.
It is then we notice how nauseous and dizzy we are and turn to examine our own injury. There is a large puddle of blood beneath us, our jeans are sullied from thigh to knee. Though our fingers shake, we lift Michael's shirt and cut a long strip from its hem, wrapping it tightly around the knife and wound in our left arm.

We're aware the reason we are still we is because the Rider is our protector from certain death by exsanguination.

Somehow, we will have to haul the incredibly heavy corpse back into the trailer, and then find a hospital. – Yes. We are still too proud to call Rob to inquire whether he had or knew any trustworthy, discreet physicians in relative proximity to wherever we turned out to be. Instead, we call Kate after having retrieved our cell phone and learning where precisely we are on the map. She groans, "Oh my God!" when we rattle through an explanation of what had occurred within the last half a day, all the while omitting Rob's involvement. Upon our request, she provides us with the address of the nearest hospital, and she instructs us to download a tracker app so she could follow our every move and call for help in case we inexplicably stopped moving.

"Kate, you wouldn't be able to call an ambulance or the police either way," we croak, growing weaker by the second. "If they discover the dead body of the owner in the trailer, we go to prison. Execution pending."

"Are you nuts?!" she shouts at me. "You must be in shock and not thinking clearly. Leave that body where it is. You aren't strong enough to pull Jabba the Hutt's 350 pound body more than an inch. If you try and aggravate that wound, you'll bleed out within minutes. You're in the middle of nowhere, no one will find him. I will jump in my car and take Blobby McBlobberson apart to –" she stops. "Wait a second, why did you call me and not Rob?" she suddenly asks. "And wait a minute, wait a minute, you texted me that everything was fine in the group chat, and so did Rob. What's going on?!"

"Kate," we breathe through gritted teeth. "I can't explain now. I have to get to a hospital, and you are currently the only one who can dispose of Michael. I promise you, I'll fill you in on anything and everything else later. No texting Rob. He's…busy."

Her reply comes hesitantly. "Okay…"

"Trust." We simply state.

"Okay," she replies, steadily this time. "Go. *Now*. Keep your phone with you at all times in case I call, and you call me right after your wounds were treated. Christ, I hope I don't have to break you out of that hospital, if anyone tries to stop me I'll burn them all." With this, she hangs up.

As we stumble back towards the car, unhooking the travel trailer before driving off, we experience another small epiphany. We'd always believed Kate to be rather low on empathy. It's true that she may be low on affective empathy, but that had never stopped her from caring by doing. Miss "I have an idea." She was a no-nonsense doer-kind of personality, always ready to help, readily making my problems hers. Her heart might not care, but her mind did. Was that not good enough? Particularly considering that *"The heart is deceitful above all things,"* according to Jeremiah 17:9? The thought of reuniting with Kate, as well as Nick, sustains us on the drive to Brookings, Oregon.

We had been rather certain that Oregon, similarly to Washington, had to disclose both gunshot as well as stab wounds to law enforcement. However, we had concocted a little scenario that we rehearsed in our head before entering the emergency room. Truth be told, we can hardly remember all of the events that unfolded at the hospital now that we had received a blood transfusion and been stitched up, floating on a cozy cloud of Percocet. A high we will not be able to enjoy, planning to escape before law enforcement finally arrive and both our cover story as well as the fake name we had given blow up in our face. Obviously, we couldn't admit to having a phone on us, as the staff and police would have used it to verify our identity. Thus, we'd availed ourself of rootkit emotions to facilitate sobbing credibly at the baffled staff in Swedish, running up to the reception desk to point at the phone, saying, "mobiltelefon" over and over, engaging in a frustrating game of charades until one of them understood we were asking for someone to hand us their phone. There's hardly any Swede who doesn't speak English, but fortunately Americans were generally a tad culturally challenged, so no one appeared to question our not speaking a lick of it. When we were finally handed a phone, we typed out into Google translator a little text about how we'd recently suffered a miscarriage and had gone on a soul-cleansing camping trip in the great American wilderness, so as to emotionally tend to our tremendous loss. Our husband had remained at home in Malmö to tend to our daughter Solveig.

And while we were in the process of preparing a meal for ourselves, we had encountered a cougar. They do range throughout the state, yet conventionally not in the Southeastern region of it. The animal's unexpected appearance had startled us so much that we had risen and stumbled backwards over the tree trunk we'd sat on, accidentally lodging the knife in our arm. While bandaging our arm in a panicked hurry, we had cut our fingers on it. An insane story at best, and weakened as we were, we'd had trouble discerning whether the staff had believed us.

The windows of our room had been restricted, regrettably, making impossible a swift and elegant escape. Instead, we had begun to cry again when hobbling towards the same nurse who'd already leant us her phone several hours earlier, asking for her "mobiltelefon" again, and then typing out that we wanted to call our husband on Whatsapp. Our eyes had lit up when "he" – in reality Kate – had picked up. We'd moved a little towards the side, the nurse's watchful eyes always upon us, at least until she had been called away. She'd taken a step towards us then, likely to request back her phone, but we'd sobbed even harder, and ultimately she just sighed, shook her head, turned and left. Immediately, we'd run towards the car, with the hospital gown fluttering in the wind, leaving our shirt and sullied cardigan, which the nurses had bagged for us, behind. Risky, albeit necessary. The SIM card had been first to go out the window, and an hour later the phone was next.

We abstain from seeking out Rob in Portland to murder him. Or at least beat him. With a shovel. The shovel we had removed from Michael's trailer, as we knew we had two more bodies to bury back in California. Too confused are we still about the fact that Rob had done both, betray and yet save us at the same token.
The long, uninterrupted road trip puts a serious strain on us, but Rider energy pushes us ever forward, its fire burning, perhaps not as brightly inside us as usual, but enough to remain conscious and lead the way to our house. Or rather, the remains of it.
We park the vehicle a way away in the woods, stalking through them to where Whithurst and Cutter would still be lying, decomposing, increasingly leaning on the shovel as though it were a cane.
We do not immediately locate the spot; it is the stench that leads us to the bodies. Rob had pulled them into the shrubbery, covering the remains up with branches, twigs and leaves. Was this more evidence he'd acted out of protection for us? Or had Michael ordered Rob to cover up the corpses while keeping him on the phone, concerned that the discovery of his foster brother and ex-girlfriend could have led to him?
A rustling inside the death nest has us take a step back. Possibly a bobcat feasting on the remains. We do not stick around to find out. For now.
As we make our way towards the house, the smell of charred wood and lingering smoke prompts us to cough. Carefully, we glide forward as silently as possible, apprehensible about encountering law enforcement or anyone else at the burn site. Other than yellow barricade tape, informing us that this was a "fire line, do not cross," nothing and no one else awaits us, however.

The house would never be linked to us either way. The bodies lay too far away for anyone to smell them out here at the ruins of our favorite home, as well, the smoky stench would likely cover up the one of rot.

But as we slowly walk back towards the death nest, we capitulate, begrudgingly accepting that we were neither fit enough to fight hungry bobcats nor to spend long hours burying a body, let alone two.

Our phone is dead by now. We can already hear Kate furiously chide us for not having gone to purchase a charger and stop long enough to keep it charged, during our drive.

As soon as we are in Sacramento, we locate a store that was open during the wee morning hours, pay for the item with our Emily Sand credit card – another risk we will have to live with – and rent a seedy hotel room, grateful for the fact we kept our ID and credit card in the card holder of our phone case.

We gulp down some of the most disgustingly over-chlorinated tap water we'd ever had the displeasure of tasting, plug in our phone and switch it on once it finally shows 1%, then collapse on the creaky hostel style wooden bed.

We want to send a message to Kate but the last thing I feel is the Rider letting the reins slip from his grasp, shuddering, shivering in exhaustion, ultimately rolling over onto the murky stone ground in front of the pit. His blackened, more solid features are visible through the diminishing smoke; he truly had burned himself out keeping us alive and going. For once it is me who reaches out to take his claw, whispering words of gratitude and healing into his ear, admitting to him for the first time how much I loved him, before we both fall into a deep sleep.

Chapter 31
Decrescendo

As I awaken I immediately experience the discontent. Today, though, it is a different kind than the Rider urge to kill. Disoriented, I look around, taking in the unfamiliar surroundings until I remember where I am, and all that had happened within the last two days. I'm jittery and have a splitting headache. My swollen, shredded fingers and arm sting, the damp, sullied bandages uncomfortably sticking to the stitches. The clock on the nightstand informs me I'd been asleep for approximately fourteen hours straight; it was just after 8 P.M.

When someone once more loudly knocks on the door of my hotel room, I understand that I had subconsciously integrated the sound into my dream before it had yanked me out of my sleep. I'd dreamt the knocking was Rob patting flat the earth atop the wooden casket he'd buried me in alive, whilst Isobel's voice had spiraled down from up above, giggling, "Yes! Bury her! It's me, Rob! It's me, bury her!" A strange twist on what had actually transpired with Whithurst perhaps thirty hours prior.

I hear a raspy male voice murmur, "It's Dr. David, please open up if you're awake."

Smart. He hadn't addressed me by name and had not given away his real name. His quick-wittedness and discretion made him an ideal ally, and friend. I roll onto my side, careful to hold up my left arm, and groan like an old hag when rising from the bed to stagger to the door.

When I unlock it and gaze up at Nick, his face falls. Tears enter his eyes, though he hastily blinks them back, squeezing into the room and closing the door behind him, before gingerly wrapping me in his arms. Something bumps into my back and when I untangle from his embrace, I see it's a grocery bag. I'd been close to collapse at the store I'd bought the charger at and had not dared waste more time to shop for food.

"Emily, you look like death itself. We were so worried about you until we saw you pop back up in the app and I immediately followed you here." His tone, as always, is non-judgmental but caring in a professional way, though nothing about our relationship was professional at this point.

"I'm sorry, Nick," I swallow dryly. "I knew my battery was dying but we were so exhausted, the Rider and I didn't think we would make it if our body stopped for even just one second to purchase a charger." I point at the bag in his hand. "Is that for me? I'm so hungry and thirsty…"

He hands me the bag. "Kate said to get you some painkillers as well. Over-the-counter medication only since I didn't think attempting prescription fraud would be a good idea, considering what's at stake should I get caught."

I nod gratefully, then rifle through the bag with stiff fingers and fish out the Ibuprofen, chasing them down with half a bottle of Schlitz. I turn the bottle in my hand to look at its label, then chuckle, "Why, you are an unconventional therapist, aren't you."

"Well, I do know you like your hard liquor," he smiles. "I thought we could meet each other halfway, no whiskey, but your favorite beer instead."

I motion for him to have a seat on the chair with the grimiest upholstery I'd ever laid eyes on, and crawl back into bed, leaning against the headboard while ripping at the plastic wrapper of a sandwich.

"I don't know where to start," I yawn. "I have a million questions. So you went up to Oregon with Rob's man. Start from there, tell me everything."

Nick clears his throat and launches into a detailed monolog. I do my best to listen attentively, but my thoughts keep wandering back to Rob. From the timeline of events, Rob had not even pulled his men from the cabin projects after Michael had called to inform him that he had abducted his wife. One of them, it appeared, was still working on my Scotts Valley cabin right outside of Santa Cruz. Which prompted yet more questions. Had Rob done so to keep up appearances or to protect me, despite having been forced to betray me? If I ever decided to speak with him again, would I even believe his answer in case I inquired?

I return my focus to Nick's account of how he had experienced the last two days, yet just as he delves into what appears could be a stammered confessional, there's yet another knock at the door.

"It's Kate," he informs me as he jumps up from his chair and jogs to the door to unlock it.

Kate squeals happily when he pulls her into a tight embrace, rocking her from side to side while running his stubby fingers through her hair, inadvertently pulling several strands out of her perfect bun.

I wolf down a second sandwich triangle while impatiently watching them giggle with each other and murmur so I would not overhear all the saccharine words they were undoubtedly exchanging.

Kate finally pries herself away from Nick, swiftly striding over to the bed to bend down and plant a lip-smacking kiss on my cheek. When she pulls back, her hand comes to rest on the side of my face and she gives me a strangely pained smile. "Have you talked to Rob?"

I avert my eyes and, not being able to conceal my irritation, toss the last bite of sandwich back down into its packaging. "You contacted him, although I asked you not to, didn't you."

Kate cranes her head to look at Nick. "You haven't told her yet?" He coughs nervously. "I was just getting to that part. Well," he seats himself on the chair again, "Kate texted me, and well, you know how she sends her messages in little installments. I sent the first two to the group chat, with some added questions, before learning you had not wanted Rob…involved. I want you to know one thing, Emily. Rob immediately confessed. His relief that you had survived was genuine, believe me. The first thing he asked was how you were, where you were, and how he could help."

I shake my head with so much gusto that the headache returns, despite the 1,000mg of Ibuprofen I had consumed less than half an hour ago.

"Anyway." My voice is bitterer than I'd intended for it to be. I scratch at the stained bandage on my itching arm and force a smile. "We have other things to discuss. First of all, how did it go with Michael and the trailer, Kate?"

She climbs over my legs to sit down on the bed and lean against the dirty white wall, her legs stretched out across mine.

"I've never had a workout quite like this," she admits, raising both her eyebrows while staring off into space. "I cried. I'm serious! I kept digging and digging and the hole was still not big enough for him. Please, please, for practicality's sake, get yourself fitter boyfriends from now on. If I have to bury another larger guy, I think my heart will give out."

I chuckle. Kate had never been particularly politically correct, but it was one of the things I liked about her. She went for the jugular, hitting below the belt, as soon as someone got on her bad side. Or mine.

"What did you do with the trailer?" I ask.

"Cleaned it inside out while wearing a forensic suit, after driving it approximately an hour South of the burial site."

I scratch my nose and whistle, impressed. "Alright. We had better rid ourselves of the car as well. We ought to take it into an alley somewhere in Whithurst's former neighborhood, and set it ablaze once adequately cleaned." I look at Nick. "You think you're up for it? I imagine Kate has had enough of a workout for a while."

But ultimately it is decided all three of us will dispose of the car together. When the sun finally comes up, bathing the room in a

Kelly-green light, thanks to the hideously colored curtains, we are all set, and Nick has helped change my bandages, for Kate had also instructed him to acquire several gauze bandage rolls, complete with scissors.

I'd treaded lightly, probing whether Nick should perhaps live at my Ames Lake cabin as a free man, being that the location minimized the risk of him being discovered by anyone he knew in Northern California, or who recalled his face from the Missing person bulletin. It had been a mere hunch that Kate might prefer Nick not to live in my Scotts Valley cabin – her metaphorical backyard – since I knew how sacred her boyfriend rotation schedule was to her, being that she was an avoidant attachment type of person. And indeed, Kate had enthusiastically agreed, then winked at me when Nick had turned to set down his water bottle on the desk behind him.

Now, you may argue that Nick would never be truly free, unless unbrainwashed. But I ask this then, had it truly been me to conduct any brainwashing? Other than implanting one single memory in his mind, a brief moment in time, five minutes or less out of the overwhelming roundabout 23,652,000 minutes he'd spent on this planet. Inconsequential to him in the large scheme of things, though a necessary failsafe for me and Kate.

Why, had I not been the one to unscramble his domesticated herd animal brain and returned, as he'd conceded all by himself, his sense of unbridled adventure, teenage wonder and unstifled creativity to him? I had separated him from his true captors and emotional hostage takers. His family.

One might even say that I had given him himself back, just as he had done with me via extensive therapy. What other than brainwashing was therapy anyway? We merely appeared to be members of two different schools of thought, and practice. His cognitive behavioral therapy was all but geared towards overriding some of the neuronal pathways in my brain in order to create healthier habits and more awareness as it pertained to my thought and emotional processes and actions. A sluggish procedure that required some finesse on his part, whereas I had been my usual juggernaut self in delivering results without delay. Hence I must conclude that we were, for all intents and purposes, liberators unto one another, though, certainly, I was the superior therapist.

Kate, with great foresightedness, had excused herself at work on the day I had called and rushed to obtain a doctor's notice that she would be sick for at least another three days, before racing towards Oregon to dispose of my deceased former romantic partner.
Thus, we venture back to Washington together. Nick's excitement about his new home is contagious, and he is delighted when Kate and I present him with a brand new laptop for the purposes of his writing the first novel of his series, tentatively titled "Mercy Woods." I liked that he'd caught on regarding how the Rider and I had always picked my aliases, particularly the last names. They were all connected to nature in some form or another, based on the one the body my smoky protector and I inhabit had been born into – Underwood. I was Emily Sand, had been Zadie Shore, and in two more locations I was Drew Meadows and Genevieve – "Just Gen" – Plains. Of course, we chose strong first names as well. Emily meant "rival," for instance. Though, we pondered whether the good doctor had gotten a tad confounded when deciding to name my fictional alter ego Mercy. However, considering he believed that I had saved him from the gallows, he might certainly view me as a benevolent and merciful Goddess of sorts.
Kate had chosen to spend another day with Nick at his new cabin, using her usual excuse that I – whom her husband only knew as Lisa – was in crisis. I would visit Nick each Friday to bring him groceries, and whatever little hedonistic pleasures he required for

his new life, as he understood he could not leave the grounds until further notice and was to never answer the landline or open the door, unless it was for me, or Kate.

And so, a week goes by, and then another, and two more, until we settle into a nice, comfortable routine, with Kate making the drive up to Washington bi-monthly to visit with her main side boyfriend and plan our next shenanigans, id est murderous quests.

I had found that my misgivings in relation to confessing I was no vigilante killer had been in vain. Kate appears to have required but a brief phase of warming to the idea of killing indiscriminately. She easily slips back into the mindset of claiming that the world deserved to be purged of the people she selected and then stalked for our joint future homicidal feats, but I can tell from the way she averts her eyes to conceal the glee in them, from the way she touches her face, nose and neck while speaking, that she is aware her reasons are devoid of credence. Sometime soon I would need to give her a lesson on how to avoid so-called manipulators, gestures revealing that she wasn't being truthful.

One night, she calls me at an ungodly hour. She says nothing of significance, but when she mentions how much she felt our friendship stabilized her, I know. She has killed on her own. Her first solo experience. My baby is all grown up and spread her beautiful razor-sharp wings to wreak havoc on the unsuspecting public.

She had also presented Nick and me with a curious proposal, which I had initially dismissed without adequately reflecting upon it. When I finally did, I acknowledge its merit. The newness of it excites the Rider and me equally. Kate had suggested our team take on cases for hire. No decision has been made as of yet, but I assure you, I shall update you on any further developments of this potential new avenue of me becoming an assassin.

Now, you may wonder about how things have gone between me and my one true love, whose name is Legion. The Rider, my

Driver, Wanderer, ruthless Protector. And I must apologize profusely for keeping you in suspense. The Rider is, as he will always be, alive and well inside me. He had fallen into a comatose sleep at the hotel in Sacramento, stirring on occasion, but remaining unconscious. I had pulled him down into the pit towards one of the little fires that kept burning throughout, so its raging heat may nurse him back to health.

He had surprised me one evening as I was sitting on the couch with Nick at his Ames Lake cabin doing crosswords after a therapy session, knocking on the rock at the upper edge of the pit, poking his head out, grinning, "Knock, knock."

We had buoyantly danced around each other a while, arms raised, our laughter bouncing off of the black walls of the pit. My body had remained calm, and my pen continued to meticulously scribble letters into the little boxes in order to form words, but Nick had immediately sensed a shift inside me, and, beholding my gentle smile, asked, "Is he back?" To which I had merely nodded in reply.

'Tell me everything!' the Rider had sung. 'I could read you, but I want to hear it from you directly.' I had briefed him, pulling memories, images, out of my head to cast them into the air so he could watch and feel a part of it all.

One weekend, Kate, Nick and I make our way to my new Medford, Oregon apartment, as we had chosen it to be our new headquarter. It was more conducive to meet each other halfway, rather than keep driving half a day to see each other in person. Some things were too dangerous to discuss via modern electronic devices, and, after all, we cherished how efficiently our team worked together in person. As well, we enjoyed each other's company; our shared laughter after talking business had become my new favorite band aid, prohibiting intrusive thoughts. I shall leave it at that.

It is a sunny Saturday afternoon, just after 1 P.M., and we are taking a break from strategizing. Kate had given Nick *the look*, after which he had immediately retracted to my bedroom.

"What's going on?" My voice is thick with skepticism.

"Look, I know you've shut down each time I mentioned his name," she briefly closes her eyes when she sees me roll mine and defensively cross my arms – so much for wanting to teach her how not to give yourself away with body language – but continues, undeterred. "But you can't ignore him. I know he tried to reach out to you, even after you kicked him out of the group chat and blocked his number."

"I don't want to talk about Rob," I reply pointedly.

"Fine, then just listen," Kate quips. "Why are you so incredibly mad at him? He saved you."

My head swivels around. "He betrayed me. He chose her over me."

Kate leans back on the couch. "Emily," she slowly begins. I can tell I'm in for a hard truth whenever she takes this tone of voice. I can almost see the different words and stats, her analyzing my body language and what she knew about me, appearing in red letters before her inner eye, as though she were the Terminator himself. "Let me ask you this. If it came to a point where you had to save either me or Nick, whom would you choose?"

I squint at her. "I'd choose you, I thought that much would be obvious."

She nods. "But you love Nick, he's your friend. But our friendship has a different quality, and you have a different kind of love for me."

I see where she is going with this, and I don't like it.

"If it were between you and Nick, I would also choose you. But I'm telling you very honestly now, if it were between you and my family, I would always choose them."

There it is. Again.

"Rob put himself and his wife and son in danger when getting out of that car to beg Michael to let him say goodbye to you," she proceeds. "Had Michael caught him slipping you that blade, we all would have died. All of us. Do you understand how much he must love you in order for him to have done that?"

Overwhelmed doesn't begin to describe how I feel.

"So you are saying... what *are* you saying!?" I yell, throwing up my arms in exasperation.

"That Rob loves you. That he worked like hell to save both his family as well as you. That he placed you right next to them when it comes to significance."

"I have to think about this. I can't think straight," I say weakly.

"Well," Kate says, as she rises from the couch, "then don't think, just feel. And I myself," she stops to type something into her phone, "will join Nick in the bedroom for a spell."

She pulls out her phone and types something into it while walking out of the living room. I hear Kate open the front door, rather than the bedroom door, but no words are exchanged, which is even stranger. A dark sense of foreboding grips me, and so I slide my hand underneath the seat cushion to feel for my Bowie knife, but before I can grab it, the Rider knocks it out of my hand when we lay eyes on the person entering the room. It looked as though the Rider was in agreement with Kate as it pertained to him.

Rob's shoulders are straight, he is walking with his usual swagger, but his face is tense. Automatically, I rise from the mustard yellow sofa, but do not quite know where to go, what to do, or what to even say.

"Hi," Rob says carefully. Softly. My God, how much I had missed his voice. He had always abhorred it due to its higher pitch, but I loved its gentle liveliness that reflected well his personality. Whenever he spoke to me, it was from his heart, the sun itself. His words were radiant, life-giving rays that warmed and strengthened me. I didn't need him, I wanted him enough to let myself need him.

I look into his clear, skylike eyes, their tiny laser-point pupils dilating conceivably with each passing second, until the crow's feet around them deepen when he shows me a cautious smile. I cannot help but return it, and as soon as I do, the orb, the orb that the Rider had never removed from my chest, and which the rage had contaminated on the day Rob had come to deliver me to Michael, explodes in light. Everything that lay incapacitated within me had now arisen.

Simultaneously to my stepping around the couch table, he takes several more steps towards me and we hug each other tight. I bury my face in the nape of his neck and feel both our anxious heartbeats slowing down with each breath we take.

"I'm so sorry, Emily, I'm sorry," he mumbles into my ear, inhaling the scent of my hair, the finger of his right hand tugging at the ends of my hair with affectionate playfulness.

"No, I am sorry, Rob. I am, for getting you involved, and for –" I pause for an instant. I still do not want to speak his wife's name. "For everything," The last part of my sentence comes out half strangled because he hugs me even tighter.

I do wonder what Michael had told Rob's wife, how the latter had explained why she was kidnapped, and who the woman he had known fifteen years, and which he had insisted on kissing goodbye, was. But I know now is not the time to ask these questions, as much as I know I'm not ready to hear the answers just yet.

When we finally release each other, it is not for long, my lips hungrily falling upon his. After a few minutes of passionate kissing, Rob grabs me by the waist and sets me back until an arm's length separates us.

"Woohoo!" He laughs and does his usual head shrug. "Okay, we better stop, I'm getting a bit too into this and we're not alone. Yet."

I burst into a school girl giggle when he winks and clicks his tongue at me, settling the matter. But then I approach again. I don't touch him, for I know he's just like me, quick as timber, and quite unstoppable once he was in the zone, but I have to tell him, and I have to be close to him when I do.

"I love you," I say, albeit a bit shyly.

Rob's eyes light up, but then he turns serious. "I do love you," he replies huskily.

"I also wanted to say, about breaking your face," I awkwardly gulp, but before I can explain to him that I had done it in order to save him from Michael, Rob grins his best coprophagous grin.

"You fuck like a Goddess, and you definitely headbutt like one too, babygirl."

I laugh. "I also kill like a Goddess,"

"I'd like to see that sometime."

Surprised, I meet his gaze. Was this an admission? He had not batted an eyelash when blazing into Grace's garage to save me, discovering Michael's mother deceased on the floor. He had been a smidgen too "business as usual" about it. He had also known that we would have to kill Whithurst after our plan to interrogate him. His men equally had expertly disposed of Grace, as well as all the body parts I had graced – no pun intended – the Pacific Northwest with over the decades.

"It would appear we have a lot to still tell each other about who we are, and what we do," I slowly say, cocking my head.

"You betcha."

"Are you seriously shooting finger guns at me!?" I cackle, and when he chimes into my laughter, the door finally opens and Nick and Kate's heads poke into the room.

"Well, hello, you two love birds." Kate's tone is jovial. "I see you made up. Excellent. Let's get down to business. I have an idea."

Of course she did.

Rob leans back on the couch, pulling me into him, while Kate and Nick take their seats on the two armchairs across from us. And while my best friend fills me in on everything she and Rob had spoken about over the past few weeks, I learn all about what I had sensed yet never known about the High House and their various international criminal enterprises, including Rob's position.

At some point, I sit back up and move to the other end of the sofa so I can drink in the sight of everyone and take mental photographs of this most precious moment.

Here they all are.

My friends.

My chosen family.

A close-knit team of perverts.

I peer down into the hole to spy the Rider, and he smirks up at me, shrugging his shoulders as though to convey he had known all along we would find our home, but that none was more surprised than him as to the fact our home was with other people.

I do not yet know how to, or if I should, reveal to Kate and Rob the existence of the Rider, or whether to share with Rob how I had sustained my hip injury. But unlike with Michael, I felt that none of it had to be rushed, and I could take my time with it, employing Nick's help in the process.

All I know, without the shadow of a doubt, is that The Rider and I are, and would always be - eternally, magnificently, irrevocably, lustily, yearnfully... Emily.

- The End -

ABOUT RAGE – The Soundtrack
available on Spotify, YouTube & all available platforms

Track #1
Violence Come Out To Play
Poetry/Lyrics: Erin Banks, music & vocals: Erin Banks & Peter Douglas

Violence, come out to play,
And sweat our sheets to a tired gray.
Haul towards the pit our strangled need,
Perpetual fire's fever dream.
Violence, come take him now,
In sickness and health as you once vowed.
Down our dismal soul, that famished den,
Pour his ashes, heal, heal us again.

Chorus:

Hail to the privation I knew not yet how to miss,
An utter desolation, mistaken, once, for duty's bliss.
They weigh like pregnant cloud banks, the humid memories,
Heaving their stomach contents — at the mere sight of virility.
Wisdom pledges anguish, a mind corset never willed,
And so knowledge begets reprisal, always by loss instilled.
Perhaps by now I should hail amnesia, a sleepy mercygrace,
Avail myself of small white pellets, to put me back in my place.

From "Violence Come Out To Play, August 5th, 2018 & August 25th, 2019

Track #2
Turncoat
Poetry/Lyrics: Erin Banks, music & vocals: Peter Douglas

Turncoat, awaken, time to leave.
Suit up in black on Mournday,
Although you have no right to grieve.
And change to white on Truthsday,
In remembrance of his shroud.
And gray for Whose- and Whensday,
To blend into the faceless crowd.
Slip into red on Thirstday,
As your tongue scrapes along the ice.
Blue, perhaps, on Fryday,
Incinerate your childhood lies.
Coffin brown on Satinday,
When laid to rest we both shall be.
In ashes dress on Someday,
When Turncoat will have found her peace.

April 26, 2019

Track #3
She's My Savior, My Perdition
Poetry/Lyrics: Erin Banks, music: Peter Douglas

She's my savior, my perdition.
My pursuits without fruition.
A luminous goddess, a slut.
Butterflies, a knife in my gut.

Perish shall I dare I beguile.
Still...probe will I and know not why.
Another credo penned in vain.
Unwavering, she yet remains.

I am the cap that crowns this fool.
The risen son on every yule.
A manifesto of regret.
Success in loss my epithet.

She is my possession, most prized.
A squalid secret glamorized.
My heroine in every sense.
The spike upon my picket fence.

Perish shall I dare I deceive.
Still...will she truly never leave?
Another promise made in vain.
Though staggering, she yet remains.

I vanish unless I repent.
Am worthless but for her lament.
Stray I must to remind myself
She is the one, unparalleled.

February 20th, 2019

Track #4

My Beloved Is A Bird Named Resentment

Poetry/Lyrics: Erin Banks, music: Erin Banks & Peter Douglas, vocals: Mirko Swo & Peter Douglas

My beloved is a bird named Resentment.
His feathers are thistles and when he whistles,
When he dances and caws, defiles with his claws,
And pecks at his compeer, songs of contempt sneers,
My world disappears.
"Why, you broke my beak, my wings and my voice,"
Squawks he who dove straight at my window by choice.
"Hold still, stupid bird, that to your scrapes I may tend!"
Tighter squeezed I 'til he lay limp in my hand.

I'm no one's beloved, my name Possession.
Drew I my conclusion, truth or illusion,
The tenderness ruse, cultivated abuse,
Through the art of stillness, transmitted illness,
My world was regained.

February 16, 2020

Track #5
How Exquisitely I Rage
Poetry/Lyrics: Erin Banks, music & vocals: Peter Douglas

What's this most indistinct of sounds?
The sigh of the lost and never found?
A trapped jayhawk's despondent cry?
A predator's most vulnerable lie?
The rhythmic hum inside the hive?
A murderer's campfire lullaby?
The anguished yelp of a fawn shot?
Whatever could it be, just what?!

Across the land, and time and space,
No border law could impair my chase,
No matter, though, how far I go,
How intently listen in my woe,
I can't detect from whence it came,
Surprisingly, due to my shame,
I turned within and found...and found,
It was my own soul which made the sound.

Oh, how exquisitely I rage!
And neatly furnished this homemade cage.
Was that love once? That trampled rug?
The heartstring curtains and skull cap mug?
The house Ted built, our legacy,
And far from reach, a finger bone key.
The house Ted built, what, what have we done.
And what's left now...to do and to become.

April 26th, 2019

Track #6
Our Love Burned Cities To The Ground
Poetry/Lyrics: Erin Banks, music: Peter Douglas

Journey northwest, towards the Cascades tonight.
Bring along your cargo, doubt and pride.
Blaze through the Taylor Mountain trails, leave your hide.
A soldier, reluctant, jaw clenched tight.

And if we could still burn cities to the ground,
Bathe our Entity in the skulls atop the mound?
If we could walk through murder suicide, our land?
If your mind and mouth cannot caress, beat me then.
Would you not grip me tighter, twirl me around,
Bed me on the pitiful husks at Puget Sound?

Chorus #1:

You are the wilderness in me,
The vaulted sphere untouched by man.
My God of serendipity,
The napalmlust of unity --
All I can neither have nor be.

Instead you flew to Salt Lake City tonight.
Left me accused -- speak, what other lie,
What treachery of compatriots, what crime
Shall I commit that warrants your faith and time?

And if we cannot still incite the vapid horde,
Then I myself will hand you crowbar and chord,
If we can't walk through rotted timber woods, our land?
If you can't see the truth for the trees, kill me then.

Would you wed my corpse in his basilica?
Bury me with your casualties at Issaquah.

Chorus #2:

You are the wind across my plains,
The longing sigh of borderlands.
You are my passions and my pains.
And all the things I've craved in vain --
My pleas as fruitful as on sand.

From Our Love Burned Cities To The Ground, & You Are The Wilderness In Me, both August 24th, 2019

Track #7
Queen Of Scum
Poetry/Lyrics: Erin Banks, music: Peter Douglas, vocals: Helena Roth& Peter Douglas

I am not a patient woman, and I have never been.
I scrape the ice off of my tongue,
Emit the embers from my lungs,
And toss the mud off of my prongs.
I am not a good woman, I am but a wasted whore.
The queen of scum without a throne,
Spit your contempt into my soul,
And take a hammer to your bones.

Chorus:

We were like mountains breaking apart.
Were pounding like fists on a slowing heart.
And touching me at a spot so wet,
You competed with years of blood I'd let.
We spun a tale of mutual rape,
Until either dawn or bones would break,
Then returned to warmth to lick our wounds,
But, once healed, longed to be hurt anew.
She is still my dripstone cave, she could never comprehend.
The self-inflicted runes I bear,
Entrust your will into my care,
You can't miss what was never there.
She is the barren dirt on which I tread, and I her plow.
Call me ye ole Silver Tongue's kin,
Clandestineness my second skin,
I am a man, the first born twin.

Chorus:

We were like mountains breaking apart.
Were pounding like fists on a slowing heart.
And touching me at a spot so wet,
You competed with years of blood I'd let.
We spun a tale of mutual rape,
Until either dawn or bones would break,
Then returned to warmth to lick our wounds,
But, once healed, longed to be hurt anew.

From "Queen Of Scum," September 5th, 2019 & "We Were Like Mountains Breaking Apart," 2009/2019

Track #8
Between The Lines
Poetry/Lyrics: Erin Banks, music: Peter Douglas

It is what any story fears,
Her sentiments might be in vain,
After all, there are no more tears
In oblivion's somberlane.

He wrapped himself inside my words.
A dusty opus, shy at first,
The writing frayed, in truth and jest,
An open book at his behest.
Absentminded, he broke my spine.
He wept then, worshipped at my shrine,
In rage my pages deeply cut,
His open palm til we forgot.
Why, won't you take me off that shelf again?
And let your blood be the ink of this writ.
But in the end... this just wasn't a good fit.

It is what any story fears,
Her sentiments might be in vain,
After all, there are no more tears
In oblivion's somberlane.

January 20, 2019 & February 2021

Track #9
Salt Of The Earth
Poetry/Lyrics: Erin Banks, music: Erin Banks & Peter Douglas

An episode carved with scalpel in stone,
The loreless maiden, entombed in a crone.
Fists clutching the sanatorium's gown,
As the man on the ledge flung himself down.
No grave did he find at the bottom red,
But surgical cotton, a makeshift bed.

Chorus:

I lied today, then lied some more, and lied again.
One reason is there for the little rhymes I pen.
Storms wane, and although try I might, I never can.
No time is lost on earth but pining over stubborn men.
I'm sorry.

The Stranger, the Hermit, the Lover, Death.
The Tower, the Prison, The Beast's last breath.
A shared soul pavilion, slightly deranged.
Indefinite, though parameters changed.

Chorus:

I lied today, then lied some more, and lied again.
One reason is there for the little rhymes I pen.
Storms wane, and although try I might, I never can.
No time is lost on earth but pining over stubborn men.
I'm sorry.

Crush the headstone, by its lesson abide,

Swallow the rock dust to soften inside.
Reach far past the pit with all its regrets,
Forgive all the world and its living dead.
Freely dispense the soot from my hearth,
So it may become the salt of the earth.

Chorus:
I lied today, then lied some more, and lied again.
One reason is there for the little rhymes I pen.
Storms wane, and although try I might, I never can.
No time is lost on earth but pining over stubborn men.
I'm sorry.

From Salt Of The Earth, August 26th, 2019 & Storms Wane, I Never Can, August 31st, 2019

Track #10
The Empty Space
Poetry/Lyrics: Erin Banks, music: Peter Douglas

They echo inside, these words most tender.
Ricocheting off the enclosure's walls,
Dancing, spiraling through the empty halls.
Seeking that high from when I surrendered.

Chorus:
But I still, I still remember!
And do you, do you miss me sometimes?

Confined to memory ever shrinking.
Lost in quicksand of a presence most bleak,
And a future past that had reached its peak.
Into the Passenger I am sinking.

Chorus

Just one more dose, one sip, that I may rest.
Sleep off the ache of another missed call,
I'm a monster dreaming it were a doll.
Any affection was but human jest.

Chorus

Autumn I am, without a September.
A poet's worst work to practice his rhyme,
Each verse carefully metered to pass the time.
It is with shame that I now remember.

February 18, 2019 & February 2021

Track #11
Emily Of Sand & Sea
Poetry/Lyrics: Erin Banks, music & vocals: Peter Douglas, Anja Axelsson

My home, my only home,
Swallowed now, by Sand and by sea.
A comfortable, homely cave was he,
Made out of word shells, prettily.

My home, my only home,
Dismantled now, and silently.
Did you forget so easily?
That my true name is Emily.

I'm About Rage, I'm last June's lust,
I am repose, I am disgust.
You cannot run, you spirit whore,
Not outcrawl me at Ocean Shore.

My home, the man you slew,
A tiny crab shell I outgrew.
But in the sky waits my forlorn,
My murder twin, a Capricorn.

April 6, 2019

Track #12
Nip From His Mind Its Blinding Light
Poetry/Lyrics: Erin Banks, music: Peter Douglas

Meet me at the cherry blossoms,
Where within, without sweetrotting spring arose.
Where scalding pleasure-ire outshone worrywoes
Meet me at the cherry blossoms,
Where as they crumblewhitened, affections froze.
Meet me at the cherry blossoms,
Where bitter winterwords left us paralyzed,
Meet me just one more time to say goodbye.

In his elegant responses, a rapture each, I rest,
Each betrayal, holy, holy, a generous bequest.
Insults, suicidal leaves, sail to their death from wanton trees,
Their irately rustling sighs a swansong in the breeze.
And once dawn subdues the moon's hyperborean ode,
I vow to dauntlessly contemplate in profound a mode,
How to everlastingly nip from his mind its blinding light,
Capture the stinging bittersweetness dripping from its hive.
Now that my filial loyalty has me stigmatized,
Here's to vengeance's hopeful chime, within you crystallized.

Meet me at the cherry blossoms,
Where within, without sweetrotting spring arose.
Where scalding pleasure-ire outshone worrywoes
Meet me at the cherry blossoms,
Where as they crumblewhitened, affections froze.
Meet me at the cherry blossoms,
Where bitter winterwords left us paralyzed,
Meet me just one more time to say goodbye.

From "Meet Me At The Cherry Blossoms," & "Nip From His Mind Its Blinding Light," both October 14, 2021

Track #13
To The Patron Whore Of Cowards
Poetry/Lyrics: Erin Banks, music & vocals: Peter Douglas

All raise your cups to the womb raider
Who stole the fruit of my hard labor.
The unwanted drowned toddler coward,
Blind to his harlot mother's favor.

What on you I bestowed, the payment you owed,
Offered up as tribute to Epiphany.
Her you accosted, yet all I exhausted
Slaughtered on the altar of Epiphany.

Apocalypse means Revelation,
Crippled slouches my Congregation.
Flaunting your sins on a silver plate,
Mercy awaits beyond death's gate.

What to me you once served, malice undeserved,
A sacrifice for my avenger, The Void.
Retribution, disdain, your cunning, in vain,
Whimper louder, you traitor, into The Void.

January 3rd, 2021

Track #14
Hold Your Hooves & Horns
Poetry/Lyrics: Erin Banks, music & vocals: Peter Douglas, additional voices: Aaron Furlong, Robert Bryce, Kacey Williamson, Dwayne Letson, Markus Brooks, Jeff Ignatowski, Chris Morgan, Chris K., William Dathan Holbert, Mike Hines, Gryff Nowicki, Mikey Allen and Joe Kellerman

Hold your hooves and horns, for he who'll bask in their fire
Will come at his own pace, and in his own time.
Hold your tongue, calm your twin bow, he who'll ride you right
Will first grant you insight into his own crime.
And, prancing around the funeral pyre of youth,
Gift you lighthearted laughter without reason or rhyme.
Forsaking sorority, another hard truth,
But how could sisters grasp the wildcat's allure?
Should we burn each other to rubble and grime,
I'll acknowledge that age hasn't helped me mature.
But this goat's about the fall in lieu of the climb.
What filthier way is there to celebrate this day
Than with the animal King, master of decay?

Interlude:

Happy birthday, babygirl. Or should I call you my sexy little slut?
I'd love to give you a fuck *and* a suck for each candle on your cake.

Verse repeat

January 8, 2022

Track #15
Shout It Louder, Sinner
Poetry/Lyrics: Erin Banks, music: Peter Douglas, vocals: Peter Douglas & Erin Banks

And maybe all these long blighted years,
The perturbed depression and the fears,
The abuse exacted and sustained,
The self-imposed loneliness ingrained,
Created this now cheerful sinner,
An inventive fantasy spinner,
A confidante, covert paramour,
A giver without the soft allure,
A taker and a keeper alike,
Eager for your every touch and strike.
And should all this turn out to be
My own hemorrhaging brain's reverie,
Then keep laughing, for I pray you knew
I spent all my carefree hours with you.

When the hours feel like days,
After all was said and sucked,
And you set that jar ablaze,
Then you, my dear, are fucked.

From "Shout It Louder, Sinner," January 26, 2022 & "You, My Dear, Are Fucked," January 12, 2022

Track #16
We Are Kayser Soze
Poetry/Lyrics: Erin Banks, music & vocals: Peter Douglas, additional voice: Erin Banks

"Remember, charge, these are your friends," Kayser said.
And though scream I could, I bow my throbbing head.
Empress of mine, there are spiders in your hair,
Weaving an elaborate web of lies to share
With our lesser Arcana, those of small mind,
Afterbirth sisters, born solely for the Grind.
Kayser Soze is a gentle trickster God,
All things coldly diplomatic I am not.

Community is another word for slavery,
Our Lady of Deceit, a beacon of bravery.
Her fickleness is the only thing reliable,
Repent, abjects, unity is still viable.
"Your naivety will aid us," she sagely smiles.
For the noble cause, shall I entertain her wiles?

"Remember, friends are foes you don't want to know.
The Chariot is prepared to take you to growth."
Empress of mine, there are spiders in your hair,
Weaving an elaborate web of truth to share,
With our major Arcana, those of sound mind,
This night I shall take the vow to join the Grind.
A gentle trickster God is Kayser Soze,
Come for us all who are insane but not crazy.

January 11, 2021 by Erin Banks

Track #17
Hell To The Liars, Hail To The Rider
Poetry/lyrics: Erin Banks, music & vocals: Peter Douglas

Verse:

Wanderer, and sometimes runner, always Rider,
Her roamer, ruthless protector, adept hider,
Faithful to the pathetic youth's pain that birthed him –
A Legion with purpose, then acting on a whim.
Neither mercy nor affection, never again,
Just a brain thrill to halt the rootkit, now and then.
Bachelor, father, sage, once his smoky tendrils rise,
A honey badger nurture, brutally concise.
Force yourself inside her corpse – he's already there,
One day, he'll guide me to the blissful neverwhere.

Chorus:

From Passenger to Driver, a knife up his sleeve,
Genuine solicitude, his greatest pet peeve.
Risen from the wreck has he to vacate their hosts,
Guest to his crimes, I stand, taciturn, on my post.
He coaxes me to watch, forces me to admit,
That without him I'm an effigy without wit.
I watch their eyes lose focus as affrighted they flee,
And inhabit them once they breathe their life into me.
Now whatever perversion I am called to enforce,
I relent to Him who delivered me from remorse.
No deformity marks us but we're disease come to life,
Whoever is so foolish to loves us will not survive.

Verse:

Wanderer, and sometimes runner, always Rider,
Her roamer, ruthless protector, adept hider,
Faithful to the pathetic youth's pain that birthed him –
A Legion with purpose, then acting on a whim.
Neither mercy nor affection, never again,
Just a brain thrill to halt the rootkit, now and then.
Bachelor, father, sage, once his smoky tendrils rise,
A honey badger nurture, brutally concise.
Force yourself inside her corpse – he's already there,
One day, he'll guide me to the blissful neverwhere.

From "Hell To The Liars, Hail To The Rider," January 11, 2022 & "Driver," January 10, 2021

Track #18
To Georgia But With The Grace Of Gods Go I
Poetry/Lyrics: Erin Banks, music & vocals: Peter Douglas;
background sounds: Michael Ghelfi Studios

He loots their wit, their rhyme,
Corrupts their pride, squanders their time.
For he is a meat suit with impeccable taste,
Despite low self-esteem.
Pridefully worthless, unredeemed,
He violates all, be they fledgling or human waste.

Chorus #1:

To Georgia but with the grace of Gods go I.
Atlas shrugged as we kept a watchful eye.
Having leverage now,
I laugh as devils laugh,
Whilst sweat forms on my brow,
Clutching the cryptograph.
Come ye, to roast the sow,
Hear its squealed epitaph!

Lo this prickly walker,
That's him, a prolific stalker,
Unlike her Holiness heroine – more… cocaine.
Thus he still rapes her psalm,
And in her storm finds he his calm.
Why go for the kill when you can go for the pain?

Chorus #2:

To Georgia but with the grace of Gods go I.

Atlas shrugged as we kept a watchful eye.
"Was it treachery though?
Treasure ye not my gift?
Word and wit from below,
From within my great rift."
You, pig, may want to know,
No matter how you shift,

You will die on this hill.

December 16, 2021 by Erin Banks

Glossary

Antisocial Personality Disorder
A cluster B personality disorder characterized by impulsivity and at times criminal behavior. People with the disorder are conventionally described as deceitful, manipulative, lacking empathy and having overall superficial as well as flat affects. A very small percentage of antisocial personalities are violent repeat offenders or serial murderers.

Borderline Personality Disorder
A cluster B personality disorder including symptoms of an extreme fear of abandonment, emotional instability, feelings of worthlessness, emptiness, insecurity, impulsivity (for instance self-harm, substance abuse, overspending, reckless sex), and impaired social relationships.

Cluster B Personality Disorder
These disorders are characterized by dramatic, overly emotional or unpredictable thinking, feeling and behavior. Included in the list are antisocial personality disorder, narcissistic personality order, borderline personality disorder, and histrionic personality disorder. The causes of personality disorders (clusters A-C) is still not fully understood, but commonly thought to mostly stem from a combination of genetics and trauma.

CPTSD
Those with complex post-traumatic stress disorder experience symptoms of regular PTSD along with additional symptoms such as difficulty controlling emotions (which may result in impulsivity), feelings of rage and paranoia. The condition is generally thought to be caused by trauma. Because some symptoms overlap with borderline personality disorder, the two

have often been confounded with each other, resulting in misdiagnoses.

Dissociative Identity Disorder
It is associated with traumatic or overwhelming events and/or abuse that occurred in childhood. A mostly involuntary escape from reality, they are characterized by a disconnection between consciousness, identity and memory. A sub-type of DID (formerly known as multiple personality disorder) is OSDD (other specified dissociative disorder), where the core persona may be co-conscious and experience an alter as a separate individual interacting with them.

Modus Operandi
MO for short, the term derives from the Latin term meaning "mode of operation," describing the procedure the offender employs. It encompasses techniques and habits and specific types of behavior.
The MO usually remains the same but may be added onto or gradually change with time as the offender develops their skills, or as their signature develops.

Mydriasis
The dilation of the pupils, mostly a non-physiological response to extreme emotions, such as stress, excitement, fear. It may also have a physiological cause, such as due to medication.

Neurodiversity
Aka neurodivergence or neurovariation. The idea that differences in brain structures are not abnormal or deficiencies. The term is used by those trying to reduce stigma surrounding conditions such as autism, personality disorders et al.

Neurotypicality
The brain structure, behavior and thought as well as emotional processes of "normal" people; in other words those who act in accordance with society's standards and expectations.

Obsessive Compulsive Disorder
A disorder characterized by obsessive and recurring, intrusive thoughts. The individual feels compelled to act out repetitive and rigid behavioral patterns, such as checking on things, neat- or cleanliness. repetitively (compulsions).

Ritual
Acts that are unnecessary for the execution of the murder, such as posing of the bodies, torture and overkill. It is fantasy-driven, compulsive and linked to the signature of a killer.

Schizoaffective Disorder
A mental health condition where symptoms of psychotic and mood disorders are present together.

Schizotypal Disorder
A cluster A personality disorder involving eccentric or unusual thinking, beliefs, perceptions and mannerisms. It is characterized by paranoia regarding the loyalty of others, as well as the belief in superstitions and special powers; for instance telepathy, mind control etc. Suspicious or paranoid thoughts and constant doubts about the loyalty of others.

Seven Phases Of Serial Killing
1. Aura Phase: The offender distances himself from other people. Beginning of obsessing over violent fantasies and living in their heads. Substance abuse may occur/intensify during this time.

2. Trolling Phase: Starting to form an idea about how to carry out the next murder – whom? When? Where? How? This phase may take anything from days to months; in isolated cases even longer.
3. Flirting Phase: This phase more often plays a role for socially adept and organized offenders. They may attempt to make contact with and/or gain the trust of their victim to ultimately lure them to the place the criminal intends to murder them at.
4. Capturing Phase: The offender reveals their true intentions to the victim. They may taunt them or do anything to draw out the moment to gain satisfaction from it.
5. Murdering Phase: The actual homicide, which may involve torture, sexual assault and post-mortem activity with the deceased victim, such as necrophilia.
6. Totem Phase: After the perpetration of the homicide, the offender experiences a dramatic emotional and psychological drop. Some describe this as "waking up" from the fantasy. To clamor to the fantasy, the offender may rely on souvenirs, trophies relating to the crime or that belonged to the victim. The memories will prolong the Totem Phase and prevent the immediate switch into the last Phase of Serial Killing.
7. Depression Phase: The offender realizes that the homicide did not still his urges and falls into a deep depression. Some consider or commit suicide. At the end of the depression phase, before he comes full circle, once entering the aura phase, during which they will convince themselves that the next murder will satisfy their urges in full.

Signature
A fantasy-driven and compulsive behavior that aids in fulfilling the offender's emotional and psychological needs. A subset of ritual in serial murders.

Trophy

Aka souvenir. It serves as a way to preserve the memory of both the crime and victim, but also signifies the power over the victim by possessing (a part of) them beyond death.

About Erin Banks

Erin Banks is a Northern German-born autistic author who used to work as a Specialist in Library & Information Sciences and simultaneous interpreter. She has lived in Sweden, Denmark, the US, the UK, and Northern Germany.
She started the CrimePiper blog in 2018, and wrote her first book on the Ted Bundy case before transitioning to fiction writing.

https://facebook.com/erinbanksauthor

*

Other books by Erin Banks

True Crime

Ted Bundy: Examining The Unconfirmed Survivor Stories

Ted Bundy: Untersuchung der mutmaßlichen Überlebenden (German translation)

Horror/Thriller

ABOUT REVENGE, part two of the ABOUT RAGE trilogy (Coming soon)

Demons Named By Zeitgeist
(Coming soon)

Books by other authors Erin Banks appears in

Horror/Thriller

Books of Horror Community Anthology Vol. 4, Pt. 2 by RJ Roles

Scorned, An Anthology of Female Revenge by C.A. Baynam

Napalm Psalms by Lisa Vasquez

Weird Fiction Quarterly: Monsters, 2024

Weird Fiction Quarterly: Folk Horror, 2024

Crazy From The Heat by PsychoToxin Press

666 Flags - A Fundraising Anthology by PsychoToxin Press

True Crime

The Enigma Of Ted Bundy by Kevin M. Sullivan

Mentally Caged by Bruce LeMaster

Paranormal

Immortal Tales by Jay Long

Poetry

A Touch Of Temptation by Jay Long

Blossom by Jay Long

Shadows of the Soul by Jay Long

Autism

Could YOU Be Autistic? by Anne Cossé

Music
Available on Spotify

ABOUT RAGE – The Soundtrack
https://open.spotify.com/album/4bsjsAkRn4pF06PHJziwR7

ABOUT RAGE – "Kate Said" (Single, teaser for the upcoming novel ABOUT REVENGE)
https://www.youtube.com/watch?v=SZZhAnUUizg

Printed in Poland
by Amazon Fulfillment
Poland Sp. z o.o., Wrocław